Deepest Desires
of a
Wicked Duke

JAN - - 2017

By Sharon Page

DEEPER IN SIN

DEEPLY IN YOU

BLOOD CURSE

BLOOD FIRE

BLOOD SECRET

"Wicked for Christmas" in
SILENT NIGHT, SINFUL NIGHT

BLOOD WICKED

BLOOD DEEP

BLOOD RED

BLOOD ROSE

BLACK SILK

HOT SILK

SIN

"Midnight Man" in
WILD NIGHTS

Deepest Desires
of a
Wicked Duke

THE WICKED DUKES

SHARON PAGE

WILLIAMSBURG REGIONAL LIBRARY
7770 CROAKER ROAD
WILLIAMSBURG, VA 23188

KENSINGTON BOOKS
www.kensingtonbooks.com

To the extent that the image or images on the cover of this book depict a person or persons, such person or persons are merely models, and are not intended to portray any character or characters featured in the book.

This book is a work of fiction. Names, characters, places, and incidents either are products of the author's imagination or are used fictitiously. Any resemblance to actual persons, living or dead, events, or locales is entirely coincidental.

KENSINGTON BOOKS are published by

Kensington Publishing Corp.
119 West 40th Street
New York, NY 10018

Copyright © 2016 by Edith E. Bruce

All rights reserved. No part of this book may be reproduced in any form or by any means without the prior written consent of the Publisher, excepting brief quotes used in reviews.

All Kensington titles, imprints, and distributed lines are available at special quantity discounts for bulk purchases for sales promotion, premiums, fund-raising, educational, or institutional use.

Special book excerpts or customized printings can also be created to fit specific needs. For details, write or phone the office of the Kensington Sales Manager: Kensington Publishing Corp., 119 West 40th Street, New York, NY 10018. Attn. Sales Department. Phone: 1-800-221-2647.

Kensington and the K logo Reg. U.S. Pat. & TM Off.

eISBN-13: 978-1-61773-097-9
eISBN-10: 1-61773-097-1
First Kensington Electronic Edition: November 2016

ISBN-13: 978-1-61773-096-2
ISBN-10: 1-61773-096-3
First Kensington Trade Paperback Printing: November 2016

10 9 8 7 6 5 4 3 2 1

Printed in the United States of America

To A. J.
And to my readers,
with deepest thanks

ACKNOWLEDGMENTS

Many thanks to the team at Kensington
for bringing this book together so beautifully,
with extra special thanks to my editor, Esi Sogah.

1

Whitechapel, London
June 1821

Portia Lamb strode swiftly along Maiden Lane, keeping to the pools of light cast by the street flares. Miscreants likely lurked in the shadows. So did poor young children who survived by picking pockets.

The children she was trying to help.

"Are ye sure about this, miss?" Pressed right up to her side—so close their skirts kept tangling—walked Merry Meadows, the oldest resident of her family's home. Merry had stayed on to help with the children once she'd turned eighteen and was becoming a capable teacher. "I think we should've waited for one of yer brothers. There could be white slavers about. Your Ma always warned us about white slavers—"

"Merry, we are perfectly safe," Portia said in brisk tones. "Yes, my mother always issued dire warnings about white slavers and brothel owners who pluck innocent women off the streets. I have been rescuing children and bringing them to the home for ten years and nothing terrible has happened to me."

But under the cover of her cloak, she clasped the grip of a pistol. It was unloaded, but she'd discovered men didn't want to call her bluff.

Mother had never wanted her to go onto the streets of the Whitechapel slums, looking for orphans and impoverished children who were in danger. Now Mother was frail and ill, sometimes so confused she often didn't remember who Portia was. But when she'd had all her faculties, Mother believed Portia's brothers should be the ones to patrol the streets. She felt a girl should stay in the house and its classrooms.

Portia had never agreed. Children were more likely to trust a young woman. Her brothers were well-meaning, but they could be brusque, impatient, and intimidating. And children were already more wary of men in the stews.

Yet now that her mother was so forgetful, Portia found she missed Mother's dire warnings.

A sound came from an alley. Someone hiding? Rats?

"I'm still frightened, miss." Merry moved so close Portia almost tripped over her.

"There is nothing to fear, Merry. We can take care of ourselves. And we're clever. That counts for quite a lot."

Merry, who possessed blond ringlets and large blue eyes, looked around and shuddered. Her hand clutched Portia's arm. "Oh, heavenly stars, there's men lurking, waiting for us, Miss Lamb," Merry whispered, her voice a mere croak. "They're in the shadows ahead."

The other children used to call her Merry the Mouse, because she was shy and fearful. Merry also had the most remarkably attuned hearing and instincts. Portia couldn't see anything yet, but if Merry said there were men in the shadows, Portia didn't doubt her.

"Move close to the wall, into the shadows," Portia instructed quietly. She drew out her pistol. She peered into the darkness ahead and made out the opening of a narrow alley. Then she heard them—the murmur of two men's voices. A low, leering laugh made a shudder crawl down her spine.

Merry let out a squeak of fear.

"I heard something," one of them said. "Think it's the lass? Think she took the bait?"

At once Portia whirled to face Merry, her finger to her lips in a warning to be silent. The girl gulped but didn't make any other sound.

The note had begged Portia to come to No. 10 on Maiden Lane, to take a young girl from a desperate mother who could not support all her children, and who was being pressured to hand the nine-year-old over to a brothel.

"It was a ruse," Merry whispered. "We must flee, miss."

Portia held her ground. "We don't know that," she whispered back. "There might really be a child in need, even if that child is being used as bait."

"We *must* go, miss."

Portia hesitated. If there was a child who needed her help, how could she turn her back and run? But if this were a trap, she wouldn't be able to save the child anyway. Pressed tight against the wall, she peered at the mouth of the alley, her heart pounding.

What should she do? What if, by running, she condemned a little girl to a horrible fate?

"You can't be foolish, Miss Lamb," Merry whispered, her face a mask of fear. "I know you want to go forward, but we mustn't. We must fetch one of your brothers."

"She'll come," said a second voice. Portia smelled smoke. The man had only responded now because he was smoking a cheroot and he'd taken it out of his mouth to speak. "Keep yer bloody voice down and wait for the signal."

The signal? Merry was tugging at her cloak, urging her to run. But what if there was a child in danger—?

A sharp whistle rent the air. Then their hackney driver flicked his whip and sent his horses galloping away, taking the hackney cab with them.

The two men ran out of the alley, faces splitting into wide, gap-toothed grins.

That must have been the signal. Their driver had been in the pay of these men. Blast!

She and Merry couldn't outrun two men. Not in cloaks. And skirts.

Why had they been tricked? These men didn't look cunning enough to have thought this up. They looked like the kind of thick-necked brawlers who worked for someone clever.

Breathing hard, she lifted her unloaded pistol and leveled it at the men. Meredith gasped at the sight of it. "You'll shoot them? Miss, that's murder."

"Not if we're defending our lives," she said, with all the calm she could muster. "If I were you, gentlemen, I would run away as fast as you can."

One man chuckled. He was the shorter of the two. Burly, with a dirty face, dark clothes, a dark cap. They were dressed the same, but where one was short and squat, the other was tall and thin.

The squat man stepped forward. "I know that pistol isn't loaded."

Portia was so scared it was hard to breathe, but she couldn't show it. *Don't panic. Keep your wits.* Father had taught her that. He'd been a great explorer before he settled down, got married, and opened the home for children. Wits were a man's—and a woman's—best weapon. In a commanding voice, she barked, "Of course it is. I'm not a fool."

"I know it's a bluff, missy. Ye never load the thing. And even if ye did, I were told ye'd never hurt anyone."

How could he know? Or was he bluffing her? She clutched the pistol grip with two hands, pointing it at his chest. "I would hurt you to protect our persons. Let us go."

"Ye've no way out, missy. We want ye, not the other one."

"Can't imagine why," muttered the tall one. "The other one's the beauty with 'er blond curls and round tits. This one's skinny and the 'air's so red, it looks like 'er 'ead's on fire."

"Shut up," barked the short one. "Now come quietly, missy, and we'll let yer maid go."

"No, Miss Lamb, I won't leave you." But Merry shook like a leaf.

"You must," Portia said. She glowered at both men—the short one who thought she was daft and the insulting tall one. She had no intention of going quietly anywhere. "Turn around and go, Meredith. Go to the High Street—it will be the safest for you. Now run!"

Merry shook her head.

Portia motioned desperately with *her* head. If Merry got away, she could make it back to the foundling home and tell Portia's brothers what had happened. "You must go! Fetch my brothers from the Eight Bells and bring them at once. Do exactly as I say and run!" She was supposed to come alone. Let them think she hadn't.

Merry, thank heaven, finally understood, Portia guessed. For Merry started to run.

Her attackers had been advancing. Now they stopped. "No one said nothin' about brothers," began the tall one, and Portia took advantage of their momentary distraction. She spun on her heel and ran for her life.

She turned at a corner and sped for the nearest alley, one that led farther into the maze of the Whitechapel slums.

She knew the stews, but she feared the two men knew them just as well. Footsteps thundered behind her and she rushed out of the alley onto the lane, holding up her hems.

Damn! One of the men was down the lane, ahead of her. He'd circled around to cut her off. She turned and ran wildly away from him, up the street. Now both men were behind her, for she was sure the short man had followed her into the alley.

She had friends amongst the people who lived here on these streets. Surely, at a house on this street, she could find refuge—

Oh, drat it, no! Out of another alley, a few yards ahead of her, the squat man emerged. He held a white cloth.

She had fallen for the same trick twice.

Portia raced blindly to the door of the house beside her. Pounded hard with her fists. But no one answered. What could she do? Then she remembered—one of the houses ahead of her had a carriageway through it that led to a courtyard. She ran.

The fiend looked short and squat, but he ran fast. She reached the carriageway just as his hand landed hard on her shoulder and hauled her back. She slammed against him. Her hood blocked her view, but she knew she was trapped against his chest. Looking down, she saw his huge, thick arm, wrapped around her like an iron bar. And she smelled him. Sour sweat. Beer on his breath.

She screamed—

A wet cloth slapped against her face. She breathed in sickly sweetness. At once, her wits whirled, her stomach lurched, and she felt as if she were dropping into an abyss.

Ether? It must be some chemical like that.

Portia shoved at the man's arm and kicked at his shins behind her. But she was sinking, weakening, falling.

His leering laugh sounded against her ear. "Next thing ye know, love, ye'll be waking up in His Grace's bed."

Desperate, she tried once more to fight. What did he mean— waking up in a duke's bed?

"The Duke of Sinclair will be right pleased." The second man laughed in a sneering tone.

The Duke of Sinclair? She had once *loved* the Duke of Sinclair. She had once agreed to marry him, but the duke had told her that he couldn't marry her, that he was going to let her go because he'd make a rotten husband. And for the ten years after, he'd proven the truth of those words, doing nothing but throw large, scandalous orgies.

But he wouldn't actually *kidnap* someone. Would he?

Blackness rose up and swallowed her whole.

Silk ropes wrapped around the Duke of Sinclair's wrists, binding them together behind the back of the chair. More rope tied his ankles to the chair legs. A blond courtesan's melon-sized breasts pushed into his face, almost smothering him. Another woman—a redhead with a spectacular rack of tits of her own—stroked his semi-erect cock. With her tongue. A third woman—a brunette—flicked his shoulders playfully with a whip.

The duke—known to intimates as Sin—was supposed to be the women's "prisoner," but he was in charge of this game. They would do anything he wanted. And he wanted them to make him forget her.

Portia. The woman he could never have.

For ten years, holding extravagant orgies or intimate ménages with groups of four or five had worked. Tonight, it bloody well wasn't.

The red-haired woman, Emmie, laved the head of his cock with her pretty little tongue. Normally, his prick would go bolt upright, hard and throbbing.

But all he felt was an uncomfortable surge of guilt and regret.

"Sorry, love," Sin muttered. "Sorry to all of you. I can't do this tonight."

"Why not?" breathed Emmie.

"Tsk." The brunette, Laurette, folded her arms over her chest and tapped the whip against her bare thigh. She arched a brow. "I know what the problem is. You're getting older, Your Grace. You're almost thirty. You get a little tired with old age."

"Thirty is not old," he growled. "And I'm not bloody well thirty. I'm much younger than that."

Emmie widened her eyes innocently. "If His Grace says so. I remember when you first came to London. The most gorgeous brown-haired lordling you was, Your Grace, with the dreamiest chocolate brown eyes. It couldn't have been *that* long ago. And he was about eighteen. He can't be more than twenty-five now?"

Sin knew she meant well—meant to imply he wasn't so old. Emmie had lovely breasts and sweet pink nipples that were long and thick when they hardened, but she was not particularly endowed in the upper story.

Laurette shook her head. "I remember when ye first came to London. Lad of nineteen ye were—and looked as if butter wouldn't melt in yer mouth. That was in 1811. See—ten years ago."

"And, thus, I happen to be twenty-nine," he growled.

The blonde, Sukey, pulled on a scarlet silk robe, wrapping it around her lush curves. "Then it's the brandy. You've pickled it. What happens when you put anything in brine? It goes soft."

He glanced at the empty glass on a nearby table. He'd downed about four. "It's not the brandy," he growled. "Tonight, I'm just preoccupied. Untie me and leave me."

"As you wish, Your Grace. But we could have had so much fun." Pouting, Laurette set to undoing the knots she'd made. Emmie and Sukey tried to change his mind, but Sin knew it was pointless. Nothing sexual was going to happen to him tonight.

The three women curtsied because he was a damn duke. Then they scurried out the door.

Defiantly, he drank some of the brandy. A man couldn't pickle his cock.

Or could he?

Hell. He put the alcohol down.

He walked to the window of his bedchamber and looked out over the gardens. It was a late spring—only the toughest of his partygoers were fucking outdoors. Music poured out from the ballroom, along with wild laughter and squeals of pleasure. His house always shook with moans and screams as people had sex and climaxed en masse.

He had an orgy under way and he had never been so disinterested in his life.

Last night, he'd gone into the Seven Dials area for gaming and he'd seen *her*. Portia had been carrying a small child in her arms—a child she had rescued from a slum tenement.

As he'd watched her go, desire for her had hit him like Gentleman Jackson's fist.

For ten years, he'd avoided seeing her again. And now that chance meeting had wiped out a decade of working to forget her.

Strangely, it just seemed to have made him want her more.

And he couldn't have her.

The irony was Portia hadn't broken the engagement with

him; he'd broken it with her. He'd chosen the orgies, the brothels, bondage, and group sex over her.

"Your Grace?"

Sin looked up. His butler, Beagle, looked as unperturbed
and rigid as ever as he performed his duties with an orgy going
on around him.

Beagle held out his silver salver, on which sat a folded note.
"This arrived for you, Your Grace. A child brought it to the
kitchen door and said it was to be delivered at once."

"A child?"

"An urchin lad. He ran off as soon as a footman took the
note."

"Before he'd received any money?"

"Yes, Your Grace. I thought that was quite suspect myself."

Sin didn't say anything, but he agreed. He picked up the
note and unfolded it with a snap of his wrist. He had to read it
twice before the words fully penetrated his brain.

> *By the morning post, you received an invita-*
> *tion to an unusual house party to be held on an*
> *island off the coast, near Southend-on-Sea. To*
> *put it plainly, the event is a bacchanalia. Miss*
> *Portia Lamb is being lured to the party. It is in-*
> *tended as a joke—a surprise to entice you. A*
> *gentleman of your considerable experience*
> *would be aware she will literally be a lamb led*
> *to slaughter.*
>
> *To protect her—and her reputation—you*
> *must attend.*
>
> *A Concerned Friend*

"What in hell—?" he muttered. Was this true? Who in blazes
was "A Concerned Friend"?

Maybe it was a joke. A joke in poor taste.

Where was that damned invitation? He remembered glancing at it, barely reading it. Last night, he'd been thinking of Portia and he'd barely noticed the invitation.

He'd tossed it aside . . . where?

Sin stalked downstairs to his study, off limits during his parties. A stack of invitations sat on the edge of his oak desk. The towering pile contained entreaties for him to attend balls, musicales, card parties, picnics. He was an unmarried duke. Every matchmaking mama of the *ton* was trying to draw him out.

He sifted through the pile quickly, invitations sliding onto the floor.

Here it was—embossed in silver on thick card.

THE DUKE OF SINCLAIR IS CORDIALLY INVITED
TO AN ORGY
TO BE HELD 21ST JUNE
AT CLIFFSIDE HOUSE UPON SERENITY ISLAND

A letter was also enclosed. Sin scanned it swiftly.

> *It's said you give the best orgies in England. I intend to steal your crown. This party will be more thrilling than any other carnal gathering you have ever attended. You will be astounded.*
> *Proceed to Southend-on-Sea, where a small craft will be waiting to transport you to Serenity Island, one mile off the coast.*
> *I defy you to refuse this invitation. I know you will not resist a challenge.*

It was signed: *W.*

At first, he'd thought *W* stood for Willoughby, at one time his best mate, when he'd first come to London. Now he shook his head. Will wouldn't invite him to an orgy. They'd avoided each other since their last face-to-face meeting—down the barrels of a pair of dueling pistols.

So who was *W*? And who would bring Portia to the event?

Now he had to go to this damn party. If Portia was being lured to an orgy for some nefarious purpose, he had to protect her. Given the way their brief engagement had ended, he expected she wasn't going to appreciate his protection.

But she was going to get it.

2

The Coast, Southend-on-Sea
June 1821

"Have you seen a young lady? About so tall—" Shouting to be heard over the screeching gulls that swooped over the shore, Sin held his hand at the level of his chest.

"Auburn hair—unruly waves and curls," he continued. "Usually keeps it pinned back and wears big bonnets. Large eyes. Looks sweet and innocent, but she's a managing sort of female."

The four old fishermen who sat along the quay looked at him blankly.

Gulls swooped around him, cawing as if laughing at him. Waves lapped at the sea wall, filling the air with the tang of brine and drying seaweed. A gust of ocean breeze almost took his beaver hat off his head and sent salty spray in his face.

"Her name is Portia Lamb," he added. Praying inside. His gut clenched in fear, even if he looked cool, calm, and ducal on the outside.

"Aye, we've seen some young lasses this morn . . ." began one of the fishermen.

The other men all made grunting sounds of affirmation.

"Were she wearing a shocking red gown?" asked the fisherman.

Sin had no idea but couldn't picture sensible Portia in one. "I doubt it."

"Then I don't think we saw the lass."

The rest shook their heads, pulled at their pipes.

"Only people we saw were toffs, Yer Grace," the fisherman said—the one who appeared to be the group's spokesman. "And ladies in some shocking dresses. Necklines cut down to their wee nipples and their tits almost falling out."

"Ladies? You daft old buggers don't think they were ladies, do you?" An older woman sat a few feet beyond, on a rickety chair, sewing up fishing nets. She laughed, spat out some tobacco, and leveled a shrewd gaze on Sin. "Those were no ladies. Not in those garish dresses."

She was wrong. Some would be courtesans, but some would be ladies of the *ton*—ladies looking for carnal fun. Portia would never wear a shocking dress, but he realized she could have been forced into one. "None of them had bright red hair and freckles?"

"One had red hair—henna-colored, out of a bottle. There weren't any natural redheads."

"Then the woman I'm looking for was not amongst them. Thank you for your help," he said, though he hadn't gotten any help. He tossed them all a few coins. "Have a pint on me."

He'd asked every person at the quay if they had seen Portia. This was the last group. He'd had no luck.

Was this whole thing just a sick joke? Maybe Portia was still in London, safe and sound in her family's foundling home. . . .

But he couldn't give up and walk away—not until he was sure she was safe.

He turned to face out over the sea.

A few hundred yards offshore, a sheer face of dark rock rose out of the water. It looked square, squat, flat topped. That was Serenity Island, though it looked ominous and stark instead of serene.

A dory was moored on the quay, waiting to take him to the island.

Portia might already be there. She could have been taken to the island at night, under cover of darkness. Or hell, even in a sack so no one would see her.

He had to find out.

Long strides took him to the stone steps that led to the small jetty where the dory was moored. Sin waved away help from one of the oarsman and climbed aboard. He settled in the rear of the craft, facing the island, and they cast off.

The two men pulled hard on the oars. A breakwater stretched out into the sea, calming the larger waves, allowing the dory to make headway over the water. But it was still a journey that took time.

Giving him time to think . . . and remember when he'd gotten engaged to Portia . . .

Ten years earlier
London, 1811

His carriage rattled along a wide cobblestone street past soaring mansions of glittering windows and crisp white stone. A huge park stretched out along the street. Earlier today, in the afternoon, he'd seen beautiful young women strolling along the park's paths. Skirts of colored muslin and silk swished around their legs and they twirled dainty, lace-trimmed parasols.

It had been astounding to Sin to see so many elegantly dressed girls gathered in one place.

Now, he stared through the window at the darkness that shrouded the park. He was in London for the first time in his life as the new Duke of Sinclair, a title he'd never expected to inherit. He was the son of a cousin of a duke, a side of the family that had been exiled long ago over some son's bad behavior. His name was Julian Markham, and he was just about to be given the nickname "Sin."

When he'd first met the bucks of London at White's Club— he inherited the membership at the exclusive gentleman's club along with his title—they expected him to be a rural rube since he'd grown up in the country, even though his father had been a gentleman and Sin had gone to Eton with the sons of peers. He could have been offended, but he let them think he was innocent and naïve.

It was a way to hide the truth about his past. About all the perversions he'd taken part in. A sordid, wicked past that he didn't want anyone to know about.

On his first visit to White's, Julian met Viscount Willoughby, a peer of twenty-four who held court in the bow window at White's, making rapier-sharp jokes about the peers strolling past. "Come with us tonight, Sinclair," he'd drawled, "for a night of deep play at a new gaming hell on Curzon Street. Have to initiate London's newest duke properly." A slow grin spread over Willoughby's good-looking features.

"I'll go," Sin had agreed. That night Willoughby had jokingly decided to call him "Sin."

That had been a fortnight ago. Tonight, he was meeting Willoughby and several other peers at a gaming hell.

His carriage traveled several more blocks, stopping in front of a townhouse with a dark-painted door. Within minutes he was inside, hunkered over his cards in a smoke-hazed room, gambling at whist with Willoughby and two other men. After a few hands of play, Sin realized the other men hoped to relieve him of some of the fortune that came with the dukedom. But one thing he knew was how to play cards—and so far, he and Will, who was his partner, were winning. After a few hours of play, Sin had downed a lot of port and was in a state that titled men called "disguised" and others called drunk, when some saucy, voluptuous women came flirting around them. Willoughby planted one on his lap and instructed one to do the same with Sin. He tried to get her to shoo. He lifted her off several times, but she kept climbing back on.

He gave up. Tried to ignore her. The girl was wriggling on his lap, squealing and giggling, when a sharp female voice demanded, "Unhand that young woman."

Startled, Sin looked up.

That was when he saw her.

At first, he saw two of her; then the two images coalesced into one surprising one: a respectable young woman, storming into a gaming hell.

A sensible gown and dark blue pelisse covered her figure, but he could see she was slender, with a tiny waist, long legs. Her face was the most striking he'd ever seen. Dark gray eyes, long and narrow and seductively tilted upward at the ends. A tiny nose and a spray of freckles. Her mouth was the most ripe, full red mouth he'd ever seen.

She stalked toward them, stopping in front of him with her hands on her hips. "I am Portia Lamb and I demand that you unhand that woman at once. Please take her off your person."

As he stared in surprise, she wagged her finger. "She has run away from my family's foundling home to launch a career as a prostitute. And, of course, there are dissolute men to make that possible. She is but sixteen!"

As Miss Lamb glared at him, he handed the would-be courtesan back. "I had no intention of doing anything to the girl." His words came out fairly slurred. "I wasn't even the one to ask her to sit on my lap."

Miss Lamb hadn't listened to him.

But he'd fallen in love with Portia Lamb nonetheless that night, while she lectured him about evils, then dragged the young woman out of the gaming hell.

Miss Lamb was so good and noble. She cared about children and rescued them. And she was astoundingly pretty with huge gray eyes and thick, curling, flame-red hair.

After that, he'd pursued her like a besotted fool in a love sonnet. He started following her on her missions into the stews to protect her. Night after night, he spent in her company. Then it became days as well. Days where he visited the home because even minutes away from her felt like too damn long.

Finally, one day, he dropped to one knee in front of Portia and asked her to be his wife.

And she said yes.

"I'll go and talk to your father," he promised. "And I'll introduce you to my grandmother and my cousins. They live in the ducal home in Mayfair."

In the carriage, he kissed her. They shared hot and passionate kisses, dueling with tongues. He was hard as a brick, panting for her.

She drew back. "Julian, we can't." She used his Christian name—she didn't know about the nickname Sin that Willoughby had given him. He hated his Christian name, but he didn't want her to call him by the nickname. It was too damned close to the truth about him, a truth he wanted to hide from her.

He held back, trying to be good, be noble. Make her believe that's what he was. He wanted her, but didn't kiss her.

Then the carriage stopped. He handed her down.

"Good heavens." She stared up at the mansion that was Sinclair House in Mayfair. Where he had been living for only a few weeks.

Tucking her hand in the crook of his arm, he showed her the house. They walked through the massive ballroom with its five chandeliers. The music room that boasted two gleaming pianofortes. The gallery filled with paintings. The four drawing rooms.

He watched her beautiful eyes and saw her astonishment. She must be thrilled to become a duchess, to become mistress of all this. Maybe that way she wouldn't leave him, wouldn't desert him, if she found out the truth about him.

"I knew your home would be grand, but I've never seen anything like this." She gazed at him with concern on her face. "I . . . I don't know anything of this world, Julian."

"That doesn't matter, Portia." He walked up to her, drew her into his arms. He could spread the world at her feet because he was a duke. And Portia deserved the world.

She looked up at him, biting her lip, gleaming with innocence. Her lashes were long, flashing over gray eyes. Her hair was a mass of unruly curls. She smiled at him and his heart almost burst. No one had ever loved him before. That this precious woman did—it meant he might be worth loving.

He started taking off his clothes. They were in one of the drawing rooms and he'd locked the door. Breathing hard, he undid his cravat with a quick tug of his fingers. Pulled off his tailcoat, then his waistcoat. He stood in front of her in his linen shirt and trousers, his collar open. He was going to marry her. He could have everything he wanted—

"Julian, put your clothes back on! Nothing can happen until we're married. I, of all people, can't make such a mistake. If I let things happen, then you won't love me anymore. Our foundling home is filled with children because of men who were filled with desire, then, after, wanted only to run."

"That's not me. I love you. I'm going to marry you. Spend my life with you." He drew his fingers up her arm. He saw the little shiver she gave. Heard her soft, throaty moan.

He felt such a strong jolt of lusty agony, he almost stumbled.

"Then we can wait just a little longer," she said. But it came out in a whimper.

"I'm not going to ruin you, Portia. I want to please you."

"Please me? What do you mean?"

He wanted her to know how good he could be in bed. That way, if she found out the truth about his past, maybe she wouldn't be as horrified if she knew how much pleasure he could give her.

Maybe . . .

He jerked off his shirt, baring his torso. His heart pounded so hard, he was surprised he didn't see it push against his chest.

"Oh!" she gasped.

"Don't be scared," he said. What he wanted was her hands caressing him. Touching him.

She bit her lip. "But if I let myself be ruined before marriage, I would be breaking every vow I ever made to myself. I would feel so terrible, facing my parents who believe I am good."

"I won't do anything wrong, Portia. I promise." He bent to

her ear—pretty little ears—and touched the lobe gently with his lips. She gave a sharp, sweet gasp. It was hard to move slowly.

But taking it slow forced him to savor everything. The softness of her skin as he nuzzled her neck. The tickle of her hair against his cheek. She smelled lightly of lavender water.

"I won't ask for more than you can give," he said. "But I need you to touch me."

"Touch you?"

He clasped her hands and laid her palms on his naked chest. Her fingers were long and slender and graceful. Feather-light, her fingertips skimmed over his bare skin. She traced his muscles.

"You're beautiful," she whispered. "I like touching you. I . . . I've never seen a male torso before. I mean, except on statues. Yours is completely perfect. Your muscles are so big and hard."

The innocent shine in her eyes hurt his heart. He wished this was his first time. That he was innocent too.

Her fingers brushed his nipples. They were tight and hard. Tentatively, she stroked them. Strummed them.

He threw back his head and groaned.

"Have I hurt you?"

"No, I like it." Then he did something hellish. "This is new to me too," he lied.

"It is?" That seemed to make her braver. To save children, she sashayed into the stews, facing pimps and madams. But here, she was nervous.

She caressed his shoulders, laying her palms on them. She felt his biceps, his chest. And he guided her hands down lower, and finally coaxed her to slip her right hand in his trousers.

She squeaked. "You're so hot."

He nuzzled her neck. "I like that. Hold my cock, love."

"What?"

Kissing behind her ear made her gasp. "Play with my cock," he urged.

"Oh, er . . ." But she did it. Her fingers slid around his shaft.

He hadn't been a virgin for a long, long time, but he almost exploded like one. He gritted his teeth, fighting for control. Did she like him? Was he good enough for her?

He knew she wouldn't let him undress her. And he couldn't take the risk that he would lose control. Since coming to London, he'd been working on developing control. That one night when he'd gotten drunk and Willoughby had sent the young prostitute to pursue him had been the only night he'd broken his vow to change. He'd given in to Will's goading to drink and have fun.

"What do I do?" she asked. "How do I touch you?"

"Wrap your hand around it and move up and down," he said softly.

She gripped him and slid her hand along him. This was different, seeing the act that had become so warped to him as it actually should be—a sharing of love. Something sweet and erotic.

"What's wrong? You just got the saddest look on your face." Concern furrowed her brow.

"Nothing. Keep touching me."

She did, squeezing harder. He'd done so much, but this— this was perfect. He had to let his head drop forward as pleasure and agony hit him.

She jerked him faster. He was getting tighter, tenser—

God, yes. His hips jerked as the spasms sent his semen rushing through his cock. He spurted out into his trousers. On Portia's hand.

She squealed and he laughed softly at the innocent sound.

"That's your seed."

"You made me come, Portia. Now I want to do that for you."

He cleaned her hand with his handkerchief, led her to the sofa. Begged her to trust him as he settled her down on its soft cushions.

Muslin fell over his arms as he lifted her skirts. He glanced up. She nodded. "I want to share this with you—I am ready." She adopted a brave look.

Grinning wickedly, he drew down her drawers. Simple white muslin with a little trim of lace. Red-gold curls made a vee between her silky thighs. He couldn't hang on any longer. Diving down, he slipped his hands under her rump and lifted her pussy as he lowered his mouth.

Her scent washed over him. Her nether lips glistened. Planting his mouth over her, he tasted her, teased her with his tongue.

"What are you—? Oh, oh . . . oh!"

She tried to slide back. Saucer-wide eyes stared at him.

"I love you, Portia. I want to show you how much. There's nothing wrong with this. Nothing wrong with pleasuring each other sexually. You won't lose your virginity. But you will have fun." He bent back to her fiery curls and licked.

She squirmed. "It is good. And I want . . . I want more."

He suckled her clit, flicked with his tongue. Slowly at first, then more demanding. He built up the pleasure. As much as his cock throbbed, he was patient. He would do this until he made her come.

And he thought, pride swelling, he was getting her close.

Suddenly her hands flailed out and hit the top of her head. She arched up, cried out. Her hips rose up, smacking him. He had to back off and watch her climax. She was so sweet, trying to smother her squeals as it happened. Surprise showed on her face, warring with the sultry look of erotic pleasure. It made him grin.

She clutched at the sofa as her body pulsed. Then she relaxed. She wriggled like a contented kitten. "I didn't know it was possible to feel like that. You made me feel . . . oh, it was lovely."

He laughed. Kissed her.

"Ooh, your lips taste all earthy."

"They taste of you, Portia. You're mine. All mine now."

He'd said that. And he'd meant it.

It was the next day, when he announced the engagement to their families and his friends, that everything went to hell.

Serenity Island
June 1821

" 'Ere we are, Yer Grace."

Jerked out of his memories, Sin looked up. The cliffs of the island loomed over their craft, sheer and gray.

"Where do we land?" Sin shouted.

"There's a cove—hidden from view until ye're right upon it." Sweat rolled down the oarsman's face.

Restless and worried about Portia, Sin shifted forward, taking hold of one of the oars. The men protested, but he insisted.

Adding his muscle, the three of them pulled hard on the oars and brought the small boat into a notch in the rock. This was the cove—rounded in shape, with steep cliffs on both sides. At the end, steps had been cut into the rock. The oarsmen lashed the boat to metal rings. Sin agilely leapt out onto the dock and took the steps two at a time. The men followed him up the steps, at a slower pace, carrying his half-filled trunk. He'd been so concerned about Portia he'd interrupted his valet to start his journey before the man had finished packing.

At the top, the stairs opened out onto a terrace that faced east, toward the open sea. The terrace was formed from the natural rock of the island, dotted with chaises and benches, and beyond that stood the house. But his attention was instantly drawn elsewhere.

Right in front of him, two men sat on a bench with a woman sandwiched between them. The woman pushed down her bodice, giggling madly. Sin knew her. A young courtesan who had magnificently large breasts. Sadie was her name, Sadie something. Bold as brass, full of fun, and on the hunt for a very rich protector. She had been trying to seduce him for a year. Not to get into his bed—to get into his pocketbook.

It hadn't worked.

Sadie lifted her tits. "This is all you can have right now. Not until after dinner, you naughty boys!"

The men leaned over and licked Sadie's thick pink nipples.

One was the Earl of Blute, a man of thirty-five, who enjoyed any sporting competition and considered an orgy to be that kind of event. The other man had raven-black hair and was loved by courtesans across London for his handsome looks and his almost freakishly enormous prick. He was the Earl of Rutledge.

The oarsmen stopped to stare at the threesome. Their jaws dropped and they sniggered like schoolboys. Until one groaned, and said, "If word gets back that we were lollygagging and watching those sweet tits, we'd lose our jobs."

"Aye, though it might be worth it." But even as the man said that, wistfully, he started off toward the house. "Some blokes have all the luck," he muttered.

Sin presumed these men would include him in that group of blokes. Funny, he didn't feel lucky.

Sadie moaned loudly. Sin realized the two men were sucking her tits, but she was staring at him. She watched him boldly as she opened the trousers of both men at the same time and reached in to fondle. She pursed her lips at him and blew him a kiss.

Sin shook his head. One quick, curt shake. Then he looked away and walked toward the house, a sprawling edifice with gabled roofs and gray stone walls. It was wide and long, with terrace doors that ran the length of the house, giving a view of the cliff edge and the sea beyond.

Where was Portia? Somewhere in the house? In danger?

Every man here better pray he hadn't touched Portia. Sin would kill any who had.

His boot soles pounded across the marble tiles. He was in a kind of gallery. The room had French doors that led to the interior of the house.

Someone cleared his throat and Sin whipped around.

A butler had materialized. Tall, cadaverous, with only a few strands of black hair combed over a bald pate. "I hope you had a smooth trip out to Serenity Island, sir. If I might show you your room—?"

"Never mind about the room. I'm looking for a young woman with red hair."

"I was informed, sir, that such events would not begin until after the first dinner. However, I do believe that several guests have . . . er . . . jumped the gun."

The butler spoke like a well-trained servant, but he was blushing. Apparently not used to waiting on people who'd come for an orgy.

"I'm not looking for her for those purposes," Sin said. "She doesn't belong here."

The butler didn't show any surprise at the statement. Merely said, "I have not seen any young lady with red hair, sir."

"It's Your Grace. I'm the Duke of Sinclair."

"Of course, Your Grace. I beg your pardon, Your Grace. I am Humphries, the butler of Cliffside House. Allow me to show you to your apartments."

Frustrated, Sin followed. The house was harsh gray stone on the outside, but a tribute to Adams on the inside. Pastel colors and intricate white mouldings were everywhere. The furniture was all white and gilt and covered in pastel blue cushions. Partway up the wide stairs, Sin asked abruptly, "Who is the host of this party? My invitation didn't specify."

"My employer is Lord Genvere. An earl. He will be joining the party tomorrow."

"He's arriving late for his own orgy?" Sin had to admit that surprised him.

"That is what he indicated to me, Your Grace."

"I've never met him," Sin said. He thought back over all the peers of England he knew. No Genvere.

"I have not yet had the privilege of meeting him either, Your Grace."

"You can't have been here long, then." The skin along the back of Sin's neck prickled. Something was wrong. Years of abuse had honed his instincts.

"I have been on the island several days, Your Grace. The house was shut up before that. I did not arrive until the house had been rented, aired out, and put in readiness for occupation."

Only several days. He'd assumed the butler would be a fixture of the house. Very few gentlemen would hire new staff for a bacchanalia. They would want to ensure the staff was loyal, discreet, trustworthy.

The man stopped in front of a white door. "Your rooms, Your Grace. I hope you will find it satisfactory. I have been instructed to not enter the guests' bedchambers. And most particularly not your bedchamber. Your trunk will be brought up to your rooms shortly."

With that, the butler bowed, then moved soundlessly down the hall.

Specifically not his bedchamber? What in hell did the servant mean?

Sin pushed open his door. A huge bed stood in the center of the room.

And a woman lay on that bed.

A slender figure of a woman, dressed in a drab gray gown. He moved closer and saw the bands of scarlet around her wrists at the same moment he recognized her.

The scarlet was rope that bound her spread-eagled on his bed. She was wriggling her wrists desperately and muttering curses, trying to work herself free.

He'd found Portia.

3

10 years earlier
London, 1811

Sin's cousin, the current Duchess of Sinclair, pushed herself up from her chair in the austere drawing room—one of six such drawing rooms—in Sinclair House on Park Lane. Tall, thin, with pure white hair piled on her head, the duchess leaned on her cane and glared at Sin with ice-cold fury in her pale blue eyes. "You are not going to marry this person," she snapped. "This girl has no breeding, dowry, or bloodlines. She is a nobody."

"That doesn't matter to me," Sin said. He was a duke—he didn't need to marry women for their money, as his father had done. A vast fortune was his to command. "I'm in love with her, Duchess."

"No doubt," she snapped. "However, that has nothing to do with marriage. When a duke marries, it is a carefully orchestrated social maneuver. You marry to increase wealth and social prestige. If you don't object to bedding the girl, it is icing on the cake."

The duchess waved her walking stick at him and continued. "My God, it is bad enough that my son was killed so stupidly—racing a dratted carriage—and I have had to see *you* become duke. The only vindication for that is that you use your handsome looks to bring about a superb marriage. You will pick the richest duke's daughter in the offing, you fool."

The duchess had told him from the moment he arrived in London that she despised him, that he was not worthy of being a duke. He came from a branch of the family that had been disowned by his great-grandfather, and his father had usually, when drunk, told him the ducal side of the family would rather split them with swords, then spit on their entrails, than speak to them.

The duchess pursed her lips. "I will not allow this marriage to take place."

That startled him. For a moment, Sin felt a jolt of panic. "You can't stop it."

"I will ensure that you see sense," she barked. "You are nineteen years of age. You have not even begun to sow your wild oats. If you're lusty, there are places you can go."

This was a conversation he refused to have. "I am engaged to Portia Lamb and I will not break off the engagement. Not for you. Not for anyone."

"We will see about that," his cousin snapped.

There was nothing to see about. He didn't care what she thought. What the *ton* thought. He wanted to marry for love. He knew what happened when people married and despised each other. He knew what happened when people married for money and social prestige—it led to hatred. Sometimes it led to death.

He turned and walked out of the room.

As he reached the threshold, the duchess shouted, "You will not marry this nobody and make her a duchess. You will marry as I wish. You know nothing about being a duke. And you have the inferior blood of your parents in you!"

Sin kept walking, her words ringing in his ears. She knew how to wound, his cousin. But his past didn't matter. He was going to start again with Portia. She was his promise of a good future.

Dejected, angry, he stalked out of the house. He summoned his carriage and called out to the driver, "Take me to White's."

Willoughby and the rest of his friends had planned to go to the staid old club tonight. He joined them at a table and ordered a bottle of the best port. One for each of them.

"Damn generous of you," said the Earl of Wintermere. "Luck at hazard?"

"No." Sin couldn't keep the grin off his face. "Tonight we celebrate my engagement."

Willoughby's cheroot fell out of his mouth. He caught it before it hit the table. "Your what?"

"My engagement. To the most beautiful and sweet girl in England, Portia Lamb."

"The girl who works at the foundling home?" Will frowned. "Our sort don't marry girls like that. Seduce her if you really want her, then pay her off with a settlement."

"What the hell are you saying, Will?"

"She's a nobody."

He was damn tired of titled people saying that. "She's the woman I love."

"So make her your mistress. That's what peers do. Fuck all the angels and whores you want, but you marry a woman who has two sterling qualities: bloodlines and money. If you find a pretty young debutant who's also deliciously fuckable, that's all to the good. But you don't love your wife. Marry Miss Lamb and you'll make a hell of a mistake."

Sin got up from the chair, a heavy weight on his heart. "I thought you'd be happy for me, Will. I don't understand why everyone is against this marriage. I'm going through with it, no matter what anyone says."

With that, he strode out of White's. He stalked down the steps and turned up St. James Street. For once in his life, he was happy. He wanted love. He didn't want to marry for duty and keep a mistress.

He and Portia would prove them all wrong. He would never

let her find out the truth about him, so they would always be happy.

The next night, his butler announced that the Viscount Willoughby had arrived.

Will walked in. "Forgive me for last night, Sin. I'm delighted to see you happy. Let me make up for what I said. Let me take you out on the town, so you can savor your last few days as a free man."

"So you approve of my marriage?"

A wicked grin flashed on Will's face. "I do. But you need to experience the wild sex on offer in London before you settle down."

"No, Will. I consider myself already married."

"Then we'll hit the gaming hells. Deep play at cards before you put on the leg shackles of marriage."

"All right. Gambling is fine. But nothing involving brothels or sex."

His friend clapped him on the shoulder. "Of course."

But after six hours of gaming and drinking, Willoughby threw his cards on the table of the gaming hell and got to his feet, stumbling. He fell back on his chair, laughing uproariously.

Sin got to his feet. The room tilted, the furniture appeared to slide.

He and Willoughby held each other up, stumbling outside. Sin summoned his carriage with a whistle—it took him three attempts to do it. He fell into it. Willoughby gave an address to the coachman and they were off. Willoughby pulled a flask out of a pocket in his greatcoat and they shared it between them.

"The carriage has stopped." Willoughby got up, lost his balance, and fell against the door. "Why'd this thing jump up and hit me?" he complained.

That seemed like the funniest thing on earth, setting Sin off laughing as he struggled to push open the door. His laughter set Willoughby off. But as the door flew wide, Sin had to grab his friend so he didn't fall on his ass. Will pointed wildly out at a building. "Here it is—the House of Discipline."

"The Who of What?"

It was a town house with a bright scarlet door. A beefy, thick-necked doorman bade them admittance and Will dragged him past statues of naked women—no wait, they were naked women. When they walked inside, the first thing Sin saw was a young blond woman on her hands and knees on a table. Actually, he saw two blondes, both blurry, but he knew there was only one. Behind the pretty blonde, a raven-haired woman with a fake cock strapped to her hips fucked her in the arse. He knew it was going up the blonde's ass, because the blonde was thrusting a thick dildo into her pink glistening pussy from the front.

Blearily, he stared at the scene, his brain taking far too long to focus on what he was seeing.

"I have to leave." He stumbled backward, and fell heavily against the doorframe as his body moved but his boots didn't.

Willoughby laughed. "If you're only here to watch and drink, what's the harm?"

"I can drink somewhere else."

"It's one of your last nights of freedom, man. Enjoy yourself."

Willoughby grabbed his shoulder and propelled him past the women putting on the display, toward a set of double doors painted white. Out of the shadows near the door stepped a young woman.

Sin blinked.

Big tits brimmed over the top of a corset that was dyed black. A leather strap was wrapped around her neck and glittering jewels dangled from it. She wore tall leather boots and a man's beaver top hat. The woman carried a riding crop. And she wore nothing else, so her blond nether curls and pussy were on display, the lips plump, pink, slick, and shining as if wet.

She tapped the crop against her hand.

"To dominate or to be dominated?" she asked.

"That is the question," Will replied, grinning. "He's new.

Looking at him, I can't tell which he'd prefer. But tonight we'll start where he's in charge. Have Mistress Bellows find him a pretty slave. He's got a ten-inch prick. He'll make any sweet, submissive whore very happy."

Sin began to drunkenly protest. For a start, he didn't like having his physical attributes discussed. And he had no intention of doing anything with any prostitute. He was about to get married. To the woman he loved.

The hell with what his cousin, the duchess said. But in his soul, he knew his parents had been warped and he feared he was too.

"What about you?" The girl eyed Willoughby. She took her riding crop and ran it up the inside of her naked thigh. Then stroked it between the lips of her cunny.

The long black rod slid in and out. Drunk as he was, Sin could smell her arousal as she sawed faster.

Willoughby grabbed the crop out of her hand. Abruptly, he replaced it with his fingers and he slid them deep in her pussy. The woman moaned and moved her hips, rocking herself on his fingers.

Sin felt his cheeks heat up. He was likely blushing. He wasn't innocent, but he'd never had sex in front of someone. Neither Will nor the woman appeared to care he was there.

Will took the riding crop and pressed it between the woman's naked arse cheeks.

"Are you going to thrust it up my bum?" she gasped.

"I've got something longer and thicker in mind for that. Take my friend to Mistress Bellows, then come back, and I'll fuck you hard up the arse and make you scream the house down when you come."

The woman trembled. She was pink with desire. She curtsied, which looked strange with her naked lower body, and she held the bottom of her corset to make the motion. "Yes, Master. At once, Master."

Breathlessly, she turned to him. "Come this way, my lord."

"Your Grace," Will corrected.

"Oh heavens. A duke," the woman whispered. "Mistress Bellows will be most happy to please you."

"Look, I'm not interested in this—"

Will moved close. "Go with her. Get a few drinks. There's gaming in the back room. Have some fun and give me some time to fuck the pretty wench."

"I'm not bedding any whores."

"No, you're going to be a staid married man instead."

"A happy married man," Sin corrected. He walked away, staggering slightly. He didn't want to look openly drunk—he'd look vulnerable to any thief who might be lurking. One thing he'd learned about London: some of the seedier brothels were filled with men and women who would steal a man's belongings, get him royally drunk, and chuck him out on the street.

"Look, I don't want to see Mistress Bellows. Take me to the door. I'll hire a hackney to take me—"

"Oh, Your Grace. If the mistress were to know I had not introduced her to a handsome young duke I would be punished. Would you please just greet her? For me?"

His brain function was not at its best. He didn't want the pretty girl to get punished. Some madams were so harsh and abusive, they made army generals look like cuddly kittens. "All right."

Hell, if anything, he felt like he was getting drunker. But he didn't have a glass in his hand.

The woman reached a door, curtsied again by holding the edges of her corset and dipping her legs and naked pussy in front of him. Then she left. She must be returning to Will.

Sin pushed open the door.

In front of him, a tall woman with silver hair piled on her head was tying a younger woman to a strange metal rack. He watched, heart slamming, as the woman looped thick black rope around the delicate wrists.

Suddenly it was like he was eleven years old. It had been

eight years, but he could still hear her voice in his ear. Sinfully silky even as she made demands. *I want you to tie me up. Wouldn't you like that? To dominate me? And if you don't do as I ask, I'll see that you are taken away. You'll find yourself in a brothel of boys who service old men. Or slaving away on a sailing ship, far away from home.*

Christ, he had shoved his memories as far down in his soul as he could. But being here, he was remembering—

"Come forward!" The silver-haired woman snapped her fingers and cracked a whip and two other women scurried forward. They were naked except for high boots with leather turndowns, black masks, and heavy diamond necklaces. Those women crouched and he saw they had sex toys sticking out of their bottoms. Long, white ivory dildos.

His cock bucked in his linens.

No, he was supposed to become a married man.

But this was like nothing he'd ever seen before. A crowd of people all engaged in this scene of sex. The room was filled with gentlemen, all dressed in the latest fashions—all obviously rich. And there were courtesans of every size and shape imaginable, most half-naked. The smell of arousal was drugging.

He knew he should leave. But he was drawn to this, even though he knew it was wrong.

The silver-haired woman walked slowly around a circle of gentlemen, wearing a triumphant smile and cracking the whip against the floor. The sound reverberated through the room. She handed the whip, handle first, to one of the men.

The man leered. He approached the bound woman, spread his legs as if he needed to secure his balance.

He raised the whip.

The lash slapped her bottom with a soft *thwack*.

The leather slid off her delicate skin. A long red line was left, where the tail of the whip had hit.

Sin's cock throbbed. He almost staggered with the sudden jolt of lust that hit him. Ever since he'd been introduced to the wildest, wickedest erotic games, he found he wanted them.

Getting married was his way of taming those needs. Of leaving the past behind. But he was feeling a powerful surge of lust.

Two women ran up to him. The two women with dildos up their arses. Each woman took his hand and placed his palms against the ends of their thick sex toys.

"Pleasure us, please, my lord. Thrust them in our bums."

His cock was pulsing like it was ready to burst. He should refuse. But he was so aroused he felt like he wanted to holler in pain.

They wriggled, using his hands to brace the sex toys and push them deeper in their curvaceous arses. One woman squealed with pure pleasure.

"Please play with us. You are so very handsome," the other begged.

Around him, he saw other people had joined into groups. Threesomes of two men and one woman. One group of five women and one man. Cocks were freed. Pretty hands stroked men's shafts. Mouths happily sucked cockheads. Breasts were bared, bouncing through the room.

Everyone around him was fucking. It was staggering to stand in the middle of so much sex.

"Please play with us," one of the girls cooed. "We like to watch, and then we get so hot, we need relief."

He didn't know what came over him. He started thrusting, just as they wanted. The girls braced themselves against the wall as he drove the fake cocks into their tight butts. They played with each other's pussy. Pinched each other's nipples.

He'd never seen anything so erotic.

His cock damn well hurt, it was so rigid, so engorged, so eager to fuck. He'd never done anything with two women at once. One set of lovely breasts, one rounded ass always seemed like enough. What would it be like to suck both sets of tits? One set was large and tubular shaped, with dark brown nipples. The other was smaller, with little dainty pink nipples.

Would their pussies feel different? What would it be like to dip his cock in one, fuck her a while, then do the other?

What was it like to bed two women?

"You want to bed both of them? Ever done that before? You can't do that when you're married, Sin. Not with a gentle and sweet wife."

Sin let go of the pair of dildos and swung around.

Willoughby stood there, holding an ornate pipe. He drew on it, closing his eyes. Will had a babyish face—a small nose, full lips, deep violet eyes. He had stripped to just his trousers, revealing a muscular bare chest, rock-hard abdomen. Will exhaled sweet-scented smoke, then handed the pipe to Sin.

"Opium. It expands your mind. Takes away all pain. If you're meant to marry, you'll know it once you've let the opium free your mind."

Sin took it, but frowned with suspicion at the beautiful pipe, with its squat bowl and carving of a dragon with coiling tail. He'd never smoked opium.

"Smoke some. I do this all the time. Helps you forget."

Sin jerked his head up. Could Will know he had a hell of a lot he wanted to forget? But Will just grinned and motioned, taking a drag of smoke from the pipe. Sin tried it. Drew in a few puffs; then he began to feel intensely relaxed.

A voluptuous woman in a shift suddenly gripped his arm. "Is this 'im? Ooh, 'e's lovely."

Sin found he was being dragged away. Will followed. Giggling, the prostitute pulled him into a bedroom, gave him the pipe. He had to admit he liked the feeling. He didn't give a damn about anything. He laughed.

Next thing he knew, they were all on top of the bed. Naked. He must have passed out for a few minutes, because he saw Willoughby holding a thick dildo.

"I'm going to stuff you more than you've ever imagined, love," Will said, and opened the woman's plump, pretty legs. He shoved it deep inside her, right to the hilt in one stroke. She squealed and Sin thought she was hurt. Until she winked at them. "I love when you do that, milord."

Willoughby sat on the edge of the bed. "Now, come sit astride me and let me stuff my hard cock up your arse, sweetheart."

"Ooh yes. With this in my cunny, I'll be lovely and full."

"Not yet, my dear. Not yet."

Sin watched her stand and walk, holding the false cock inside. The jewels winked through her blond pubic curls. She got astride Willoughby, with her enormous bare breasts facing him. He gripped his cock, she held the cheeks of her ass apart and she slowly took him inside. Sin heard her moans and Willoughby's grunt, and a spasm of agony shot through his legs.

Sin could see just a couple of inches of Willoughby's long cock, where it was revealed by her parted cheeks.

"Now you get in her, Sin. We're going to fuck her arse together."

God, his brain was fogged. What in Hades was Will saying? "How—?"

"She can take us both. Rub some of the oil on your big prick and get over here."

God, he was so aroused his legs were shaking. Join Willoughby in her ass? It was forbidden. Wicked.

He was going to drown in wickedness.

He grabbed the vial, slicked up his cock. The woman—he didn't know her name—watched him rubbing his shaft with bright eyes. "Oh, you're huge," she gasped. "I don't know if I can take that monster inside as well."

"You can," Willoughby said gruffly.

With his cock slick and leaking fluid out of its tip, Sin got beside her voluptuous ass. Willoughby rocked back, lifting her. Sin pressed his cock in the valley of her rump. He slid, hitting Willoughby's cock. Buried inside her, his friend's cock was completely rigid. He tried to force his way into her snug hole.

"It won't go in."

"Keep working." Willoughby grabbed her full ass cheeks and pulled them wide. Sin held his cock hard and pushed it. Then he felt the pop and the sudden hot, tight grip.

She squealed. "Oh! Oh! It's too much."

"I'll take it out."

"Don't. Let her get used to it."

She was gasping and sobbing, but suddenly she stopped and she wriggled again. "Oh yes. Two enormous pricks in my ass. I never dreamed of such a thing."

"Slide in, Sin. Go in her to the hilt."

He realized his cock was nosing in beside Willoughby's. He was being caressed by the hot walls of her ass and by his friend's shaft. God, he was being squeezed tight. He fought the almost instant desire to come.

He managed to fuck her for five minutes before he exploded in orgasm. The orgasm seared him. Burst inside him. The opium in his system made coming feel like he'd glimpsed heaven.

The instant his climax finished, guilt crushed him. He had to wait for Will to withdraw as well. Will grinned, looking like a naughty boy. "All this can be yours whenever you want. In London, you can experience any sexual adventure that money can buy. Anything you can dream of. Any number of whores. Any type of orgy."

Any sexual experience. Anything he could imagine. Two women and him. Four women. A dozen women.

Sin threw on a robe and got the hell out of the room.

He'd given in to lust, when he was supposed to be in love. But the experience—it had been beyond anything he could imagine.

Downstairs in one of the drawing rooms, he commanded brandy. He flopped into a seat. Drank and kept drinking.

He'd been driven to come here by his cousin, the duchess. Today, she told him she knew everything about his past. When she'd learned he was going to inherit, she had hired investigators and she had bribed the past servants of his parents' house. She had even found the lady's maid who had served his brother's wife, and for a small fortune, the maid had revealed everything. Things he had no idea anyone else knew.

The duchess had called him a monster. Told him she was re-pulsed by him. Insisted he must marry well—marry the daughter of a duke or an earl—to ensure he had an heir with good bloodlines.

He'd told the old hag she was insane and stormed out.

But damn it, he was beginning to think she was right. He was a monster. . . .

He had given into lust. And he wanted more. He wanted to go to a damn orgy. He wanted to do the wildest, kinkiest things. . . .

Sin didn't know what in hell happened to Will—when Will left the brothel or where he went. Sin was still there when the sun came up. Sitting in a chair, his head hung down, empty brandy bottle dangling from his fingers.

He knew he was going to come back to this world. He knew he wouldn't be able to resist.

Some "gentlemen" would still marry Portia, and leave her at night to fulfill their sexual cravings. Easy to justify—a gently bred girl shouldn't know anything about these things. She shouldn't be putting her mouth on a man's cock, or letting him tie her up and fuck her in the ass. A man was supposed to get that elsewhere.

But he couldn't do it. He couldn't leave Portia at night to give his body to other women. Nor could he change—he'd wanted to stop his sinful sexual lusts, but he hadn't been able to do it. It was as if he was addicted to sex.

And because he couldn't change, he couldn't marry Portia.

4

Serenity Island
June 1821

The red ropes were soft, silky, and didn't hurt, but the knots were secure and as much as Portia had struggled, she hadn't been able to get free. It was infuriating.

Now the tall, broad-shouldered, dark-eyed Duke of Sinclair—the man who had ordered her kidnapping—stood at the foot of the enormous bed, staring at her.

Portia knew she should quake in fear. But this man had broken her heart and she wouldn't break down in front of him. Fury commanded her as much as fear.

"God in heaven," he muttered, in his husky baritone voice. "What happened to you?"

At once, he stalked to her right hand, drawing a knife out of the leather turndown of his boot. A knife with a long, thin blade and silver handle. He came to the bed, over six feet in height and muscular, leaning over her. She squeaked in alarm. In real fear, so sudden and shocking, it left her horribly immobile. She was utterly vulnerable, but somehow she was going to fight him if he tried to hurt her—

With one swipe, he slashed through the rope.

He was letting her go?

The duke moved to the rope that bound her right ankle before Portia remembered to breathe again. She'd read Minerva Press novels—stories of innocent girls kidnapped by deformed monks and taken to gloomy castles to satisfy the cravings of strange, wicked gentlemen. The girls in her family's home devoured those stories and she always laughed at how ludicrous they were.

But now that she was living this, she knew the authors had never adequately described how it really felt to be confused, exhausted, scared, and angry all at once.

She met the duke's brown eyes—dark, mysterious eyes the color of melted chocolate, surrounded by long, long lashes—and tried to see if there was anything in there of the sweet, wonderful man she had once agreed to marry.

His eyes looked at her with such tenderness, her throat went dry.

Ten years had changed the Duke of Sinclair. The years had broadened his shoulders, widened his chest. The youthful beauty of his face had hardened into grizzled handsomeness. Wicked handsomeness. It seemed to cast a spell. Otherwise, why would she be studying his wretched looks when he'd broken her heart ten years ago and right now she had no idea whether he was the villain or not?

His gloved hand touched hers after he cut the rope away from her left wrist. Slowly his long fingers traced her palm through her thin gloves. Sensations tumbled. The pressure of his fingers, light and gentle, made her hot—

Really, what was she thinking? "How could you do this to me?" she cried.

The Duke of Sinclair moved to her foot. He freed her ankle, then frowned. His dark brown hair fell over his brow. Ten years ago she used to love to watch the way his thick, silky hair fell over his brow. Her heart would almost explode for he looked so handsome that way.

That scared her more than anything. That right now, when she should be like Merry, reacting in fear with the desire to run, she was remembering this man when he'd been young and sweet. When she had called him by his Christian name, Julian.

This wasn't like her. She was the girl who carried a pistol and who had men believing she was willing to use it.

The Duke of Sinclair had broken her heart once, and she was never going to let him think she felt anything for him but utter disdain.

He held out his hand to help her sit up, but she ignored it and struggled up herself, thankful she wore only light stays instead of a tightly laced corset. Another sign of her practicality.

"I should think I deserve an answer," Portia said tartly.

The duke raked his hand through his hair, making the coffee-brown tresses catch the light of the fire, before they fell back across his aristocratic forehead. He let out a sigh. "You really think I would be responsible for this, love?"

Love. That word—it fluttered inside her, touching her heart like a magic wand and making it swell and ache. Reminding her of how very much she'd once loved him.

"Don't call me that," she cried angrily. "Not *ever*. Not after what you did."

He gave a stiff, abbreviated bow. "My apologies. I will not use the term of endearment again."

He looked hurt? How dare he?

Something inside her snapped. She was always calm and in charge, but right now, fury was washing through her like an unstoppable wave.

"Why shouldn't I think you responsible?" she demanded. "I was told I was being kidnapped for you by the two men who took me. And why did I believe them? Because you told me that you are debauched!"

Ten years ago she had been too shocked when he broke off the engagement to really say what she had felt. Now, all the pain bubbled over.

"Don't you remember?" she demanded. "You said you liked to be tied up, and to tie up women, and have orgies. You said you wanted things that no gently bred girl should ever know about. So when I was told I was being brought to your bed, I assumed that kidnapping for ravishment was one of those things."

He leaned against the bed column, slouching in the way only a man now accustomed to being a duke could do. He looked carelessly elegant with his long legs crossed at the ankles. His brow furrowed and pain turned down the corners of his lips.

"I'm sorry, Portia. I'm sorry about the past. I'm sorry I let you go. But I believe I did the right thing. When I met you, I thought I could be tamed into matrimony. When I realized I wanted all the vices London had to offer—that I needed them— I knew I couldn't marry you. I would only end up hurting you more."

"More than breaking my heart?"

"Wouldn't it have broken your heart more to have married me and to have me leave you at night to go to places where I could indulge my needs?"

"But why do you have such needs?" she asked. "Why couldn't we—us—have been enough?"

He looked down. "It's just the way I am."

Now she was utterly exasperated. Her life was about education. About growth and development and change. "That is ridiculous. People can change. I find children in the stews with no hope and I help them become educated—I've helped them become teachers, physicians, governesses, notaries. Of course you can change!"

"I can't."

"Pah," she said. Not the most clever of retorts, but she was not at her best at the moment. "Anyway, none of this matters. Why am I here?"

Then his gaze lifted, holding hers. Those gorgeous, melting, chocolate-brown eyes . . .

His voice dropped to a deep, hypnotic murmur. "I don't know why you are here. I had nothing to do with it. But you deserve to know I've always loved you. I just can never have you."

Portia's eyes went wide.

For ten years, she had dreamed he would realize he'd made a terrible mistake. Dreamed he would come crawling back and she would tell him, with pride, that he was too late. What woman who'd been jilted didn't dream of having the last laugh when the man in question realized he'd been a complete fool?

And now he was telling her he loved her.

Yet not apologizing for breaking her heart.

"How easy that is for you to say!" she cried.

She had never married. Never had any children of her own. She'd devoted herself to her family's foundling home. She'd had one night of wicked pleasure with Julian, yet he'd bedded scores of women over the last ten years. Portia had never even kissed anyone else. For ten years—over three thousand nights—she'd gone to sleep in her cot, yearning to know love and knowing she never would.

"You've had everything you've wanted for ten years, Your Grace. I've had—" She was about to say "nothing at all." But that wasn't quite true. "I've watched other people be happy, fall in love, marry. I've had my work. I've saved children. But I'm a spinster who had the misfortune of learning what it might have been like if I wasn't one."

"You're not married?"

"Don't sound so surprised," she said bitterly. "Of course I'm not married."

"Why not?"

He was so exasperating! "I couldn't!" The moment the words left her lips she wished she could pull them back. What was she thinking to admit that to him?

"Why not? You weren't ruined, Portia. I wanted you to be

free to find a good man who would give you the love you deserved."

"You really don't understand." Portia realized with shock that he had an entirely different view of the last ten years.

He didn't understand that he could have broken her heart, yet she could still love him. And when she finally didn't love him anymore, she knew what love had felt like. No other man made her feel like that.

So she'd waited.

Waited until she knew she was on the shelf. Until her only means of happiness was to watch others find love and marriage, to find those things that she knew were so very precious.

"Then I was an utter fool, I suppose," she said. "After you, I never gave my heart to anyone else. While you threw scandalous parties and did all your wicked, naughty things. Saying yes to you was a mistake. You *weren't* worthy of me—you were absolutely right."

She launched up from the bed, ignoring how her legs still felt a little weak from being tied up. "If you had nothing to do with this, Sinclair, why did those men tell me I was being brought here for you?"

"Portia, I don't know. Given they kidnapped you, I wouldn't say they were the most morally upstanding of men. They lied to you. As for why they did, I have no bloody idea."

She wanted to take him at his word. Her heart wanted to believe him. And that made her panic.

"Well, I am going to go out there and find out the truth. Now that I am no longer tied up, I will find out who brought me here. And why."

She stalked toward the door.

Sinclair lurched away from the bed column, but Portia hoisted her skirts and she rushed to the door. She grasped the handle and yanked it open.

The door across the hallway stood open. And she could see into the bedroom.

A blond woman was astride a young gentleman, her pink muslin skirts in a frothy tumble. The blonde rode the man the way ladies rode horses. Her bodice was pushed down and her breasts—plump as two musk melons—bounced as she moved up and down. The black-haired man, utterly naked, wore a delighted grin, watching the wobbling dance of her breasts. Portia couldn't tear her gaze away from his muscled arms, the glimpse of his long legs, the devilishly pleased expression on his handsome face. Then the man sat up, buried his face in between the bosom, and waggled his head back and forth so her breasts slapped his cheeks.

Portia stood in the doorway, shocked and transfixed.

Sinclair's arm went around her waist and he pulled her back so fast that her shoulders bumped his chest and her bottom hit his groin. He smelled of lush, exotic sandalwood—that had to be his soap. She could breathe in the astringent witch hazel he must have slapped on his freshly shaven jaw that morning.

She remembered those scents. Remembered how delicious they were on the night he proposed, kissed her senseless, then made her climax for her very first time—

"You can't go out there." His voice was a low rumble near her ear. His breath stirred the wisps of hair on the nape of her neck. "Your reputation will be ruined."

He pulled her back a little farther into the room, so they were clear of the door; then he slammed it shut.

Portia couldn't help it. She couldn't forget the sight of the eager young man slapping himself with breasts.

She should be shocked.

Instead she started to laugh. She just dissolved into giggles and pushed away from the duke, falling with her side against the wall.

He must have thought she was hysterical, her once fiancé, for he lifted her into his arms, carried her across the room, and deposited her on the settee in front of the fire in his rather spacious room.

Being carried in his arms silenced her wild giggles. She couldn't giggle with her heart racing so fast.

He left her and went to a small table, on which sat a silver tray and a glass decanter that reflected the light of the lamps and the fire. It was summer, but there was a fire in the grate. No doubt because of the damp of the ocean.

She couldn't help watching Sinclair's lean, powerful body as he moved.

Next thing she knew, the duke was pressing an enormous snifter of brandy into her hands. "You're still in shock, Portia. Drink this."

She never took spirits. Having spent ten years collecting unwanted children from the stews, she'd seen the evils of alcohol. "I don't want this."

"I promise you I didn't drug it," he said dryly.

She had been staring suspiciously at the glass with her nose wrinkled, she realized. Portia smoothed out her features. "I did not suspect you had, Your Grace." She was simply suspicious of brandy as a concept.

He settled in the wing chair opposite. His broad shoulders filled the backrest. His long-fingered hands curved over the ends of the arms. Sitting there, Sinclair exuded the power of a king. Under his scrutiny, she sniffed the drink. And blinked away tears as her eyes watered.

His voice was a soft ripple in the room. "You used to call me by my Christian name."

"I can't. Not anymore. And we would never have seen each other again, if I hadn't been kidnapped and deposited on your bed. For whatever reason—"

And then an idea struck her as she watched him, remembering he was a gentleman. Gentlemen made ridiculous wagers. They would bet thousands of pounds on dice and cards. On bedding a woman. On which cockroach could race across the floor fastest. "What if this was a wager? Perhaps one of your foolish, drunken friends bet the others that he could kidnap me and tie me to your bed?"

"Perhaps." Frowning, his rubbed his hand across his jaw. "That is possible. But I heard nothing about it."

"Someone here at this party must be involved. That's why I went out there—I have to find who."

"And what will you do when you do find out?"

"I could have that person arrested for kidnapping. Couldn't I?"

"All the men here will be peers of the realm. You were not hurt. That person would argue it was just a joke."

"And my word would be powerless against the word of a peer. Who would listen to me or care about what anguish I went through." She said it bitterly. Frustrated, she took a sip of the brandy. Maybe she did need alcohol—

"It's like drinking lye!" She stuck out her tongue and almost put her hand up to paw her tongue clean.

He quirked a brow. "You've never had brandy before?"

"No, apparently I have not missed a thing."

"Sip slowly."

"There is no danger I would do anything else."

A smile tugged at his lips.

"How can you smile right now?" she demanded.

"You are adorable. I'd almost forgotten that," he said softly. "But you are right. This is no time for smiling. And I assure you—if one of my friends is responsible for this, he will pay."

His eyes narrowed and they were so dark suddenly they were points of black. A hard, ruthless look crossed his face. He'd never looked like that, ten years ago, when he was only nineteen and he'd been so young and sweet. That expression made a shudder run down her spine.

"But to find out who did this, I need to know everything that happened to you, Portia. I need to know if you were . . . hurt in any way."

"Hurt?"

She tried another sip of the brandy. Now that she expected to drink something that she was certain had the same taste as paint, she was prepared. And she just dipped in her tongue. She tried a bigger sip but still shuddered as it went down.

She held the glass away from her. "If I drink all this, I will be as drunk as a skunk and you could easily have your wicked way with me. I'd be too poddled to stop you."

"Poddled?"

"Drunk," she explained. "Inebriated. Foxed. Addled. Soused. Sozzled."

His brow lifted. Apparently he was astounded she knew so many words for drunkenness. But one did, living near the stews.

He sighed. "Portia, I can't believe you think so little of me. I don't get women drunk to get them into bed. I don't need to."

"Of course you don't," she muttered.

He leaned closer, hands on his knees. The concern in his eyes made her heart flutter strangely.

"Portia, damn it, just tell me what happened."

"You needn't swear. I'm going to. I was lured to a house in Whitechapel by a note that begged me to come to a child's rescue. But it was a trap. I was knocked out with ether. When I came to, I was in a carriage at the quay. My hands were bound and I was loaded by masked men onto a dory and brought out to the island. Once we docked, I was knocked out again by that horrible stuff. And when I awoke, here I was."

"Why didn't you call for help?"

She arched a brow. "I was told this was a bacchanalia, Your Grace. Given I was tied hand and foot to a bed, and utterly defenseless at that time, I thought if I called out for help, I might toss myself into a worse pickle."

"Yet you just went storming out to confront people."

"I'm not tied up now."

He made a sound—distinctly like the grinding of teeth. "Having your hands free will not offer you much protection."

"At least this time I could run. And I assure you I am spritely."

"Might I point out you were captured before? This is an island—eventually you'd run out of places to run. Now, in all seriousness, Portia, did those men touch you? Hurt you?"

"Other than slapping an ether-soaked rag to my face, then carrying me upstairs in their arms, my kidnappers were actually perfect gentlemen. Oh yes, and telling me that I was going to wake up in a duke's bed. Which they found uproariously funny."

"So you weren't unconscious the whole time?"

"No, but I rather wished I was when they brought me on the boat."

"Portia, this is not a joke. This is damnably serious."

"I know that." She put her hand to her mouth. A giggle snuck out the side.

Now she realized that half the brandy was gone. She'd drunk much more than she'd expected. Strangely, she felt much different about the kidnapping. More cavalier. Braver.

She had to admit his point about the island was quite true. No matter which direction she ran, there would be the sea. But there must be a boat. Somewhere.

"Explain what happened step by step," he said. "Every detail."

She tipped up her brandy for a little more before she began. Wait, where did it go? There wasn't any left. She held out the glass. "More first."

"You've had enough."

"This is for medicinal purposes." But it came out *medishnal porpoises.*

"No, Portia—"

"You won't give me any until I tell you. Oh, all right." She took a deep breath. "I received a note, delivered by a boy from the streets. The missive asked me to go to Maiden Lane, as there was a young girl there about to be sold to a brothel. I hired a hackney—"

"You went alone."

"No, I took Merry—a girl who works at the foundling home. And a pistol for protection."

"But it didn't protect you."

"Well, it wasn't loaded. And the men who kidnapped me knew it wasn't loaded."

"Interesting," he murmured.

"*I* thought so," she said. "I mean, how would they know that?"

"When did these men approach you?"

"If you let me continue with my story, Your Grace, I will tell you. Before I reached the house, the two miscreants slunk out of the alley and confronted us. I attempted to bluff them with the pistol, but was unsuccessful. Anyway, at that point they let Merry go. I ran and they chased me. One managed to catch me, said I'd wake up in the Duke of Sinclair's bed, then slapped an ether-soaked cloth on my nose and mouth. Before the bed, I woke up in a rocking dory. I was sick, really sick in the boat. I was knocked out again. I remember going upward. I would have thought I was ascending to heaven, if it weren't so jostling and uncomfortable. Apparently, that was when they carried me up to this house. After that, I did indeed wake up in your bed. I remember the men perfectly well. One of the men was tall and thin. He had black hair, a crooked nose, and he was missing several teeth. He had a scar on his right temple. The other was short and fat. So fat, he didn't have a proper neck at all. Just a roll of fat that connected his head to his shoulders."

"Would you recognize them if you saw them again?"

"Oh yes. That was an incident I'll never forget. Their faces will be etched in my memory forever." She held out her glass again. "You owe me more given everything you've put me through."

"Portia, you are astounding. You've had—" He broke off.

How odd. The room was tilting to the right.

Then she was looking at the ceiling. It was revolving slowly. Blech. That was the only way to describe the horrible sensation that suddenly gripped her. The room was moving and she wanted it to stop. She closed her eyes.

No, not seeing the room move didn't stop it, didn't make her feel one jot better—

Oh no! Her stomach was attempting to escape. She clapped her hands to her mouth—

"Hell," Sinclair growled.

He hauled out the porcelain chamber pot and held it in front of her. She stared at him helplessly. She wasn't going to be sick.

Oh wait, she was.

5

Sin drew the counterpane over Portia. Bending over her, he brushed back her hair, damp from when he'd bathed her with water from his ewer. Admittedly he'd poured her a generous glass of brandy. It had never occurred to him it would be enough to knock her senseless.

"Sorry, love."

She didn't protest the endearment. She couldn't—she was unconscious. Carefully, he tucked the cover around her. That meant leaning over her. With his lips mere inches from hers. She had rinsed her mouth and had kept her hand over it, before she'd passed out.

He wanted to kiss her anyway. On her lips. Her soft cheeks. Her cute nose. Her fluttering lashes.

And he had no right.

At least she was in no fit shape to go questioning people at the orgy. He suspected it wasn't just the brandy. She must be exhausted from the fear and shock of her ordeal. By the time she woke up, he intended to have found out what in hell was going on.

Heading to the door, Sin jumped when he found the butler standing on the other side. What was the man's name? Humphries.

Humphries held a silver salver on which was a thick, folded note, sealed with scarlet wax. The butler bowed. "These messages were instructed to be delivered to each guest at precisely six o'clock, Your Grace."

Sin grabbed the message but didn't open it. He'd been preoccupied with Portia and hadn't thought about the mystery of this party. Now that he'd heard her story, he was damned interested in their host. "It's not just that I haven't met the host, Humphries. I've never heard of a Lord Genvere."

Why would Genvere sign a letter with a *W*? If it was the man's Christian name, the familiarity was lost on him, because he didn't know the man.

The butler took on a worried look. "Nor had I, Your Grace, before I was offered employment. His lordship's secretary contacted me while I was still with the Marquis of Barrow-Ffinch. Lord Genvere made a most astoundingly generous offer for my services, one I could not refuse. My first action was to peruse DeBrett's for further information on his lordship. According to that revered tome, Genvere was a line that had died out. When I was hired, I was told that the new Lord Genvere had resided in the West Indies and had only lately been discovered as the heir to the earldom. I believe he owned several lucrative plantations on the islands."

"And he's supposed to arrive tomorrow?"

"Yes, Your Grace. In the morning, via the dory from the mainland. I was given precise written instructions on how to proceed this evening, in the absence of Lord Genvere. At exactly this time, I was to deliver these messages."

"Lord Genvere tends to be eccentric?"

"I really could not say, Your Grace. Though this arrangement is not the sort to which I am accustomed. I find it quite odd."

Sin was surprised the butler had revealed so much. Humphries had dropped the perfect servant expression and looked uneasy. But then, as if he'd remembered his place, he became expressionless once more and bowed with stiff correctness. "I must deliver the remaining missives, Your Grace." He moved down the corridor, on to the next room.

Sin wanted to talk to the other guests. Doing that without Portia made the most sense.

He had to admit Portia's strength and courage impressed him. Those attributes had drawn him to her ten years ago. She hadn't changed at all.

And hell . . . ten years had only made her more beautiful. She'd matured from a pretty girl with large eyes and flame-colored curls into a voluptuous woman. Her hair was still rich and red. Her large, uptilted eyes, full lips, and spray of freckles gave her a startling beauty—a combination of sweet and sensual.

Which definitely meant an orgy was no place for her.

As he went down the stairs, Sin tore open his letter. A second sealed note fell out and landed on the step. He bent and picked it up.

Miss Portia Lamb was written on it.

What the hell—? Their host knew she would be here. Genvere had to be responsible for her kidnapping.

Bastard.

Whoever the hell this man was, he'd have hell to pay when he arrived.

Sin looked down at the first sheet, the one addressed to him. Three sentences were written across the page.

I know all your sins. They will soon be
revealed. And you will pay for your crime.

What in hell was this?

Sin had reached the first floor and he stood, staring at the blasted letter. He had a boatload of sins to his name. But no one could know about the crime. That wasn't possible—

A hand grabbed his arse and squeezed hard.

"What the blazing hell—?" he snapped, and spun around.

A woman had her hand on his buttock. She tittered behind her ruby-encrusted fan. Her long lashes fluttered at him. Har-

riet Barker was one of London's most successful brothel owners. She had started as a prostitute in the House of Discipline,
took it over when the former madam died, and had taken control of dozens of brothels in London. She ruled her empire like
Bloody Mary had ruled England.

She had come to many of his orgies, though he'd never been
intimate with her.

She was too old for him. Too ruthless.

She reminded him of—no, hell, he wasn't going to think of
his brother's wife.

Harriet folded her fan, but still had hold of his ass.

Usually, when he went to an orgy, he did not object to being
fondled. Touched. Admired. Right now, it made him want to
grit his teeth.

He moved her hand away.

Harriet laughed. "Your Grace, how delightful to see you
here. There are several charming young gentlemen here, but
none as handsome and delicious as you."

Could this woman be involved in Portia's kidnapping? Harriet Barker was not adverse to hauling innocent women off the
streets of London and forcing them to work in her brothels.
She had a private army of thugs and criminals.

So how did he handle this? Ask her bluntly? She wouldn't
admit kidnapping Portia and it would put her on guard.

He bowed over her hand, kissing it lightly. "And you are
ravishing as always, Mrs. Barker." He was very practiced at
meaningless compliments.

"Do call me Harriet, my dear Sin."

"I found an unusual gift in my room, Harriet. But no calling
card, so I don't know who to thank for its delivery."

She was waiting for him to offer his arm, so they could stroll
together. But he played obtuse.

"A gift?" she squawked. "*I* didn't receive anything." She actually pouted. "Our host must have wanted to reward a duke."

"I wondered if it was from you," he said, though from her

reaction he doubted it. He didn't think Harriet was smart enough to display such genuine acting.

She frowned. Lines puckered her forehead. "I am afraid not, my darling duke. But I should be happy to give you a gift later. A very special gift. I am aware of how generously endowed you are. I could swallow it all for you. Every inch."

"Er, yes. I imagine you're skilled enough to do it."

"Shall I show you now? A little aperitif before dinner is served?"

No, he really couldn't see Harriet Barkder being responsible for Portia's kidnapping. Portia would be competition.

He managed to get away from Harriet, telling her he had to speak to the butler. He found Humphries as the man emerged from the servants' stairs, carrying a tray with a decanter of sherry.

Sin cornered the man, who swallowed and said nervously, "May I help you, Your Grace?"

"What do you know of the woman in my room? You gave me a note with her name on it." In fury, he loomed over the butler. "Do you know how she was brought here? Unconscious and against her will? She was kidnapped."

The man's jaw dropped. His face went pale. "I don't understand, Your Grace. How can that be possible? I had no idea—no idea. In my instructions, I was told that you would have a Miss Portia Lamb joining you. I was told to give you a box when you informed me of her arrival, and to tell you that it is specifically requested that she come to dinner tonight. All guests are to attend, I was told. An important announcement is to be made."

"Then he did arrive. Genvere. Where is the bast—man?"

"He has not arrived, Your Grace. I have a sealed letter, and I am to read it in his stead. Please excuse me one moment, Your Grace, while I fetch the box. All the guests are to enjoy sherry in the drawing room, as they arrive, before dinner."

Sin barely heard the last bit. Too many thoughts were racing through his head. He was expected to bring Portia downstairs? What the hell? Why was someone doing this? *Who?*

The object appeared to be to ruin Portia, but he couldn't see who would engineer all this for that end. And what would be the point—Portia was a spinster. She'd said she would not likely marry. It had taken money to hire men to kidnap her and bring her here. As well, this party had required a great deal of money. This had to be the work of a gentleman. What gentleman would want to destroy Portia's reputation? Or see her ravished at an orgy?

Was she right—was all this over a wager?

Sin followed the butler to the drawing room. Seething. He barely noticed the décor of the house around him. Modern, with delicate plasterwork and pale white-painted mouldings, all light colors. White marble statues of well-endowed naked gods sat in niches.

The butler opened white double doors, revealing a large drawing room. A glossy-painted white piano sat off to the side. The room was blindingly white. Sin was the first guest to arrive in the drawing room, a room lined with arched windows that looked out to the sea, away from shore. Dark clouds massed on the horizon, high, gray, imposing. A storm was coming.

He waited, pacing in front of the windows. If a storm hit, he wouldn't be able to get Portia off the island.

High-pitched giggling told him a woman was coming. And he was right. Two courtesans strolled through the door, arm in arm, whispering to each other.

"Your Grace!" At the sight of him, they both dropped into deep curtsies.

He knew them. They were London's darlings of the courtesan world at the moment. One was Sadie. With pure golden blond hair, she looked like an angel, but she could be coarse and blunt. Men liked the contrast between her sweet-as-pie appearance and her brazen, wanton behavior. She wore a tight scarlet dress, with her large cleavage jiggling over the low neckline. When she curtsied she dropped low, so he could see down it. He took one glance, remembered Portia in his room, and looked away. Sadie stuck out her lower lip, playfully wounded, he was sure.

She'd been to his parties and he'd seen it all before. And given Portia needed a protector, he had to put other things on his mind than sex.

For him, an unusual undertaking.

The other woman held out her hand to him with more elegance and aplomb than a royal princess. "Your Grace. How delightful," she crooned, in her posh, throaty accents.

She was Clarissa Carrington, London's most sought-after Incognita. Dark haired with large green eyes, she was elegant and lovely. She dressed exactly like a young lady of the *ton*. And looked like the sort of blue-blooded heiress a peer was supposed to marry, except she had bedroom talents no girl of the *ton* would ever learn. Men adored her. Clarissa claimed she'd received marriage proposals from every eligible peer and had turned them all down. It was a lie—Sin had never proposed to her.

They were the sort of courtesans invited to any and every orgy held in London. But at no other bacchanalia that he'd attended had one guest been kidnapped.

Clarissa sidled up to him, her green eyes glowing at him. "I had no idea you were to be a guest. What do you think of the island setting? It's rather isolated." She gave an exaggerated shudder. "I find it rather frightening. But perhaps you shall protect me?"

"From what?" Frowning, he looked down at her. He'd thought her fear was just a ruse to snare his attentions for the party, but she looked pale. Did she know something?

"Did you receive a note?" he asked abruptly.

She blinked her huge green eyes. "A note? What kind of note?"

"One from our mysterious host."

"Is he mysterious? I was told he was delayed and will arrive tomorrow. I have never met him. Of course, you must know him well. Given this is to be the grandest orgy ever held in England, I assume he must attend your famous parties all the time."

"I've never met him either," Sin said. He watched her eyes.

"Did he send you a note in which he threatened to reveal your sins?" He gambled and revealed, "I received one also."

"If he wished to list your wicked sins, it would take him weeks to do so." She laughed a silvery laugh. "I have nothing to hide. I don't think I am a sinner in any way. I'm a survivor."

Sin glanced to the other courtesan. "Do you know if Sadie received a note?"

Clarissa narrowed her eyes, looking instantly much tougher. "Darling Sadie Bradshaw got something all right. She says it was a request from the host that she join him tomorrow night when he arrives. But I think she's lying."

"Our host appears to be playing some kind of a game," he said darkly.

"Yes." She slipped her arm through his, taking him by surprise. "It all seems rather silly. Perhaps he means to tease us, then have our 'sins' be particular carnal games we are to play. I took part in an erotic scavenger hunt once. All over London there were clues, and we were dared to do erotic things to get them. Very naughty fun."

It made sense. But why include Portia?

He was trying to ease his arm free of Clarissa when Sadie sashayed up to him and grabbed hold of his arm on the other side.

"Are you monopolizing our steamy duke, Clarrie?" Sadie demanded as she plastered herself right up against him, squishing her bosom to his biceps.

He tried to peel her off, but it was likely extracting a small boat from a large squid. So he questioned Sadie while he tried to get free of her, and her hand drifted closer and closer to his ballocks.

Sadie hadn't met the host, Genvere, either. She couldn't even remember hearing of him in London.

Sin finally growled in Sadie's ear. "Let go of me now, love, and I'll reward you later."

"Coo, all right." She released him and fluffed her blond curls. She shot a smug look at Clarissa. Then she widened her eyes. "Perhaps Lord Genvere is a deformed recluse," she said breathlessly. "He is so hideous he cannot go to London's parties. Even brothels would turn him away.

Clarissa laughed. "You should write Minerva Press novels, darling. How debauched. Do you think he will also chain us up in the dungeon?"

"Perhaps. And perhaps he'll use his whip and crop." Sadie ran her tongue around her lips and Sin saw she was looking right at him. "I do love to be punished by a big, strapping gentleman with a huge cock, Your Grace."

"Good for you," he muttered. Normally he'd play along. Tonight he was too worried, too frustrated. "Even though neither of you know Genvere, do you know what kind of entertainment he planned here? Anything involving virgins?"

"Virgins?" Clarissa echoed. "Here?"

"Virgins are dead boring," Sadie declared. "I hope there aren't virgins here. Men are so fascinated with them. Possibly because men know a girl with her cherry unpopped will have no frame of reference."

Before Sin could answer, a masculine voice asked, "Sin, what are you doing here?"

The last time he'd heard that voice, he'd been staring down the muzzle of a dueling pistol.

Sin turned and faced Willoughby, his former good friend. The man who had introduced him to London's vices. Who had ruined his engagement to Portia.

Though that was ultimately his own damn fault.

But still he saw red. Maybe the reason Portia was here was due to a wager amongst his drunken friends—his *former* drunken friends.

He was about to stalk over to Willoughby to find out if the man had arranged Portia's kidnapping, when he just about choked.

Portia stood in the doorway. She wore a cloak, with the hood up, so her face was slightly hidden at least, but not much. If

Willoughby turned around, damn it, he would see her. Willoughby would remember her.

But what in hell was she thinking?

He stalked past Willoughby, felt his former friend's stare on him as he did. He moved fast to block Will's line of sight. Portia's lips parted as he reached her, but he shook his head, warning her not to speak. He grasped her arm as she started to protest and hauled her away from the drawing room door, out into the corridor.

Several squawks of protest came, but he ignored them. He dragged her into a darkened room he assumed was empty.

When he saw his good friend, the Duke of Saxonby, thrusting into the beautiful widow, Lady Linley, from behind, he knew his assumption had been wrong.

The most beautiful woman Portia had ever seen leaned over the arm of a sofa, braced on her hands. Her pale gold hair was pinned up in curls, decorated with diamonds, and one loose tendril dangled and bounced by her face. The woman's face, in profile, was as lovely as an angel's, even as she cried out, "Oh yes, Sax. Harder!"

Then Portia stopped looking at the woman's face and realized what the woman was doing.

Her gown of white silk with gauzy gold lace was open at the back and spilling down her arms. Her skirts were thrown up, revealing a naked, heart-shaped bottom. Her bosom was naked too, except a man's hands were in there, cupping the woman's breasts from behind. . . .

While he thrust into her from behind with long, powerful strokes. Powerful enough to make the sofa shake and a painting rattle on the wall beside them.

The man had pale blond hair—no, it was silvery blond on top, but black below, where it fell against the nape of his neck. His lashes were long and pure black, his brows dark, which looked striking against his pale and dark hair. He whispered gruffly, "Play with yourself, my angel. Stroke your clit and come for me again."

He hadn't removed a stitch of his clothing and there was something about the contrast of a softly curved, naked woman and a fully dressed, powerful-looking male that made Portia's breath catch in her throat.

She felt rather trembly inside.

The woman's hands slipped beneath frothy petticoats and moved vigorously. Her moans grew louder.

Portia's heart palpitated.

"Oh yes!" the woman cried, with such breathless agony that Portia felt a jolt of desire and her legs almost buckled beneath her.

Sinclair's arm went around her chest and she was hauled away yet again.

Out into the corridor. Down the corridor. Her sensible shoes were barely touching the floor, he moved her so hastily.

She had come downstairs feeling rather sore in the head from the brandy. Now she felt a different ache coursing through her. A throb down low in her belly. She'd forgotten all about that slight pounding in her head.

All she could think of was the way that handsome man with unusual hair had thrust into that receptive woman.

Her face flamed. Suddenly she realized what she had done. "I shouldn't have looked. I invaded their privacy."

"Don't worry, Miss La—my dear. That's the point of an orgy. To look."

Sinclair dragged her farther away, down the corridor, when someone cleared their throat and the duke just about jumped a foot. She knew, because he almost pulled her with him.

The butler stood there, carrying a large, flat box on his silver salver. "Your Grace? This is the box intended for Miss Lamb."

6

Portia was whisked back up the stairs by the duke, whose dark brown eyes gleamed. He looked tremendously annoyed and she couldn't think why.

She tried to dig in her heels at the top, but that was impossible in the carpet runner. Sinclair pulled her down the hall, back into his bedchamber, and slammed the door shut behind them.

His face looked as stormy as the view through his windows.

Sinclair had grasped the mysterious box, which he now held just out her reach as he shut the door to the room.

Portia reached for it, and he lifted it. Without thinking, she launched up on her tiptoes, almost lost her balance, and had to put her hand against his chest.

She felt the hardness of his muscles even through his coat, waistcoat, and shirt. Her breath caught, her heart wobbled.

She remembered how their friendship, their courtship had blossomed slowly. She truly had not believed a young duke was falling in love with her, not when he was surrounded by pretty debutants in fancy gowns. He was so earnest and sweet, helping her rescue children. Then one afternoon, he'd teased her playfully, annoyed her until she had glared at him and he'd burst out laughing. Then he'd kissed her and—oh—it had been heavenly. And hot. So very hot. Suddenly she'd realized why men were rakish, why women fell in love.

The next day, he'd proposed—

Portia pushed those thoughts away. She stepped back and crossed her arms over her chest. "Are you going to give me the mysterious gift or not?"

He also crossed his arms over his chest. Glowered. "What in the name of sense did you think you were doing? I told you not to go down. Any one of those people could have seen you. Your reputation would have been ruined."

"I have learned to take charge of my own life. I've had to fend on my own for years. I certainly do not believe in cowering and relying on a man to protect me."

His dark brow arched.

He looked as if he was about to say something, and she could guess what it was. "I wasn't accustomed to brandy. I'm normally far more sensible." She was always sensible, unless she was around him. Now she knew to be extra careful. "Anyway, I am now considerably more knowledgeable about intimate relations between men and women—I thought it was simply beds and a woman lying down."

A flush touched his high cheekbones. That startled her. Was the Duke of Sinclair actually blushing?

"Please give me my box," she said.

"I'm going to open it," he insisted.

"Why—do you think a snake will spring out?"

"Someone kidnapped you, Portia, and I intend to keep you safe from now on."

If only he'd been so protective, so stubborn ten years ago. Why now did he act as if she was responsibility?

"You are not my husband. You don't dictate to me."

She saw him wince. "I'm not," he agreed. "But I'm taller than you, which means I get to decide who opens the box."

"You are infuriating."

He tugged the large silk bow and the ribbon fell free. Then

he pulled off the top of the box, still holding the wretched thing over her head.

Portia quickly concocted a plan. She moved close to the window. Gasped and peered down.

"Oh my goodness, look out the window! On the terrace, six women are doing things to that naked man—"

Sinclair came at once to the window to look at the shocking sight she had not actually seen. As he did, peering out the window to find people who weren't there, he lowered the box.

Portia grabbed it. She hurried away from him, looking into the box. She pulled out tissue paper, sending it fluttering behind her.

"Portia, blast, give me back that box."

She ignored him. Frowning, she picked up a sparkling item that sat within. "It's a mask."

In her moment of confusion, he took it right out of her hand. He studied it, then handed it back.

"Indeed, it looks like a mask," he said. "Hold it up to your face. I'll tie the strings behind your head."

She stepped in front of the cheval mirror in its huge gilt frame. Sin was reflected behind her, his long-fingered hands holding the white satin ties of the beautiful white mask. It was made of papier-mâché and white and gold paint, decorated with pearls and ribbons of white satin. It suited her very red hair—most things didn't.

Sin's hands moved to her shoulders, but he didn't quite touch her.

Stop it, Portia. You don't want his touch. Or his kiss. Or his... his anything else.

She'd overheard what that courtesan had said. Shocking things. A huge ... cock, she'd said. Portia remembered when he'd dropped his trousers in front of her, ten years ago. ...

She had to stop thinking of things like that!

The duke stepped back without touching her.

It was for the best. She might touch him back. Maybe she was still a little drunk after all.

"Your dress is wrong," he said, rubbing his jaw. "With the mask, you could pass for a courtesan, but not in that gown. I'd never let any woman of mine wear a dowdy dress like that."

"Well, I am not your woman. And this is a practical dress for practical and important work. It's also all I could afford." Which was true. Of course, her brothers were married and they were always fashionably and respectably dressed, for they had to attend parties and drum up donations for the home. Portia, as an unmarried woman, didn't make house visits or attend balls and parties, so she had no need for anything but sensible clothing. Which meant drab.

Whenever she felt a little tug of longing over a fashionable dress, she remembered that she did good work. And didn't need bright plumage.

"I wonder if our bizarre host thought of this," he said. "If he gave you a mask, it means your ruin is not his intention. I wish I could figure out what in hell his intention is."

She didn't reprimand him on his language as she rather agreed.

He left her and walked through a doorway into a second room. She had explored while he was downstairs. That was a dressing room, with several wardrobes and a cushioned bench for one to sit while being dressed by a servant—something she'd never experienced. All of the wardrobes were empty. No servant had arrived to unpack his belongings.

A shiver ran down her back. Suddenly she didn't want to wear the mask. She wanted to rip it off.

But Sinclair was right. She couldn't let people know her identity. She would be ruined. And that would ruin the foundling home.

A knock came at the bedroom door. Portia opened it a crack.

"Pardon me, but this was to be delivered to His Grace." A pretty face was behind the door. A young housemaid. Over her arms was the most beautiful gown Portia had ever seen.

"Thank you." Portia held out her arms and took it, turning

and shutting the door as the duke came out. "A dress was delivered."

"So Genvere did realize you would need one." He shook his head. "I don't like this."

"It's a beautiful gown. It must have cost a fortune."

"We'll put it on you."

"*We?* I am not stripping to my undergarments in front of you. I will dress myself."

"No, you won't."

"Yes, I will," she said firmly. "I will do so in the dressing room."

But as she struggled to get into the dress, she understood why he'd said she couldn't dress herself. She couldn't reach the fastenings. This was a gown intended for a woman who had a lady's maid to help her dress.

And she would have to use the duke.

Oh bother.

Pinning her dress against her front with her hands, Portia went back into the bedchamber. Swallowed hard. Sinclair was stretched out on the bed, his booted feet hanging off the edge, a glass of brandy in his hand.

"You were correct," she conceded. "I need your help to get dressed."

"Then come over here." His voice was low and husky.

She didn't want to approach him on the bed. Didn't want to *think* about him on a bed. Trousers covered his long legs and he wore his tailcoat, waistcoat, and shirt. He was utterly the opposite of naked. Yet he looked so informal and relaxed on the bed, it felt far too intimate.

With a grunt, he sat up. His hand settled on her hip and she jumped, clutching the dress.

She stood on the dress and almost pitched forward, but his hand slid around her middle, supporting her, and he set her back on her feet. Carefully, he drew the soft, satiny fabric up on her shoulders, drawing the lace-trimmed edges together. His knuckles skimmed the nape of her neck.

Portia bit her lip. Just that touch seemed to set her skin aflame.

But he'd broken her heart. She'd been so hurt by the duke she would never let herself feel desire for him again.

She would have to *stop* it. By force of will, she would make it go away.

Adeptly, he managed all the fastenings. He was very good with women's clothing. She supposed he'd had lots of practice.

The dress was rich ivory silk decorated with pearls and black lace. The neckline scooped shockingly low. As he tended to the fastenings at the back, it pulled the fabric snug to her back and made her breasts appear plump and rounded above the neckline. The skirt fell in shimmering beauty over her hips. She'd never worn such a dress. In the warm-toned embroidered silk, with the white and gold mask, she looked both innocent and exotic. Her flame-red hair looked lovely and wild, instead of just an untamed, unruly bother.

His hands brushed her low back as he finished the fasteners. A shock rushed through her. She was so aware of his hands, her heart was pounding, her whole body tense.

"Done," he said, and it came out strangled. He was breathing hard.

While she fought to control her breathing. He could carelessly feel desire—she would not allow herself the same.

"You look beautiful, Portia." His voice dropped to a whisper of a growl. He bent to her ear, where his breath brushed over the back of her neck and she felt like a helpless puddle of wax approached by a flame. "So very beautiful."

The caress of his warm breath made her ache. She felt a sharp pang right through her—right down to her intimate place.

"Don't."

"Don't what?"

"S-speak so close to me." Her voice shook.

She stepped away from him, aware of the sensual rustle of silk. The stunningly soft way the fabric caressed her skin—

Then she realized something. She turned in front of the mirror, her heart pounding. "It fits me perfectly. As if it was made to my measurements. Who could do that? I mean, how could anyone know?"

Sinclair shook his head. "I don't know."

She stared at him. Of course, even he couldn't know her measurements. Had someone watched her and guessed? But this gown must have taken days to make. How long had someone been watching her?

A shiver went down her back. It felt like a spider crawling along her neck—which had happened the time she'd decided to clean the foundling home's attics.

"This . . . this is unsettling," she said. "Perhaps a bit . . . disturbing."

"Unsettling? A bit disturbing? That is your description for this? Any other woman would have had the vapors. Long ago."

"That would be pointless. Besides, you might give me more brandy." Ruefully, she touched her head. "I never intend to do *that* again."

His gaze moved slowly over her, and it heated her in its path.

She both liked it and desperately wished he would not do that. "There. I am ready to go downstairs. Down to the orgy."

But before she could take a step, his hand was on her wrist. "I want to know the truth, Portia. Why are you so determined to go down to an orgy?"

Sin couldn't stop suspicion from rising. Along with another part of his anatomy.

Portia was breathing fast and her cheeks were pink. He could sense she was hiding something. He'd learned from living with his family how to tell when people were lying to him— people he had trusted and loved.

Could Portia be in on some kind of game to hurt him? She had every reason to hate him. She hadn't forgiven him. And why in hell would she? He'd broken her heart.

Was her kidnapping fake? Was that the reason a dress was provided that fit her perfectly?

So damn perfect it made his mouth water?

She moved away from him, but she stopped in front of the mirror. Stared at herself as if she couldn't believe it was her reflection. She was a beautiful creature. In the pale ivory with the gleaming mask, she looked like an angel who had come down to sin.

"I am willing to endure it," she said briskly. "To find out who kidnapped me."

"I can find that out. You can trust me to find information for you."

His suspicious nature, honed by years of hell, wondered if she needed to be downstairs to contact a conspirator.

No, this was Portia. Innocent to the core. What was wrong with him?

His childhood had poisoned him. Made him suspect rot and evil everywhere.

Just as he was considering that, she said, "I don't know that I can trust you. How do I really know you are not involved?"

"If I really had you kidnapped for nefarious purposes, don't you think I'd be having my wicked way with you by now?"

"There is no need to take offense at my doubt," she said firmly. "After all, you brought it upon yourself."

He groaned. "Yes, I know this. Let me make amends then."

She studied her masked face in the mirror. "No one will recognize me, will they?" she asked. "So there's no danger."

"There is a hell of a lot of danger."

"Of what sort?"

"You're trying to flush out a kidnapper. Dangerous by definition. And the danger that men will take one look at you in that gown and want you."

Her lips parted. Her mouth alone—Christ, it was gorgeous. There were men who would sell their souls to kiss those lips. Having her eyes and cheeks masked made her lips all the more erotic.

"I can avoid such men."

He rolled his eyes. "You can't."

"But if I went downstairs, would you—protect me?"

"With my life."

Her chest rose with her sharp breath. Her neckline was cut so low, her breasts lifted, wobbled, and almost bounced up over the neckline. His sharp eyes detected the dark pink hue of her nipples, barely covered by the lace of the gown. He had to grit his teeth as the desire to taste those nipples hit him. "But since I'd like to keep my life, I need you to stay up here. Locked in this room."

"But I want to go!" she cried.

Sin blinked. "You want to go?"

Below her mask, he could see her cheeks turning bright pink.

"Why is that such a surprise to *you?*" she exclaimed. "This is what tempted you away from me. I've always—I've always wanted to know. I want to just see . . . what it's like. I'm just . . . curious."

She couldn't have shocked him more if she'd suddenly hit him in the face with a shovel.

"You're curious," he repeated slowly.

Hell, he'd never dreamed of that. Portia had always been so good. She was as far from his dark, tormented world as he could imagine.

And she was curious about an orgy?

His cock responded. His brain said: *Look, this beautiful, tempting woman wants to know all about wicked sex.* At the same instant, his prick stood proud, saluted, and was ready to offer its services. Blood raced down so fast it physically hurt as his cock bolted into hardness.

Sin drank in the sight of Portia in front of her mirror. The bodice of her fashionable dress cradled her breasts, lifting them high. The fabric skimmed her rounded hips and fell in a sweep of glimmer along her legs.

He wanted to take the dress off her. Reveal every inch of her soft ivory skin. Kiss her everywhere.

He'd seen hundreds of women naked. Given the size of his orgies, possibly thousands. But he'd never seen Portia naked.

He was just seeing Portia's bare neck and a little bit of naked shoulder.

And he was on fire.

She squared her shoulders and stared him in the eye. "I wanted to know what was so fascinating about them. What made you want them so much."

Sin couldn't resist. He bent and pressed his lips to the nape of her neck. She tasted fresh and clean. Like lavender and a sweet English spring. "God," he muttered. "I made a hell of a mistake. I should have married you and dedicated my life to giving you pleasure."

She froze.

He nuzzled her neck, just behind her ear.

She whimpered.

His cock throbbed and he could barely think. One delicious fuck and she would be his forever—

She pulled away from him. "No! You wouldn't have done that. You would have preferred to go to brothels and had your naughty parties. I wouldn't have kept you interested."

"Yes, you would."

She shook her head fiercely. "It's too late. Too wretchedly late."

She started for the door.

"Before you go storming away, Portia, you need to read this." Sin drew the sealed note addressed to her out of the pocket of his waistcoat and handed it to her. "I was given a note by the butler, from our host, Lord Genvere. Enclosed in mine was this note, addressed to you."

"I don't know Lord Genvere. . . ." She tore it open. "Goodness, what is this? It makes no sense at all. "It says: '*I know all your sins*—' "

"'*They will soon be revealed. And you will pay for your crime,'*" he finished.

"How did you know?"

"Mine said the same. This note means our host must be responsible for bringing you here. He's not coming until tomorrow morning. I don't care for Genvere's sense of humor."

"I no longer think this could be a joke." She pointed to the bottom of her note. Unlike his, hers had a smear of color on the paper. A thick, inconsistent line of dull red-brown ink. No, not ink. Blood. As if the writer had wanted to punctuate the message with a fierce underline of blood.

"This is a threat," she whispered.

7

I made a hell of a mistake. I should have married you and dedicated my life to giving you pleasure.

Portia kept hearing his words in her head. Each one punctuated by the thrumming beat of her heart as she walked downstairs.

She should have been thinking of the horrible note she'd received. The bloody print on it. The threat. Sinclair had believed it was paint, not blood. But she suspected he was lying to keep her from being afraid.

The threat made him become terribly protective and insist she should stay locked in the bedroom. She'd insisted it was all the more reason to go downstairs.

Finally, he had relented. Sinclair said he was reluctant to leave her alone, even if locked in her room, because she could be in further danger. He wanted her where he could see her.

Really, how dare he think he had to give her permission! He had surrendered that right on the night he had broken their engagement.

On the other hand, the thought of someone cutting a finger to draw a line of blood made her worry. It seemed . . . mad.

Still, the uppermost thought on her mind was what he'd said. *I should have married you.*

Too late, too late, too late, she thought, and swept downstairs.

She turned the corner at the bottom of the steps, waiting for an orgy to leap out at her.

One didn't exactly, but there, beneath the stairs, a courtesan was playfully spanking the tight bottom of a dark-haired gentleman who looked like a grown-up, stubble-covered version of a naughty little boy.

He was the one who'd been in the bedroom with the voluptuous blonde. But this woman was quite different. Tall, dark-haired, dressed in a gown that would have made a duchess weep with envy. How could this woman be a courtesan? She looked more regal than the Princess.

"You shouldn't be watching that." Behind her, the duke's voice was curt, low.

Exasperation—and a strange wound-up tension—made her snap, "Why not? They are fully dressed and she is spanking him the way she would discipline a little boy. That I have seen before."

Sinclair had just teased her with the life she could have had. Hinted at the pleasure she could have spent ten years enjoying—her whole, entire youth. But she would never have that life. Never know that pleasure.

She was nine-and-twenty. Portia had given up on love, on making love. She'd pushed aside marriage as impossible. As for children . . . that was a thought guaranteed to bring her to tears if she didn't remain staunchly stoic.

Drat him. Of course her tongue was sharp.

"Not that I condone that in our foundling home," she continued briskly. "There is no corporal punishment allowed. But really—why on earth would he find it pleasurable to be treated like a misbehaved toddler?"

Sinclair stood at her side, watching the spanking from under thick, dark brown, curling lashes. Tension was written in his expression—in the lines around his mouth, the way his eyes narrowed. "That I can't explain for you," he said.

A gong rang at that moment.

"What does that signify? What are people about to do?" She looked around, heart pounding. Did they all race to a bed?

"It signifies dinner, love."

"Dinner? They have *dinner?*"

He shook his head, looking bemused. "You thought they just had sex and never stopped to eat?"

"Well, er—yes."

"No gentleman would put up with that. He expects to be well fed, and given damn good port as well." Sinclair offered the crook of his arm. "We are supposed to go into dinner in order of precedence."

"And you are a duke."

"I am expected to escort one of the high-ranking women into the room. But I'm not letting another man lay his hands on you," he growled.

The guests were gathering, but Sinclair swept her into line before she had a chance to really look at them. One man went in before Sinclair, which meant he had to be at least a duke in ranking. He was the tall, broad-shouldered man with the unusual silver and black hair, and he was almost as handsome as Sinclair. Under long dark lashes, the man studied her curiously. His intense stare made her fear he could see through her mask.

Impossible, of course. Or so she prayed.

Sinclair called him "Saxonby," nodding curtly. The other man returned the quick nod. Obviously they knew each other.

She'd wondered how people greeted each other at orgies. Did they trade commentary about the weather before . . . before watching each other do something naughty to someone's private bits?

They were approaching the enormous dining table and the balding butler stepped in front of them.

Sinclair growled—he seemed to be doing a lot of growling. "She sits beside me."

But the butler rushed in. "My apologies, Your Grace, but that is not possible. Seating has been arranged by Lord Genvere, based upon precedence." The butler waved his hand and a handsome footman, dressed in livery, came forward to direct her to her seat.

A footman, whose impassive expression kept changing into a smirk, led her to a chair positioned between two young men—a tall, slim man with golden blond hair, a baby nose, and huge blue eyes, and the raven-haired man who had been spanked. He possessed a gentleman's jaded expression.

With wide blue eyes, the blond man introduced himself by lifting her gloved hand—in fine white silk gloves—and bestowing a kiss. He smiled at her. His eyes shone at her. "I am Viscount Sandhurst."

Portia floundered. She couldn't give her name, and she'd never thought of that. Sandhurst was young, but dressed in elegant, stunning clothes. Diamonds glittered on his buttons and gold thread adored his silk waistcoat.

"I am Miss . . . Miss Love."

"What a delightful name." Sandhurst grinned. "I saw you come downstairs with the Duke of Sinclair. Throws fantastic parties. I've never been, but I've wanted to go. Are you his special mistress? You are lovely."

"I—" Being Sinclair's mistress would be safest, wouldn't it? There was irony. "Yes, I am exclusive to him."

"A dashed shame. You have the prettiest lips I have ever seen." He leaned close. His breath tickled her ear.

Of course that was all of her face he could see. Should she run? No, she couldn't do that. She couldn't flee in a panic after only minutes here. However, she was used to dealing with unwanted male attention with a pistol. Here, she was devoid of weaponry.

Young Sandhurst whispered, "I have to admit I've never been to one of these. To a scandalous party. What happens? How do people begin to have sex with each other? I feel too dashed awkward, not knowing how to begin."

She had no idea. She could be truthful. But it was too tempting to make fun. How *did* people go from sitting calmly around a dinner table to doing carnal things . . . in a group? "I believe sometimes an announcement is made. Something like: 'Begin Rutting in Three seconds.' Then a countdown ensues. A horn might be blown, as if signaling a hunt."

"Ah." He nodded. "I wonder what will be done here. Have you met our host?"

Heavens, this young man was naïve. "No. Do you know Lord Genvere?" she asked.

"Never met him. Dashed surprised to receive the invitation, but since I've been eager to attend a sex party, I accepted at once. At least he's invited attractive guests."

She glanced around the table at the glittering crowd. Yes. And some he brought against their will.

Soup was served. A lobster bisque, rich and velvety.

She got that feeling—the prickling awareness that someone was watching her. Looking up, she met Sinclair's intense, chocolate-brown eyes. He shot a glare at Sandhurst.

She knew what she must do. Find out what she could from the young viscount. But how did she do it? She couldn't ask: Did you kidnap me? This young man looked too callow to be a dastardly kidnapper with a warped sense of humor.

She touched his wrist to get his attention.

Sandhurst jerked around so quickly he almost knocked over his wineglass. She snapped her hand out and saved it.

He was staring so intently at her, he hadn't even noticed. "Yes, Miss Love?" he asked. He looked boyishly hopeful.

With a pang, she remembered Sinclair as a young man of nineteen. He had been so boyishly gorgeous too.

"Did you receive a note from our host? An odd and unsettling note?"

"The note? I thought it was a hint we would be doing sinful things tonight. We will, won't we?"

A hint. She hadn't thought that. But then this young man hadn't been kidnapped and tied to a bed. Yet, that could have been a sick joke as well.

"Did you know anything about my arrival?"

"No, I wish I had. Of course, I guess you're the property of Sinclair. And he's known to be a crack shot."

"So am I," murmured the black-haired man at her side. He leaned close to her, his lids half-covering his green eyes. "I can also boast the best endowment of any man here. I've seen my competition and it wilts before my impressive prick. I possess thirteen inches. In this instance, my dear, thirteen is very lucky."

He grinned. Smugly.

Portia slowly put together the words he'd said. *Prick. Endowment. Thirteen inches.* Suddenly she knew what he meant.

Her gaze went down. She couldn't help it. She was utterly shocked. She used an inch ruler for school lessons and she knew how long one foot was. His was even longer . . . ?

Heavens, what must such a thing look like, sticking out from him and swinging about—?

"You have the most stunning eyes," he murmured. "What do you really look like under that mask, Miss Love?"

"Like myself," she hedged.

The man's black brow lifted. She saw he had scars on his cheeks and down his jawline. From battle with Napoleon? Duels with rapiers? Fisticuffs? Or perhaps not so romantic—perhaps his valet was clumsy when he shaved.

The man leaned closer. "I am an earl. I can be generous. Having found coal on my estate, I can be a damn sight more generous than Sinclair. I'm not afraid to fight for you, my dear. If I decide I want you."

If he decided—? Despite leaning close and trying to look down her bodice, he was also looking down his aquiline nose at her. Arrogant nuisance.

"Perhaps you should not trouble yourself to decide." She said it with complete sweetness. "The Duke of Sinclair is the most wonderful protector a girl could ever want. He is the perfect man. Generous and handsome. And he's a duke. What girl would say no to a duke?"

His eyes narrowed, and she felt a tiny triumph at pricking his arrogance a bit.

"Most women do not say no to me," he stated imperiously. "I can fuck you better than he can, I promise you. Meet me tonight. After you've been filled by my thick staff, you'll never want any other man again."

Oh goodness. What in heaven's name did she say? "I . . . I assure you that the Duke of Sinclair is like a stallion. An absolute stallion."

Thank heavens for the mask. Her face was so hot from blushing, she was actually perspiring.

Portia was used to herding children, thus she was able to line up the guests in her mind. There were thirteen guests altogether—including her.

Seven of the guests were gentlemen, all titled, ranging from dukes to viscounts. The eldest was a marquis who had to be over sixty. He bore a haughty expression and was still rather handsome, with a lean, straight form and thick white hair. He used a gold-topped stick for walking.

There was another earl, a brawny middle-aged man with barrel chest and huge shoulders. He looked like a pugilist, a boxer, but dressed like a gentleman. He was handsome, but more grizzled with auburn-brown hair. Then the Earl of Rutledge, with his coal-black hair and emerald green eyes—and his colossal arrogance. The Viscount Sandhurst, obviously the youngest gentleman, who wore a wide-eyed expression and was thoroughly beautiful with his full lips and long, curling lashes. Sinclair and Saxonby, of course. There was another man with dark gold hair—darker than Sandhurst's tresses—but she couldn't see his face.

And then there were the women. Portia was awfully curious about them—what kind of women attended orgies? Could a woman be behind her kidnapping?

Five other women sat at the table. Five women, each completely different from the others. Portia watched all the women, straining to listen to their conversations.

One of the women appeared to be a real lady of the *ton*. She had entered the dining room on Saxonby's arm. Portia tried not to stare as she recognized the woman—the one who had cried out in ecstasy as she was made love to from behind by Saxonby. The lady possessed golden blond hair, large blue eyes, and a slender, but lovely figure clad in white silk. Portia felt a stab of jealousy as the woman leaned close to Sinclair and he turned at once to speak to her, their heads close together.

Why should she care? It was all in the past, everything between her and Sinclair.

Sandhurst leaned toward her. "She's lovely, isn't she? You'd never guess she was a widow. She's barely twenty-three. She is Countess Linley."

Wonderful. A woman of Sinclair's world exactly—titled, beautiful, and wanton.

"The man she's talking to now is the Duke of Saxonby. He's one of the Wicked Dukes. But of course you know that—so is the Duke of Sinclair."

Portia looked up to realize Lady Linley had turned her attention to Saxonby. She felt foolishly relieved.

She did know about the nickname, the Wicked Dukes. She'd read it in gossip columns. She would sneak peeks to see mention of Sinclair. Not that she would ever admit she did so. She did not want anyone to think she still cared.

Because she did not still care, of course. She had just been curious.

"Who are the others?" she asked. "I haven't been introduced."

"This is Sadie, beside me," he said. He ran his finger around his cravat as he looked at Sadie.

"Miss Sadie?"

"Miss Bradshaw, I guess," he said, looking at her in confusion.

But oddly, it bothered her that Sadie, even though she did

look scandalous, did not even merit a proper introduction. Then she got rather a good look at Sadie and her dress.

The bodice was . . . well, as good as transparent. The filmy red lace barely covered her large, tawny nipples, not that it mattered, since one could see the nipples' shape and color through the fabric.

Portia knew this was supposed to be an orgy, and she shouldn't look disapproving if she was going to be disguised as Sinclair's mistress. But she couldn't help it.

And deep down inside, she couldn't stop remembering what Sadie's breasts looked like naked, for she'd seen them engulfing the face of the Earl of Rutledge. Now she was putting them on display for everyone, even strangers.

Portia felt disapproving, as one would expect.

But she felt something surprising. She felt rather hot and tingling about the idea of sensuality being so open and free.

What would it be like to be so bold?

Exciting? It seemed frightening, yet that made her heart beat faster and it made her feel . . . hot and squishy. The same way she used to feel when Julian—*Sinclair* kissed her.

Sadie was young—perhaps nineteen—with fluffy blond curls. As the course was cleared, Sadie leaned over toward the Viscount Sandhurst, lifted his hand, and slipped it somewhere down in her lap.

He went red as a beetroot.

A few moments later more food came, so Sandhurst had to use both his hands to eat. Sadie turned to her food, so Portia, blushing fiercely too, leaned to him. "What about the other women? Who are they?"

She was squirming with embarrassment, but she had a mission. To find her kidnapper. To find out who had sent those eerie notes.

"The older courtesan sitting beside the Duke of Sinclair is Harriet Barker." The lad blushed even redder, now looking like a prize tomato.

Harriet Barker wore so many diamonds, Portia was surprised she didn't fall over from the weight. She wore black— pure black satin, cut low to reveal a cleavage like two plump pillows. Her hair was henna red. She had a beautiful face, but it was lined, and she wore rather a lot of rouge and lip color.

"She looks like a madam," Portia said. In the stews of London, She had seen a few madams trying to steal hapless young women off the streets.

"She is a madam. I lost my virginity at her establishment."

Wine sputtered from Portia's lips. Really, she thought she was naïve in this world. He was even worse.

Across from the young courtesan Sadie, sat the elegant young woman who had spanked Rutledge. Portia thought she must be a lady, but her position at the table belied it. She was exotic and beautiful with dark eyes and she swept her lashes over them in a sultry way. Yet she could not be a lady, or she would be sitting much nearer to the dukes. Portia had heard of women called Incognitas. They were courtesans but were as well-dressed and well-mannered as ladies of the *ton*. So this woman was the Elegant Incognita.

"She is Clarissa Carrington," Sandhurst whispered. "And across from her is a courtesan I don't know. I've never seen her before."

The courtesan Sandhurst didn't know had brunette ringlets, and a darker complexion—a light caramel color. The young woman's eyes were almond shaped and exotic. She wore not a gown but a silk wrapper in a stunning turquoise color, belted tight around her.

At that moment, Sadie leaned over toward Rutledge, so her bosom pressed to the table. Portia couldn't see, but she suspected the breasts had almost popped up and out of Sadie's bodice. Rutledge was staring. In her mind, Portia named her the Brash Courtesan.

The Brash Courtesan giggled at the earl. "I think we should have a competition. Are you really as generously endowed as the rumors say? I think we should view the delightful pricks on offer and award those that please us best. Perhaps it's time that women chose the gentlemen as opposed to the other way around."

Portia sat stunned. How could she be that brash?

Naughtiness gleamed in Sadie's eyes. "You claim to have thirteen inches, Rutledge. But is it true? Is there anyone here to beat you? Perhaps it's not the length, but the thickness. Perhaps fatter is more pleasing?"

"It's not size," cooed the sultry dark-haired woman, the Elegant Incognita. "It is skill."

"A large man can be like a bull, and make a woman cry out in pain, not pleasure," declared the Old Madam. "But any lightskirt will take that man again, fascinated by his fearsome size, certain that the next time such a huge club will give her the orgasm that lets her see heaven. We're all searching for that. The exquisite little death where we do indeed glimpse heaven." She laughed loudly, riotously after this.

"That is true, Mrs. Barker. I know the endowments of every gentleman here," said the Incognita. "Except Viscount Sandhurst." She teasingly fluttered lashes at him. "I do hope to rectify that situation during this event."

The lad blushed. Tugged at his collar. "Well . . . well, indeed. I should oblige." Then he turned to her, Portia. "Unless I am claimed by another delightful lady."

Oh dear.

The sound of glass shattering made everyone gasp. Sinclair growled, dropped his broken wineglass, and mopped up his hand. The footman rushed over to assist.

Someone laughed. A deep, throaty, husky chortle.

Portia looked toward the sound and saw the gentleman who'd laughed was staring at her.

It was the man with the darker gold hair. She hadn't been able to see him well before, because he'd been leaning toward the woman beside him.

Now he watched her, leaning back casually in his velvet-cushioned chair. A smirk touched his lips. He brushed back his hair, the dark gold tresses falling over his brow. His eyes appeared to be violet. A startling color and probably just a reflection.

Then she gasped. She knew him. It was one of Sinclair's old friends from ten years past. Viscount Willoughby.

But why smirk? Was it because he was responsible for bringing her here?

Ten years ago, the viscount hadn't approved of Sinclair marrying her. She knew Willoughby had been the one to take Sinclair to scandalous brothels. Oh yes, it had been Sinclair's fault because he had gone, but the viscount had been determined to corrupt him.

Could he be behind her kidnapping?

Somehow she had to question him.

Willoughby looked away from her. "The problem here is that there aren't enough women. It's damned disappointing."

"What do you mean?" demanded Miss Bradshaw, the Brash Courtesan. "There's one of you for each of us."

"Almost, darling," corrected the Incognita. "There are six of us, seven of them."

"I like satisfying a group of women at once," Willoughby said carelessly. "I never fuck less than three. Having only one woman is damned dull."

Portia gritted her teeth. She hadn't liked Willoughby then for his arrogance. It appeared he was no different now.

The footman—there was only one—cleared away the course. Humphries followed, serving the next one. He held a plate in front of her. It held pinkish red lobster tails, stuffed with something and delicately arrayed with green sprigs of an herb. She took one.

At the foundling home, she'd always eaten simply. She had to run the foundling home on a meager budget now. Her brothers now had families to support, so they had to receive incomes, else how would they and their families live? They had found careers—one of her brothers had trained to be a physician, the other owned a print shop that was favored by the *ton*.

But with wives and children of their own, they could spare little time for the foundling home.

Portia lifted her fork and took a nibble of the filling of the lobster tail. Heavens, it was succulent shrimp, rich and almost sweet.

She closed her eyes and sighed. She couldn't help it.

She'd never had such delicious food in her life.

The Brash Courtesan suddenly squealed in delight. "Oh, Sinclair, if your mistress goes off with Sandhurst, then I would be more than happy to please you. After dinner, I would be delighted to suck your cock."

Portia's eyes had snapped open. And both her fork and a piece of shrimp had gone spinning out from her hand and were now flying across the table.

Sin caught Portia's flying fork and tossed it to the table. The footman brought her fresh silverware as everyone else looked from her to Sin, then from him to Sadie.

Sadie wore a smirk like a cat that had not only gotten into the cream but who had given a standing order to have it delivered every morning.

"This time I'm devoted to my pretty mistress," he said smoothly.

"That isn't like you." Sadie pouted, watching him. "You're not even faithful to a partner at an orgy for longer than it takes to make her come."

He saw Portia wince.

This conversation needed to come to a halt. "After dinner, Sadie, we'll see."

"We'll see?" She put her hands beneath her bosom, lifting it. "You can't be turning shy now. Not after all the wicked things you've done. You're like Willoughby. The rumour is you never sleep in your bed unless you have four others sharing it with you. But with you, not all of your bedmates are females."

Portia stared with wide eyes.

"Exaggeration. I'm not as legendary as that."

"But you are," murmured Clarissa. "You are quite legendary, Sin."

"Enough," he growled, his voice a warning.

Another course came, interrupting the conversation. The first meat dish. What startled him was how red-faced and shocked Portia looked. Their eyes met. She looked . . . so unhappy, so disappointed.

It couldn't be because she cared about him.

No—he'd broken her heart once and she'd told him it was now too late.

The guests attacked their food. Sin lifted his wineglass to his lips. He was supposed to study the guests, but he kept staring at Viscount Sandhurst. Sandhurst was drooling over Portia. Sin glared at the lad over his wineglass. Glowering.

The lad was kissing Portia's hand again. She was looking impressed by his attentions.

Sin tossed back his wine. He had cost Portia more than he'd expected. He had assumed, when he'd broken the engagement, that she would meet another man and marry.

He'd never dreamed she wouldn't.

Guilt sat on him. Hard.

How did he make amends for taking ten years of her life?

First, he could find out who kidnapped her.

Across the table, he noticed Sax's gaze falling on Portia. On her full, natural pink lips. On her rounded bosom and the obvious slender grace of her figure. His friend's brow rose in appreciation.

He'd been surprised to find Sax here. In truth, he didn't know why his initial reaction had been shock—Sax enjoyed bacchanalias as well as he did. They had only a chance for brief conversation. He had mentioned the notes, the absent host. Sax had also received the note. And Sax was in agreement—something was off about this party. They had a missing host and the kidnapping of Portia.

Right now, he didn't like the way Sax was studying Portia. The mask covered most of her face, revealing only the soft curve of her jaw and delicate chin, and her full, generous pink lips.

He caught Sax's eyes. Across the table, he mouthed, "Mine."

Instead of looking challenged, Sax just grinned.

He could trust Sax not to reveal the truth about Portia's identity. And not to try to seduce her away. His warning hadn't been necessary. Or had it?

After all, when he and Portia had seen Sax with Georgiana, Lady Linley, he'd heard Portia's sharp intake of breath. She was staring at Sax. Just because she'd never seen a man fucking? Or because she liked the way Sax looked while he did it?

The man was damned handsome with white-blond hair, but long, dark lashes. At his orgies, women always swooned over Sax. It was irritating.

Now, he felt a sharp slam in his gut. What if Portia looked at Sax and wanted him? What if she wanted Sandhurst?

His plan had been to portray her as his mistress to the guests—with all the exclusivity that came with such a title—but she wasn't his mistress. She was free. And, in that mask and gown, she was stunning.

Jealousy hit him harder than guilt.

The butler appeared. "Port will be brought in for the gentlemen. Sherry and coffee are available for the ladies in the west drawing room."

An untouched dessert sat in front of him. The lone footman was moving from female to female, drawing back her heavy chair.

Sadie cooed, winked, and waggled her fingers at him. Ignoring her, Sin got up and went to Portia, who was heading for the door.

He stood in front of her. Through the holes of her mask he could see her huge gray eyes. "Where are you going?"

"For sherry and coffee with the women. As I'm supposed to do."

"I don't like you leaving my sight."

"I shall be with all the women."

"Women can be more dangerous than men, Portia."

"Well, I shall take care of myself."

Pulling away from his hand, which he'd settled on her arm, Portia followed the women. Sin wanted to go after her, but he realized this time alone with the men, before their brains focused on rutting, would be profitable. A time to question them.

At that moment, Sadie ran back into the room. Sin tensed, expected she would do something bold and daft, like jump on him. Instead she went to Sandhurst, who was still seated, and whispered in his ear, ensuring her tits pressed against him.

Sadie's bosom just about swallowed up the lad's head. Sadie left; then, blushing and swallowing hard, Sandhurst stuttered. "Have to excuse myself for a moment—have to go—something to do—"

"Know exactly who you're going to do," Rutledge sneered. "Though Sadie needs more than a boy just out of short pants. That girl can fuck until your head's ready to pop off. Doubt you have it in you to keep up with her."

Sandhurst gulped. But he headed out of the room anyway.

Sin went back to his chair, leaned back in it. Angry. Irritated. He used to love a good orgy. Now, he just wanted to get Portia out of here, take her home—

But without sex, how did he get the guilt and regret out of his head?

Portia had felt a quiver go down her spine at Sinclair's intense look. *I don't like you leaving my sight.*

Of course, that was just because he was being protective. She followed the women toward the drawing room, trailing behind the others. Then she spotted Sadie, alone, down the hall, looking furtive.

Why wasn't Sadie with the viscount? Why did she look so guilty? Was their meeting for another reason than a romantic tryst? Curious, Portia followed. No one would suspect they were meeting about her kidnapping—everyone would assume they were doing something naughty.

Portia approached, then slipped behind a marble statue of a nymph that stood in a niche so Sadie would not see her. The nude nymph's full figure and huge bosom could hide a small horse.

In the hallway, the young, bosomy courtesan met Viscount Sandhurst. "Quiet and come with me," Sadie commanded, and she led Sandhurst by the hand down the corridor.

Blast. Portia still didn't know if they were going to meet for pleasure or to discuss a plot that involved the kidnapping of innocent women.

She couldn't picture blushing Sandhurst, who seemed to be only thinking about sex because he was so young and fascinated by it, being a clever villain. And she felt there was an intelligent, evil person behind her kidnapping. Though, that was just a guess. Just an instinct.

Sadie didn't seem to have any thought beyond seducing a man with a title.

But was that true? Or just a very good act?

The problem was—how could she follow them without being spotted? She could hardly walk in on them if they were having a passionate encounter.

She went back into the drawing room. And walked in on yet another shocking thing.

Harriet Barker and the young courtesan whose name she didn't know were kissing while sitting on the sofa. A sloppy, openmouthed kiss with lots of moaning.

As Portia almost stumbled over her feet, they broke apart. "I thought you were one of the men," rumbled Harriet. "What's taking those blasted gentleman so darned long?"

"Maybe they're kissing each other while we're not there," suggested the very lovely widowed countess. Her soft laughter fluttered through the room.

The countess leaned against an enormous white piano, polished to a mirror finish. The whole room was white. In blinding daylight, it would hurt the eyes. In warm, golden candlelight, it was rather stunning.

"Ooh, I'd like to see that. Gentlemen kissing. Yummy!" declared the Unnamed Courtesan. She jumped up from the sofa, her brunette curls dancing. She discarded her wrap. Good heavens! Portia gaped. The woman wore only a corset embroidered in fanciful colors—turquoise, lavender, scarlet. Peacock feathers streamed down from the bottom of the corset, covering just her privates and her bottom. Her long, shapely legs were revealed. In a world where it was shocking to show an ankle.

Also, could such a woman be a kidnapper? She seemed only to care about gentlemen. All the women here seemed to be thinking only about the men—or was one woman faking her interest, and she was behind Portia's kidnapping and the notes?

But who could be likely—?

"Who are you?"

The sudden, abrupt question startled Portia. Sherry flew up out of her glass and landed on the pale carpet as she spun around, wishing she could swallow her heart back into its place.

The Elegant Incognita stood behind her, watching her suspiciously.

"Me?" It took her so long to answer she knew she looked exactly as if she was lying. "I am Miss Love. The Duke of Sinclair's mistress." Summoning courage, Portia lowered her voice. "I've heard that a woman was to be kidnapped and brought here. Part of a game. Did you hear any such thing?"

The woman's brows lifted. "No, but perhaps Genvere likes women to be unwilling. Some men do. But now that you have your hooks into Sin, you'll never want for anything again. Will you?"

The woman peered at her, as if trying to see through the mask. "A woman wears a mask at an event like this to protect her identity. Which means she has something to lose."

"Or she just likes to wear a mask," Portia retorted. Though it wasn't the cleverest thing she'd ever thought of. Still in her thoughts was the scene of the two women kissing. She knew there were women who loved other women, who had Sapphic feelings. But those women had kissed to entice the men. How odd to think men would be aroused by such a thing, since it appeared that men were not to be involved.

It interested her. She knew a proper woman should not be curious.

But she was.

She also knew she had no idea how to question anyone. How to find clues or even, through extreme cleverness, get a person to reveal secrets. But she had to try.

Twirling a curl around her finger, she asked in a careless tone, "So it would not bother you if a woman was brought here against her will?"

"Of course I would find it stupid and tedious. But if a courtesan is to be successful, she has to feign enjoyment of stupid and tedious things," the woman said lightly.

These answers weren't helpful at all. Portia tried to think of something else to ask, when the butler cleared his throat from the doorway. "The gentlemen will be joining you momentarily—"

A scream came from outside the room, cutting off his words. The butler jumped a foot. It was a screech of terror.

Everyone ran for the door, to see what was going on.

Out in the corridor, the beautiful viscount lay on the carpet. Sadie lifted her two naked, melon-sized breasts off his youthful face. She clutched her bosom with both hands and threw herself back, falling on the floor on her bottom. Wildly, she looked around and her gaze locked on them.

"Oh my heavens, he's dead!" she cried. "I think . . . I think my bosom killed him!"

8

Moments after Sadie's panicked cry filled the room, thunder boomed. So loud, it seemed to shake the stone walls of the house. A gust of wind flung open the glass doors of the drawing room. Candles went out.

They were not plunged completely in the dark, but into a shadowy gloom, and one that was quickly split by a second ear-shattering scream that made Portia almost leap out of her slippers.

"I'm going to be hanged for killing him!" shrieked Sadie. She began to run about, rather like a headless chicken, if said fowl was clutching a dress to its bare bosom.

The young woman was stark white, squealing in terror. Even though Sadie held up her bodice, she was crushing her breasts flat, which made most of her bosom stick out the top and the sides and wobble about like aspic jelly.

The men, instead of one stepping forth to act as knight errant, appeared frozen with shock.

No. Portia realized several of the gentlemen were staring at the enormous breasts that jiggled to and fro, up and down. Even the butler, Humphries, stood with his jaw dropped and his salver tilting off his fingers.

But Sinclair was not looking at the breasts. Or at Sadie. He had gone to the eerily still body of the young viscount.

Someone had to take charge of Sadie. No one seemed to care the poor young woman was in a terrified panic. Portia went to her and put her arm around Sadie's slim shoulders. "You must calm down. And you must stop making this racket. Come with me and sit down."

Sadie stared at her in confusion. "I can't! I can't!"

Saxonby, the duke with the striking silver and black hair, tore his gaze from a barely dressed Sadie. He hurried over to join Sinclair.

To Portia's surprise, Sinclair dropped on one knee and tore off his leather glove. She expected him to search for a pulse, but it was obviously hopeless. The young man's eyes were wide open and blank. But Sinclair studied Sandhurst's face, leaned close to the viscount's mouth.

Checking for breathing, she assumed.

"He is dead, isn't he?" Sadie whimpered.

"Yes, he is," Sinclair said matter-of-factly.

That set Sadie shrieking again. Oh heavens. Portia put her arms around the girl. Suddenly Sadie, bare breasts and all, was plastered against her.

She heard a man making a groaning sound. The white-haired marquis stared at their embrace with bright eyes.

"Really," Portia said, appalled. She propelled the young courtesan away and hoisted up Sadie's gown once more, then pressed the girl's hands to the fabric to keep it up. "Calm yourself. Now come with me. You ... you need something for shock."

"But I'll 'ang, won't I?" Sadie squealed. "For I killed 'im. Smothering 'im with these!" She slapped her hand over her chest. "I didn't mean to do it! It was an accident! But, oh bloomin' 'eck, 'e's a viscount. I don't want to 'ang!"

Sadie's accent had gotten much rougher in her panic.

Portia put her arm around the girl's shoulders once more. "It was an accident. And I don't see how you could have ...

uh, smothered him. Wouldn't he let you know that he was in distress? Did he try to . . . to free himself from under your bosom? What exactly were you doing to him?"

She'd asked that without thinking.

Sadie looked up. "I were just riding him. He didn't even know a woman could go on top, the poor sweet thing."

Oh dear, she really had not wanted to know.

"I doubt he would've stopped her," the old marquis barked. "Once his prick began to do the thinking, the daft lad could've died without realizing it."

"I do not believe that," Portia said, primly. "I am sure a lack of air would have been uppermost on his mind."

"Doubt it." The marquis glared at her. "Are you implying this young woman murdered the man by holding her massive rack of tits over his mouth and nose, even as he struggled?"

That set Sadie wailing. "Of course not," Portia declared, loud enough to be heard over the crying. She then dragged Sadie to a small brocade chair by the wall and forced her to sit.

"I doubt he was smothered." Sinclair's cool voice cut through the wailing. And everyone appeared to accept his word on the matter.

Portia waved at the butler, but he was staring at the body and did not notice. Sandhurst had been so alive, so handsome— she hated death. Sometimes, in their care, children got ill and they couldn't save them all. That was horrible. So horrible. She couldn't bear the pain afterward. And the anger. She would throw herself into work at the foundling home, so she didn't have to face the loss.

She felt just as sorrowful at Sandhurst's untimely death. He seemed far too young. But she really had to deal with Sadie.

"Will one of you noble gentlemen please fetch her some brandy?" she asked loudly.

No one even appeared to hear her. They were either gaping at Sadie's breasts as she sobbed into her hands or at poor Sand-hurst. Portia was rather fed up with noble gentlemen—and even with the ladies.

But Sinclair lifted his head. "Yes, fetch something to calm the girl down."

The butler jerked. "Of course, Your Grace. In one moment." He scurried away.

Portia grabbed a small throw of tasseled silk from one of the wing chairs. She draped it around the courtesan's shoulders. "This will warm you up." *And make you more decent,* she thought. "You must calm yourself. I assume he met his end in another way. An apoplexy. An explosion of a blood vessel in his brain. He must have had some kind of weakness."

Sadie wiped at tears. "Really?"

Bending, the butler presented a silver salver with a snifter of brandy atop it. Portia handed it to the young woman. And gave some hard-earned advice. "Don't drink it too quickly."

"Listen to her. She is a bit of an expert on that matter." The deep voice with the lightly teasing note belonged to Sinclair.

His expression did not match that wry tone. Lines furrowed his brow and his mouth was held in a tense line.

He straightened away from Sandhurst's supine form. Portia had intended some kind of rejoinder, but his expression stole her words. The way he looked as he elegantly rose to his feet, like a lion stretching, robbed her of breath.

His long strides brought him to Sadie. Saxonby followed and asked the butler for more brandy as Sinclair squatted in front of the courtesan, to bring himself level with the girl's huge blue eyes. Portia heard Sadie catch her breath and let the throw slip open a little.

But the Duke of Sinclair didn't look down at Sadie's breasts. He didn't take his eyes from the young woman's face.

It was something Portia didn't understand. Given why he'd broken their engagement—addicted to carnal games, he'd said—she was surprised. He was not acting as though he was attracted to Sadie in any way. "Tell us exactly what happened," he said softly.

"I'll tell you. You've always been so kind to me, Sin," Sadie purred. She batted lashes, having transformed from terrified to temptress because she had a duke in front of her.

Always been kind? Goodness, had Sadie gone to his orgies? Probably she had. Had he touched this woman's body when she was naked? Played with the large breasts? Made love to her?

"I'd feel so much safer in your arms," Sadie cooed. "I could sit upon your lap. I know you do like that. Especially when I am—"

"That's enough," he said abruptly. "This is not the time or place."

Well, she had her answer. Sadie and Sinclair had shared intimacy of some sort. She rather wished she'd asked for brandy too.

Sadie gazed at him adoringly. "I only invited Viscount Sandhurst to play to make you jealous. And 'e's rather sweet. And terribly 'andsome. I mean 'e was—" Her large blue eyes filled with tears. "I was riding on top of 'im, and 'e looked as 'appy as a clam. Then suddenly, 'e jerked beneath me. I thought 'e'd come. But 'e made an 'orrible sound. Then didn't move at all. So I got off him. And 'e was staring upward with those blank eyes. And blue lips."

Sinclair nodded thoughtfully. "I believe Sadie is correct. He had a sudden seizure."

"So likely his heart," said Saxonby. "Or a blood vessel bursting in his head."

"So it wasn't not my fault?"

"Not your fault," Sinclair said gently.

"That is what I conjectured," snapped the old marquis. "I don't see why we're wasting all this time. The lad is dead."

"But what do we do with poor Sandhurst, Your Grace?" asked the Elegant Incognita.

Sinclair exchanged glances with his friend, Saxonby. "I think we should take him upstairs. Wait for the boat to arrive tomorrow, then take him back to the mainland. What do you think, Humphries?"

"Your suggestion is most excellent, Your Grace. A most intelligent solution."

"Are there other footmen to help?"

The butler shook his head. "There is only one footman, myself, a maid, and the cook in the house."

"No other servants?"

"No, Your Grace."

"Strange." Sinclair frowned. "Genvere expects four servants to tend a houseful of guests."

"We are extremely capable, Your Grace. In fact, I believe the four of us can move the unfortunately deceased Viscount Sandhurst."

"Probably you could. But Saxonby and I will carry him."

Willoughby stepped forward. "I offer my services."

"Fine. You take one leg, with Sax. I'll get his shoulders."

They took their positions, crouched, then lifted poor young Sandhurst. Willoughby puffed as he helped carry one leg. Saxonby looked barely encumbered, but what amazed Portia was Sinclair. He carried the young lad as if he were weightless. They moved Sandhurst to the stairs and Portia felt tears on her cheeks. Sandhurst had been like a naughty boy, but he was young and handsome and he hadn't meant any harm. This seemed a tragedy.

She stared blankly at the place Sandhurst had laid. Something incongruous caught her eye. A dash of pink on the carpet. Portia bent and picked it up, the satin of it sliding smoothly over her fingers.

A small piece of ribbon. Probably torn from Sadie's dress.

Portia frowned. But Sadie's dress was scarlet. This pink would clash garishly. Perhaps it came from Sadie's undergarments—

"Madam?"

She whirled around.

The butler hovered behind her, salver balanced on thumb and fingers. "I do not know who to ask, madam . . . should I summon the guests into the drawing room for coffee or a restorative brandy?"

She looked around at the remaining guests, who looked pale and shaken. "That is an excellent idea. They will all need something to take their mind off the shock."

The butler looked around. "When Their Graces return, there is something I must tell them."

"What is it?"

"No, madam, I could not trouble you with this. It is something I was given and I am concerned about it. Gravely concerned."

"If you would tell me what it is, no doubt I could help lift some of this concern with helpful advice." She almost pointed out that she was quite used to managing things but stopped herself just in time.

Humphries was perspiring. His face was an odd color—pale but mildly green. She did not like the look of him.

Firmly, she led him to a seat and told him to sit.

"Madam, this is quite improper."

"I don't care. You look very ill. And unless you tell me what the problem is, I shall help by keeping you in this chair."

He looked around, but no else was paying any attention. The remaining guests were engaged in conversation, speculating on what had happened. He sighed. "All right, madam. It is this. I wished an opinion from one of the gentlemen, as Lord Genvere is not here. I was given this to read after dinner. I looked at it several minutes ago. I found it shocking."

"Is it rude?"

He jerked. "Rude? It seems in bad taste. And it is odd. And also—I don't know how Lord Genvere could have known what was to happen tonight—"

"Can I see this note?"

Humphries hesitated. But she had learned how to have children obey her. She behaved the same with the nervous butler and he handed her the note.

She read: *He has paid for his sins*.

"Who has paid for his sins?"

"I thought perhaps Lord Sandhurst was indicated. But now, of course, I see I leapt to a conclusion. It could mean anyone."

"It could. But if it does mean Sandhurst, you are correct: How could Lord Genvere have known?" She looked around, uneasy. Heart thumping. "Could Lord Genvere be here, and we simply don't know it?"

"There are no other buildings on the island, madam. And I was given the letter in the packet I received when I arrived on Serenity Island. That was four days ago."

She had promised to dispense advice. At this moment, she had none to give.

"What do you think of this?"

Portia hurried to Sinclair as soon as he walked in the door, and thrust it into his gloved hand, giving the explanation for it as rapidly as possible. His brown hair was in disarray, tumbling around his face. He was breathing hard. And his eyes held a dark, determined intensity.

He took it, and at once she asked rapidly, "Do you think he could be referring to Sandhurst? If so, how could that be possible?"

"Por—Precious, I just carried a man up a flight of stairs. I need a second."

Precious. He had almost slipped up on her name but had covered up well.

She watched his deep brown eyes scan the page. He looked up at the butler, who was leaning over as he read, clutching his silver salver.

"Miss—er—Love says you were told to read this in the drawing room."

"Indeed. That was the written instruction left by Lord Genvere. With the small number of staff and the unfortunate and untimely demise of Lord Sandhurst, I was so occupied I admit I almost neglected the task." The butler withdrew a handkerchief and blotted his forehead. "What do you think of it, Your Grace?" the man asked worriedly.

"It's a mystery," Sinclair muttered. He rubbed his jaw. "I doubt Genvere can read the future. The likely explanation is that the note had another meaning. Sandhurst's death is an unfortunate coincidence."

"Do you really think that?" Portia asked doubtfully.

"I don't know. Genvere isn't here—unless he's in hiding. It looks like Sandhurst died of a stroke or a failure of his heart—" The duke broke off. "What were the exact instructions you were given? Was something supposed to happen first? Who were you to read it to?"

"The assembled company after dinner, Your Grace. I was simply told to read the letter at half past ten. I was to break the seal and read its contents immediately before that. Miss Lam—"

"Love," Sin corrected. "Her name is Miss Love."

"The young lady believed I should bring the guests into the drawing room for brandy."

"I thought it would take the minds of the guests off the tragedy. They are all stunned."

Sinclair looked up at her. "That's a good idea."

She met his gaze. She'd never seen him look so serious. For the last ten years, he had been painted in the gossip papers as a scandalous rogue who thought only of vice and pleasure. She'd been never sure that was really true. Did he really just want orgies for pleasure, or because, as he'd explained to her, he could not resist them? She had realized the difference, even as she read of his exploits, tried to ignore the pain in her heart, and tried to congratulate herself on a lucky escape. Except she didn't feel lucky.

"Should I read the note in the drawing room, Your Grace?"

Humphries words jerked Portia out of her thoughts.

Sinclair rubbed his jaw again. "It will upset them, but I would like to see all of their reactions. Yes, read the note as you were instructed."

The butler bowed. "Of course, Your Grace. I will announce that brandy will be served."

He did so and the guests filed into the drawing room.

"I don't like this," Sinclair growled as they entered the room.

"I highly agree," she threw back. He had said it before and she understood why. She felt as if someone was walking over her grave. This event was eerie, disturbing.

Sinclair handed her a brandy from Humphries salver.

The Earl of Rutledge approached her in the drawing room. "Why are you masked, Miss Love? Who are you really?"

"I shouldn't think that of importance," she said carefully. "Not after the tragedy of poor Sandhurst."

"But what a way to go," declared Rutledge, "buried under Sadie's fabulous tits. Magnificent things. Designed to strain a man's heart to the limit. Can barely hold one of them with two hands." And he laughed.

"That is distasteful and you should be ashamed of saying such a thing!" Portia cried. She began to move away from him, offended—just as she remembered she was supposed to question people.

"Wait," Rutledge said quickly. "I apologize. You're right. It was tragic. But it reminds us to live for the moment, doesn't it? To enjoy life's pleasures while we can." He moved close. "And sex helps one forget tragedy."

Those words speared Portia to her soul.

She remembered Julian—Sinclair—coming to her, his face a mask of agony as he told her that he couldn't marry her.

Had the reason Sinclair couldn't resist London's sexual vices been because he was using them to escape memories? Was that why he had orgies? Was he trying to bury the pain of a tragedy?

She felt a spurt of pain around her heart. But it wasn't one of anger. She could picture Sinclair, naked and beautiful, surrounded by naked bodies, but distant and hurting. A tragic hero looking over naked, heaving bosoms toward a distant horizon . . .

Heavens, how could she be feeling sympathy? Inventing a past filled with tragedy for him. She knew his cousin, the duchess hadn't approved of him, hadn't liked the fact he'd become duke, but that was hardly a tragedy. Yet the foolish thing was she wished he had a tragic past, and she would have an excuse to forgive him—

Suddenly she saw Rutledge's hand lift toward her face. Toward her mask!

She quickly took two steps back. "Leave the mask. I . . . uh, like to be mysterious," she said evasively.

"I'd like to see you."

"No, you wouldn't! I'm always masked. I have scars. I was in a . . . a fire. And I have scars on the side of my face and I always wear a mask to cover them. So I mustn't take it off. They are not awfully disfiguring, but I am ashamed of them. And Sinclair allows me to keep them covered."

"Of course you must." Rutledge grimaced. "What a shame. With that mask on, you looked like you had so much promise."

Of course he found her distasteful now. She felt very indignant. Men with scars could still be adored by ladies. But if a woman had any flaw in her looks, she was cast aside. Usually into homelessness and poverty.

Bother. She wasn't here to crusade.

Rutledge was leaving and she had not asked him a question. Acting on instinct, she rested her hand on the crook of his arm, stopping him. Her heart pounded. "Have you heard there is a wager—a joke to be played on the Duke of Sinclair? A woman to be brought and delivered to him?"

The earl stared in surprise. "Delivered?"

"Yes, brought by men. I heard this was to happen at this party."

"Didn't know that. If that were true, why did you come along?"

Drat. She had no answer for that.

He continued on, though, without caring that she'd done nothing but move her lips helplessly.

"If women are being delivered, I might order one or two. Not enough women at this event so far."

"So you think like Lord Willoughby," she said, her voice dripping with disapproval. She couldn't help it. "I thought Lord Willoughby sounded greedy."

"Pah. He likes two women in his bed. I can roger five women at once. Now that is fun. Five eager courtesans, all pleasuring me at once. After you've had five pretty whores, you find one or two is boring."

She blushed fiercely. And she wanted to smack him. He was even more arrogant than Willoughby! But inside she wondered—was that how Sinclair felt now? He might have started using sex to escape memories of a tragedy, but would he now not want anything less than multiple women? Or maybe that had been the lure of brothels and orgies all along.

Why then did he say that ending their engagement was his biggest mistake?

"So . . . impressed by my endurance?" Rutledge smirked.

"I have only your word for it. You could also claim to be able to swim the English Channel."

"I'd be more interested in plumbing the depths of your tight channel. I can fuck you better than Sinclair."

She was still reeling at his appalling pun. "I think not. That boat will not float," she muttered. It was time to get away.

Hastily, she turned and collided into a broad chest. Her heart just about stopped as she feared a man was about to give her another proposition, when she looked up and met Sinclair's deep, beautiful coffee-brown eyes.

He gripped her wrist and dragged her away to one of the drawing room windows, where they were away from the gathering of other guests. His eyes blazed. They might be dark, but they were obviously burning with great emotion.

"What were you doing with him?" he growled.

"Questioning him, if you must know." She had actually been delighted when he'd dragged her away, but she wasn't going to admit it. It would be admitting weakness to a man who would use that as reason to lock her in a bedroom. Alone. For her own good. "Why do you look so troubled? Sandhurst's death was tragic—"

"His heart might not have given out. He might have been poisoned." Sinclair spoke softly, so only she heard.

She stared at him, openmouthed. "Why would you think such a thing?"

"I've seen it before. Just like this. But I'm not sure."

"You have seen someone who was poisoned before? How can that be? Who?"

He started as if his thoughts were somewhere else. "It's not important. But I believe it to be true. That note of Genvere's . . . either he can read the future, which I doubt, or he knew someone was going to die. Which means he engineered Sandhurst's death."

"What?" Portia gasped. "But how?"

"I don't know how he did it. He must actually be on the island now. But I don't know how he got the poison to Sandhurst, if he did. How Sandhurst was poisoned and no one else. If it killed a young, healthy man, it should have killed others. So food or drink was not randomly poisoned. It had to be directed at Sandhurst. Something he alone consumed was poisoned."

"Why would anyone want to do such a thing?"

"I don't know, Portia."

"But who—how do we find who did this? Should we not assess what Sandhurst ate and drank? Shouldn't we speak to the cook?"

"If she poisoned the food, we'd all be dead. The truth is, I am likely wrong. The most likely answer is that he died of an attack of his heart or a stroke. Yes, that is what must have happened."

"You don't truly believe that. You are saying that to placate me."

"No." He met her gaze without even a look of guilt as he lied. "That is what I believe."

She was about to argue when a loud "Bah!" interrupted.

The old viscount had spat the word, as he stood up from his seat. "I'm not letting young Sandhurst spoil my fun. We came here for carnal sport—hard, punishing sexual sport. If he was too much of a weakling to keep up, that's not my problem. Feel sorry for the lad, but there it is."

There was silence.

"I came here for an orgy," his lordship snapped, "and I intend to have one."

Portia now knew what the marquis's name should be—the Cruel Marquis.

"There's a diamond bracelet in it for each lady who wishes to entertain me tonight."

At once Sadie jumped to her feet. "Cor, for a diamond bracelet, I might be tempted."

"It would help us forget this sorrowful and tragic thing," drawled the Elegant Incognita.

"Yes." Sadie nodded her head, curls bobbling. "Let us have some fun. I shall give you a lot of fun, my lord." She started toward the marquis.

But Harriet Barker, the Old Madam, jumped in front of her and reached him first, before the Elegant Incognita and the Exotic Courtesan wearing the costume could even move. "I can pleasure you in ways you don't even know exist, my lord."

The marquis looked doubtful, and the woman leaned over and whispered in his ear. His brows shot up under his white hair. He stamped his ornate walking stick against the floor. "Finally," he barked. "Let the orgy begin."

Then Humphries returned, but Sinclair told him to go.

9

"Let it begin indeed, my lord," the Old Madam declared.

She stood up, tugged on her dress, and suddenly her gown fell away. She wore nothing but a scarlet corset beneath and scarlet-and-white-striped stockings. Her large bosom was lifted high, her waist nipped to a tiny circumference, her hips generous. She stood before them all in the middle of the ornate drawing room, glowing with confidence. Portia would have sunk through the floor if she was so undressed before strangers.

The Old Madam grabbed the white cravat of the Cruel Marquis, pulled him to her, and wrapped herself around him like a blanket as she gave him a fierce kiss.

She undid the knot in his cravat with incredible speed and skill. Portia supposed Harriet Barker must have undressed a lot of men.

The Old Madam looped the cravat around his neck. "I'm not going to let the other women here witness my rather special, private techniques."

With that, she tossed her elegant coiffure, smirked at the other women, and, using the cravat like a leash, led the marquis away.

Sadie retreated to Portia's side. "Wretched cow," the girl sniffed.

"What can she do that is so special? Well, let her have the old crock. I'm going to have two handsome dukes tonight!"

Sadie reached around and began to undo the fastenings of her gown, strategically placed so they swiftly fell open and more and more of the girl's smooth, dewy, curvaceous body went on display. It didn't fall away quite as quickly as Harriet's. "Are you ready, Sax and Sin?" Sadie cooed.

Portia swallowed hard. Now she was going to see what an orgy was—whether it was anything like she had secretly imagined.

By seeing Sinclair take part.

She suddenly felt sick, the rich dinner curdling in her stomach. She'd been kidnapped, there might have been a murder, but the real reason for the pain in her tummy was jealousy.

Foolish, useless jealousy.

"Not tonight, Sadie," Sinclair said.

Astonished relief flooded Portia. A silly emotion to have, when she knew this was his world, and before she could respond, a hand snaked around her waist.

"I'm going to claim this little temptress," rumbled a husky, masculine voice. A voice that didn't belong to the Duke of Sinclair. "Tonight this luscious mystery woman is going to be shared by Sin and me."

"The lucky cow," Sadie whined, again bestowing a bovine comparison.

Portia was struck dumb. She couldn't have heard that right. Portia whirled around just as Sinclair hauled the hand of the Duke of Saxonby off her hip.

"What in hell are you doing, Sax?" he rumbled. "She's mine. Keep your hands off her."

Saxonby moved closer to Sinclair, who had curled his black-gloved right hand into a fist. Fury emanated from his dark brown long-lashed eyes. Heavens, she hadn't expected a fight to break out over her.

Lowering his voice so no one but the three of them could hear, Saxonby said, "You told me she'd been kidnapped and brought here. My goal was to remove her from a potentially ruinous situation. Or do you want her to take part?"

"No, I damn well do not. But it's *my* duty to protect her."

Portia did not appreciate the two tall dukes speaking over her head. "It is not anyone's duty to do that," she whispered, "especially when I cannot trust anyone here."

"You don't trust Sin?" The Duke of Saxonby frowned, black brows drawing together.

"I do not yet know, Your Grace. He tells me he had nothing to do with my kidnapping. I would like to believe him—and there is much evidence he is telling the truth. But I can't be too trusting."

She saw Sinclair flinch.

Bu what did he expect? He had broken her heart once, and she'd never seen it coming.

Still, the argument was strong for his innocence. If the Duke of Sinclair had nefarious plans for *her* innocence, wouldn't he have done something by now?

Or would he, now the orgy was starting? Maybe when the orgy started, everything would change. . . .

Both men had positioned themselves so she could not see past them. As she stood more in the corner of the room, she couldn't tell what was happening. What people were doing . . .

"You can also trust Saxonby," Sinclair said. "I've known him since I went to Eton."

"I have not, Your Grace, so I must reserve judgment."

The Duke of Saxonby inclined his head. "She's right there, Sin. You shouldn't trust anyone, Miss Lamb."

"It is 'Love,' " she said.

"Pardon?" asked Saxonby.

"I am going by the name of Miss Love. And it is my hope to question these guests and find out who, if anyone, knew of my kidnapping. Find out if any of these people are involved."

Saxonby frowned. "Willoughby," he said. "This sounds like the kind of thing he would do. Willoughby is dangerous, Sin. You need to keep her away from him. If he had some warped idea of a wager, or cruel game, he could ruin Miss Lamb's reputation. Or worse."

"What do you mean—?" she began, but Sinclair growled.

"I know what Will is capable of. I will protect her."

"Why don't you take her upstairs, lock her in your room, and pursue Willoughby?" Saxonby asked. "That seems the most logical course of action."

She opened her mouth to protest when Sinclair said, "Miss Love wants to see what this world is about. I give her about two minutes after the rutting begins to beg me to take her away from this."

"She wants to watch?" Saxonby's dark brows disappeared under his silvery hair.

Oh fie. They were making fun of her. "I suppose I wanted to see the world that lured away the man I might have married."

She could not believe she was being so blunt. Certainly, when it came to rescuing children and running the foundling home, she was direct where needed. But she didn't quite know where her courage was coming from.

"But you are an innocent," Saxonby protested.

She was about to protest against his protest, when Sinclair said, "I hurt her a great deal and I have since discovered I stole many things from her."

Saxonby frowned at him. "What are you talking about, Sin?"

"If she wants a little naughty voyeurism, I will allow it—and protect her. But I know you—" Sinclair turned to her. His lips looked soft and they turned down at the edges. It reminded her of how vulnerable he had looked as a nineteen-year-old, new to London and despised by his cousin, the Duchess of Sinclair. "You will discover very quickly what I took ten years to learn. This is athletic, but not all that arousing."

"Then why did it matter so much to you?" Her heart raced. Would he confirm any of her conjecture? Would he reveal a tragedy in his life?

He hesitated. "That I can't explain," he said.

Her heart sank. But did that mean he just couldn't reveal his past to her—or did it mean there was no tragedy that had driven him to blank out his heart and soul with erotic activity?

"So you really want to see it?" he asked.

"Why shouldn't I?"

Even though she couldn't see around or over the men to view what was happening, she realized she could *hear* things. The rustle of clothing. Sighs. Whimpers. Moans.

She hadn't been focusing on them before. The sounds, even the softest ones, seemed to spear through her.

"All right. You can take a peek, angel."

Saxonby looked shocked. "Sin, you should prevent this. Take her upstairs away from harm."

But Sinclair shook his head. "I have no right to dictate to her."

"Her innocence is a remarkable thing," the other duke protested. "She joins that orgy, even watches it, and that innocence is gone forever."

"I am tired of missing out on life to protect me and my innocence," she threw out.

"You can't mean that," Saxonby sputtered. He was going to stop her, she knew, but Sinclair stopped him.

And then Sinclair moved aside. She looked, filled with confidence, until she saw—

The handsome, raven-haired Earl of Rutledge lying on his back on the floor, his trousers pushed down to his boots. His coat, waistcoat, and shirt dangled from the backs of chairs. From the side, Portia could see his long legs, splayed apart, the smooth, sculpted torso. A leaner frame than Sinclair's, but with remarkably defined lean muscles.

He appeared to be holding a bat—

Oh. Oh dear.

That was his erection. Portia couldn't forget his boastful words in the dining room. The thing was huge. Remarkably thick at the base, tapering to a smallish head. Thick dark hair surrounded it—

Sadie, as naked as the day she'd been born, sat over the earl's face, and she held up her full breasts, so they plumped up like peach-colored cushions. The Elegant Incognita, also nude and displaying a curvaceous form with a nipped waist, generous hips, and a large bottom, knelt between the earl's long, well-muscled legs and—

And half the length of his . . . thing disappeared into the Elegant Incognita's mouth.

As Portia stood, frozen in place, the other earl, the auburn-haired one, a Sporting Corinthian type, ripped open his trousers and roughly massaged the Incognita's dangling breasts, which were tubular shaped and topped with large brown nipples. The nipples grew startlingly long—longer than thimbles and rather closer to pinecones—as the earl played with them.

The Incognita bobbed on Rutledge's shaft. The Corinthian grasped her hand and wrapped her fingers around his—his part, jutting out of his open trousers. Then he slid his fingers up the skirts of the Wanton Widow, moving his hand beneath the silks. The widow squealed and moaned, and the young, dark-haired courtesan in the costume moved around behind Sadie. She held something up—a long white wand. Licked it and sucked it. Then Sadie grabbed it and she slid it into her privy place. Balancing it on Rutledge's chest, she bounced on it and smacked his face wildly with her large breasts. While the dark-haired, peacock-costumed courtesan slid her fingers into . . . into Sadie's bottom. And touched herself with her other hand.

"Oooh, yes, Nellie," Sadie cooed. Others moaned. Some made deep, throaty sounds, some squeaky sounds.

Drugging, rich smells filled the air.

"I know where I want to shove my cock," Willoughby said. At once, he dropped his trousers. He got behind the Incognita, behind her rounded bottom, all plumpness and smooth, lovely skin. Willoughby patted her cheeks, took his erection in hand, and pointed it at her from behind. He thrust his hips forward and the Incognita let go of Rutledge to cry out, "Oh yes, fuck me arse with your huge staff."

Portia made a little strangled sound.

Then Willoughby looked up. He looked right at her. He grinned and crooked his finger, inviting her to join.

That was what it took to make her run.

Leaving Sinclair and Saxonby, Portia sprinted out of the room. Once she reached the hallway, she realized what she'd done.

Given herself away!

She'd run like a panicked innocent. Everyone who saw must now know that's what she was. She didn't even know why she had run. Those people didn't care that she saw them. That was the point.

She had known an orgy was about people in a group doing intimate things that were supposed to be enjoyed in private by a husband and wife.

She'd never expected how it would make her feel. She had run, panicked, because of what happened to her as she'd witnessed all those people making love together. A wash of heat that melted her from within. A pounding of her heart. A pulsing, throbbing ache inside her.

"Angel, are you all right?"

She could barely breathe. She couldn't speak. Sinclair had pursued her and she didn't want him to know what was happening to her.

She had almost wanted to go to Willoughby when he'd crooked his finger. She wanted to be touched everywhere by women and men. She wanted fingers to caress the place between her legs that absolutely screamed with agonized need. She wanted to feel someone pounding deep inside her.

She wanted it to be Sinclair.

Oh God.

Portia hurried away from him as fast as she could, passing through the room across the corridor. She'd walked into a gallery, one devoid of paintings. Glass-paned doors lined the wall. She pushed one open and stepped outside. Into a fierce, salt-filled breeze. Her skirts whipped around her. There were no trees on the rocky outcrop that was Serenity Island and gusts blew up to the house, tugging at her hair. Water droplets blew into her face—from rain or from the sea, she didn't know.

Sinclair came up behind her. "Don't run, Po—Miss Love. Are you all right? Did that shock you?"

She couldn't run anymore. Not in the wild wind. So she turned. She lifted her chin. "Did you really do things like that at your parties?" It was a silly question. Of course he had.

He looked suddenly awkward, which surprised her—that he would be self-conscious. "Yes, Portia. That is exactly what happens in orgies."

She lifted a brow. "Is that really better, more exciting, than sharing lovemaking with someone special, someone you love?"

He didn't answer, but pain was written on his face.

She pulled her hair back—a curl had blown into her face. "That's what you traded my love for? Women who put their breasts in your face, then into the faces of other men?"

This was wrong of her—she was behaving judgmentally when she'd almost been crippled with lust and desire just watching. She had never been hypocritical in her life.

He took a step closer and bent his head so he could look her right in the eye. "I was wrong. I was a damned fool."

She couldn't admit it to him, but when she saw Sadie on top of the earl's face, she'd remembered Sinclair doing that to her.

And when she saw the Incognita take that long thing into her mouth, she'd thought . . . what would it be like to do that to Sinclair? Would it thrill him? What would it feel like? Taste like? She had held his erection in her hand. She remembered how big and hard it had felt. How hot it had been against her palm. The thought of sucking on it and making him moan? Meltingly arousing.

His lips were close to hers. His wide, soft lips. Ten years ago, he'd kissed her and made her melt.

She hadn't kissed for ten years. Ten years!

She couldn't *stand* it anymore.

Her fingers went up and she touched his jaw—the strong

line of his jaw. The bristle of his stubble tickled her. "You truly regret ten years of sex with women like Sadie and her dangerous bosom?"

"Yes." It came out husky and deep. He was so close she heard it over the wind. "It was like an addiction for me. When I lost you, I gave in to it."

"An addiction? I don't understand."

"It's a craving, like one for alcohol or opium. It consumed me. I needed wilder and wilder things to arouse me and capture my attention. I did things—things I will never talk of. What you saw tonight was simple, mild group sex—"

"Mild!" she gasped. Her cheeks burned.

"I'm sorry you were shocked."

"Not shocked . . . exactly." The words came out in breathy patches.

He stared. "You weren't shocked," he repeated.

"It was . . . actually interesting."

"Portia, you were aroused by it?" He looked stunned.

She blushed ever harder behind the mask.

Then he closed the last inch of distance between them, with the wind howling about them, and his lips gently caressed hers. It was like she'd touched a shooting star with her mouth. Heat and sparks rushed through her.

Sinclair deepened the kiss, opening his mouth, and kissing her in a lush, earthy way. His tongue came into her mouth, warm and teasing.

It was so intimate to be kissed with her mouth open. So scandalously intimate. Portia moaned. She leaned against his chest. She slipped her hands up to his shoulders. Firm and broad. Wider and more muscled than they were when he was a young, beautiful man of nineteen.

She kissed him back, moving her mouth and moaning softly. Devouring him like he was devouring her.

He'd kissed her like this on the night they became engaged. Kissed her senseless. Until she ached and was so scorching hot, she was surprised she hadn't set the sofa on fire.

Her fingers trailed along his shoulders, sliding along the exquisite fabric of his tailcoat. His mouth teased and tormented hers, making her throb deep inside. Throb with need.

He lifted her suddenly, his hands under her bottom. She loved the sensation of his large hands there. He carried her and she suddenly felt the stone wall of the house press firmly against her back.

Would he do as he did on the night he asked her to marry him? Make her come, as he'd called it?

She panted into his mouth. She wanted to come again. To feel that glorious explosion of pleasure. But she'd loved him back then. They didn't have love now. How could she still want pleasure with him?

She was being dangerously weak.

She pushed against his chest—it was rock hard under her palms.

Sinclair drew back, breathing hard. "What's wrong?"

"I can't do this. With you, I turn into a hen-witted fool. I suddenly am willing to do erotic things with you, even though I know there will never be marriage or love or respectability. I feel this wanting deep inside, but I know I'm just being a complete idiot."

Portia turned and walked away from him, toward the terrace doors. Footsteps pounding on the flagstones told her he was following yet again. "What if I'd realized I love you?"

Oh Lord. Such words. They gripped her heart. They begged her to stop and listen.

No.

"It's too late. I couldn't trust you. This is your world—you'll go back to it eventually." She kept walking. A stone wall edged the terrace and she followed it with no idea where she was going to go. She wouldn't be able to talk to anyone tonight. She stopped and turned. "I want to go to bed—to sleep. I'm exhausted. I can't face anything more tonight. But where can I sleep? There is only your bed."

Suddenly, she was almost in tears. She felt both hot and ice-cold inside.

"You may have it," he said gallantly. "I'll find another bed tonight."

"I suppose you can find one easily." She hated how obviously hurt she sounded.

Yet he appeared oblivious. He nodded. Then said, "There are a lot of empty rooms in this house."

He meant an empty bed? Not one occupied by another woman. Or women. That startled her. Yet she was not going to be in love with him ever. Why should it matter to her?

She'd had a wonderful kiss—but there could never be another one.

He grasped her hand. "Portia, lock your door tonight. The more I think about it, the more likely I feel Willoughby is involved. I saw how he invited you to join in at the orgy. He was watching you. Kidnapping you is the kind of nasty thing he would do. I intend to confront him over this. But I need to know you are completely safe."

"I'll lock it, push a chair against it, push the wardrobe against it, if I can."

"Good."

With that, he escorted her upstairs. Once he left her in the room, she diligently turned the key in the lock.

But she knew that was she really wanted to do was protect herself against this mixed-up feeling of emptiness and need, of fear and yearning.

It was the most frightening thing she'd ever felt. Wanting to go back to where she was ten years ago and feel passion all over again.

Even knowing how horribly it had ended.

Portia couldn't sleep. Even though she was exhausted from having been kidnapped, from being tied to a bed, from witnessing a man's death—and some rather shocking sexual antics—she just could not fall into slumber.

She lay with her eyes wide open.

Had Sandhurst been poisoned?

By whom? Which of these people who had come to an orgy for wanton sex had done such a thing?

The door rattled.

Oh heavens, who was there? Her heart thundered. She sat up in bed, staring at the door handle. It was locked, the key on her bedside table.

The rattle sounded again, sharp and urgent.

It wasn't coming from the door.

Glass-paned doors led off Sinclair's bedroom to a small balcony. The wind off the ocean buffeted them, pushing them to strain against the bolt that held them closed. That was causing the rattle.

Portia got out of bed. She'd slept in a filmy white silk nightdress. It had been brought to her by the maid who told her it had also been left for the guest of the Duke of Sinclair. She had questioned the maid, whose name was Ellie, but the young woman had known only what she'd been directed to do by written instructions from Lord Genvere.

Where was Sinclair? Had he gone to the orgy after she'd gone to bed? Was he in bed now? Was he really alone?

He'd kissed her and perhaps he'd wanted to seduce her, and she'd turned him down. He must have been lusty and frustrated, and there were plenty of women here who would be delighted to satisfy him.

Portia went to the window.

The storm had broken overnight. She couldn't see the sea for rain and cloud.

There wouldn't be a boat coming from the mainland. She was trapped here for another day. She slumped down on the window sill—she who had braved the slums.

Lightning flashed, making her jump. The whole island lit up with cold white-blue light. In that burst of light, she saw a shape on the lawn—a long, dark shape. At once, she was plunged back into darkness. As she struggled to make sense of what she'd seen, thunder crashed. Like the gods playing cymbals, her mother used to say.

She thought she saw someone lying on the lawn in the rain. It must have been one of the guests. He must have passed out there—

Or he was *dead*. Like Viscount Sandhurst.

She waited. Another flash came and she strained to see. It was so brief, just for a second, but she was certain now. There was a man lying in the grass. Probably a drunken orgy guest. But what if he wasn't?

What should she do? *Get help, goose.*

Yet another burst of lightning and she saw a man running out through the rain; then she jumped at an almost instant explosion of thunder. The storm must be right over them.

The man she'd seen running out had dark hair and he was tall. Her gut instinct screamed that it was Julian. The Duke of Sinclair, she meant.

But it could be someone else. There were other brunette men in the house. Still she hurried to her door, unlocked it, and headed for the stairs.

Portia reached the bottom and made her way through the dark house to the terrace doors. One was opened, snapping against the stone wall of the house, flung back and forth by the wind. She grabbed it and held it.

There were no lights on, and she should have had the sense to bring a lamp. A dark shape against the black rain-filled night sky, the man came in, staggering slightly under the weight of the apparently unconscious man he carried over his shoulder. He made his way to the settee. Another bolt of lightning in the background illuminated his face from the side.

"Sinclair!" she gasped.

His face was stark with shock and pain. "It's Willoughby. He's been attacked. Beaten badly."

"Heavens. By whom?" She quickly moved toward him to help.

"No, Portia. Go back upstairs. Don't come here. You shouldn't see this."

"I've dealt with violence before."

"Nothing like this, I'll bet." He shouldered Willoughby's limp body to the settee. Ignoring his warning, she went forward and around him and she got a glimpse of Willoughby. She let out a cry, then clapped her hand to her mouth to smother it.

His face . . .

It was all darkness. A strange circle of black and shadow. There were no features. There was *nothing* there.

Sinclair's body loomed in front of her. His arm went around her, holding her up. Suddenly Portia found herself sitting a large wing chair—Sinclair had deposited her there. "I don't understand," she breathed. "Where is his face?"

Pain flashed over Sinclair's face. Then she understood. "Someone did that to him? That's awful. Horrible!"

For the second time that day she had a glass of brandy pushed into her hand. Sinclair hadn't said a word. He'd just poured a brandy for her and pressed the plump balloon-shaped glass against her palms. She took one burning sip. It didn't calm her. Nothing could.

"I'll take you back upstairs," he said. "It's too late for him."

"He *is* dead?" But given what she'd seen, she knew he must be. And if he hadn't been . . . it would have been worse.

"I can't believe this. Earlier tonight he was alive and . . . and . . . doing things in the drawing room." She had no words to describe what he'd been doing in the drawing room. Not any words she could actually say. "Now he's gone."

"Sip the brandy," Sinclair said.

"No, I think not," she said as she put it down.

Sinclair had turned on a lamp and had removed Willoughby's coat while examining him. Now he went back and laid the garment over Willoughby's body, covering the destroyed face. Portia forced herself to get up and go over to help him. But she'd never seen such horrific damage inflicted on a human being, and her knees kept wobbling.

She had to stop and grip the chair. She wasn't as strong and tough as she thought she was. It was an infuriating thing to discover.

For a moment, the sky brightened with lightning. Wind buffeted the house and rain slammed against the glass, as if trying to break in and invade.

Sinclair came and stood over her. He stripped off his gloves and tossed them aside. Warm, strong, his hand stroked her face. She should say no. Tell him to stop. But she couldn't.

A second death in the space of hours. Suddenly, she needed to press tight against Sinclair. She turned his face into his chest. Strong and safe, his arms went around her.

She needed to be touched. She hadn't experienced comfort for five years, not since Mother got very ill and confused.

Thunder came then. Delayed and fainter. The boom still made her gasp in surprise, but she knew the storm had passed them. It was going farther away.

At her gasp, he bent over her. He pressed his lips softly to the top of her head. Oh, what that did to her heart.

No, she had to stop this. She moved away. Spoke with the crispness of a school mistress. "I am quite fine now. I had a bit of a shock, but I am all right now. Do you need me to help you?"

"You need to sit. You are not fine. I'm not." He directed her back to the chair, sat on the arm of the chair, beside her.

Large. Strong. Warm. Male.

She leapt up as if shot from a cannon. "I don't need to be hugged and coddled. There are far more important things we must focus upon. Such as—who did this?"

"That is not for you to worry about. It is my fault you are involved in this—and I will make this right."

"How is it your fault?"

"You were brought here as some kind of joke against me. Now this has happened—I don't know who is responsible for this, but there's a murderer on this island."

"It is not your fault!" She cupped his face, feeling the scratch of stubble against her hands. She shouldn't touch him, but he looked so white and shocked and in pain. He needed to be touched.

To her surprise, he drew her hands away. "Don't. I'm not in the mood."

"I didn't mean—"

"I know what you meant. To make me feel better when I don't deserve it. Protecting you is what matters to me, Portia."

"Sinclair, for ten years I have looked after myself," she argued. "I can do so now."

The she saw something white on the carpet, near the settee. She stared in disbelief, already certain what it was. "Look. It's another note."

Sinclair bent and grabbed the paper. "Where did it come from?"

"It must have been with Willoughby. When you carried him, perhaps it fell."

"It's sealed with wax again." He tore the paper open. She leaned over his arm to read.

A second sinner has paid for his crime. He will not be the last.

10

Crossing his arms over his broad chest, Sinclair drew his dark brows together in a frown. "If you won't have the brandy, I'll go down to kitchens and brew you tea."

Despite the horror of the night, Portia had to smile. "You are a duke. Do you even know how to make tea?"

"I wasn't always a duke, and I learned in my youth how to brew a cup of tea. For you, Portia, I'm more than willing to hoist a kettle and draw some water."

He gave a gallant bow.

Her heart wobbled. Once she had felt so close to this man. Over the last ten years, she'd believed she had never understood him. Yet now she saw in him the young man she'd adored.

She shook her head again. "I am fine. I don't need anything." *Except you*, thought her traitorous heart. "But what is going on here? Does it mean someone killed both Sandhurst and Viscount Willoughby?"

Sinclair stood in the middle of the room, grinding his fist into the palm of his other hand. But she didn't think he realized he was doing that—instead he was looking at Willoughby, a sad, pitiful shape covered by a coat. "I don't know," he said pensively. "I intend to find out."

It was all he said, but Portia knew he had more thoughts. She could tell by the distracted way he answered her. It startled her to realize she *knew* this man. Ten years ago, when they were falling in love, he would tell her so many things. He had revealed how the duchess, his cousin, hated him. Revealed how awkward he felt being a duke, dealing with the business of the dukedom when he'd never been trained for it. How awkward he felt being in London. He'd told her that the only time he felt happy was when he was with her.

But that was in the past, no matter what he said now.

She almost touched his forearm. She stopped herself. "I can tell you have ideas—suspicions, Sinclair. You're just not telling me. I believe I have a right to know, since I was kidnapped and brought here."

He hesitated, then shook his head. "I have no idea what's going on. Or what the notes mean. In truth, Willoughby was the man I suspected of orchestrating your kidnapping. Now, I don't know. Someone did that to Willoughby." He shook his head. "*You* should go to bed."

"I can't sleep. And I won't leave you down here alone—not when the person who did that could be lying in wait."

The fist stopped grinding. He snapped his head around to look at her. "What do you intend to do, Portia?"

"First, I am going to do this—" She stalked to the unlit fireplace and grabbed the poker. Made of heavy brass, it was a cold weight in her hand.

"You're going to protect yourself with a fireplace poker?"

"I don't see why that won't work. Now I am going to help you. I'm going to help you tend to Willoughby. Then find out the truth."

"Tend to him?"

"Do stop repeating everything I say as if it's shocking. I don't think I'm shocking you."

"You'd be surprised," he said.

"Well, we—we can't just leave Lord Willoughby there."

Sinclair scrubbed his jaw. "I'll get the butler to help me move the body."

Another flash of lightning made her almost leap out of her skin. Instinctively she swung the poker. Sinclair stepped back abruptly. "Careful with that thing, love."

Love. That name had irritated her before. Now it made her think again of what he'd said. That he regretted what he'd done.

Bother. He could call her "love" all he wanted. She was not going to let it affect her.

The silver-blue burst of lightning had stolen her ability to see in the dark. Now she couldn't see anything outside the windows. Just her reflection in the glass.

She swallowed. "Do you think there are other people on this island? That someone came up to the house, found him outside, and robbed him?"

"I don't know, Portia. I don't know why anyone would have gone out to the terrace tonight, in a storm, without good reason."

"Maybe he went out for a breath of air after the . . . the things he was doing."

Sinclair shook his head. "I don't believe that's likely."

"We should lock the terrace door."

"Agreed," he said. He crossed over and did that. She felt safer once he tried the handle and checked it was locked.

But then, Viscount Sandhurst had died in the house. And Sinclair had believed he was poisoned.

Could that really be true? Or was it an attack of his heart?

But the author of the letters had foreseen it. And knew almost exactly when the young viscount was going to die.

That had to be murder, didn't it?

Was it Sadie and she had actually smothered a grown man with her bosom? And was lying to cover up her deliberate crime . . . ?

Portia almost let out a desperate, nervous giggle. That was madness. Sadie, a criminal who had engineered the viscount's death? Why even would she do it? She seemed desperate to snare a man's attention, not murder him so he would be unable to give her money and gifts.

Portia looked up. Sinclair had gone back to the body. He'd lifted the coat and looked at the face again. By the light of the lamp, she saw him grimace.

He dropped the coat.

"I'm sorry," she said.

Willoughby had worked to break up their engagement, but he hadn't deserved such a horrible death.

"Sorry about what, love?" Sinclair looked up.

"I did not hold him in high regard," she said softly, "but I know he was your very good friend."

He frowned. "He was once. Our friendship ended when we faced each other over dueling pistols. I shot wide. He didn't."

"Good heavens, he shot you?"

"Obviously not fatally." He smiled, a small upturn of his lips that disappeared quickly.

"That is not the point. What on earth did you fight about?"

His broad shoulders shrugged. "He's dead now. It's of no consequence."

"Was it over a woman?"

He didn't answer, but she saw it in his dark brown eyes. It was. She felt it again—the agonizing twist of jealousy.

"Was it a courtesan?" she asked softly. "Who was she?"

What woman had he risked his life over? When he had so easily left her, who was the woman who had been worth his life in a duel?

Slowly, Sinclair walked back to her. He moved with grace, as always, but his expression was stark.

He came to her until they were only inches away. Until she had to crane her neck to meet his gaze. He was so close she could see droplets of water that still dripped from his hair.

The hard anger gleaming in his eyes made her take a half step back.

"Will had deliberately ruined a young woman," he said, bitterly. "He pursued her, made her believe he was in love with her. She was a rich merchant's daughter, a naïve and pretty young heiress. She fell for him, went to bed with him. The moment after, he broke it off with her. Her father had died, leaving her a fortune, but she had no strong family to pressure Willoughby into marriage."

"So you tried to."

"What I did was a damn stupid thing. The indiscretion could have been covered up. By dueling with him, I made the girl's disgrace public. She . . . she took her own life. And the fault was mine."

The emptiness with which he spoke stunned her. "You tried to help, Sinclair—"

"Portia, I don't know if that was the real reason I dueled with him."

"I don't understand."

"Will made a game of conning innocent girls, getting them into his bed, then abandoning them. He made wagers with his bas—I mean, his friends. I was angry that he was so callous and I called him out. But maybe I did it because I wanted vengeance for being lured to brothels, for his part in ending our engagement. It was stupid, because the fault was mine."

She drew in a deep breath. She knew it was true, but the pain in his eyes touched her heart. "What happened between us is not of consequence. You did champion that poor girl. You risked your life to force Willoughby to do the honorable thing. That makes you the hero—"

"Angel, of all people, you know I am not heroic."

She didn't know what to say.

"Do heroes break women's hearts and hold orgies?"

"No," she said. "I suppose not."

"Exactly. But I am aware of when a man needs to take action." Lifting a brow, he looked toward the door.

Then she knew. "You're going out there? In the storm?"

"To hunt. I don't know if I'll find anyone out there, but the other option is that someone in this house killed Willoughby."

Rain again lashed the panes of the doors. Portia clutched the fireplace poker. "Whoever wrote these notes must have done it. Sadie was alone with Sandhurst."

"You think Sadie a murderess?" His brows shot up.

"I don't know. It seems madness. But she could have fed him something or given him a drink once they were together."

"I saw no used glassware near him. And he didn't go into the drawing room."

She stared at him. The fact that he had thought to look surprised her.

"I don't see how he was poisoned during dinner, if in fact, he was," Sinclair continued. "No one else was near his plate or glass. The butler or footman could have given him an individual serving of food that was poisoned, I guess. Sandhurst left before port was served. He could have had a doctored drink before dinner. There could have been poison in the brandy in his bedchamber. Or Sadie could have done it."

Then he added, "But it would have been impossible for Sadie to overpower and attack Will."

Portia nodded. That did seem logical. She looked up at the ceiling. Above her were all the bedchambers. "Still, it had to be someone . . . here. In this house. One of the guests. Or one of the servants."

"Not necessarily. It could be someone not in the house. Someone hiding on the island. This mysterious host of ours, for instance."

"If it was someone outside. . . ." An idea hit her. One she wanted to grasp at. "Perhaps it was someone else who lives on the island. Who found Willoughby and decided to attack and rob him." But that would not explain Sandhurst's death.

"No one else lives on this island. That was what I was told, when I was searching for you, asking fishermen on the quay."

"You were searching for me? Before you reached the island?"

"I was sent a note that told me you'd been kidnapped. It was the only reason I came to this place—I was told you were in danger."

He'd only come here for *her?* That thought rushed through her, intense as lightning.

He'd come close to her, and she was enveloped in awareness of him.

"What do you think, Portia? To have found Will in a thunderstorm outdoors, the killer had to know where to look. That's why my suspicions lean toward our unknown host. Someone brought us all here for some purpose."

He was telling her of his thoughts. Wanting her opinion. "Wasn't the orgy the purpose?"

"That's what we all thought. Now two of us are dead." He rubbed his jaw again. "I wonder if our host has arrived and he's hiding somewhere out there." He sighed. "It's time I went out and looked."

"I'm coming with you. With the fireplace poker."

He began to shake his head, but she marched to the door. "You are not leaving me in here all alone."

He rolled his eyes to the ceiling. "You will get soaked to the skin, Portia."

"As will you." She said archly, "You do remember I wanted to marry you once. I don't now, but I still would be hurt—heartbroken—if anything happened to you."

Then he said the most shocking thing, just before opening the glass door and stepping out onto the rain-swept terrace. "You give me hope, angel."

"Please cease to say things like that," she said, following him out.

As she passed through the open terrace door, she walked into the sudden embrace of his tailcoat, which he'd worn under the great coat he'd draped on Willoughby.

Sinclair drew his warm coat around her. But despite being swathed in his great coat, her face was almost instantly wet. Her hair was quickly catching up. Already, it clung to her cheeks. Rain dripped from her eyelashes and pelted against her eyes.

She'd thought the rain was coming down like a sweeping

gray sheet. She'd been wrong. Rain seemed to drop in quantity, like an entire sea flooding the terrace from the heavens. His brown hair was plastered to his brow. His shirt, where not covered by waistcoat, went transparent.

Completely. It clung to his shoulders, his biceps, his forearms, like a teasing veil revealing hints of bronzed skin and dustings of chocolate-brown hair.

"You can't give me your coat," she protested. "You'll be soaked."

"Look down, Portia."

Confused, holding his coat on her shoulders with one hand, she did. She had run out in the borrowed white nightdress without even thinking. Rain. White fabric. His shirt looked positively proper in comparison to the way her nightgown's skirt clung to her legs. She could see the pink skin of her thighs through the clinging fabric. Tummy, bosom—wet fabric clung to every curve she had, revealing all. Her nipples were visible. Almost. A little longer in the rain and she might as well have been naked.

"Oh."

Then, realizing he could see all, she went, "Oh," and pulled the coat tighter.

He held out his hand to take hers.

"I can't. Between holding your coat and the poker, I haven't got any free hands."

"Wait here, then," he said. Then he turned and he was gone, running across the stone terrace in the rain. She could barely see him. There was some light spilling from the house. The stone terrace was large and rimmed with a carved stone balustrade. Ornamental vases of stone held flowers. Beyond the terrace, there was a stretch of lawns, but then there was the rough, craggy surface of the island, all mounded rock and small shrubs. That disappeared into darkness. Over the drumming rain, Portia faintly heard the crash of waves. The winds of the storm would be driving the seawater hard against the rocks.

There were some trees, but they were stunted, lichen-covered things with black trunks and twisted limbs and few leaves. No one could be hiding up in one of them, she was sure. And why would someone, in all this cold, pounding rain?

Holding the poker up, she hurried out after him. It was so hard to see she almost stumbled over him. He was crouched on one knee, running his bare hand over the grass.

She bent over. "What are you looking for?"

"Any kind of clue. Something left behind by Will's attacker."

She peered down at the wet flags. An uneven line of darkness ran along the stones, moving with the rain. Oh heavens, that was blood. "I don't see a thing."

"Neither do I." He stood, straightening to his full height right beside her.

There was something about the sight of him wet—

She didn't know what it was. The way his hair was sleek and shiny. He flicked his hair to send it flying back, away from her so she wasn't hit by the spray. Droplets ran along his lips.

He must look rather like this after a bath—

A man had been killed! And she was certainly never going see the Duke of Sinclair after he had bathed. A wife barely even did such a thing—

It was the things he said. They made the daftest thoughts come into her head.

She was never going to marry the Duke of Sinclair.

He turned and strode toward the end of the terrace. She wanted to shout to him, but she was afraid of alerting someone. A killer, for example.

He paused, waiting for her to catch up. As she hurried to him, she saw him look down at her legs. She felt the fabric clinging to her. He looked pained.

"What's wrong?" she asked, as she reached him. "You look as if in agony."

"I am. Seeing you in a skin-tight, wet white nightgown. This is punishment for every sin I've ever committed. To discover how lovely you are, when I can't touch."

"No, you can't. At least, not my legs." Touches were something she craved, but they were so very dangerous to her heart. "Are you really intending to search the island tonight?"

He frowned. "That was my plan. Yet you make it sound idiotic."

"It's pouring rain and pitch-dark. Would someone really be out here? If they are, they must have taken refuge."

"We'll hunt for other buildings." He took the poker from her hand and clasped her wrist.

She felt safer being hand in hand with him. Though it spoke of joining, of partnership, and she fought to ignore that.

He took her down the terrace and they followed the lawns toward the edge of a cliff—the end of the island, where the rock was a drop to the sea.

Her slippers (also left for her, since she'd worn sensible half boots into the stews) squished with each step. That felt worse than wet clothes. They were also as slippery as metal runners on ice, and she was careful as she ventured near the edge of the cliff. Below, in great bursts of silvery white, waves crashed on the rocks, sending spray up to collide with the cascading rain.

It might be June, but outside, wet to the skin, she found it freezing. Sinclair was looking below, over the edge of the cliff.

"No one could be there, could they? They'd fall and be killed. It must be slippery and deadly on the rocks."

"True," he murmured. She barely heard his deep, low voice over the rain. He held her hand tightly, and his was warm, despite the cold rain running between their palms. "We'll work around to the house."

She had insisted on coming out with him, now she knew she'd been mad. She'd thought London rain—cold, dreary, and filled with the soot from all the fires—was awful. This rain felt like icy needles jabbing her. She sneezed.

Brushing back his hair, the duke stopped. Looked down at her. "Damn, you're soaked through and you're going to catch cold. I need to get you back to the house."

Before she could protest—or even agree—he scooped her into his arms. The cold ridge of the poker was pressed between his palm and her bottom. But she barely noticed that. She couldn't stop thinking: *I'm in his arms, held tight against him.*

He carried her toward the house. She hated to give in and she was used to being tough, but for once in her life she wanted to be safe inside and dry. Well, as safe as she could be.

How strong his arms were. She felt the hardness of them, his unyielding muscles pressing against her. His hands were splayed under her bottom. Even though she was very practical—she'd been raised to be practical—she couldn't help but melt at being swept off her feet.

They reached the terrace, then the doors, and he set her down. She skidded a little as wet slipper sole contacted even wetter smooth flagstone. Skidded and slid so she fell against him, dropping his coat—an accident. It meant her wet night-gown pressed right against him, with her in it.

His hands went around her waist, drawing her close to him. The poker hit the flagstones with a clang. Another ridge, almost as hard as the poker, pressed to her from the front.

His mouth touched hers. Warm lips caressed hers. As if ten years hadn't happened—

He pulled back. This time he was the one to do the sensible thing. "You need a hot bath. Then bed."

"A bath? It's the middle of the night. The poor maid will be asleep. I can't bear to wake her. I'll towel off and be fine." She stopped on the threshold of the door. Perhaps, inside, there was a murderer. Waiting. Or perhaps he was out here. . . .

"Do you really think there is someone hiding on the island?" she asked. "Or do you think it's one of them? If Willoughby did awful things, like ruin women, perhaps one of those people wanted revenge."

"Possible. So it's a good thing we're sharing a bedroom tonight."

"What?"

"You'll sleep in the bed, after we've gotten you dried off. I'll sleep on a chair. But with the door locked, I'll know you're safe."

Portia knew she would be safe, even locked in a bedroom with the notorious Duke of Sinclair. She knew he would be a perfect gentleman.

But she had kissed him again. And, as wrong as it was, she'd wanted *more* than that brief, soft kiss.

Would she be safe from *herself*, locked in a bedroom with Sinclair?

She was curled around her pillow, sleeping like an angel, except she looked like a temptress in his bed. The silky sheets had slid down off her body.

Sin was sprawled in the wing chair. After returning to the house, he and Portia had woken Humphries, and he and the butler had carried the body up to Will's bedroom, where they'd laid him on the bed and covered him with a sheet. Shocked, appalled at Will's death and fretting over their bedraggled condition, Humphries had certainly looked genuinely surprised and horrified.

Portia had insisted she didn't need a bath, and the butler had given her a stack of thick towels to dry herself. After that, she'd gone to bed.

Then Sin had planted himself in the chair. For hours, he had not looked at her. But with daylight—a gray gloomy light—illuminating the room, he'd given in to temptation. Twice, he'd gotten up and pulled the sheets up to cover her. Then she'd wrestled around until they'd slid down.

With her nightgown soaked through, she'd taken it off in the dressing room, then pulled on her shift. But that had ridden up. Fortunately she held the pillow tight to her and it covered her nether curls and her pussy. But he could see the voluptuous curves of her ass and he didn't have the courage to try tugging it down without waking her up.

He'd barely slept, his brain going mad.

Who could have kidnapped Portia?

Who had battered in Will's face?

Who'd killed Sandhurst, who seemed like a daft, inoffensive lad?

It was like all those years ago, when Sin had been a boy. So much death ... death wrapping around him. Then it had all culminated in that moment he'd been standing across from his own brother, aiming a dueling pistol—

His door rattled. Once. Then twice. The knob turned. Then footsteps moved away. The maid laying the fires? A murderer hoping to catch them asleep in bed?

Sin launched to his feet. He ran to the door, turned the key, and opened it. The hall was empty. But from the stair landing, he could hear voices. The appetizing scents of cooked food had begun to slip into the room. Breakfast was being served.

Groaning, he closed the door, locked it again, and went to the window.

The torrential rain had stopped, but gray clouds hugged the island and the sea tossed. No boats would be coming today. He couldn't get Portia to the mainland. Their host would not be arriving. . . .

Unless Genvere was already on the island.

It was time to wake Portia and take her downstairs. Tell everyone what had happened to Will. Start questioning the guests.

Sin looked longingly at the bed. If he hadn't been such a damn idiot ten years ago, and if they weren't on an island with a lunatic, he could be in bed with Portia right now.

Then pain hit him, pain and anger.

"No," he muttered. "With the perverse things you did as a boy, you could never have had Portia. You're damaged, just like she said, Sin. You're not a hero, you're a sinful bastard."

Maybe the lunatic was getting to him. He was talking aloud to himself. At least Portia was asleep. She hadn't heard.

11

Sin walked downstairs with Portia to join the other guests for breakfast, his jaw clenched with tension.

He should have never allowed this. He could have demanded that Portia stay in the bedroom. He wasn't nineteen years old now, a new duke who had no idea how to be in command. Now, at twenty-nine, he knew how to give orders and have them obeyed. In the decade after he'd lost Portia, he'd learned how to make his cousin respect him, his servants snap to attention and respect him, and he'd learned how to make every gentleman of the *ton* envy and admire him.

The only man who didn't envy him was himself.

In their bedroom, with her determined, brilliant gray eyes locked on his face, Portia had insisted she should speak to the other women. It was the best solution, the logical thing to do. To have a woman try to get information from the women.

He'd helped her back into her ivory gown, tightened the ties of her mask. All the while, he'd fought not to fall into the glittering beauty of her eyes. "Let me do this, Sinclair," she declared. "I am comfortable on the streets of Whitechapel. I can take care of myself."

"I could seduce information from the women."

"I doubt they'd tell you they'd done something heinous, even in the throes of ecstasy."

"Would they tell you?"

"I can be clever. And I can simply climb down from the balcony and go downstairs if I wish, even if you lock me in."

"Damn it, all right."

The reason he'd let her come downstairs was that she was right. Portia had the finest brain of anyone he knew.

But the more time she spent with the guests, the more she risked revealing her identity. Portia could end up ruined.

After what had happened to Will, and if Sandhurst had been poisoned, ruination was their smallest concern.

Now Sin watched her walk ahead of him into the dining room, his every instinct on edge. He found the other male guests loading their plates at the buffet. The women were already seated, nibbling from tiny plates of food.

Crayle, the marquis, whom Sin privately called the Marquis de Sade, sat down with a plate in which food had been placed with geometric precision. The Earl of Blute, the muscular, auburn-haired Sporting Corinthian, was piling his plate with gusto, creating towers of kippers and sausages. Rutledge was taking coffee from the urn and holding his head. The sign of a man suffering the aftereffects of drinking. Sax stood at the buffet of warming dishes, selecting sausages.

Sin considered the food. Could it have been poisoned? Portia walked to the warming dishes and picked up a plate. He lunged forward and caught her wrist, ladling spoon clutched in her hand. "Watch for a few moments," he muttered. "Let them eat. See how they fare."

She gulped. "Oh, I see."

Her tummy made a rumbling sound and she stared at the dishes. Damn, he knew she was hungry. How long would it take poison to act? Longer than mere minutes. But he could see the appetizing smells were getting to Portia.

"Do you really think all the food could be poisoned? Though

Lord Rutledge is not eating. Do you think that means he is wary of the food?"

"Or that he drank too much last night."

He saw her gaze longingly at the food. Sighed. Softly he said, "Even if Sandhurst was poisoned, we think it was likely not in the food. I'll taste some. Then you can eat if you want."

He knew it would likely prove nothing for him to test the food, but he guessed she was hungry. And the poisoner last night hadn't seen fit to try to kill them all.

He put a little food on his plate. She did the same. After he tried it, at the table, and nodded, she ate a little.

The women began to leave the table. "We are retiring to the drawing room," Clarissa announced.

Portia set down her knife and fork. "I should go too," she whispered. Then she jumped up and followed.

Sin couldn't tear his gaze from her, from the sway of her hips beneath silk skirts as she sashayed out. Reluctantly, he knew he had to let her go. Then, on a grunt of frustration, Sin got out of his seat and went to the head of the table.

"Last night, Viscount Willoughby was murdered," he announced bluntly. "He was attacked and savagely beaten on the terrace outside. I found him dead."

He glanced at each man—even Sax. A kipper fell out of Blute's mouth. Rutledge sputtered over his coffee. The marquis looked unmoved. Sax blinked.

Sin mentally assessed the men. Willoughby liked pugilism and was a bruising rider. Will had been strong.

Crayle, the marquis, was over sixty, with a thin build. However, Rutledge, Blute, and Sax had the strength to take Willoughby.

He and Sax had been friends for a long time. Since they had all gone to Eton. They were members of the group of friends called the "Wicked Dukes" by the *ton*. He doubted Sax would kill anyone, even with strong motivation. But he couldn't know for certain.

He was considering suspects based on their physical strength. On the other hand, any one of them could have taken Will by surprise, clubbed him over the head first to knock him out, and then beaten him with a weapon. None of the men could be exonerated—including the butler and the footman. And if the killer had taken Will by surprise, the women were suspects as well.

Damn it, he should never have allowed Portia to come downstairs—

"Someone attacked him? You are saying there is a murderer on this island?" barked the marquis. He stood up from the table, tall and straight, his white hair flowing back. "It must have been a footpad who attacked him to rob him. I'd run through any bastard who assaulted me."

"I doubt that, in a thunderstorm, someone attacked him to rob him," Sin answered. "I think someone had a motive to want Will dead."

Sax frowned. "You mean someone in this house. One of us."

"Unless there is someone else on the island," Sin said. "I searched as much as I could last night, but that wasn't particularly effective, in the driving rain."

"Then we should carry out a thorough search this morning," Crayle barked. "I will help also. There must be some ruffian on this island. Perhaps several. We will catch them and string them up."

"String them up?" Sin repeated.

"I had arranged to entertain the lovely Sadie this morning. I came for sexual sport. Having to delay my satisfaction is putting me in a very bad mood," Crayle snapped.

"If we find this person, we will wait for justice until we can take him back to the mainland. Understood?" Sin said.

He glanced toward the door. He couldn't go and search now—he'd only allowed Portia to go and speak to the women alone because he was close enough to hear her scream if she was in trouble.

Portia would never forget what she'd overheard Sin say this morning.

The perverse things I did as a boy. . . .

What did he mean? She knew there was no point in asking. Knew he wouldn't tell her. She had pretended to be asleep, so he wouldn't worry that she'd heard.

What could he have done as a boy that was so bad?

But for now, she had to focus on questioning the other women. She sailed into the drawing room, confident she could do this. Determined to find justice.

But as she entered the drawing room, she suddenly remembered that some of these women, or even all of them, might have made love to Sinclair.

She stood in the drawing room, wearing her elegant gown and mask, and she felt tremendously tongue-tied. Did some— or all—of these women know the Duke of Sinclair more intimately than she ever would?

The Incognita wore a day dress of the sort that a royal princess might wear. Elegant and fashionable, it was pale ivory with a delicate stripe of blue, and followed her every curve. But it was cut so low Portia could see the dusky pink of the woman's nipples.

The Old Madam, Mrs. Barker, paced the room, glaring outside the window through a glittering, bejeweled lorgnette, her skirts swishing around her. She wore a bronze gown, the neckline cut low as well. Her bosom was like two enormous pillows stuffed within. An elaborate turban adorned her head. "What in heaven's name is taking those gentlemen so long?" she snapped, without looking at the others in the room.

The young and bosomy courtesan Sadie giggled. She wasn't wearing a day gown. She had on just a thin, silk robe, belted at the waist. She sprawled on the settee, the robe slightly parted to reveal her shapely legs and plump thighs.

The widow stood near the fire, studying it, playing with the pearl choker around her neck.

Portia knew it was time to speak. "They are discussing what happened to Viscount Willoughby."

"What happened to him?" The Old Madam whipped around and looked at her sharply.

Portia told them, as bluntly as she could. It was tough to do, but she had to see their reaction.

The widow, Lady Linley, turned from the fire and stared. "Killed? Deliberately?" She took a step forward; then her legs crumpled beneath her. She fell to the floor, because no one was close enough to reach her, but she did it as elegantly as a feather fluttering down.

The Incognita rolled her eyes. "For heaven's sake. I suppose we must come to her rescue. Miss Love, would you help me lift her and take her to the settee? At least she's not heavy."

She helped, though even working together, she and the Incognita had to drag the widow. Portia ensured the widow had a pillow. "Do you think she's all right?"

"I'm sure she will be fine. I wonder if she even really fainted. She wants to look delicate, fluttering around in front of our two available dukes." The courtesan's tone was dry, sarcastic.

"Surely, if she hadn't fainted, she wouldn't want to be dragged," Portia observed. Was the faint a sign of guilt? A woman who easily shocked would hardly beat a man to death, would she?

Portia wondered if she should poke the widow to check if she had really fainted, when the Elegant Incognita touched her arm.

"My dear, I know why you are wearing a mask. You are respectable and innocent, and you don't want anyone at an orgy to know who you are. I take it you were the woman brought here against your will."

"Er—" She had to distract the woman and think quickly. "Of course not. I came with Sinclair."

"No, you did not. I saw him arrive from my window. He came up with the oarsmen who were carrying his trunk. You were not there. Is he the one who had you brought here unwillingly?"

"No!"

"Well, Sinclair always did enjoy strange games. And punishment."

"Punishment?" Portia echoed.

"Didn't you know? He came to London at nineteen, looking so sweet. But he loves pain. He'll give it and he'll take it. He used to like being cut, liked feeling the blade of a knife part his skin. Of course, he also used to like opium. I am sorry to shock you—I can see you are shocked, even with your mask. But Sin is wild. Wild and impossible to tame. I am surprised he's been so dedicated to you here. It's unlike him. He usually has four or five people in his bed with him. Anything else, he finds deadly dull."

Portia had thought his life was shocking. But nothing like this. He found being cut erotic? She fought the dizzy, buzzing feeling in her head. She said, "Perhaps he's changed." But it sounded idiotic, even to her ears.

"Yes, some men do change. As they grow older. Or if they truly find love. But some men never do—they are driven by something that is deep in their souls. Sin is a man like that. Enjoy him while you can, dear. But you'll lose him in the end."

"Were you ever his lover? Were you Willoughby's lover?"

The Incognita smiled. "You *are* innocent."

What did that mean? That she was Sin's lover? "Do you know anything about Lord Willoughby's murder?"

"Are you asking if I murdered him? I would hardly tell you."

"Someone did. Someone on this island." Portia watched the Incognita's beautiful green eyes.

And she saw it. The flash of fear. Of wariness.

"This wretched party is cursed," Clarissa said carelessly. "First Sandhurst. Now this. I suppose we must all leave. I shall be glad to go."

"We can't leave. The sea is too high. We are all trapped here," Portia pointed out.

"We can't leave?" The Incognita bit her lip.

"Ooh, look who's finally arrived."

The bubbly voice belonged to Sadie, who came up beside Portia.

Portia looked to the door. Sinclair stood on the drawing room threshold, looking slightly disheveled. She was the reason for that. Her stomach had rumbled and he'd brought her down without bothering to shave. Or put on a cravat.

The hint of stubble along his chin was gorgeous. The glimpse of his bare throat in public rather shocking.

"At least we have such a strong, handsome duke to protect us," Sadie cooed.

Then Portia felt a hand where it shouldn't be. On her bottom.

It was Sadie, and startled Portia turned around. The most wickedly naughty look came into Sadie's huge blue eyes.

Suddenly Sadie lunged forward. The girl's bosom smacked Portia's chest. Sadie's soft, puckered lips came to hers. Slanting her head, Sadie kissed her. Her mouth was hot, tasted of sugared coffee, and her tongue was small and playful inside Portia's mouth.

Portia stood, feet riveted to the floor. Sadie moaned, moaned softly in pleasure, and Portia blinked and suddenly all she could see was Sadie. The girl's lashes trembled. Her lovely eyes filled with pleasure.

Sadie's arms were around her. Then Sadie cupped Portia's bottom and her left breast.

Portia made a squeak of shock. Heavens, a thrill went through her as Sadie caressed her.

Sinclair's jaw dropped so precipitously she was amazed it didn't hit the carpet. A pained look flashed over his handsome face. He scrubbed a hand over his jaw. His dark eyes glowed as if lit by fire.

The desire in his expression stunned her. Then propriety hit.

She shouldn't be doing such a thing—not in such circumstances. She tried to ease away from Sadie, but the girl stuck to her like treacle.

Oh. Blast.

She put her hands firmly on Sadie's shoulders and pulled back. Sadie released her.

What did one say at such a moment? What was proper? "Thank you."

Sadie laughed. "How polite. I do wonder who you are."

Sadie was never going to find out.

Still laughing, Sadie turned and blew a kiss toward Sinclair as she twirled a golden curl around her fingers.

At once Portia understood. Sadie's steamy, lusty kiss with her was a way of flirting with the duke.

Suddenly Sinclair was right in front of her. Hand on her elbow, he pulled Portia away from the others and led her to the window. His wide chest blocked her view of the room. Looking up, she saw the stubble—little bits close enough to his lips that if she kissed him, it would scratch and tickle.

His hair was in a tangle as he shoved it back with his hand. "What are you doing?"

"I was speaking to the women, Your Grace. Then Sadie kissed me." Then, she couldn't help it—he'd broken *her* heart ten years ago because he'd wanted wicked pleasures. Lightly, she added, "Kissing Sadie was rather nice."

"It was?"

She'd meant to tease, but raw feeling strangled her. "It wasn't as fiery, as intense, as powerful as kissing you. And for feeling that, I'm an utter fool. But unfortunately I haven't had a chance to talk much to the women. The Wicked Widow—I mean, Lady Linley, fainted when I said Willoughby was dead."

"Wicked Widow?"

Her cheeks burned. "A nickname. But I'm sure Lady Linley couldn't be capable of killing Lord Willoughby."

"If she snuck up on him and knocked him out, it could be possible. However, we're going to search the island."

"That is fine if it was someone from outside. But what if it *was* one of them? You will all be out there—" Her imagination quickly supplied the frightening image. Sinclair searching along the cliff edge, then a figure stealing up and hitting him over the head—

The mere thought made her feel as desperate with fear as when children in her home got sick. "You can't! You will be outside and vulnerable. It's too dangerous."

"We'll go in pairs."

"And you might be paired with a murderer. I'll go with you again. With the fireplace poker."

"Por—my dear, I don't think you and your fireplace poker could do more than I."

"You would be surprised."

A smile played on his lips. A grim one. "The island isn't large. All of us men will go together. You will stay here. But watch out for the women. . . . Hell, I still don't like leaving you alone."

"I guess, if you are all together, you will be safe. All of the other men can't be involved."

"I damn well hope not."

Her heart wobbled. Wobbled terribly. "Do be careful."

"It's all right, angel. I have a pistol."

"A pistol?"

"Brought it because I knew you were in danger. And, Portia—be careful kissing the women. One could be our suspect."

"I'm not . . . I . . ." She sputtered, allowing his to be the last complete and coherent words.

He strode away and rounded up the other men. Saxonby, Rutledge, the Cruel Marquis, the Sporting Corinthian earl—they all filed out through the terrace doors with Sinclair.

"You really are in love with him, aren't you?"

Jasmine perfume teased her nose and Portia whirled around. She faced the Incognita's green eyes. "I'm not. I am not that foolish. I won't forget what you said."

"You won't forget it, but I suspect you will ignore it. Let me tell you more about Sin."

"We should check where Will was found," Sin said to the other men accompanying him. Even the footman and the thin, aging butler had come out onto the terrace to assist the search. The ocean wind whipped around them, the air filled with moisture and the tang of salt and dead seaweed.

As Sin looked across the terrace, he wasn't seeing the smooth flagstones, the grass beyond. He was seeing Portia's wide-eyed look of sweet surprise, then the sultry look as she kissed Sadie. He was remembering the press of Portia's rounded breasts against Sadie's full bosom. Sadie's hand cupping Portia's bottom.

He had to stop thinking about it. He had a murder to solve. Murder had touched him before, a long time ago, and he couldn't let himself think about that either.

Sin started across the terrace with long strides, slowed down, and held back, letting the other men overtake him. He watched. Would any of the men go instinctively to where Willoughby's body had lain?

One did and it surprised him. The old butler walked to the spot on the still-damp grass and halted. Then he jerked his head around nervously and met Sin's cool eyes.

"Your Grace, where exactly was the young gentleman found?"

"You're standing there," Sin answered. "So you obviously know."

"I observed the depression in the grass, Your Grace."

"There wasn't anything obvious. The rain beat down all the grass." Straightening, Sin moved to the butler and glared down at the man. "But you knew where to come."

"I . . . It was pure chance—"

"I don't think it was. Why did you kill him?"

"K-Kill him?" The man's eyes bulged. "I did not. You must believe me! I would never murder a peer of the realm! I had no argument with Lord Willoughby! I looked out last night. I saw him there. I saw two people—one must have been Lord Willoughby."

"Yet you didn't reveal this before. Did you see Will be murdered?"

"No, Your Grace. No—if I had known the viscount was in danger, I should have sounded the alarm. Gone to his aid at once. I believed the gentlemen were speaking. And I was warned that on occasion there might be . . . certain behaviors between the male guests. Lord Genvere's instructions quite clearly stated I was to show utmost discretion at all times. I simply closed the drapes and continued with my duty—which was to ensure all windows were closed for the night."

"You thought Will and this other man were having an assignation."

The old butler turned red. "It occurred to me that I might be witnessing such a thing, Your Grace. Thus I decided to apply discretion and afford the gentlemen privacy."

"Who was the other man with him?"

"I can't say."

"You bloody well will. That man might have murdered Will."

"I mean, I cannot say, Your Grace, because I did not clearly see him."

"Was he taller than Will? Bigger build? What about his hair color?"

"Perhaps similar height to poor Lord Willoughby. He wore a great coat and hat and with the heavy rain, I could make out little."

An eyewitness who could give them nothing. Damn it.

"Did you see him walk? What kind of gait did he have?"

"They did not walk. I would say I believed him to be inebriated. He staggered once under my observation. I am afraid I can help no further."

"All right. What we will do is search the grass for clues."

"And if I were the murderer," barked Crayle, "wouldn't I pocket any incriminating clues?"

"I think it was someone from outside. Not one of the guests."

"Could be the bleeding footman," Crayle snapped. The footman had moved off to scour the ground for clues. "Willoughby could have suggested some sport with the footman's arse and the lad took objection."

"Possible," Sin agreed. "I'm watching him, to see if he hides anything."

"Eh, you won't be able to watch him every second. Let's get this blasted island scoured. Then I can get back to fucking."

Sin jerked. It figured the marquis was still thinking of that after Will had his head cleaved in. Once he would have been like that. Strangely, he wasn't anymore. The main thing on his mind—Portia.

As a group, they searched the grass. Sin walked around, eyes on the ground. There—footprints. Several, evenly spaced in a stretch of mud, as if two people walked together, side by side. Did they belong to Willoughby and his attacker? Or had the attacker followed Willoughby? Sin crouched and studied the prints. Both appeared to be made by a man's boot. One set larger than the other.

"Interesting," he muttered.

"What did you find?" Sax asked.

"Footprints. Apparently made by two men." He straightened and continued his search, to see if he would find anything else.

The island itself wasn't large and was mainly rock and scrub grass. There were few trees and none provided a hiding place. With the weather improving, Sin tried rappelling down the safer parts of the cliff, hunting for caves, for steps, for rock shelves where a man could hide.

Sax and Rutledge helped haul him up after his last descent. They had taken turns, exploring all the accessible areas of the cliffs. Sin wanted to rappel down the riskier spots, but Sax shook his head. "Too risky. And if we're afraid to go down there, who else would do it? How could they get back up?"

"There could be caves there. There could be safe ways to ascend the cliff, using rope, that we can't see from here."

Sax shook his head. "It's too wet. And I think unnecessary."

"But it means we've combed the island and found nothing except two sets of footprints," Sin pointed out. "No sign of anyone else on the island. If that's true, it has to be someone in the house."

12

Curiosity was driving her mad. But Portia tried to appear blasé, tossing her curls and sipping the sherry handed to her by the Incognita. Syrupy sweet sherry. Gasp. It burned like sin going down, but she held in the splutter she almost made.

"What do you wish to tell me about Sin? I'm sure it's nothing I don't already know."

The Incognita smiled. A wicked smile. It only made the woman look even sultrier. "So you've done that shocking thing that he likes best?" Clarissa continued.

"Oh—er."

"I had never done anything so naughty in my life. How did he want you to do it? What position?"

Oh ack. This was maddening. She had to play along, but what was she going to be claiming she'd done? What was the thing Sinclair liked best?

She was so curious, but also afraid to find out.

The Incognita nudged her. "You must tell me how he wanted you to do it. I thought I'd gag. It was far too huge of course."

Gag? Huge? Did she mean taking Sin's erection in her mouth? Portia had taken him in her hand. On the night they got engaged.

"And then with the rope," continued the Incognita. "I mean, really."

Rope? "Oh, er, yes."

"And then, involving the hounds. Utterly shocking."

"The *hounds?*" Her sherry tipped over and spilled on her skirt.

The Incognita took Portia by the arm and led her toward the windows. "You have no idea what I'm talking about, do you?"

"Of course I do," Portia insisted, but knew it was a losing battle.

"I made all that up, darling. But I've never known Sin to want an innocent. He likes his women tremendously experienced. He liked punishment, as I said. Whips, spanking paddles, riding crops. Even blades. I've seen him endure all kinds of cuts. I would be sick with pain and fear, but he was aroused. His cock was harder than I'd ever seen it. And then he climaxed with so much force, he broke the chair he was sitting on."

"Oh God," Portia muttered.

"Would you be willing to share him with other women? What about other men?"

"Other men? I don't understand what you mean—"

"Innocent, just as I thought. Why are you here, darling?"

"Because someone kidnapped me in London and brought me here," Portia said. Her heart still pounded from the things the Incognita had said. But she had had enough. "Were you responsible for that? Someone was. Have you ever met our host, Lord Genvere?"

"You were kidnapped. What are you—a virgin dragged off the streets?" Clarissa's dark brows shot up. "You are!"

"I am not—oh, er, I don't know." Did she admit to innocence here?

The Incognita tapped her lip. "And Sin came to your rescue? He can be dreadfully noble when he wants to be. He's more fun when he's naughty."

"I am going to find out who is responsible for kidnapping me." Portia watched the woman's green eyes.

"So you should. If I can help you, I will."

"You will?"

"I do not believe women should be subject to such danger. I was innocent once. Dragged off the street, as well, only I was sold to a brothel. Sold, like a slave. The money was handed over to the man who had no rights over me. In those first days, I wanted to die. Then I wanted revenge—and to get revenge, I needed money, power, and my freedom. I achieved all three."

"Did you get revenge?" Portia asked. The woman's story had her under its spell.

"I did."

"You had him arrested."

"Arrest would do no good. He is dead now."

"You killed him—"

"Oh, my darling, I would never admit to that. Suffice to say his greed and brutality were his downfall in the end."

Portia stared. The Incognita was smiling. Humming, actually. She looked utterly proud of herself.

She was astoundingly ruthless. Portia opened her mouth to speak—

The doors leading to the terrace opened. Drapes tangled in the wind, and the air blowing in was cold and wet.

The Duke of Saxonby came in first, holding his hat to his silver hair. The Cruel Marquis followed, muttering, "Damned waste of time."

White-faced, the butler entered, along with the handsome dark-haired footman who had a few grass stains on his breeches. The Earl of Rutledge came in, followed by the Earl of Blute, then Sin.

Sinclair, she meant.

"Bollocks," barked the marquis. "Have no idea who attacked Willoughby, but I came for an orgy, and I'm damn well having one. Willoughby would. He wouldn't sit about, mourning. He'd be buried deep inside some lass, pumping as if his life depended on it. *Carpe diem*. Seize the tarts and rut all day, I say. I'll be more than generous with the woman who satisfies me."

Sadie launched up. "I will," she simpered. She slipped her hand in the crook of his elbow, and with that, the marquis and Sadie left the room.

The Earl of Rutledge growled. "The old bugger is right. Come, Clarissa. Come and please me. I've got some fun games in mind with your pussy, my cock, and a dildo."

Blute grabbed Nellie's bottom—apparently that amounted to a seductive invitation in his mind, for he then hauled her to him and began kissing her neck with loud suction.

Despite her previous experience, Portia actually wished she had more sherry. She needed that bold courage she'd felt before.

Someone was going to notice how shocked and awkward she looked. She'd been curious about the orgy, but now knew this wasn't for her.

She should talk to the servants. In a household, servants knew everything. The maid could know something—could have seen her be brought here. And there was the cook. Portia couldn't see how the cook could poison Sandhurst without killing everyone else, or why she would want to poison him, but—

It was an escape.

Portia slipped out of the drawing room, heading for the baize servants' door.

Just as she reached it, someone put his hand out behind her and prevented her from opening it. "Understand this," growled Sinclair. "You are not going anywhere in this house alone. If you think you can escape me, you are mistaken."

"I wasn't escaping you. I was escaping . . . what was about to happen in the drawing room."

"I thought you wanted to watch," Sinclair said coolly.

It was embarrassing to admit, but she couldn't bring herself to lie. Sighing, she shook her head. "You were right and I was not. I don't belong in this world. I'm not right for it at all. I'm dull and proper and boring. Working like a maid in a home is what I was meant to do."

"Damn it—" He grabbed her.

His hands clamped to her bottom and he dragged her right against him. Something huge pressed against her tummy. It couldn't be him, could it? They must have got the fireplace poker stuck between them somehow. . . .

No, heavens, it was him.

Hot, demanding, his mouth claimed hers. His tongue teased, tangled, thrust, and made her weak in the knees. If his tongue hadn't been in her mouth she might have . . . might have begged him to take her.

Suddenly he let her go. Moved his mouth, his hands, his body. She almost staggered and fell. Only the wall, that she slapped her hand hard against, saved her.

"I hope that proves you aren't dull and boring," he said. "And that it proves I kiss a damn sight better than Sadie."

She was not going to let him know how he'd made her feel dizzy. And so, so lusty.

"I doubt the Marquis of Crayle would agree about your kissing," she said evasively as she pushed open the baize servants' door. A staircase led downward. The walls were stone and only one lamp lit the space—it was placed below, so walking down felt like entering the pits of hell. She spent so much time downstairs at the foundling home, she should not be frightened to enter a basement. Ahead she could smell the warm scents of fires in the stoves, of fresh cooking. And she could smell the salty damp of the sea.

Portia made her way down briskly, with Sinclair behind her. She did feel safer having him with her.

At the bottom of the stairs, in the basement, Sinclair had to duck. He rested his hand on one of the thick wooden beams of the ceiling. "What do you hope to learn from the cook?"

"I don't know exactly," she admitted. "I know that if she poisoned Sandhurst, she would hardly admit it. And why kill him and not the rest of us—if she's mad enough to do such a thing? As for Willoughby, why would a cook attack him?"

They approached the kitchen. Huge, black iron stoves stood along a stone wall. Large fry pans hung from hooks in the ceiling, as did drying herbs. She looked at the frying pan. "I suppose, if she'd wanted to hurt him, she did have weapons."

"I am astounded you can assess this so coolly."

"I've read a lot of gothic novels. I feel like I've fallen into one. All I need is a handsome but tormented earl who wants to ravish me—"

"You already have that. Any man here would want to ravish you."

She knew she'd blushed. "Not with those other voluptuous, experienced women here."

"Yes, any one of those men would bed you in a heartbeat. Willing or not."

"Even Saxonby, your friend?"

"No, Sax wouldn't. Willoughby would. I saw him looking at you last night. At dinner. I didn't like the way he was doing it."

"He smirked at me once."

"He was looking at you like he wanted you in his bed. Pure lust."

"What? At me?" she squeaked. "I never noticed."

"I did."

Sinclair had seen Willoughby looking at her. Had that made him angry? Had it raised his suspicions?

The worst thought went through her head. Could Sinclair and Willoughby have argued? Fought? Then—

No. It was not possible. Portia pushed those awful thoughts away. "I also wondered about the maid," she said. "There's only the one, so she works all over the house. Maybe she saw something. Overheard something—"

She broke off as a low, masculine laugh came from a doorway. So did the smell of smoke. She peeked inside the room.

The young, black-haired footman sat at a wooden table, having a cup of tea. A cheroot rested between his fingers, smoke rising. Grinning, he reached for the pretty housemaid, catching her by her hips. "Come sit on my lap, love."

The young woman—she must be close to Portia's age of

twenty-nine—pushed his hand away. "I haven't time for the likes of you. I have to do all the work upstairs. I never would have taken this position if I'd known I would be the only maid for a house party."

"Orgy, you mean," the footman sniggered. "Don't see why they get all the fun. They're not going to notice if you're not there. Even that old bugger was going off with two women."

"Does Lord Genvere have parties like this all the time? What is he like? Is he handsome?" the maid asked.

Portia strained to hear, curious.

"Hopeful?" mocked the footman. "I don't know what he's like. I started the day before you came here, love. Never seen Genvere."

The maid hesitated. "What do you think about that toff being murdered outside, Reggie? The other one—well, Cook figures he must have had a weak heart, for he was so young. But do you think one of them upstairs is a murderer?"

"I don't know," Reggie answered slowly. "I took a good look around this island when I first got here. Slipped off in the afternoon. There aren't any other buildings on the island except this house. There's no one else on it but us."

The maid had gone white.

"I'll watch out for you, Ellie," the young footman promised, cockily.

"And who will keep me safe from you?" she asked pertly.

So the maid was Ellie, the footman Reggie.

Reggie took something out of a pocket of the coat of his livery. He threw it on the table. "Did you leave this for me?"

Portia stared. It was a folded note on thick white paper, with the red wax seal.

The maid gasped. "Of course not . . . what did yours say?"

"A warning about all my sins." His grin widened. He leaned back in the chair. Winked. "What are your sins, love?"

"I don't have any sins. Those notes are silly. I thought . . . I thought the butler might have left them. To frighten us, so we work harder."

"Why would you be frightened, Ellie, if you have no sins to hide?"

"I . . . oh, never mind."

The maid headed for the door, so Portia moved back, into the shadows around a corner. She realized she stepped right against Sinclair. The duke really was a tall, well-built man. Ellie passed them without seeing them, hurrying to the stairs.

"I'm going to talk to the cook," Portia whispered to him. "Can you question the footman? Perhaps he saw something—or he might even be the man who attacked Willoughby."

"I will question him. I'll have the butler send him upstairs."

She frowned. "But he's right there."

"And it is customary for me to make a request to a footman through the butler."

"That's ridiculous."

"It's what the footman will expect."

She sighed in frustration.

"As for the footman, did you recognize him as one of your kidnappers, under the wig and livery?"

"The two men who kidnapped me were quite unappealing in their appearance. And their smell. It couldn't have been the footman—he's far too handsome."

Sinclair did not look pleased at that observation. "I will go with you to question the cook."

"That's not necessary."

"A house like this has to be filled with hiding places. That's why I'm going to watch over you. Whether you like it or not."

"I doubt Genvere or someone will leap out at me from a cupboard."

"That footman might. I've seen him watch you with a lusty look on his face."

He looked so annoyed, so possessive Portia's anger flared. "Well, I wouldn't want to keep you from taking a group of men and women into your bed. And you can't do that if you're following me around."

She tried to walk away, but his hand caught her waist and he pulled her back. "What are you talking about?"

"I was told you always take groups of people to your bed. Rather like a dinner party under the covers."

"Actually nothing like a dinner party under covers," he muttered.

"What you told me—about regret—how can that be true?"

He frowned, looking like an angered lion. "It is true." Then his expression softened. Slowly, so slowly, his fingertip traced her lip.

"But don't you want that now? Isn't that what you would be doing, if I weren't here? When you're surrounded by all these beautiful women."

"Around you, Miss Love, I can't even see anyone else."

"I will go," she whispered. She had to. Before—before any good sense melted away like sugar in rain. She left him, quietly going into the kitchen.

Ahead of her, a full-figured woman leaned over a wooden work table. The woman's back rose and fell as she vigorously drove a rolling pin over dough, flattening it. Obviously this was the cook.

"Hello?" Portia said tentatively.

The cook jumped, clapping her hand to her heart. She turned, waving the pin. "Keep back or I'll—" The woman, her voluptuous form covered by a gray striped dress, reared back. "Oh, I'm sorry, miss. I feared it might be this murderer. He killed that poor, handsome viscount. He's not going to get me. I'll bash his wits with this rolling pin if he even tries."

Portia stepped back as the woman waved it menacingly. Then the cook pushed back her glossy black curls, leaving a streak of white flour along her temple.

"I wondered if you had any clue as to who did that horrible crime, Mrs.—?"

"Mrs. Kent, miss. And you are?"

"Miss—uh—Love."

"I can tell ye I have no idea, Miss Love. I don't see anything down here. There's barely any windows. And I've got so much work to do, I barely have a minute to think, much less be peering at things that aren't my business. Murderers are not something a respectable woman concerns herself with. Besides, he was murdered in the night. I were asleep then. I doubt I'll sleep well ever again. Too afraid I'll be killed in my own bed."

"You heard about the other death. Viscount Sandhurst."

"Aye, the other young peer. You're not going to tell me he was murdered too!"

"We aren't sure. We fear he may have been poisoned—"

"Poison? Ye think I caused his death. That my cooking killed him!" Mrs. Kent waved the rolling pin about in her excitement and Portia had to dodge it.

"No, of course not."

The cook dropped the implement to the table, then reached for her apron ties. "Perhaps I shouldn't do any more cooking, if ye think I'm killing ye."

"We don't think anything of the sort. Please do not take offense. Your cooking is delicious. I've never had such lovely dishes."

"Well, if ye think that . . ." Mrs. Kent fiddled with a locket that hung around her neck. It was gold and a small pink ribbon was tied in a bow on the chain above it. Portia stared it the ribbon, remembering the one she'd found when Sandhurst died.

"What are you staring at?" the cook asked.

"Your ribbon. Is it something special?"

"Just a bit of ribbon I found in the house. Too small to use for sewing. I didn't think Lord Genvere would mind."

Had Sandhurst got the ribbon from the house too? But for what reason would he have tucked it in his pocket?

"What is Lord Genvere actually like?"

"I've no idea, miss. But surely you know him. I thought his lordship was only inviting friends to his gathering."

Portia shook his head. "That can't be so. Many of the guests have never met Lord Genvere. I certainly don't know him. But then, I wasn't invited here. I was kidnapped and brought here against my will. Were you told about that? To expect another person for dinner, a person being brought here against her will?"

"Good heavens, miss, what on earth do you mean? Are you saying that Lord Genvere had you kidnapped? Surely not. Perhaps it was just a game? There are courtesans here—" The woman sniffed. "I don't like serving them. They're no better than they ought to be. But I need this position. If you're one of them, perhaps he bought you from your madam."

"I'm not a courtesan. I'm a respecta—" She broke off. "I don't have a madam, and no one bought me. I was snatched off the street and brought here. So I want to know everything I can about Lord Genvere."

Portia half expected what the cook would say and she was right. "I can't tell you anything," Mrs. Kent said. "I've never seen him. In the time I've been on this island—only a few days, I admit—he's never been here. The butler and I were hired and came here at the same time."

She tried more questions, but learned nothing more. She thanked the cook and left. Outside the kitchens, Portia sagged against the stone wall. Mrs. Kent seemed so normal—surely she wasn't poisoning food and killing viscounts. So who was?

She heard low voices and saw Sinclair speaking with the butler—the thin, balding butler must have come downstairs.

Questioning people was exhausting. She'd thought it would not be so difficult—she liked to solve puzzles. She'd always insisted she had as good and clever a mind as her brothers.

But now she realized she had no idea how to lure someone to incriminate themselves.

She knew she should wait for Sinclair—

What on earth was that sound? It sounded like someone struggling to breathe.

It came from a doorway that stood across from the one that led to the kitchen. Portia hurried there, even though she was alone.

Cautiously, hands on the rough stone blocks, she peeked around the door into the small room—it was some kind of pantry.

There was panting. There were naked male bottoms. There was the lovely widow, sandwiched between the muscular, raven-haired Earl of Rutledge and the sinewy, handsome, equally raven-haired footman.

13

"Both men were—were thrusting into her. How on earth can they do that, if there are two of them? Do they take turns? Does one stop to allow the other his chance?"

These seemed perfectly logical questions to Portia. Given Sinclair had spent ten years holding orgies, she thought he would answer. But he caught her elbow and hauled her away from the stunning scene, taking her into shadows under the staircase.

As he did, she could see the sweep on color following his high cheekbones. "You're blushing."

"I am not."

"Yes, you are! Are you really shocked?"

"No, damn—I mean, no. You want to know what they are doing?" It came out hoarse and harsh. "They do not take turns." Sinclair's finger went around his collar. "One man fucks her in her pussy. The other in her rear."

"In the rear? What on earth do you mean? Do you mean he goes in from the rear?"

"Are you trying to kill me, Portia?"

"Of course not. Why are these questions painful?"

Hair-raking ensued, as did pacing and growling. Sinclair paced like a caged lion, in a slow but lithe movement in front of her, spiking his fingers through his hair. He paced through the shadows beneath the stair, his boot soles striking the flagstone floor. The basement smelled of damp and the sea, of fires and hanging, dried spices.

Finally Sinclair stopped. "You want the truth of what they are doing? Both men are making love to her, in her pussy and arse. One is inside the hot grip of her pussy, the other man has slid his staff up her butt. She is being doubly penetrated, which is an intense, arousing sensation for most women."

For some reason, his words came into her brain slowly. Pussy. Staff. Butt. It took a few ragged heartbeats for her to understand what he meant—

Oh!

Of course, she'd heard whispers that two men could do intimate things together, but she'd never really grasped how it could happen. And now she—

Oh my. *My.*

What would that feel like?

Her blush swept over her like a raging fire touching dry hay.

In the other room, the widow cried out. It was a shriek of sensual agony that made Portia's legs wobble.

She wanted to see how this . . . worked. She moved toward the doorway again. Sinclair hauled her back. All of a sudden, all she could see was his dark gold waistcoat with fanciful embroidery of lions. Her heart beat rather swiftly. The soles of her feet tingled. That was mystifying. But suddenly her whole body felt aware.

"Protecting you from men is not my only duty, Portia," he rumbled. "I also want to protect your innocence. You should not see things like that."

"You look. You do that all the time at orgies."

"It's different for—"

"For men. Of course. It *always* is." She crossed her arms over her chest. "My life is entirely different from my brothers' lives. I have to be maid, cook, schoolteacher. No man would ever do that. He would think he was far above all that. Besides, what man could actually do it all?"

A smile touched his lips. "I meant that it's different for me. Since I'm an unrepentant sinner. Hence the nickname." He frowned. "It sounds as if you are worked like a slave."

"It takes rather a lot of work to run the home. And, if I wanted to, I could just step around you and go and see what the Wanton Widow is doing," she added stubbornly. "Why shouldn't I know what it's like for a woman to have pleasure?"

"You should be shocked," he growled.

"Maybe I'm not. It's exciting to see two men serving her, caring about giving her pleasure. They have put her desires above their wants. They are willing to not fight over her, to work together to please her. It's rather stunning."

Partly she was teasing him—but partly, she ached so much, it was crippling. It hurt.

His brows shot up, to vanish under his wind-swept chocolate brown hair. His gaze went over her, slowly. Something changed about the air—it became thick, hard to breathe, and felt as if it was charged with static, could spark and shock them.

In the shadows beneath the stairs, she put her hands on his chest, her fingers stretching over the embroidered lions, touching the solidity of the duke, the warmth through his clothing.

That touch was like striking a match and having the sudden whoosh of heat and flame.

He bent to her. His lips so soft, his lower lip slightly thrust forward, ready to claim her mouth.

No, no.

Yes.

Look at the Wanton Widow. Was she tying herself in knots over what she should or should not do? Not in the least. She wasn't waiting for another marriage. She was enjoying her pleasure.

Portia knew she didn't belong in the world of orgies. But right now she wanted Sinclair. She ached for him.

What if she kissed him? With no fears, no worries, no expectations. What if she just kissed him . . . for fun?

She slipped her hands to Sinclair's shoulders. And kissed him. She opened her mouth. Parted her lips. Let her tongue slide into his mouth to play with his. Their tongues tangled and she felt the ache intensify. She pulled closer to him, pressing against his broad, hard body.

His hands slid down to her waist, skimmed over her hips, cupped her bottom. She knew his next move—to lift her so she was poised over the hard ridge in his trousers, where she would be going half-mad feeling him press against her.

What if she caressed him instead of the other way around?

Her palm pressed against the thick, firm bulge contained behind the fine fabric of his trousers.

Taking charge was fun, after all.

"Touch me," he murmured. "Stroke me, love."

She moved her palm over the length of him, until she felt a change in shape. A ridge, then a rounded shape, and she knew she'd reached the head of it. Rolling her fingers around the bulge, she explored its girth—rather big. It was hot even through his trousers. Oddly, with each stroke she was sure the length and girth changed. For the larger.

Sinclair moaned.

The hoarse, deep, vulnerable sound of it drew a moan from deep inside her. A whisper of a moan, answering his because she'd made him feel like that.

"It's good, Portia. I love your touch. For ten years, I dreamed of having you touch me."

She wanted to shout at him: *For ten years, I could have been touching you everywhere. Except you didn't want it.*

No, this was about fun. Meaningless fun. Her heart wasn't to be engaged. Or threatened.

She was going to behave just like him. For once.

Her hand stroked, squeezed his erection, while she was panting into his mouth.

He kissed her, a long kiss that seared her. He squeezed her

bottom, drawing her close, until her hand was trapped. Squished between her soft tummy and his rigid ridge. He retreated, so he was back against the wall.

Daringly, she squeezed him harder.

His mouth moved from hers on a ragged moan—

Next thing she knew, his mouth closed around the bodice of her scandalous gown and he sucked. She felt the tug on her nipple through silk and muslin. She was gripping his erection hard, but it was as much out of shock as to pleasure him.

"I want you. Can't have you, but damn I want you."

Even as he spoke, Sinclair gently tugged her bodice down. It was so scandalously low, it didn't need much effort. As it went down, over her breasts with a slight rending of seams, her breasts popped up. They sat on top of the taut fabric of the bodice, pointing right at his mouth.

Her nipples tightened. They blushed dark pink. And the right one vanished into his mouth.

Portia went weak. "Oh . . . oh, please suck me."

His lips pursed around her nipple. The dark, faint shadow of stubble scraped sensitive skin. Her sensitive skin.

She liked scraping.

Two men—how greedy was that woman? One man's mouth on her nipple, his hand on her breast was enough to make Portia see stars.

Her head fell back and she moaned. Much louder.

Wait, her skirts were going up. Her bodice was down, her skirts being lifted to meet it.

His hand, strong and large, slid between her legs. He touched her between her thighs where she was hot and wet. But the ache didn't feel relieved, it got worse, and she rocked against his hand.

He stroked her nether lips.

This was beyond scandalous. They were hidden beneath the stairs, but not completely hidden. True, they had been engaged before. But that wasn't the same as wed. Now that she was unmarried and on the shelf, and this was something she was not supposed to do. She was a fool to even dream about it. . . .

But, oh, she wanted it.

His fingers slipped between her nether lips, which were slick and sticky at the same time. He rubbed his fingertip harder—

She gripped the hard, strong biceps of his right arm . . . and his erection. She held tight, as he rubbed more and more. Her hips were rocking. Moans and whimpers filled the air.

Oh no, this wasn't fun. It went beyond fun, into someplace where pleasure and need were like wicked drugs and she knew something wondrous was just around the—

Oh goodness.

Fireworks. Explosions. Any form of combustion paled by comparison to the burst of pleasure she felt. It brought sobs from her throat. Made her wits evaporate and made her fall against him, and he sucked her nipples—both of them, back and forth—while she was rocking with pleasure and floating in weakened joy. She didn't care if everyone heard her.

He rubbed again and she gasped his name. "Sinclair. Julian. Oh, oh heavens."

Gruff and low, his laugh spoke of the intimacy of this. Shared just between them, because he'd touched her in a way no one ever had.

He lifted her off her feet. Cradled her in his arms and buried his face in the crook of her neck.

"You know," she said, "I had decided orgies were not for me. Maybe I was wrong."

He lifted his head. His eyes narrowed. He was about to speak when footsteps clattered on the steps, heading down.

"Stay here," he growled.

"No."

He pointed through a doorway. It had to be the sitting room of a butler or housekeeper for there was a mirror over a small fireplace.

Portia saw her reflection. Mussed hair. A crumpled gown. Her bodice still down. She put her hands over her breasts. Her face was all red.

Oh dear. She'd felt like heaven. She didn't look it.

With her hands clamped over her breasts—they were warm, heating from her pleasure, but not as hot as her cheeks—she nodded. "Oh, all right. Go."

He lifted her bodice with one efficient tug; then she set to ensure it was as far up as it could go—and that it would stay up.

She heard Sinclair shout up the stairs. "Who's there?"

Portia couldn't stay put. Praying her dress didn't flop down as some seams had torn and she didn't know which, she emerged and reached his side. Just then the maid hurried down the remaining steps. Pale as well-cleaned sheets.

"It's me, Your Grace. I were upstairs, doing the empty bedchambers, when I heard a woman's scream. The most bloodcurdling sound, it were. I came down to find Mr. Humphries. I weren't going to take a look on me own!"

"You go and sit down. I'll go. Which room?"

"The one belonging to that old marquis."

Cautiously, Sin opened the door that Ellie told him was the one for Marquis of Crayle's bedroom. From the corridor, he saw Sadie was on her knees, nude, her hands braced on a chair.

The marquis stood behind her, fully clothed. Thank the Lord—Sin hadn't wanted to see Crayle naked. Then he saw the large bullwhip in Crayle's hand.

Hell. If Crayle was hitting Sadie with that thing . . .

Crayle moved and Sin could see Sadie's back. Welts, bruises, small cuts made a pattern on her ivory skin.

He was ready to launch forward and physically stop the marquis with a punch in the man's arrogant face. But was Sadie a willing submissive?

The feminine gasp beside him made him freeze.

"Oh my heavens!" Portia whispered fiercely. "He's beating her!"

He'd told her to stay downstairs—to not follow him to investigate the woman's scream. He should have known she would not stay put.

Portia brandished a poker. She must have snatched it up from the fireplace.

Sin grabbed her arm to stop her rushing in and she stared at him as if he were mad. "Why are you stopping me?"

He'd hesitated because he had seen these scenes before. He'd done this before. Not with as big a whip, not as brutally. But he'd had to make sure that—for all her cries—Sadie wasn't willing.

The next blow let him know. She wasn't.

"I'll deal with him," he said shortly.

Two strides took him in front of Crayle. He ripped the crop out of the man's hands and turned to Sadie. She was on her knees, hair in a messy tumble around her face. Tears streaked her cheeks—they'd taken the kohl around her eyes with them, making wet, dark lines down her face. "Get up, Sadie. Get up and get the hell out of here."

"I . . . I didn't know he would truly hurt me. I never wished for this—"

Portia was there. She helped Sadie up and put her arm around the girl's rounded white shoulders. "I will tend you. We'll bathe you and bandage you. Let us go to your room." Portia looked up at him, admiration shining in her eyes. "Thank you for coming to her resc—" She broke off, eyes widening.

He had no idea why. Until he saw the crop jerking in his hand. He was shaking. Shaking in rage—and more. He knew what it was like to be hit until his skin broke. Until he bled. He'd been the victim in strange games. Not just when he went to the House of Discipline. Long before that.

He snapped the crop over his knee, ignoring the pain of striking himself hard enough to break it. "Touch a woman like that again, and I'll meet you over pistols," he snarled.

Crayle was white. Shaking also. Fear and rage, Sin guessed. "Damn you, Sinclair. No right to spoil my fun. You'll pay for this."

His hands fisted and he was sorely ready to punch Crayle in his face. Not caring that the man was so much older. Weaker.

"I'd suggest you get the hell out. Before I knock your teeth out of your head."

It came out low, smooth, calm.

That had its effect. Crayle backed away. But gave one last parting shot, to stand on pride. "You will pay for this."

Turning, Sin stalked out of the room. Took the stairs upstairs and found Portia as she was giving direction to the young maid to fetch warm water, cloths, towels, bandages.

Sadie was on her knees at the side of the bed, resting her chest on it so her back could be tended. "Look at my back," Sadie whispered. "It's a horrible, ugly mess. He's ruined me. My back was lovely—perfectly shaped, without a blemish. He said it would just be a game. Then he turned vicious, trying to hurt me."

"I'm sure it will heal," Portia said. "We'll clean it up and bandage it, and you will heal."

"I'll be scarred. Forever. He'll pay for this. He owes me for this—I'll never find a good protector now!"

"Calm down, Sadie. I'll take care of this," Sin growled. She deserved something to make amends for what he'd done.

The maid appeared, puffing, carrying a large porcelain basin filled with steaming water. Aware she was struggling with the weight of it, Sin lifted it out of her hands and carried it to the vanity. The maid followed, towels over her arms. Her gasp of shock made Sadie start crying again.

"Look how horrified she is! I'm ugly now." Sadie's hands flailed and she began to slap her own head.

Portia grasped her hands, stopping Sadie from hurting herself. "The marquis did a terrible thing, but it looks worse now than it will be. We will tend to you. That way you can begin to heal. If necessary, I can stitch wounds and that will help them heal."

"You can do that?"

"I've done it for children in the foundling home—that I once was in." She added that swiftly. A smart and quick reaction. Sin was fairly sure she hadn't given herself away.

"A surgeon taught me how to do it, so I can do it very neatly," Portia continued.

But Sadie peered at her. "A foundling home? I was in a foundling home. A long time ago. It was run by a family."

Portia jerked. Sin saw her sudden reaction. She was soaking a cloth and water sprayed. She looked startled.

"Do you know of it?" Sadie asked her.

What would Portia say?

Softly, she said, "I knew of homes like that, of course, because I grew up in one."

Not a lie, but not the exact truth. Delivered smoothly. Sin had no idea Portia could lie so well. With him she always seemed to be completely honest. Brutally honest at times.

"What family ran the home, Sadie?" Portia asked softly.

"They were named Woodcock."

"Oh, that was not the one I lived in. But of course, if we had been in the same one, we would have known each other. Now, you must lean over the bed and grip the sheets," Portia instructed. "If it hurts, do try to bear it. It's important to clean the wounds. But let me know if it is too terrible."

With a cloth, Portia began to bathe the wounds. Sadie cried out in pain.

"Too much?"

Sadie nodded.

"Can you bear it? We must clean them. I could give you brandy—"

"I will be all right," Sadie muttered.

Portia set back to work. Suddenly Sadie said, "If you were in a foundling home, I guess you never knew your mother or father either. Were they dead or were you just abandoned?"

He saw a look a panic flash on Portia's face. She could lie, but he saw she didn't like it.

"I know very little—"

"They told me almost nothing about my past."

"Perhaps they didn't really know," Portia said softly.

"It's hard not knowing who you are. I used to dream—" Sadie broke off abruptly. She looked scared, and he thought it was not just because of her wounds.

"It was hard to not know my mother," Portia said. "To know she would never come for me, but to wish I could see her. And of course I entertained silly thoughts that she had been forced to give me up, but she would come back to me."

Sin could tell Portia hated to lie. He was astounded that sounded so believable. So natural.

"But she didn't, did she?" Sadie asked bitterly.

"No. But were you happy there? At the Woodcock home."

Sadie winced. "I don't know. How could I have been happy? They wanted me to do lessons and be respectable. They told me I must hope to become a governess or nurse or companion. But that's really just a servant. I wanted so much more than that. And now . . ."

She began to sob.

"Shhh," Portia admonished. "I am almost done cleaning you. You don't need many stitches. The wounds are not large. Not as terrible as I thought."

"But they will scar, though, won't they?"

Sin watched Portia command boiling water from the maid. "I don't know if I can ask for that in the kitchen now, miss. Mrs. Kent told me not to disturb her."

"Mrs. Kent must accede to my request. I am sure she is busy, but I must ensure the thread and needle are both clean."

"She won't like it. She acts like a duchess, that one. And Humphries has given me a million tasks to do—"

"If you could do this for me, we shall speak to the butler and insist that you can no longer be run off your feet. And that Mrs. Kent behave decently to you."

The maid shook her head. "He won't do a thing. One maid there is—me!—and he acts as though there is a staff of twenty!"

Off she went and she did return quite quickly. "Mrs. Kent was boiling water for tea and it had just boiled when I got there. She let me take it when she knew it was for a wounded girl."

"Very good of her," Portia said, rather distractedly, as she took the basin and set it down.

Sin went over. "I'll help."

Portia washed the needle and thread she intended to use. "My father always insisted that everything be clean. He had noticed that if it is not, there is always infection."

Sin intended to help, but there was little for him to do. He held things. Portia was in charge, working swiftly but carefully. As she concentrated, her tongue dabbed her lip in the sweetest way.

Soon she was done. "You should rest, Sadie," she said.

"Am I ugly now?"

"Of course not. There may be scars, but they won't be large. We shall have to wait and see."

"He's going to pay. Crayle." Sadie shook with rage. "I want him to pay for what he's done to me. He gave me nothing but promises, and I won't accept having my career come to an end with nothing!"

Portia shushed Sadie. Helped her into her bed, where she lay on her side.

As they closed the door, Sin heard Sadie's sobs.

Hell, he'd never thought much about Sadie before. She came to his orgies because he invited dozens of courtesans. Variety was the point of an orgy—he needed large numbers of willing women. He realized he'd thought of her simply as a creature who could provide sexual favors, and who enjoyed sex.

Watching Portia tend to her had made him see that Sadie was a person. Right now, a frightened one.

Portia's hand touched his. A flare went through him as he turned to her, outside Sadie's closed door.

"It must be him," Portia whispered. "Surely it must be the Cruel Marquis who attacked Willoughby, for some reason. He must have taken Willoughby by surprise."

"Cruel Marquis?"

She flushed. "I gave them all names in my head. Identities. Sandhurst was the Innocent Viscount. Sadie is the Brash Courtesan. Then there's the Elegant Incognita, the Cruel Marquis, the Peacock Girl, the Wicked Widow. And the Old Madam."

"Harriet won't appreciate that. Sax wouldn't appreciate Georgiana's moniker, but it's apt." He knew it was a stupid thing to do, but he asked casually, "Do you have one for me?"

"Why would I? I know who you are."

"You know their names as well." How did she see him? Heartbreaker? Swine? The Dastardly Duke?

"Their nicknames help me to remember the kind of people they are. I don't need that for you."

"Come on, love. You must have thought of one for me."

She shook her head, and asked, "What should we do? About the Cruel Marquis?"

"We don't know Crayle is responsible. He's the type to abuse people weaker than him. A woman like Sadie, yes. I doubt he would attack Willoughby."

"If he took him by surprise."

"It's possible. I'll find him and question him. I need to make him promise a settlement for Sadie. She won't heal fully and there will be disfiguring scars. I know you were trying to make her feel better. I intend to find him and make him pay."

"Sinclair, the scars truly weren't as bad as I feared. And what do you mean—you intend to make him pay?"

"The way honorable men do."

Panic flashed in her eyes. "Oh no, you can't."

"I can." On that, he stalked away.

It took him half an hour to locate Crayle. What he didn't expect was to find the man hanging by his neck in an unused bedchamber.

"Oh my goodness," Portia said.

Sin whirled to block her view of the sight in the room. The sight of Crayle hanging limply, rotating slowly, his neck broken, his eyes bulged, and his tongue hanging out.

"He hanged himself," she whispered. "Out of remorse."

But Sin didn't believe it. A peer like Crayle believed he

would have divine right to do whatever in hell he wanted, including abusing a woman like Sadie. As he turned Portia away, he had the nagging doubt that something was wrong.

There *was* something wrong—

Could he believe the marquis had tied a rope from a hook in the ceiling of the room—where in hell did he get a rope? And why was there a hook there? He would have brought a chair over, stood on it, positioned the rope around his neck. Would he even have decided to kill himself over whipping Sadie? If he had, he would have tightened the rope, then kicked the chair—

Damn. That was what was wrong.

"There's no chair in the room." As he said it, the full impact hit him. "There's no chair. He didn't hang himself. He would have needed to climb on something to put the rope around his neck. If he'd kicked the chair away, it would still be in the room. If he'd used any other piece of furniture, it would have been dragged close. I don't believe he took his own life, Portia."

She wrapped her arms around her body. "You mean you think that in the time we were away from the room, someone murdered him."

It sounded mad, but he said, "That's exactly what I am saying."

"I think you are right." Her voice was just a whisper. She pointed shakily to the bed, which was stripped and covered in a white sheet.

In the center of the bed lay a piece of pink ribbon.

14

———————

The mysterious death of the Cruel Marquis—and Sinclair's announcement to the guests that it was murder, not suicide— changed everything.

Outside, rain pounded, running down the glass and turning the outside world into a blur of darkness.

Inside, the guests huddled in the drawing room. The butler had built up the fire into a grand blaze, but Portia couldn't feel warm. From the way they shivered, the other women also looked ice-cold and frightened.

Even the gentlemen were white faced. Rutledge and Blute held drinks, but did so with shaky hands. Saxonby was pale as a ghost.

Curled in Portia's hand was the piece of pink ribbon she had found on the bed. In the room that hadn't been used by anyone.

She stroked it—it was just a tiny scrap with ragged edges and her thumb ruffled them. Had it fallen on that bed? Had it dropped from the marquis? By why would he have been on top of the unmade bed?

She had shown the ribbon to Sinclair, but he'd been in a hurry to go downstairs and tell the other guests what had happened. He had ordered Humphries and the footman to find them all and have them assemble in the drawing room. She knew he'd wanted to see if guilt could be read in one of the guests' faces.

Heaven only knew what carnal activities had been interrupted.

While Sinclair had told the guests, Portia had studied each person: Blute, Rutledge, Saxonby, the women. They had all looked equally shocked.

Was one as good as Edmund Kean at acting? Or was it one of the servants who had done this? The butler, the footman, the maid, or the cook?

But why?

The blond Wanton Widow was pale, curled up on the settee. Saxonby was tending to her, fussing over her. He had brought her a thick velvet wrap, and now he fetched glasses of sherry. Portia wondered if he would mind knowing the widow had just been made love to by two men.

The Old Madam, the Peacock Girl, and the Elegant Incognita sat on a settee. The Old Madam was dabbing at tears with her handkerchief. "I can't imagine why you are crying," drawled the Incognita softly. "He was a horrible man. He lived violently and I, for one, am not surprised he died that way."

"What an awful thing to say, Clarissa!"

"You didn't care for the man either," Clarissa said. "But you did have an eye on his money. I can't imagine why. The wretched man thought any woman over twenty-one was too long in the tooth for him. He wanted the youngest, the prettiest, and he believed he could own us body and soul. So I shouldn't waste my tears on him if I were you. He would never have made you his mistress."

"Cat," spat the Old Madam.

"Realist," Clarissa returned.

"Let's not fight over him now," grumbled Nellie, the Peacock Girl.

The Old Madam got up and stalked over to the sofa where

Rutledge was sitting. She put her hand on his knee. He moved her hand. She replaced it.

Sadie was not there—she was fast asleep upstairs. She didn't even know the marquis was dead. She had collapsed after her wounds had been cleaned. Portia had put her to bed.

"We're running out of gentlemen awfully quickly," piped up the Peacock Girl. Her almond-shaped eyes narrowed. "What kind of orgy is thish?" Her words slurred, and she tossed back the last drops of her sherry.

"Shut up," Clarissa snapped, not emulating a lady at that moment.

Portia shuddered. The girl was right. Of the thirteen guests at the beginning—seven men and six women—there were now only ten. Within the space of a day, three guests had died. Three men.

Good heavens—had someone killed the men so there would be more women each? No, that would surely be madness.

At that instant, the Old Madam murmured, "Are you certain he did not take his own life?"

"That old sadist would never feel an iota of guilt," Clarissa muttered.

"Remember what Sinclair told us." Saxonby stood up and walked over from where the widow was seated. His eyes were alert with interest. "The point about the chair is a good one."

The old madam asked, her voice quavering, "But that would mean someone lifted him up and put him in the noose. Wouldn't he have struggled?"

"He could have been knocked unconscious," Sinclair said, his voice low and quiet, but filling the drawing room because everyone went silent when he spoke. "Or he could have been strangled with a cord or a wire, then put up in the noose to hide the evidence of strangulation."

The thought was sickening, but Portia knew about violence. She had seen it in the stews.

Rutledge suddenly leapt to his feet. He waved wildly at the window. "We scoured this island for a criminal and found nothing. What are you saying, Sinclair? That one of us has murdered three peers of the realm? What are you going to do next—accuse me?"

"I wouldn't blindly accuse anyone. I want proof. For a start, did any of you hear Sadie scream?"

Several guests nodded their heads. "Was anyone off alone during that time?" he asked.

Sinclair naturally took charge, Portia saw. And all seemed to accept his authority.

"Georgiana was with me," Rutledge said. And he shot a triumphant look toward Saxonby.

It turned out that all of the guests had been within sight of another guest. No one had been alone and unaccounted for.

"There is the possibility someone else is hiding in this house," Sinclair said. "Given what's happened—"

"I suggest we all search," snapped Rutledge. "Shite, I don't care if I have to tear the house apart stone by stone. We need to hunt this bastard down."

"Language," Saxonby warned. "In front of the ladies."

The earl sneered. "These women aren't ladies."

"Rescind that insult, man." Saxonby was on his feet, but Sinclair stepped between them.

"Enough. We need to direct our energies to figure out what is going on."

"I meant most of these women aren't ladies," Rutledge said sulkily. "My fair Georgiana is a goddess. I wouldn't imply anything less, Sax." He turned to Sinclair, glowering. "Maybe it's time we accused you, Sinclair. Three men have died and I know you had reasons to want each one dead."

Startled, Portia met Sinclair's dark brown eyes. He looked as if hit in the face. "What are you talking about?" he demanded.

"You were overheard shouting at Crayle. I was Willoughby's second when you faced him at Chalk Farm to duel, when he shot you. And I know you were angered by Sandhurst's attention to your masked mistress. If there's a murderer amongst us, it's likely you."

"It is not, damn it."

But Portia saw the guests all stare at Sinclair, eyes narrowed with suspicion.

Before she'd had a moment of doubt. Did she now? No—because Sinclair had been angered by the Cruel Marquis's treatment of Sadie.

She believed him innocent.

"I assure you I did not kill anyone," Sinclair said. "I've had ample time to seek revenge on Willoughby if I'd wanted. As for the marquis, if I wanted retribution from him for what he did to Sadie, I wouldn't kill him. A flirtation with my mistress is not a reason to kill a man." He looked around. "Do the rest of you believe this?"

"Of course not." Portia stood. "You could never have done such things. To think it is madness. You are not that kind of gentleman, Your Grace. And if you are going to search the house, I wish to go too. To help."

"Absolutely not."

Of course he would say that. "I could go on my own, the moment you are gone. I think it would make far more sense to work together."

Portia stayed with Sinclair and Saxonby as they searched the house. The two gentlemen were extremely intelligent, but needed a woman's touch when it came to assessing a house for its hiding places, she quickly realized.

She knew where children would choose to hide—either for games or to escape punishment for pranks. She set out the search agenda. Up to the attics first, then working down through the house. They looked in every room, every wardrobe, behind curtains, under beds. Any place someone could hide.

The Earl of Rutledge helped with the attic search for a half hour, then grunted that he needed a drink and disappeared. Blute did not join them at all. He remained in the drawing room with the other women, who had elected to stay there. Together. As she, Sinclair, and Saxonby passed the drawing room,

Portia saw all the other guests seated inside. Tea had been served, but no one was touching it. They all had liquor in their hands.

Sinclair paused just beyond door, and Portia realized he was listening to hear what was being said.

"We'll only drink from fresh bottles," Rutledge muttered. "Heard Sinclair say he thought Sandhurst had been poisoned. As long as we open sealed bottles and drink in front of each other, we've got nothing to fear."

The others answered in muted, emotionless voices. The tones of people in shock. No one was touching or having sex. They all sat grim-faced, watching each other.

Then Portia found herself dragged away from the drawing room by Sinclair. He stopped with his hand on her low back to confer with Saxonby. His touch made her think of the most inappropriate things. Such as the wonderful, thrilling way he'd made her climax—

"We've got to do this floor, then the basements," Sinclair said. "I want to search this story and the upper one again. I want to check more thoroughly for hidden rooms or passageways. My gut instinct says there are some in a rambling house like this."

"What if we don't stumble on the mechanism that opens doors to hidden rooms?" Saxonby asked.

"We measure the rooms," Sinclair said.

Saxonby groaned. "That will bloody take forever."

Portia knew how he felt. But—"What else can we do?" she asked. "I'd rather work like a fiend than be killed."

Sinclair's hand pressed with gentle firmness against her back and moved a little, in a caress. She almost gasped and her whole body tingled, just having him touch her.

"You will not be hurt," he growled. "I would never allow it."

It touched her heart, made it wobble. But he couldn't promise such a thing.

He moved to the bellpull with a panther's lithe, muscular grace. But before pulling on it, Sinclair made a lower grumble in the back of his throat, then said, in his deep, melodic voice, "Come in, Humphries."

Portia whipped toward the door as the butler walked in. The man was blushing—even his balding pate looked pink. Humphries had been skulking outside the door.

Why? To overhear what had been said? Could the thin, aging butler be involved in these crimes?

Sinclair walked away from the group of guests with the butler, close to her. She and Saxonby could overhear their conversation, but none of the others could. Yet the others watched them. In silence, drinking liquor or tea, they watched. And their gazes flicked to each other, narrow with suspicion or wide with fear.

"Any secret rooms or passages in the house, Humphries?" Sinclair asked. "Any priest holes? Or doors that are cleverly hidden in walls?"

The butler's heavy black eyebrows shot up, as if he'd expected different questions. "I have no idea, Your Grace. I was never told of any such thing. Nor have I discovered any. Now, I must clear tea." He scuttled away, sideways like a crab, as if he was still trying to hear what they said.

Portia said, "He could be lying."

Sinclair said it at exactly the same time.

He flashed her a smile. "You are clever, love."

Then he stalked away, stopped, turned. "Come, angel. You as well, Sax. Time to hunt."

Determination gleamed in Sinclair's dark brown eyes. He looked so different—she'd never seen him like this. She'd always thought of him as sweet and naïve. She'd even really thought that was why he had orgies—because he'd been bowled over by freely available sex and adventure.

Now, she saw he was even cleverer than she'd thought. And his mind seemed to race swiftly, assessing, figuring, planning.

She and Saxonby had to race to catch up to him.

Then the work of measuring began.

Portia carried paper and a quill pen. She drew pictures of the rooms, wrote down all the measurements. The three of them added figures to see if there was any place where outside and inside dimensions did not make sense. Sinclair was astoundingly good with figures—he could juggle several numbers in his head and do mathematics almost instantaneously.

Nothing came to light. The measurements showed no discrepancy that could be a hidden space. Not in room after room. They did the attics, the basement and kitchens, where the cook demanded to know what they were doing.

"The Marquis of Crayle was murdered," Sinclair told the woman bluntly.

The woman clapped a flour-covered hand to her mouth. She slumped back onto a stool. "Blimey? Murdered? Like that one last night?"

"Different," the duke said. "Crayle was strangled, then hanged."

"Oh dear heaven." The cook reached unsteadily for a bottle and slopped a good amount in a glass. It was the cooking sherry, and Mrs. Kent began to knock it back.

After that, Portia went with Sinclair and Saxonby through the bedrooms—easy to search with the other guests downstairs. As they measured and searched, she saw Sinclair swiftly search drawers. "No one can hide in there."

"Weapons. Poison. I'm searching for those."

He even searched the marquis's room. She ignored the body under the sheets. She had to admit—going through the man's bedchamber taught her rather a lot about gentlemen of the *ton*. The marquis, cold and arrogant, had feminine lace-trimmed shifts, corsets, knickers, and gossamer-thin silk stockings shoved in a drawer. "For the courtesans?" she wondered.

"Or himself," Sinclair remarked lightly.

She jerked up her head.

He gave her a wry look that made him unbearably handsome. "Some men have the desire to wear women's clothing, especially their lacy underclothing."

She thought of the Cruel Marquis dressed in such a way.

Given his vicious behavior to Sadie, the image she conjured was not flattering. Wrinkled skin, paunchy stomach, white hair, then filmy lace. "Oh dear."

Sinclair took the corset she held and put it back in the drawer.

"Er, yes, thank you. I'd rather not be touching that." She looked up into his dark brown eyes. "But why?"

He lifted his brow wryly. "Everyone has their deepest, hidden-most fantasies."

"I guess yours are all the naughty things you've done," she said. "I don't have any."

"My deepest fantasy is something I've never done before, Portia. And you have to have hidden fantasies. Everyone does."

"I do not."

"Not even two men making love to you?" he asked softly. Saxonby had moved on to the next room. Sinclair came close to her, enveloping her in his scent—sandalwood and the warm, sensual scent of his skin.

No, she didn't really want two men like the Wanton Widow. All she wanted was Sin. Sinclair, she meant. But she couldn't admit that.

"We should look through Willoughby's bedroom," she said crisply. In the hall, they discovered Saxonby was searching the bedroom belonging to the Old Madam, and they went to the viscount's room.

No frilly, pretty undergarments graced his drawers. But when Portia checked the drawer in the bedside table, there atop an assortment of riding crops and ropes sat a piece of pink ribbon.

She lifted it out. "Ribbon again!"

Hands settled on her shoulders, making her gasp. Not with fear, with a sudden rush of awareness. It was Sinclair of course. "Portia, you shouldn't be looking at those things. You're inno-cent—"

"Never mind those. It's the ribbon that's important."

"The ribbon?" Sinclair stared like he couldn't believe what he'd heard.

"I found pink ribbon on the floor near Viscount Sandhurst's body. And there was a piece on the bed in the room where the marquis . . . died. The cook had a piece too—she found it in her room."

He frowned. "You think the ribbon was a warning?"

"I don't know. We didn't have any in our room. I found the ribbon on the floor near Sandhurst, not in his room. Perhaps it fell out of his pocket. It must mean something."

Sinclair took it and she watched his fingers stroke it. "It's a girl's hair ribbon, isn't it?"

"It could belong to one of the women here," Portia began. "But this would be for a younger girl—"

"Some women dress up as young girls to arouse certain men. You think one of the women committed these murders and left hair ribbons?" Sinclair's brow rose.

Could a woman have done it? "I suppose it seems impossible for a woman to have lifted Crayle."

"Agreed."

Did that mean it was the mysterious Lord Genvere? A thought struck and she gasped out a little "Oh!"

Sinclair looked at her in surprise.

Why had she not thought of this before? She used false names in the stews to get access to places where she feared she might not. She'd even used disguises—dressing up as old ladies or servants.

"Maybe there is no Genvere at all. There is just us. And a killer." At his questioning look, she explained, "Perhaps one of the guests brought us all here, creating invitations with a false name. I've yet to find anyone who has met Lord Genvere. Not even the servants."

A grin spread over his handsome face. "Brilliant, Portia."

That smile, those words sent a warm glow through her, despite the chilling thought she'd had.

"When we found no sign of anyone on the island, it seemed logical the killer has to be one of us. I hadn't discounted Genvere altogether, but you're correct. As far as I've been told, no one has ever met him. But there are sections of the cliffs I haven't checked. I want to be positive there is no one hiding on the island. When the weather clears, I'm going to search for caves again. I'll rappel down the cliffs and search."

Her glow vanished. "You are going to do *what?*"

"Take a rope, lower myself down, look for caves—"

"Suspended over the rocks and sea? You could be killed."

"Not if I use stout rope. And Sax will be on hand to help."

"It's too dangerous," she cried. He could be killed. She couldn't face that. Couldn't. "You're utterly mad. You cannot take such a risk."

"I'm trying to stop a murderer. And find the bastard who kidnapped you."

"It is not worth risking your life."

He touched her chin, tipping it up. "For me, it is."

She wanted to protest, but the Duke of Saxonby came into Willoughby's room. "The storm's eased a little, Sin. But—"

"Good enough. I wanted to wait until the storm ended. But that isn't occurring. Given what's happened, I think I need to search now."

"No," Portia gasped. He would be putting himself in terrible danger. "No, I won't allow it."

"Angel, you have no choice."

Dressed in her hooded cloak, which had been left in Sinclair's bedroom, Portia had also acquired an umbrella from the handsome footman, Reggie. She'd blushed terribly when asking him for one, for she kept picturing him with the widow and Rutledge. Embarrassment had made her forget the word *umbrella,* so she'd tried to make hand motions, which only made the whole thing worse. Reggie hadn't been embarrassed at all. He'd winked boldly at her.

Sinclair had warned her that an umbrella would prove useless. Stubbornly, she'd tried. And of course, the wretched brolly whipped inside out and was ripped out of her hands. It tumbled across the terrace and he ran to catch it.

But it was destroyed and he let it go.

"This is madness," Saxonby stated, as Sinclair came running back. "How can we search the cliffs in weather like this?"

"What choice do we have? Miss Love's idea is that there is no Genvere. That he doesn't exist and our killer is one of the guests or the servants. But if there is a Genvere, he has to be a madman who appears able to get into the house without being seen. We've searched the damn house and found no sign of an intruder, or anyone hiding in it. So either he doesn't exist or he's hiding somewhere else. I want to eliminate all possibilities. If there's anywhere on this rock where someone can hide, I suspect it's a cave."

"You looked before and found nothing."

"I wasn't able to search all along the cliffs."

"If the cave is so well hidden," Saxonby said. "I don't see how the murderer gets out of it, up the cliff, and into the house without being observed."

"True. It makes sense that it's one of the guests, Sax." He looked to Portia. "As my clever Miss Love has deduced. But which of them could orchestrate three murders and carry them off seamlessly? Murder is a difficult thing to do. Hard to do without leaving a trace. I talked to Humphries after we searched the rooms. He says all other guests were in the drawing room. Sadie was the only guest alone when Crayle was killed."

"But Sadie was lying in bed in pain," Portia protested.

"What of the servants?" Saxonby asked.

"Humphries had gone upstairs after telling off the footman for joining . . . uh, in a threesome. The maid, Ellie, was tidying in the dining room. On her own, so she has no alibi. However, she is a slender female who doesn't look particularly strong."

"There is the cook, too," Portia said suddenly.

"That rotund, middle-aged woman? Unlikely she could string up the marquis either. Or would want to. If she wanted to kill us, she could poison us."

Portia swallowed hard. "Like Sandhurst."

"If he was poisoned, the most likely method was to introduce the poison to his drink."

"So not the cook. She was downstairs. And not the maid either."

Then she thought of what Sinclair had said. Murder is a difficult thing to do. He hadn't said it with a speculative tone, the way he'd talked about the guests.

He said it in a matter-of-fact way. As if he knew . . .

Ten years ago, he'd told her a little about his family. His parents had both died suddenly. It had been unexpected. It had been two weeks later he'd learned he was now the duke.

Had his parents been murdered?

Shocked, she looked up at his face. He looked cool, emotionless, determined.

No, she was letting her mind think of mad things.

Sinclair clasped her hand as they walked across the grass, which made her heart leap and places tingle. He walked slightly ahead of her, trying to block the wind and rain. The three of them made their way across the island, struggling against the wind.

"I've already searched close to the house," Sinclair shouted over the wind. "We'll go out further. There are no buildings on the island other than the house."

The surface of the island was not large and mostly it was a stretch of rock and grass. They soon reached the edge of the cliff. Only a few trees grew along the edge, leaning out into space. All Portia could hear was the roar of the wind across the exposed island, the pounding and smashing of the waves on rock.

If she held one of the trees, she could go close to the edge. And look over.

A flash of color caught her eye. Something pink on one of the branches, fluttering in the wind. More ribbon?

Portia took a step toward it and her leg bumped something, startling her and throwing her off balance. She tumbled forward, slipping on the wet grass. Sinclair's arm shot out and his hand grabbed her wrist to keep her from falling. He was hauling her back toward him as the strangest sound came to her ears—a sharp, mysterious twang.

"Bloody hell," he barked.

She almost flew through the air. Sinclair had jumped to the side, pulling her with him. He landed on the grass with a thud and she fell upon him. Landing hard enough that she lost her breath.

His hand was on her head and he pulled her down hard, just as a sudden whoosh of wind passed over her head. Wet leaves splashed against her, cold and horrid. Water rained down on her. A tree branch rested over them, along with a dripping length of rope.

"Heavens, that would have hit me if you hadn't pulled me away. I would have fallen off the cliff. You saved my life, Sinclair."

His hands stroked her back. She was trying for calm, and his touch was so soothing. But also slow, enticing . . . How could she think of that when she could have died?

"I saw a piece of ribbon," she said shakily, "and took a step toward it."

"It was a trap," he said huskily. "Rigged to be set off by someone walking there. What you saw was intended to lure you—or one of us out there."

His hand cradled her head. His fingers twined in her hair and he drew her into a kiss. Hot, scorching. The rain turned to steam on their lips.

After danger—in the middle of danger—how could she want to kiss him? But she did, hungrily. She cupped his face, delighting in the scratch of stubble on her palms. He was flat on the ground underneath her. She could have been killed! Yet instead of panicking, she was kissing him like mad. Her lips on his. Their tongues tangling. She wriggled on his strong, hard body. She loved the way her breasts were squashed against him. She wiggled her hips—and discovered he liked this too. She was straddling a very obvious erection—

"Ahem. I thought you two were dead. I called to you and neither answered. I thought you'd gone over the cliff."

The smooth, urbane tones belonged to Saxonby. With a tiny "erk," Portia tried to scramble off Sinclair. Almost impossible to do with a cloak and wet skirts.

Sinclair lifted her. She had no idea how, since he was on his back. He moved her over onto her bottom; then he sprang up and clasped her hand, helping her to her feet.

He had saved her life.

"I had best get to work," Sinclair began.

"You cannot rappel down the edge of the cliff now!" Portia cried.

"Portia, I must."

"No! Not when we know there are traps."

"I'll be careful."

"You will be dangling off a cliff!"

"With care."

"No! You can't risk your life. And why should you? The victims were selfish men. The marquis was horrible and abusive. Sandhurst was innocent, but he was only interested in his own pleasure. And Willoughby was a horrible man who lured and ravished innocent women. All of those men deserved what happened to them. They had committed sins—"

"They didn't deserve death even then, Portia. Who gives this person the right to be self-appointed judge and jury for them? This person is mad. Dangerous. And what of you? Was it allowable for someone to kidnap you, as long as he murders men to whom you object?"

"No . . . of course not. But it might not be the same person."

"We have both a kidnapper and a killer on the island? I am not going to stand by, waiting, Portia," he growled. "You could have been killed today—swept off the cliff by that trap. If I hadn't realized the branch was pulled back at a strange angle just before you stumbled—"

"I think we should go up to the house," Saxonby said, breaking into the argument.

She saw Sinclair glance, nod, and she knew. "You both are trying to get me out of the way. Then you will return and do something mad and risky. You cannot do this—"

"To the house," Sinclair repeated.

Sinclair's arm slipped around her waist, surprising her. He tried to draw her to walk with him, but she dug in her heels. He gave her a wry look, then started walking away. "Watch her, Sax."

Bother it! She couldn't just let him go—couldn't let him walk into danger over her.

She hurried after him, cloak and skirts swishing around her. She followed him to the terrace, where he turned and lifted her into his arms. He carried her around to the stone wall of the house, where they were sheltered from the wind and rain. Where there was the roof overhanging, keeping them dry. There were no windows. And Saxonby hadn't followed.

There were just the two of them.

Sinclair backed her up against the stone wall. His hands rested against the wall, trapping her. All she could think of was him. Powerful arms that had scooped her from danger. A broad chest to break her fall. His mouth—his beautiful, sensual, oh-so-talented mouth.

He leaned to her, his face showing pain. "Portia, damn, I let you go once. I can't face losing you. Not forever. I could survive because I believed you were happy—"

His words startled her. But she said, "I was quite fine."

He growled. A low, dangerous sound. "You were meant to be mine, angel. All mine."

Those words—they set her utterly aflame.

"That's very lovely, but—"

Then he had her pressed to the wall. His legs were spread, bracketing hers. His chest pushed against her bosom. His mouth—

Oh Lord, his mouth was on her neck.

On sensitive skin that loved the touch of his lips. He skimmed his mouth up to her earlobe and she almost slithered down the wall. Heat trailed and she wanted this, wanted his kisses. His warm breath caressed her ear and she moaned.

"Do you want this? Do you want me to pleasure you?"

She was lost. Wanting all the pleasure he'd given her, wanting the searing, fiery, tumultuous explosion of pleasure she'd known on the night they'd gotten engaged.

Your heart will be broken.

She didn't care.

She nodded, jerkily.

Sinclair lowered to his knees in front of her. She knew what he would do, and she began to draw up her skirts. Tugged at the fabric hurriedly. Grinning, he helped her pull them up. She gazed down at the dark slashes of his brows, his high cheekbones, full lips, the curl of his long lashes. And then—

Ooooh.

Slowly, he teased her with his tongue. She pressed back hard against the wall. Clinging to his shoulders, she closed her eyes. Savored. This—this was delicious. Just slow and tantalizing and perfect. She wanted more and she wanted it just like this.

She was supposed to be good. A paragon. The only time she'd tumbled was when she'd fallen in love with Sinclair before—and she'd paid the price. For years, she'd told herself that.

But now, she thought: *Why is it so wrong to want pleasure? To be physically loved?*

No one was being hurt. They were surrounded by murder— by true evil.

This was not wrong.

She knew it now.

She threaded her fingers in his silky brown hair, massaging his head through the thick strands. Gently, she stoked him, while she saw fireworks and stars—with her eyes shut.

Portia felt too shy to look.

Bother it! Cracking her eyes open, she looked down. Entranced by how his mouth moved over her.

He drew her away from the wall and she took an unsteady step. With his strong hands, he cupped her bottom and lifted her.

Oh my heavens, he'd lifted her off her feet. Putting her cunny entirely, heavily, on top of his mouth. He couldn't breathe, she was sure.

Then she realized—

She couldn't escape.

Balanced over his mouth, she couldn't move away. Even though she was on top of him, she was entirely at his command. Her skirts fell down, plopping on his head, spilling down over her bottom and legs. But still his tongue teased her, sawing across her.

She began to move on him, her hips rocking to drive his mouth harder against her. She must be suffocating him . . . it was terrible of her . . . she couldn't stop. . . .

She clutched. Moaned. Had to shut her eyes once more.

She was coming. Falling.

He held her and they were both falling backward to the grassy ground. She flopped down, straddling his face. Bracing her arms on the wet grass, she rode out her pleasure on him. Limp, spent, she could barely move, except she knew she must.

Pulling at her skirts, she lifted off him, so wet she hardly cared that she was curled up on the wet grass. "Goodness, are you all right? I was so scared you couldn't breathe."

He rolled on his side, stained with mud, and he grinned at that. "A small price to pay to hear you come, angel. You make the most erotic sounds."

"You must have heard lots of sounds that women make."

"True, but many are exaggerated. More performance than genuine. I like yours, because they are real. Honest moans and cries and adorable squeaks."

"I squeak?" She had no idea. Then remembered—she did make high-pitched sounds.

She stroked along his arm, feeling the bulge of muscle. "I realized I could lose you. I could be killed and never know pleasure—"

But Sinclair got to his feet. "You won't be killed. I promise you."

"But I'd like to pleasure you. I want to—" Could she do it? Without marriage? It would go against everything she believed, everything she advised to young girls. But she had the terrible sense she was running out of time.

"I think I want to make love." Then she added, hastily, awkwardly, "With you."

"No, Portia, love. We are not going to do that. I won't ruin you."

"You have orgies. How can you be noble?"

But he lifted her to her feet once more, and she knew, gritting her teeth in frustration, red with embarrassment, that he could be noble.

To cover up the flaring humiliation, she babbled. "What do you think the pink ribbons mean? I think it must be something to do with a girl. But a young girl—only a very young girl would use such a color. Unless Sadie does, but I've never seen her in pink. Do you think—one of the women here could have a child? There is the old madam. And the Incognita. Sadie could be old enough. I don't think the maid, Ellie, is old enough. Unless the child were very young. And there's the cook—but cooks are never married. They are called "Mrs." That's to accord them respect. But when they work in a house, they aren't married."

Sinclair sighed. "Angel, slow down."

They'd reached the terrace doors. "You're going to rappel down the cliff faces, aren't you?" she asked. "What about the rain? Won't you slip?"

"I'll tie the rope around my waist and use a couple of lines. Sadie doesn't know the marquis is dead. I'd like you there when I tell her."

"Oh. Of course." It meant there would be no money for Sadie from the marquis to ease the horror of her injuries. The girl would be angry and upset.

They passed the drawing room, now empty. Went upstairs.

Portia rapped gently on Sadie's bedroom door, then turned the key in the lock and opened it. "Sadie?"

No answer. She saw the girl's form under the sheets. She quietly approached.

Stopped dead. Her stomach plunged. Sadie lay on her back, the sheets tucked up just beneath her chin. But her eyes were wide open. Large, blue, and staring blankly at the canopy above.

Portia froze. She had to grab the bed column. Sadie was dead. It couldn't be—

Gathering her wits, Portia hurried to the bed. Was Sadie dead because of her wounds? Surely not. Sadie wasn't that badly wounded.

Then she saw it.

The ring of bruises around the young woman's neck. Marks that looked like fingermarks on her throat.

Portia stepped back. Something crunched beneath her foot and she jumped. She looked down, afraid to discover what she'd stepped on.

It was crumbs on the floor. It looked like a biscuit.

Then, as she looked up again, as Sinclair went to Sadie's prostrate body, she saw a tiny piece of pink ribbon sticking out from beneath the pillow.

15

_____

He expected Portia to be horrified. Frozen with shock and fear. Sin didn't expect her to cry out, "Crumbs! That's it! There are two clues, don't you see?" she went on, breathlessly. The piece of hair ribbon and the crumbs."

She pulled out of his arms. Sin wanted to soothe her, but she was gone—and his arms felt empty. Then he spotted the crumbs. A stretch of them strewn over the carpet. Bending down to them, he was about to ask Portia why she believed they were so important, when he heard the click of the door latch.

She could move like a streak of lightning when she was doing something he intended to expressly forbid. When he reached the corridor, she'd gone. Damn it.

He caught movement of the baize door at the end of the corridor—the servants' door.

If crumbs had set her off like that, and she'd gone to the servants' stair, she had to be going down to the kitchens.

He followed. Drawn to her. And not just to protect her.

He'd had women in every way possible. On top of him, riding him while pinching their own nipples for his delectation or squashing full breasts in his face. Below him, with legs wrapped around his neck so he could pound deep. Two women, three women. One time six women, while he lay on a large bed. One woman riding his prick. One fingering his anus, sliding three fingers inside. One sitting on his face, so he could lick her pussy. Two using his fingers for pleasure, in their cunts and asses, and the last one to slip her hand in between all the bodies to fondle him. He'd even had women strap on false cocks to penetrate him while he made love to another woman.

But he'd never known the pure agony of wanting a woman he couldn't have except with Portia. He'd never wanted any other woman like he wanted her.

Focusing on the baize door, he almost crashed into a figure who emerged from a bedroom. His chest almost collided with a protruding bosom and he caught himself just in time.

It was the Old Madam. Mrs. Barker, who he now thought of by Portia's nickname.

"What is it? Where are you running off to, Your Grace?" she cried.

"There was another murder. Sadie. Strangled," he bit out. He tried to sprint around the older woman, but she clutched his arm. With a grip like an iron hook driving into his flesh.

"One of the women? Oh! Oh! We're all to be killed! One by one. For our sins." Her eyes goggled, bulging out and looking like billiard balls. "But who hasn't had to commit a sin or two in life? I did nothing wrong. . . . I had to remove those girls. They were suffering. Sick. Wounded. What else could I do? If I'd sent them to hospitals, they would have talked and powerful gentlemen would have been destroyed. I had no choice, Sinclair. No choice! I protected those men. Those lords. Why am I paying the price? Why aren't they?"

The Old Madam was screeching at him.

He actually longed to smack her face to stop her wailing in his face in a high-pitched, panicked scream that almost shattered his eardrums. But her words . . . Hell, he understood what she meant by "removed." "You killed women. Girls you dragged into your bordellos?"

"I had no choice. When they were whipped badly, I couldn't let anyone see the wounds. I simply gave them something to make them sleep and not wake up. I found new girls. Strong, new, pretty virgins."

He wanted to vomit listening to this. He wanted to belt the woman. "Go lock yourself in your room and pray you're not dead in the morning," he said harshly.

He had to find this killer. Not to protect women like the madam, but to keep Portia safe.

The victims were all sinners. But Portia wasn't. She should not be in danger, but she'd received a note. That made no sense to him.

It also hit him cold—the murderer considered him as immoral and sick as the Old Madam, who had killed young women hurt by her clients.

In the eyes of the murderer, he was as bad.

But for which sins? The sin of holding orgies? Or for the old sins from his past?

A crazy idea leapt into his head. He'd sinned against Portia. Broken her heart.

Was that his sin?

He couldn't hear Portia's footsteps ahead of him on the stairs. This drove him to run down the steps, three at a time. He reached the kitchen floor, stepping onto the flagstones.

Then he saw her.

Dangling feet, swaying as the suspended rope twirled.

Oh God, Portia.

Suddenly, she was pulled back and all she could see was Sin's white shirt. He'd pulled her to his chest, blocking her view of the body that hung right in front of her, just as he'd done before. But Portia pushed away. She recognized the plain skirts. She didn't even have to look up.

It was Ellie the maid.

"Don't look." His chest rumbled with his husky voice.

"I have to. I can't cower in fear. I've been far too afraid."

"No, you haven't. You've been remarkably brave." He looked at her with admiration.

This was once what she'd dreamed of. Having the Duke of Sinclair realize he'd made a terrible mistake.

But now—it didn't matter. They were surrounded by horror and that was what mattered.

She forced her gaze to go up. The girl hung from a noose attached to one of the thick, large beams.

Suddenly, she couldn't stop speaking. Speaking made it so that her mind would not take in what she was seeing.

"I noticed the crumbs on the floor in Sadie's room when I went to her bed and stepped on them with my slipper. You see, they weren't there earlier. They couldn't have been, or else I would have walked on them then. Someone brought food up to Sadie. It could have been the maid—and perhaps she saw someone. Perhaps she saw the killer. And that's why she was killed."

Wait . . .

"No, that's not right," she said, her voice hoarse. "She received a letter warning her about sins. But how could she have sins? What could she have done? Stolen something from an employer? Ruined herself with a man? How could anything be worth—" Words failed. Her throat hurt too much to speak.

Sinclair's arms went around her again. "Don't talk. You are in shock."

She shook her head. "I can't be in shock anymore. I've been through this five times now. I don't think I have any capacity left to feel shock."

"Yes, you do," he said firmly.

She was sure he was going to march her back to the room. He was already turning her. She couldn't see Ellie's dangling form anymore.

But no, she had to have strength.

"I must talk to the cook. Especially now!" Portia cried. "Perhaps one of the guests came down and asked for biscuits, offering to help Sadie. If it was one of the men, surely it must mean he was a murderer, for what man would worry about such a thing? If it was a woman . . . well, it could mean she was the killer, or was being solicitous. Though, would any of these women be worrying about Sadie? Ellie would be the obvious person to take the biscuits upstairs, wouldn't she? And now she's dead. I think she is dead because she knew who the killer is—"

"Reason for you to leave this alone, Portia. I demand that you do. Upstairs for you now. I will deal with this."

"I'm just supposed to meekly let you order me about."

"Yes."

"No, I won't. I have had to be in charge of my own life for years. I've had ten years to realize I will be alone for my life. Surrounded by children and people in the home, but alone. And to be alone means you must have courage to protect yourself."

"You are not alone, Portia. I will deliver you from this hell. No matter what it takes." Ruthlessness touched his expression. His eyes went cold.

She shivered. "What do you mean?"

But he didn't answer. He lifted his head. "Did you hear that?"

A soft groan murmured through the silence.

"There's someone else down here," she whispered.

"Ooh, me head," complained a female voice.

"The cook," Portia gasped. She ran into the kitchen, even though Sinclair barked, "Portia, wait!"

Within, the cook was pushing up from the floor weakly. Dipping to her knees, Portia helped the woman, who gazed at her with rueful eyes and touched her head. "It 'urts something fierce."

Sinclair's polished boots moved beside the injured cook, and he lifted the woman to her feet. His gloved hand came down, Portia clasped it, and he lifted her as if she were weightless.

"You should sit," Sinclair instructed to Mrs. Kent. He helped the woman to a stool. "What happened to you?"

Her white frilled cap was askew and Portia helped her right it. The woman looked at her gratefully, then turned to Sinclair.

"I . . . I don't know exactly, Your Grace. I . . . I blacked out. No . . . no, something hit me. That's all I remember. A sharp pain, then the whole world went black right before my eyes."

"You were attacked," Portia said. "And Ellie—"

"What's happened to her?" The cook cried, her eyes wide with shock. "Oh my heavens, was she hurt too?"

Portia opened her mouth, but the duke said, "I will explain it, Miss Love. It's not for you to speak of such gruesome things."

He wanted to spare her. In all this horror, he was thinking of her.

"It was just as with the Marquis of Crayle," he said gruffly. "Ellie has been hanged, but there was no stool or chair in sight."

Portia saw how intently he watched the cook. But the woman went white and sagged on the stool. He had to grasp her arm so she didn't slide off. The cook didn't faint, but it looked like a near thing.

"I'm sorry to be so blunt. Now, do you know what you were struck with?"

"I don't know. It slammed on me 'ead like a ton of bricks. A pan? A rolling pin?"

Together with Sinclair, Portia looked around. Nothing lay on the floor. The wooden worktable was clear. "There's no sign of the weapon."

Something else was missing. "And no ribbon," Portia breathed. "I don't see any pink ribbon."

"Ribbon?" Mrs. Kent repeated slowly. She touched her locket. "There was this. Do you mean this ribbon? It was left in my room. I meant no harm in taking it."

"Of course you didn't," Portia assured the woman, who looked blank and confused. "As Mrs. Kent said, a piece of ribbon was left in her room before. But there wasn't any now. What could that mean?"

"Possibly that the intent was not to kill Mrs. Kent." A frown pulled Sinclair's brows together. He gave a half shake of his head. "Or the killer felt it was sufficient she had a piece of the ribbon tied to her locket. Whatever this madman is trying to say, I can't fathom it," he growled. He turned to the cook, addressing her gently. "Was there anyone else down here with you?"

"There was. That footman. And the butler. I overheard that footman flirting with Ellie. Said he'd received a letter threatening to reveal his sins. Ellie admitted she'd gotten one too."

"Did you get a letter like that?" he asked.

Mrs. Kent shook her head—then winced and stopped. "There is no point in lying, is there? Aye, I got one. What sins could a woman like me 'ave committed? I work from dawn until evening. I've no time for sins. I've never even made a soul sick with my cooking. Never poisoned anyone, if ye're thinking that's my sin!"

The woman had a bruise on her head and she looked white as a sheet, swaying slightly on her feet. She looked like a woman who had been attacked. But so far, the murderer had used bludgeoning only once. And when the killer had struck Willoughby, it had been with excessive force. Vicious force. The killer had certainly ensured Lord Willoughby was dead.

"Strange that the murderer left you alive," Sinclair said, and Portia jumped, startled he was thinking the exact thing as her. "That the killer did not ensure the attack was successful."

The cook sucked in a deep, desperate breath. Suddenly she made a loud, keening wail. She got up off the stool, rushed blindly toward the door, crashing into the silver-laded table.

Portia rushed after her and got her to halt. She put her hands on the woman's shoulders to soothe her. "Please calm down. That didn't happen, thank heaven. You are perfectly safe now."

"With a killer on the loose? I'm about as safe as a lobster dangled over a boiling pot," the cook cried.

"We intend to keep you safer than that," Sinclair said. But he was still frowning and he shook his head. "Our villain has been damned clever up until now. Why has he made a mistake?"

The poor cook looked ready to swoon. Portia held on to the woman, to keep her from slumping to the floor. The woman stared wildly at Portia, and cried, "Perhaps the fiend intended to strike again, but ran off. Or thought 'e'd done the job when I fell. Or Ellie saw 'im and 'e went after 'er instead. 'E must 'ave thought 'e'd done me in. Oh—oh my Lord, if 'e 'ad checked, I'd be dead."

"Your ideas could be right," the duke said thoughtfully. Portia wished he was not doing this in front of the cook. It was frightening the woman. "Perhaps Ellie did walk in and the killer had to attend to her. The murderer could have assumed one strong blow to Mrs. Kent's head was enough to kill her."

The woman made a helpless scream of fear.

Portia wished he would realize he was frightening the woman.

"Well, you are not dead, thank heaven," Portia said firmly. "And that is what matters. There's no point in dwelling on this. She's told us what she knows."

But Sinclair bent to be eye level with Mrs. Kent. "Why do you say 'he'?" he asked softly. "You said you did not see anything. What makes you think it was a man?"

"I . . . I don't know. I don't know who it was. I just thought it must be a man. Who else would be so vicious and evil?" The cook peered at him, looking up from the stool. "Ye think it's me, don't ye? Ye think I did these 'orrible things? Why would I? I'm innocent! What about 'umphries, always creeping about! If there's anyone mad, it's 'im! Or that Reggie. 'E's a strong one."

"And both men were down here. So why haven't they come out now, to find out what all this noise is about?"

The cook clamped her hand to her mouth.

"Stay here," Sinclair instructed. "Wait for my return."

The cook moved her hand. "I'm not staying 'ere with a lunatic on the loose!"

"Bring her with us, P—Miss Love. Let me go first. If there's anyone waiting to attack, I'd rather be the one he—or she—strikes."

Portia helped the cook to her feet and put her arm around the woman's waist to help her walk. "Do you think someone is waiting?" She glanced around.

"It's too damn quiet," he muttered.

Five minutes later, they found the butler. Sprawled on the floor of his pantry. He'd been struck over the head by a silver candlestick.

"One blow," Sinclair muttered. "One blow killed him. The killer's strong. Knows what he—or she—is doing."

The cook gave out a cry of horror. She clutched the table on which lay all the silver, half-gleaming, freshly polished. " 'Im too! I could've been dead. It was just by luck that I survived. That footman was down 'ere with us. 'E's strong. He must be mad. Utterly mad."

Then she spotted it. A swash of color. Sinclair saw it too and he bent and picked it up off the floor.

"The little ribbon clue," Portia said softly. "But there had been no ribbon near you," she said to Mrs. Kent.

Portia realized Sinclair had left the room. Hard footsteps on the flags made Portia jump. Someone was coming and she and the cook were alone. She grasped a heavy silver serving dish with two hands. She wielded it over her shoulder, ready to protect Mrs. Kent and herself—

Sinclair came back in. "The rear door that leads out to the kitchen gardens was open."

"You didn't go out, did you? It could have been a trap!"

"I was careful, love. I saw a fresh-looking footprint in the earth. Then spotted a set of white gloves tossed to the ground at the base of a shrub. White and stained with rust-red blood." These he tossed onto the butler's table.

"What are those?"

"The footman's gloves. He appears to be gone."

"Gone?" Wild thoughts went through her head. Why was the footman gone? Was he the killer? He was young and strong. A match for the men. And he could have taken all of the servants by surprise.

But why? Why would he do this? Revenge? Anger? Madness?

There had been no ribbon near the cook. If she'd been struck over the head by the killer with the intent to kill her in the same way the butler had been murdered, why was there no clue left behind?

The cook peered at Sinclair. "Gone? What do ye mean gone?"

"He appears to have gone outside."

"So 'e's the one?"

Was he? Portia knew, from the stews, that a woman could be a villain. Puzzled, she moved back toward the kitchen. Could it mean the cook was the killer? That the woman had not really been hit and had faked everything?

But she was a large, heavy, middle-aged woman. Could she really have killed Willoughby, who was young and strong? Could she have lifted the marquis and placed him in a noose?

It seemed impossible.

If the cook was supposed to be a victim, like Ellie and the butler, shouldn't there be a ribbon? The cook was wearing a little scrap of the ribbon on her locket. Was that enough for the killer? Or had the killer intended only to knock out the cook, and kill the cook later?

Portia left the butler's pantry, returning to the place in the kitchen where they had found Mrs. Kent. Was there any clue there? Any clue that pointed to the footman being the culprit? She simply wouldn't have thought him clever enough to have killed five people and have done it without detection—

"Oh my heavens." The cook had come in behind her. Now the woman passed her and pulled something out from beneath a pot. Her fingers caressed it.

Portia saw the flash of pink. "So you did get one."

"It were under the pot. A bit of ribbon, just like ye said. But why is it there? What is it? It looks like a child's hair ribbon."

"Yes," Portia said. "And these were left for each victim."

The woman turned white. "But why would I be given this? I've no daughter. Not even a younger sister. There's no one left in my family but me."

"It's a clue," Portia said. "The murderer wants us to understand why he—or she—is doing this. It is something to do with a girl. Perhaps a girl who wore this hair ribbon."

"But what could all of us have to do with a girl?" Mrs. Kent asked frantically. "Why should we be killed?"

Hinges creaked. A gust of cool air flowed in. There was the smell of dampness, the salt tinge of the sea.

Portia jerked. Sinclair must have gone out again. Gone in pursuit of the footman. A man who might be a fiendish killer. And he'd gone alone.

She rushed out the open door and almost fell over as a gust of sea wind hit her. There was no rain anymore, but the sky was a deep iron gray. Huge, dark clouds still massed around the island, as if trying to swallow it whole. The wind snatched at the door, tearing it from her hand, slamming it shut. Then she saw him. Sinclair returning to her. Alive.

She'd thought her heart would slow down from its frantic pace once she saw him and knew he was all right. But her heart thundered even faster with dizzying relief.

She ran toward him.

"You didn't find him?" she shouted over the sound of the wind. "We must organize a search. If we all look—" *All of us who are left,* she thought, panic touching her. But she fought it down. "We'll find him, surely."

"I did find him. He's not our killer."

One look at his face, hard, carved of stone, and Portia knew. "He's dead. Of course he is." Then, with an eerie sense of exhaustion, of finality, she asked, "How? How was he killed?"

But then, beyond Sinclair's tall form, she saw the footman's body sprawled on the lawn. She ran around Sinclair toward him, but as she grew close, her steps slowed. Her legs felt numb, her heart so filled with pain and horror, she could not comprehend what she was seeing.

His trousers had been torn down. There was darkness. A stretch of naked thighs and a stomach and then . . . blackish redness. Blood. She was looking at blood and—

Sinclair dragged her away. "Don't look. He's been cut. Badly."

"Around his front—his private parts."

"He's been gelded."

"Oh. Oh goodness." She did not look again. She had seen enough.

She needed to touch Sinclair. Put her hand over his heart. As if to reassure herself he was still alive.

The boastful footman. Now he was gone too. In a horrible way.

"Stay there," the Duke of Sinclair commanded. "Where I can keep watch over you every moment."

She did, her skirts whipping and snapping around her in the wind. She watched him return to the body. He crouched. Touched the wet earth. Then straightened and carefully and deliberately placed his foot in a muddy spot. The footman lay near the edge of the terrace, where there was a spot of wet mud between the stones and the lawn.

"A man's footprint," he called. "Slightly shorter than mine."

"Could it be the footman's prints?" she shouted back.

Sinclair shook his head. "I don't think so. I think he walked out here from over there."

"So we know it is a gentleman."

"Or a woman wearing a man's boots." He grimaced. "No clue gives us certainty."

"Would a woman have done that?"

"An angry, jealous, scorned woman might."

She met his gaze as he straightened and strode toward her. "Perhaps," she yelled, over the roar of the wind. Portia had never hurt so much she could turn to violence. But maybe some women did. "We are running out of suspects. Soon we'll know— because there will only be us and . . . and the killer."

He moved quickly, running to her. Her voice had become panicked. He caught hold of her hands. "No, it isn't going to be that way, love. No harm is going to come to you."

"I can't simply rely on you to do that."

He looked hurt.

"I have to rely on my wits as well. I have to think a way out of this." She looked out toward the sea. "Is there any way we could get to shore?"

"No boat. Sax checked that this morning. And I doubt any boats will come out to us. The seas are too high. I would have tried rowing back if there was a boat, but that's because I'm more desperate than anyone from the mainland coming to us."

"Are you certain there are no boats?"

He jerked up his head, silky brown hair falling across his brow. "You think Sax lied?"

"If he is the killer, he could have done."

"Sax is no madman."

Of course he would think that about his friend. "The hair ribbons. This is about a girl. Whatever our sins are, they are related to a girl or a young woman. Could there be a young woman in Saxonby's life that he is willing to kill for?"

Her words impacted Sinclair. He stepped back as if they'd struck him with force. "I don't know," he admitted. "We've been friends since Eton days. My father sent me there, even though our side of the family had been disowned. But I have to admit—I don't know about every detail of Sax's life." He looked to the open kitchen door and she looked too. Framed in the doorway was the pale, wounded cook. "We should go back to the house."

"Not yet. I can't go back yet. As mad as it sounds, I feel safer out here. I feel is if someone in the house is waiting, watching us, preparing to strike."

"Portia." His arms went around her, comforting her. "That's what I don't understand about this," he said softly. She realized he was leading away from the horribly mutilated body, but not toward the house. They were still out on the open lawn, where surely no one could sneak up and attack.

"What don't you understand? The *whole* thing seems a perplexing, horrible mystery to me."

"I don't understand why you are here. What sins could you have? You rescue children."

"Maybe this is about a child I couldn't rescue." The idea came to her suddenly. She had been brought here very deliberately. It hadn't been for an orgy, she knew. It had been to make her a victim.

"What do you mean?"

She met his darkly lashed, stunning brown eyes. "A child who died at the home, perhaps. Sometimes that happens—from illness. Or, when we rescue the child, the poor thing has been so starved or abused, the child can't recover."

Those were the worst agonies.

"But that would mean we all have this particular girl in common," he said. "What girl would we all have in common?"

"I don't know. Willoughby ruined innocents. The old madam snared young women for brothels. You gave orgies. It could be a girl who went to orgies."

He stiffened. "I never allowed young girls into my events. I employed dutiful servants to ensure the only women in attendance were of an appropriate age."

She saw hurt in his eyes, but an indignant one, not a vulnerable hurt. He felt judged. "I mean, I have been rescuing children since I was eighteen. A girl of ten then would be twenty-one now."

"Sadie," he muttered.

"Not Sadie. She is already dead." Portia tapped her chin, staring at the house. "But why? Could she have hurt this girl in some way? I could see the Old Madam or the Incognita killing Sadie out of jealousy. Or could one of them be related to this child. Even the Elegant Widow. She could be the sister to such a girl."

"Perhaps. We have to question the guests," he said. "And talk to the cook. She is the only person who has survived an attack. I know you don't want to go back to the house, but I'd like to talk to her, and I'm not leaving you out here alone."

"I can go now. With you. I can face it now."

They went back to the house, back in through the open kitchen door.

But the cook couldn't add a thing. They already knew she hadn't seen whoever had come up behind her, but Sinclair asked if she heard anything, or had smelled anything—the hint of a perfume or gentleman's shaving lotion. But Mrs. Kent had been utterly oblivious to everything that might have given them a clue.

"Who took biscuits up to the room used by Sadie Bradshaw?" Portia asked.

"Biscuits? No one asked me for biscuits, miss."

"But where are they kept? Who could have found them?"

"They're kept in a tin in the pantry. Ellie knew where they were." Tears gathered in the cook's eyes. For all she'd spoken to Mrs. Kent before, this was the first time Portia noticed the woman's eyes were large and green. They were quite striking. There was something about cooks—they were usually short-tempered, tough task masters, and always in charge of their kitchens. Often one forgot they were also women. And Mrs. Kent had probably been quite a pretty woman.

Then the woman put her hands on her hips and looked annoyed, as cooks so often did. "And what am I going to do now the other servants are gone? Am I to cook the meals, make the beds, dust and serve table all by myself?"

"We'll fend for ourselves," Sinclair said. "We have greater problems than worrying about laying fires and making beds."

The cook wagged her finger. "You say that now, Your Grace, but when there's no fire to ward off the cold sea air and your sheets stink, you'll think differently. Oh, oh blast—" The woman's brave anger vanished. Suddenly, Mrs. Kent began to cry, then pulled out a handkerchief and dabbed her eyes. "I want to get away from this godforsaken place."

"We all do," Sinclair growled. "But we can't."

There were nine guests left, including her and Sinclair and Saxonby. And on top of that, there was the cook. It had to be one of them, didn't it? There was something nagging at Portia, something that didn't seem right, but that was foolish—*all* of this was wrong. "I fear we'll know when we're the only ones left," she said softly. "Except for the murderer."

"No," Sinclair growled. "We'll stop this fiend before then. I am going to stop this damned villain now."

16

Sin stood in a shadowy corner of the foyer. Once he and Portia had come up from the kitchens, she had seen Nellie Upton, who wore a gown of translucent white lace that showed off her exotic, dark-toned skin.

She had gone to ask the girl a few questions. He'd waited, watching, thinking. He remembered his first orgy ten years ago.

He'd spent the whole night fucking as many people as he could before collapsing—he'd gone through a lot of French letters, but he couldn't remember how many partners he'd had. All the sex had helped him forget his past. Forget how, when he'd been young, his father had abused him, his mother had used him, and his brother's wife, Estella . . . she had destroyed the very last of his soul.

All his life, Sin had hated himself for letting them use him. For not standing up for himself. He had played their games—

That was what he was doing here, he realized. The killer was always ahead of them, always in command. He and Portia were playing the killer's game.

He had to get the upper hand. He had to twist things up, take charge, throw the killer off.

That was how he'd finally gotten free when he'd been

young. He had stood up to his father. He had told his mother he hated her for what she'd done to him. He'd told Estella that she could not touch him anymore. He'd finally stood up for himself.

It had set off a chain reaction of disaster that left his father and mother dead, but he had been free. Finally. He still felt so much guilt for being such a coward before. But he had only saved himself when he had stopped playing their games.

He had to do that now.

But how did he throw the killer off guard. How did he take control of this?

An idea occurred to him. A way to confuse the killer. But he would need help for his plan. He couldn't reveal it to Portia. But he could trust Sax—

"Sin. Sin, I've got to talk to you."

It was Sax, who looked like he'd seen a ghost. Sin came out of the shadows, just as Portia left Nellie. They both hurried toward Sax, and somehow Sin knew, before his friend even said a word, what had happened.

He could see it in Sax's eyes. He knew that look—he'd worn it years ago, when he was young.

It was lost hopelessness.

Saxonby came toward them and Portia hurried forward, laying her hand on the forearm of Sinclair's friend. She'd never seen a man look in so much pain as Saxonby. "What has happened?"

Sinclair was right behind her. In a raw voice, he asked, "Sax, what in hell is it?"

In the gray daylight falling into the corridor, Saxonby looked as if his heart had been torn out by vicious hands. "It's Georgiana. She has been killed. Poisoned, I think."

Portia felt her knees weaken. Four murders in mere hours—or mere minutes, really. How was it possible?

A spasm of pain passed over Sinclair's face. "I'm sorry. Damned sorry." Then, in a low growl, "How did it happen?"

"She had a decanter of sherry in her room. Took a drink even though I'd warned her not to touch anything. I found her lying on the bed, neatly arranged. With a damn pink ribbon lying on her breast."

The Duke of Saxonby was lifting a glass to his lips. Portia gasped, and said, "Don't touch that," but Sinclair had already knocked it out of his friend's hands.

"What the—? This was a fresh bottle placed in my room. I opened the seal, Sin. You didn't need to break my damn glass. I need a drink. I can't believe this happened to Georgiana. God, she was lovely. I was already half in love with her and falling fast the rest of the way. I could have happily married her—if I could marry, she would have been the girl for me."

If he could marry? Portia noted those words, but saw nothing in Saxonby's grieving expression of what he meant by those words. And what did it matter now, when he had lost the woman he loved?

"What do you mean the sealed bottle was placed in your room, Sax?" Sinclair asked, frowning.

"There was one left in my bedchamber this morning. A bottle, with the original seal in place, and a note that stated this was a fresh bottle, that it would be ungentlemanly to poison a man's brandy when he would soon need it. At the time, I had no idea what the note meant. It was signed by Genvere."

"You shouldn't be drinking it. Hell, Sax, it was likely tampered with."

"After I found Georgiana's body, I didn't give a damn if the stuff was poisoned. Since I'm still alive, I assume it was not. Or it will kill me later. But I guess that was Genvere's idea. He knew I would need a drink once I learned about Georgiana. I intend to drink the whole blasted bottle and either end up plastered or dead."

"We can't get drunk, Sax. We have to keep our wits to survive." Sinclair rested his hand on his friend's broad shoulder. "The butler, maid, and footman have also been murdered. But

I'm so sorry for your loss, Sax. I know how much this must hurt you."

"Do you? I'm in damned agony. There was a letter with that fucking ribbon."

Portia flinched at his language.

"A fucking letter that claimed she'd paid for her sins. God, I want to find this bastard and throttle the life out of him. I want to rip him limb from limb, then tear out his heart. I want him to die in the most painful way possible."

"You won't have to do that. I will," Sinclair said gruffly. "I don't have much to live for, Sax. You have your life ahead of you. I'll get vengeance. Don't worry."

"What do you mean that you don't have much to live for?" Portia breathed. She didn't understand.

But Saxonby broke in, "I'll get my own fucking revenge."

"No, you're my friend. You've been one of the best friends I ever had. You were there for me at Eton when . . . suffice to say you know more about me than anyone. I never could explain it to you, Sax, but you helped me in ways you don't even know about. You saved my life. If it weren't for you . . . I would have been dead before I was fifteen years of age. You indeed saved my wretched bloody life. I was the one who fucked it up years later, but I still owe you."

Portia gaped at him, mystified.

"Have you been drinking, Sin? I don't know what in blazes you're talking about," Saxonby said.

"It doesn't matter," Sinclair muttered. "What matters is that this has to end. Por—Miss Love was almost killed by a trap. Georgiana, who meant so much to you, is—is gone. I'm tired of being a step behind this fiend. I have an idea—a plan." He leveled his intense gaze at his friend. "There is a clue here, an important clue, and I think I've finally seen it."

Portia felt as if she'd been buffeted to and fro by the hurricane-like sea winds. Dizzy and knocked about and unsure what was going on. "What clue?" she cried, then realized she shouldn't be shouting such things.

But Sinclair, infuriatingly, only shook his head. "I can't reveal my plans yet."

Those words made her freeze. "Why can't you? I thought we were working together," she said, much more quietly.

"My duty is to protect you. I am not going to let anything happen to you."

"As I failed Georgiana?" Saxonby asked grimly.

"Not your fault. You didn't know what was to happen. And you warned her—" He broke off. "I wonder if she heeded your words. I suspect she didn't drink willingly, but was forced to consume it."

Saxonby jerked his head up, his eyes empty. "Forced?"

But how could the killer have done that, when the killer was in the kitchens?

Portia was about to ask, when Sinclair said, "I need an idea of when she was killed, Sax. I know it's hard to think of this, but I need to know. When did you see her in the morning? When did you discover her body upstairs?"

"She went to her room an hour ago, to rest. I found her about five minutes ago."

"An hour ago," Portia echoed. "The murderer could have forced poor Lady Linley to drink the sherry before going down to the kitchens. But that . . . that is horrible."

Sinclair gave a curt nod of his head. At the same moment, Saxonby made an agonizing, keening cry. "I'm going to find this bas—"

Sinclair grabbed his friend's arm. "I don't want you to do something stupid, Sax. Something that would see you hanged. I believe I can catch this bastard. But first, if I may, I would like to see Georgiana."

They walked up the stairs, Portia at Sinclair's side. Saxonby marched grimly up ahead of them, still drinking.

Sinclair had tucked her hand into the crook of his arm, then rested his hand over hers. As if making sure she was definitely at his side. The tender gesture made her feel breathtakingly close to him. The words he'd said made her feel a thousand miles apart.

"What did you mean that Sax—Saxonby, I mean—saved your life when you were at school?"

"I was lost, depressed, hurting. Saxonby helped me. I don't think he even understands how much he did for me."

She sensed that was all he was going to tell her. Curiosity ate at her, but it wasn't proper to pry.

"Why did you say you don't have much to live for?"

He met her gaze, his eyes filled with such longing, it twisted her heart.

"I lost the only person who made my life worth anything. That was you, angel. I can never have you now."

"I think you've changed," she whispered. "You have changed for the better, Julian." There, she called him by his Christian name. She had not dared to use it before now because it touched her heart too much. "I know you have."

He shook his head. "I've learned about regret. But I still could never have married you. I would have ruined you."

"Ruined me how, if you had married me?"

"You were good, kind, innocent. I would have destroyed you."

"Why?"

"I would have broken your heart, Portia. I would have made you cynical. I would have gone to brothels and orgies. I would have tried to fight the urges, but they would have beaten me in the end."

"I don't believe it. You could have fought—if you really wanted to."

He inclined his head. "True. But I'm weak, love. And . . . hell, stupid when it comes to sex. But I have to show some intelligence in this, our hunt for a killer. I have to figure out what this bastard wants. I have to try to understand his—or her—motivation for killing, try to figure out who will be attacked next. The fiend leaves no clues—except the one clue of the ribbon that we are supposed to find."

She stared, wide-eyed. "How can you know who will be next to be attacked? I never dreamed someone would want to murder all the servants at once."

His brows drew together. "That's the damnably strange thing about this. Why try to eliminate them all?"

"I don't know." Desperately she tried to think of a reason. What would the guests do now without servants? There would have been no meals. No maid. No footman. It eliminated a strong man in the footman—was that the idea? "Maybe it was to make us more vulnerable."

His brows rose. "What do you mean?"

"The footman was young and strong, so he could have helped capture the killer. Without the cook and the maid, the courtesans and gentlemen would have to fend for themselves."

"That is a good point. But the attack on the footman looked more driven by rage than by logical plan."

She shivered. "Who could have thought of doing such a thing to a human being?"

"It's amazing the ways people can think to torture others. And enjoy it."

Those words made her blood feel ice-cold. He spoke as if he knew. Then she remembered the things—the shocking things— he'd told her he needed, that he went to brothels to get. "I know there is something you are not telling me. I wish you would trust me."

He shook his head. "There are things I can't talk about. That I've never told anyone."

They'd reached the top of the stairs and were walking down the corridor. As they passed the rooms, Portia wanted to speak with Sinclair, but all she could think of was that there were bodies lying on beds behind some of those closed doors.

They passed Willoughby's door and Sinclair hesitated. "Of any of the guests I would have pegged as a murderer with a sadistic sense of humor, it would have been Willoughby. But he's dead. Lying on an upstairs bed."

"With his skull cleaved in. There's so much of his head missing, we know without a doubt he's dead," Saxonby muttered.

"Sax, careful. Portia is tough, but she is too sensitive for blunt talk."

"I am not," she said.

"I covered up Georgiana," Saxonby added gruffly. "She will lie there too in her room."

Sinclair's eyes softened. "Hell, I am sorry, Sax."

Desperation spiked through Portia. She longed to ease Saxonby's pain, but what could be done? "We must figure out who is behind this," she cried. "There is the Incognita and the Old Madam. But are they capable of this? Do they have the strength? Of the men, we have two earls left. Both are strong enough, but is one this clever . . . ?"

"And there is Sin and I," Saxonby muttered.

"I can't believe it of . . . of either of you." She gazed at him. "I know you, Sinclair. I knew you ten years ago. I knew you weren't capable of such things. When you came to London, you seemed so . . . so sweet."

Saxonby gave a pained grin at that—one that vanished quickly. "Sweet? Yes, you did seem to be a complete innocent when you first came. But Willoughby lured you into destructive vices. Worse than anything the Wicked Dukes had done. Which again makes Willoughby the most likely suspect."

"You were unlike any gentleman I'd ever encountered," she went on. "On the very first night I met you, you saved my life from a pimp. And I know you would never hurt anyone else."

Sinclair shook his head. "That is not entirely true. I wasn't innocent then. I had hurt people. I had hurt members of my family." He looked agonized. "I had even been called out in a duel with my own brother. Will didn't lure me into hell. He just pointed me in the right direction. I craved all those things. I don't want you to believe I'm something I'm not, Portia."

"Are you telling me that you are the killer? Because I can't believe that. I won't."

"Not the killer," Sinclair said. "But I'm not the man you believe me to be. I let you believe things about me that weren't true. I proposed marriage to you knowing they weren't true. I'm sorry. I just want you to know I'm not worthy of you." He cleared his throat. "I don't want you to think I don't trust your deductive skills, Sax, but I'd like to see Georgiana's room for myself. I have an idea—it could be wrong, but there's something I need to see. . . ."

Portia wished he would share his idea. But she would watch him to see what he did, what he looked at. And she would figure it out.

Why? To protect him, that was why. She was in danger, yes, but Sinclair was speaking about going after this killer by himself. That idea terrified her.

"After that, I should question the guests," Sinclair said.

"See which ones are left alive," Saxonby said heavily.

Then she heard Sinclair murmurer quietly to his friend, "You know, I have an idea to flush out the murderer. Portia is right. It doesn't seem likely to be one of the people left. The madam, the cook, Rutledge, or the other earl. If Will weren't dead . . . Hell, there's something I want to know—"

Sinclair sprinted up the stairs. Portia caught up to him. He stood in Willoughby's room. Walked over and drew down the sheet. Portia stayed in the door, but still gagged at the awful odour. Then he pulled the sheet back up.

Rubbing his chin, he walked back to the door. "Now Georgiana's room. Sax, would you come with me? I need to ask you . . . uh, something about this morning. And, Portia, I need you to stay in our bedchamber. Where you will be safe."

She sputtered, but Saxonby said, "Do as he asks, Miss Love. He only wants to protect you."

So she agreed to wait in the room, but only because it would upset poor Saxonby if she had an argument with Sinclair. The men waited while she locked her door; then she heard their footsteps recede as they went away together to Lady Linley's room.

What was it Sinclair wanted to do that he did not want her to see? Why had he gone to look at Willoughby again?

She'd thought they were partners in this. So why was he being so secretive?

* * *

Portia had almost worn a hole in the floor from pacing. It had been two hours since Sinclair and Saxonby had gone off. Had something happened to them? Her stomach plunged to her toes; then she heard loud voices outside her door.

"Of the remaining guests, you have the wit and strength to carry this out. You're the only one capable. I know you have lost women in your life, Sax. You could want revenge. These people could have hurt someone you love."

Was that Sinclair? Shocked, she hastened to the door and yanked it open.

Saxonby looked stunned. "What in hell are you saying, Sin? We've been friends since Eton. You can't seriously think me responsible for this."

Both men stood outside the door. Sinclair wore such a ruthless expression, she felt chills.

"It's the only damn solution," he said. "You're the only one with the brains for this. I don't know your motive, but I know no one else could be capable of such brilliance."

"And I'd kill Georgiana?"

"Love can turn to hate easily enough. We both know that. Georgiana had sex with other men here."

"So what are you planning to do about this mad accusation?"

Portia felt disorientated, as if she'd walked in on the middle of a play. This all felt surreal. These men were friends. What had happened between them? Why did Sinclair think it was Saxonby? What had he discovered? Could he be right?

"I have to stop you, Sax. I challenge you to a duel. Pistols. On the lawn by the terrace."

"A duel?" Portia heard her voice rise to a screech. "You can't do this!"

But Sinclair's dark eyes burned with a wild fury. "You've done this, Sax. You're mad and I am going to stop you."

17

It wasn't dawn, but Sin's thoughts kept going back to the only duels he'd ever had. One had been Willoughby, over the innocent young lady Will had ruined. The duel before that had been when he was sixteen. His brother's wife, Estella, had revealed to his brother than she'd been sleeping with Sin since he was a boy of twelve. Sin had known it was wrong, but somehow he couldn't say no to her. Estella used to threaten him to get what she wanted. At fifteen, he'd refused to sleep with her anymore. He found the courage to say no. She told his older brother about the affair out of spite.

And at sixteen, Sin had faced the hellish choice of shooting his own brother on a dueling field or letting himself be killed. . . .

Christ, he had to keep focused.

"Take your position," he growled to Saxonby. His good friend. They'd been boys together at Eton—boys with dark pasts, with secrets they wanted to keep hidden. They'd met two other boys who also had secrets to hide: Grey, now the Duke of Greybrooke, and Cary, the Duke of Caradon.

Fog wreathed around he and Sax, like ghosts ready to welcome one of them to hell. Cold, damp air clung to the back of his neck, left a film of water on his face.

They had taken a position on the grass beyond the terrace, halfway between the flagstones and the edge of the cliff. It was close enough for them to be seen by people in the house.

He heard Sax puff out a long, harsh breath.

Sin stole a glance at the house—in the cold light he could only see reflections of the iron-gray clouds on the window panes. Was anyone watching them?

The remaining guests had to be.

Sax was a damn good shot. He knew it. But Sin was also an excellent shot. Even as a young man, he'd been good enough to deliberately miss his brother. His brother hadn't missed him, however. . . .

Focus, damn it.

The terrace door shut with a bang. Through the mist he could see a dress of ivory, thick auburn hair. Portia had come out on the terrace. Damn, he'd told her to keep away from this.

"We'll count off twenty paces," he growled. Sax's shoulders bumped against his as they stood back-to-back. "On the count of three, we fire."

"On whose count?" Sax demanded.

Before Sin could respond, Sax said, "Wait. It's Miss Love."

Portia was running toward them. Her hair was falling out of its pins. Her face was almost ghostly white, and she looked likely as scared as he had been on that morning at Chalk Farm when he was sixteen and knew he was damned—whether he won the duel or not.

Guilt hit him with crippling force, but he shook it off.

Sax turned to Portia. "Miss Love, will you do the honors? Tell us to start walking. Tell us when to fire."

"This is madness!" she cried. "People are being murdered, and the two of you are being preposterous. Sinclair, please."

"He's a madman, Portia," he barked at her. "Keep out of this."

"I think *you* are going mad," she shouted back.

No doubt that was what she thought. But he had to go through with this.

"I'll count," Sax shouted. "Since you're going to cheat any-way, aren't you, Sin? You are as mad as a hatter. You think I'm a killer, without any evidence. Without reason. And I fear you plan to shoot first."

"You can do the count." Sin didn't answer the damning ac-cusations.

He began to stride away, counting off twenty paces. His boot soles thudded on the flagstones. He heard Sax's steps.

Ten . . .

Eleven . . .

He continued to pace. His heartbeat sped up.

Nineteen . . .

What should she do? Run in between them and try to stop this madness? Run to Sinclair and stop him? But that left him at the risk of being shot.

Portia stood on the cold, stone terrace, frozen to her very soul, while Sinclair and Saxonby marched away from each other across the grass. She heard their voices count off the paces, muffled by fog.

She knew how to end battles between children—she did that in the foundling home. She had even divested angry boys of weapons. But those weapons were rulers used as swords or spoon-catapults fashioned to throw porridge. Nothing like a pistol.

She'd held one—an empty one. But she'd never fired a real one. Though she had an idea how much damage one could do.

"Sinclair, this is not the answer!" she shouted. "Come back here at once, both of you! This behavior will not be tolerated."

Children had the sense to listen. Men did not.

"Nineteen," Saxonby called out.

She had to do something. Throw something? Scream and get their attention? Yet she was terrified. What if she tried some-thing and only Sin looked at her, and he got killed?

She had the bravery to rescue children. Now she was stand-ing, frozen.

"Twenty!"

Before her eyes, in glimpses through the mist, she saw Sinclair stop. Saw him turn with his pistol raised. Saw the grim, ruthless look on his face. The wildness of his eyes—her heart shattered.

"No!" she shouted.

"One," Saxonby yelled, drowning her out.

Before he could call out the number two, Sinclair roared, "You damned murderer." And he fired.

His shot went wide. Though the veil of mist, Sin saw Sax flinch as if the shot had come close. He knew it hadn't.

"You damn, mad bastard," Saxonby shouted.

Sin heard the roar of the explosion that propelled the round metal shot at him. He jolted back, knowing this was what happened when a man took a pistol ball. He'd taken two in his shoulder in past duels after all. He staggered.

He was falling and he couldn't stop himself. His back hit the ground hard, he lost all his breath. Gasping to fill his lungs again, Sin put his hand to his heart. Red. His shirt, his waistcoat soaked through, and when he lifted his palm it was slick and red.

Portia. She must be going through hell.

He wanted to talk to her. Kiss her. Say something. But he moved his mouth and dribbled red fluid.

He closed his eyes. Getting shot in the heart didn't come without a certain amount of pain.

A hand touched him. A soft hand.

He couldn't open his eyes. His heart felt like ice. It hurt like hell. He was going to lose her. And he couldn't say anything to her.

He went completely still.

"What have you done?"

Portia fell to her knees in the grass—squishy and cold from the rain. She leaned over Sinclair. His eyes were closed. His shirt and waistcoat were soaked through red. Was he breathing? With fumbling fingers, she tried to get her hand in under his collar, which was cinched by his wretched cravat.

She could barely see him. She was looking at him through tears, a watery wall of them.

Blood dribbled from his mouth, but she wouldn't think of what that must mean. "Sinclair! Wake up!"

Come back to me. She couldn't say that. He had to be still here. He *had* to be.

Through tears, she stared at the red on his chest. Wet, sticky . . .

Vomit tried to climb up her throat. Her heartbeat slammed in her head, sounding as loud as gunshots. She had to regain control.

"God. Christ Jesus. What in Hades have I done?" The Duke of Saxonby dropped down on one knee beside her, beside Sinclair's body.

The duke pulled her back, away from Sinclair. "He shot me first. I lost my head. I thought—in that moment, I thought he had set this all up to kill me. That he was the killer and had arranged this damned duel to shoot me. I thought he'd killed Georgiana."

Portia struggled to break free of Saxonby's grip. "You didn't have to shoot to kill him. He shot first—his pistol was spent."

"I lost my head. I panicked and I wasn't thinking. It's not so easy to aim to just maim a man with duelling pistols."

She pulled back so violently she lost her balance and fell on her bottom, sliding on the grass. Saxonby looked at her sadly, then reached over and touched Sinclair's neck.

She touched his neck too. She couldn't feel anything. No pulse.

It couldn't be. It must be her fingers were too cold to feel. Or she hadn't put them in the right place. He couldn't be dead.

Someone was sobbing. Salt dribbled into her mouth. She was the one crying, and her whole body seemed to dissolve into tears. She fell against Sinclair's chest. He was still warm. She held him tight, mumbling his name against his bloodstained shirt.

"You have to be alive," she whispered. "You have to be. I just want you to be alive."

Saxonby's hands gripped her. He lifted her to her feet and this time she didn't have the strength to pull away.

"My God, Miss Love, I'm sorry. But he shot first. We have to face the fact that Sin might have been behind all of this."

Clumsily, she swept her hands over her face. Fiercely wiping tears away. "What are you talking about?" Anger flooded her voice now. Anger at this man. Even despairing anger at Sinclair.

"Don't you see?" Saxonby said earnestly. "He pushed us into this duel with illogical, unfounded accusations. Breaking the rules that conduct a gentleman, he shot first. I believe it was his intent to murder me. The duel was a smokescreen for my death. I believe Sinclair may well have been the killer."

It was as if she were standing on an island made of fog and it just dissolved beneath her. Portia's stomach dropped sickeningly. "I don't believe that. I'll *never* believe that."

"If he's not, we're still in danger. I vow I will protect you with my life."

"You killed Sin. I don't want you near me. Stay away from me."

She took a step back. She didn't want to leave Sinclair's body, but fear was clutching at her.

"If he hadn't shot first, I wouldn't have killed him," Saxonby muttered. "I would have known he was still . . . Sinclair. The honorable man I knew."

Saxonby bent and lifted the—the body. He staggered as he did, but he was strong enough to do it. She wanted to be sick, but she also had to be strong. She had to be composed. For that was what she did—she did not fall to pieces.

Yet she wanted to.

Saxonby let Sinclair's lifeless form fall over his shoulder and she felt almost as lifeless. "I'll take him up to his room, like the others—" He broke off. "No, not his room. That is your bed-chamber as well. I'll take him to one of the empty rooms."

Numb, she followed Saxonby. Carrying Sinclair's empty pistol.

She didn't know why she'd picked it up. She was cradling it against her chest, holding it with two hands.

He couldn't be dead.

This had to be a nightmare.

She pinched herself. It hurt, so this was real, but she couldn't even squeak at the sharp pain. She was too empty. She trailed behind Saxonby, who was still carrying Sinclair's body over his shoulder, straining because Sinclair was strong and powerfully built.

Through the terrace doors. Into the hallway and to the stairs, past frightened faces. And frantic whispers.

"He killed the Duke of Sinclair!"

"Sinclair shot first. So who is the killer? Could it have been Sin? Or Sax?"

"I say, Saxonby, halt where you are!"

That was the Corinthian Earl. He barked, "You've just killed a man."

"And what in hell are you going to do about it?" Saxonby demanded. "It was a duel—a duel and Sin damn well cheated. I am not the lunatic who has murdered people on this island. But this insanity has just caused me to take the life of my good friend. Now, leave me the hell alone, and let me take Sin's body upstairs."

At Saxonby's angry bark, the earl glowered.

"Let him go," Portia said.

"You could be the madwoman behind these killings, Miss Love," the brawny earl snapped. "No one can be trusted. I trust only myself."

He lunged toward her pistol.

She gasped and jumped back, holding the pistol away from his reach. "It's empty! Don't be daft. We must keep our heads." That was what Sinclair had not done. Now he was gone. . . .

Pain almost made her fall to her knees.

"For all I know, you're going to reload that blasted thing and shoot the rest of us," the Earl of Blute spat.

"This is utterly insane," she said firmly. "You suspect me when I would never hurt a living soul. I suspect you and I know nothing about you except you are arrogant and strong. We're all fearful of each other. We can't attack each other, for heaven's sake. Let's not do the killer's work for him. Or her."

She couldn't say any more. Not around the swelling of her throat. Grief gripped her heart like desperate, clutching hands. Tears spilled over and rolled down her cheeks once more.

"Leave her," the Elegant Incognita warned. "Leave her alone. She has lost someone."

"She could be the killer," Blute insisted.

"Then be careful and watch your back, my lord." Clarissa gave him a wry look. "The mysterious Lord Genvere doesn't even exist, I'm sure. So the genius behind this sadistic madness could even be me."

"I doubt that," the Earl of Rutledge snorted.

"Do you?" snapped Clarissa. "Never underestimate a woman, Rutledge."

Everyone glared at the Incognita, then at Portia. She had never been stared at so intensely and with such cold, hate-filled eyes since she'd gone into gaming hells and taverns to rescue young women from prostitution. Yet she had done nothing. It was just mad, dangerous suspicion. It was like an infection, spreading and turning foul.

Saxonby made his way up the stairs with Rutledge, both of them now carrying Sinclair. She followed. She never dreamed it would be so hard to lift her feet. She felt so heavy.

He was gone. Julian was gone.

He was Julian again to her for that moment—the beautiful, beautiful man she had fallen in love with.

Rutledge and Saxonby puffed and grunted to the end of the corridor, to the empty bedrooms. In moments, Julian's body was laid on the bed. A stripped bed with a white sheet.

She flinched at the sight of the blood on his waistcoat and shirt. "I should bathe him. Clean him."

"No." Saxonby gripped her shoulder and pushed her out of

the room. "You are in shock. You need to recover, and seeing his wounds is not going to help you."

He closed the door. Shooed her away. She turned, intending to argue, but he turned the key in the lock, then pocketed it.

"I would like to be able to see him."

"That will only bring you pain, Miss Love." Saxonby steered her away from the room. "I should have some food brought to you—"

"Brought by whom, Saxonby? The servants are gone. They've been killed. And cooked by whom? The cook has said she won't return downstairs, because she's too afraid. Besides, would anyone trust any food brought to them anymore?"

Strangely, thinking of this took some of the awful pain away—it distracted her. People needed to eat. Managing meals at the foundling home was one of her largest tasks.

Food was needed for survival. The innocents amongst these people needed her. "I need to think of what we must do for dinner."

Saxonby stared at her, stunned. "You've just lost Sin, but you are thinking of dinner."

"I've spent my life managing a foundling home," she said quietly. "I know that, even in grief, such things have to be dealt with."

"You didn't care about him. You couldn't have done—not and be so calm now."

Something snapped inside her. She physically felt it, within her soul.

Suddenly, she lunged at Saxonby. It seemed to happen without thought. Her hand was raised, her palm flying toward his face. Portia stopped it before she slapped him.

Once, she'd been to Brighton and she'd played in the sea with her father and a large wave had knocked her down. Grief and pain and a pit of shock and sadness swallowed her up, just like that wave had done.

"He's gone. I'm never going to see him again. Never hear him laugh. Never get exasperated by him. Never—never kiss him."

It felt like she was freezing inside. Her whole body was turning to ice.

"I'm sorry," the Duke of Saxonby muttered. "I had no right to say that. It's obvious you are in pain—"

"Leave me alone!" she cried. She rushed into the bedroom and slammed the door behind her. The key was in the lock on the inside, and she turned it. Though her hands felt frozen and it was hard to make her fingers move.

Portia stood in the bedchamber, shaking. She'd lost children from the home. She'd lost her father. Her mother was ill and often completely forgot who she was.

She'd always found strength to endure.

Hollowly, she looked at the bed. Heavens, she could picture Julian's grin—wicked, bracketed by deep, seductive lines. She would never forget how he looked with his long body stretched out on the bed. Or how delicious it had felt—all tumbling nerves and awareness—when he'd helped her with her dress for the first time. When she'd almost melted at the touch of his fingers.

Oh . . . oh goodness.

She didn't just love him. She loved him even *more* than she had when she'd thought he was a sweet and innocent nineteen-year-old lad.

She fell to her knees by the bed. Buried her face into the counterpane. She remembered the warmth of his body against hers as he'd held her. The delectable male way he smelled. She remembered touching him, wanting to savor those moments.

She sobbed and sobbed. And when there wasn't anything left in her anymore, no more tears, she stayed utterly still, as the light faded from the sky.

18

Hell, he couldn't do this.

Sin leaned back against the stone wall, whipped by the howling wind, dressed in his black trousers, with a black coat over his red-soaked shirt. Unbeknownst to Portia, he watched her through the glass panes of the bedroom's balcony doors. Also unknown to her, he was alive.

Dumbfounded, he'd watched for more than an hour. All the while, she'd cried. She would raise her head for a few moments, as if gasping in air, then her shoulders would shake and she would bury her lovely face into the bedspread again.

After a while, she stopped shaking and she was motionless, with her cheek pressed against a soaking wet bedcover.

Watching her cry was like having his heart yanked out of his chest.

He moved to the window, lifted his hand to tap—

"Damn it, what in hell are you doing?"

The harsh half whisper, half bark came from below. Sin leaned over and saw Sax standing there, arms folded over his chest, a glower on his face. His friend scanned the grounds, watching in case someone saw them.

He had to make Sax understand. Heavy with guilt, Sin clambered over the railing of the balcony. He grabbed the thick stalk of ivy that he'd climbed up, set his boot against the cut stone wall, and climbed down the wall.

He and Sax retreated into the swift-growing evening shadows, hidden by a clump of straggly bushes near the house's wall.

"What in blazes were you doing up there?" Sax demanded. "What if she saw you? What if someone else saw you? Our insane killer, for example?"

"She was sobbing her heart out. Over me."

"What did you think she would do, once she thought you dead?"

"I don't know. I never thought she'd be heartbroken like that."

Saxonby rolled his eyes to the sky. "She said yes to your proposal ten years ago. Didn't you know then that she was in love with you?"

"I never knew for certain that she was really in love with me."

"What kind of stupidity is that?" Sax demanded.

"I never dreamed she would care about me now. Besides, this doesn't mean she loves me. It means I've hurt her. I can't do this. I've got to tell her the truth—"

"No," Sax broke in. "You can't do it yet. Her reaction will assure the killer you are actually dead. You shouldn't have even left your damn bedroom yet. What if our lunatic goes to check on you? To see if there is actually a body in the room?"

"You locked the door earlier. I presume you took the key and didn't leave it in the door. I came out through the window and climbed down the wall. I kept away from other windows. Dressed in black, I think I'm well disguised."

This had been his plan. Fake his own death and, with the killer thinking he was out of the way, watch from the shadows. "I'm going to watch Portia from the balcony tonight," he said defiantly.

"What if you have to force your way in?"

"I carried a fireplace poker up there, to break in through the door."

He saw the doubt in Sax's expression. "Don't try to stop me, Sax. I'm afraid this fiend will try to attack her tonight." His heart thudded. If Sax tried to stop him, prevent him from protecting Portia—

Hell, what would he do? Fight Sax? Knock him out? Duel with him for real? He gripped his friend's shoulder. "Now that I'm out of the way, why would he wait?"

Sax frowned. "Even with you supposedly dead, it might not be his or her plan to attack Portia. She will likely be perfectly safe and you risk exposing the plan on the first night."

"I refuse to risk her safety." He glowered.

Sax groaned. "I wish I could have protected Georgiana. How can I ask you to let Portia be at risk?"

He rubbed Sax's shoulder. "Sax, hell, I'm sorry Georgiana is gone."

"I will look after Portia, Sin, but I understand what you need to do."

"Thank you. Would you take her down to the kitchens so she can get some food from the stores you locked up? Then bring her back up to her room and make sure she locks herself in."

Sax nodded. They parted and Sin climbed back up the wall again.

She must end this. End it before everyone went mad and attacked each other.

It was the only thought Portia would let herself have. Anything else spiralled into thinking about Sinclair and the pain— the pain would swallow her alive.

With shaking fingers, Portia fumbled with her dress fastenings. She moved as if she were a hundred years old. Horrible dress—it was a nightmare to remove. She'd needed Sinclair to help her fasten it and she couldn't manage it herself.

Oh heavens, she remembered when he'd helped her that very first time. When his lips had brushed her neck. Tears fell and she was just about to sink on the bed and have another crying jag when there came a sharp rap on the door.

"Miss Love? I thought you need help getting undressed." The voice was a woman's. Cultured.

It could be a ruse, but she just didn't have the energy to care. Portia opened the door, staring into the Elegant Incognita's lovely face.

"I assume you do not trust me to allow me in, so I can unfasten the dress here."

"Thank you," she whispered. Perhaps she would turn her back and the Incognita would slit her throat. But she found it hard to care. She just felt so empty.

But Clarissa didn't murder her. The woman simply helped by undoing the fastenings she couldn't reach. "I'm so sorry," Clarissa murmured. "You should get some sleep." And she closed the door.

Portia locked it. Then she pushed the dress down and stepped out of it. It should be hung up properly and she tried, but tears came before she did, and the dressed ended up draped over a chair along with her simple stays, designed so she could do them herself.

She tried to brush her hair. Two halfhearted passes with the brush before she let it fall to the vanity top. The mirror reflected her face—the pale white face of a woman who looked as if she were staring into hell.

Her whole body felt heavy as she slid into bed wearing her shift. She pulled up the counterpane.

She rescued people—it was what she'd always tried to do. There were innocent people here who deserved rescue.

There must be a way to figure out who was responsible for these horrible murders.

In London, there were Bow Street Runners who pursued criminals. How they caught lawbreakers, she had no idea. If a crime was committed in the stews, Portia would know people who would know the identity of the perpetrator. Sometimes she did endeavor to find out, if a child required protection. She knew who to ask to find out which madams were snatching children into brothels. Or who to stop if young children were being recruited to be pickpockets.

What did she do when she had to rescue a child in the stews—when a child's future, or even life, hung in the balance?

She bluffed.

She had faced terrifying men with only an unloaded pistol. But holding an unloaded pistol on the guests wouldn't help her now.

And then—

The idea came.

She closed her eyes. Swollen, terribly puffy, her eyelids ached. But even with her eyes shut, even dizzy with exhaustion, she felt her wits work. She had an idea, a tiny inkling. Fear slithered over her as if snakes crawled on the bedsheets. But she had to fight fear and find the courage she used when she rescued children. . . .

Goodness, she must have fallen asleep after all. Portia opened her eyes and saw gray light glimmering at the edge of the curtains. It was morning.

Purpose gave her strength. She pushed back the bedcovers. Threw on her gown. Pushed open the door and stepped into the hushed, elegant corridor.

There, ahead of her was the bulky form of the cook. The woman stood at the top of the stairs, clad in a gray shapeless gown. Mrs. Kent gasped as Portia emerged, clapping her hand to her mouth.

"Oh, miss. You startled me," she muttered as she dropped her hand.

Portia didn't know grand houses, but she knew enough to know the cook didn't come onto the level of the guests' bedrooms. Servants' rooms were upstairs. "Where are you going?"

"Oh . . . er . . . the truth is, I'm afraid to be upstairs on my own. I'm afraid to go up the servants' stairs alone. Could I use one of these empty bedrooms? I know it's not what is usually done, but I don't think people are usually murdered in great houses."

Portia had to carry out her idea. "Mrs. Kent, I will arrange for you to have a bedroom. But will you come down to the kitchen with me?"

"Oh, miss, I can't make any breakfast. I can't face going down there."

Portia held out her hand reassuringly. "Well, we cannot starve. And there is safety in numbers. We shall go together—"

But Mrs. Kent made a small cry. And dug her heels in the soft carpet of the corridor. "But, miss, how can I know you will not kill me?"

Portia let out a huff of frustration. Yet it was true. How could any of them trust any other? The only person she trusted was Sin—now he was gone.

"Then we should all go," she said firmly. "All of the innocent people should be able to overpower one guilty one. And if we all eat the same food, in front of each other, then we will know the food is not poisoned. The killer won't want to eat, if it is."

That was what they did. Portia cooked porridge in front of all the others. They all held their bowls to their mouths, shoveling in food. They looked like rats, holding their plates close to their chests, with eyes shifting rapidly and fearfully about, watching each other.

Then Portia set down her bowl. She took a deep breath. "May I have your attention?" she said firmly. "Listen to me, please! I know who the killer is."

All of them—the four women, the two earls, the Duke of Saxonby—stared at her in shock.

She knew what she was doing. She just did not know who the killer was. But that was part of the plan.

"Who?" cried the cook.

"How could you know who it is?" shouted the Old Madam.

"I now know what the killer's motive is. This is about a child. A young girl. She was sent to a foundling home. Perhaps she is dead now—I don't know that. But she must have been hurt very badly. All of us have been accused of sins. We are all here because these supposed sins are related to this poor girl. Lord Willoughby was notorious for ravishing innocent women. The handsome Viscount Sandhurst might have been a seducer also, or perhaps he broke the girl's heart."

Portia watched the women as she spoke. The Old Madam and the Incognita were of an age to be the child's mother. The cook was too, but would Mrs. Kent have moved in these circles? Would a cook have come up with the plan to hold an orgy, invite people one hated to it, and eliminate them one by one?

The young courtesan, Nellie Upton, was the right age to be the child.

"The Marquis of Crayle," she continued, "Perhaps he took advantage of a young girl and carried out his perversions on her. Perhaps he whipped her."

She watched for a flinch. A flicker of the eye. A sharp breath.

Nothing. Each woman—including the cook—stared at her, glanced at each other, and showed nothing at all in their faces except surprise.

"She could not have been very young," Portia went on. "A long time must have passed since she went to the foundling home until she was old enough to go to orgies. Perhaps that was why Sinclair was brought here. The girl went to his orgies."

She pointed at the Old Madam. "Perhaps you dragged her into one of your brothels?"

"I have no idea what you are talking about! Who is this girl?"

She looked at Nellie. "Perhaps it is you."

"Not I," the girl said huskily. "I was born on a farm. I know who my mother is—I grew up with her, me dad, four brothers, and two sisters."

Which could, of course, be a lie. Portia looked at the Incognita. "You might have introduced her into this world. Maybe that was your sin. Or you worked against her, jealous of her youth, and you forced her to end up on the street."

She watched Clarissa's up-tilted green eyes. Was that a touch of sorrow that she saw?

"Is this girl alive or dead now?" She walked back and forth, as if thinking. But she was watching. She watched the two earls too. One could have a sister who had been ruined and had fallen into disaster.

Then she turned to the Incognita, aware of the woman's look of sadness. "Did you ever have a child? A daughter?"

"I did." The woman's voice was husky. "I had two children. A girl. And then a boy. And both were stillborn. Both of them."

"We have only your word for that," Portia said. She believed the pain in the woman's eyes. Yet Clarissa did not say she had *only* two children.

"You said you know who the killer is," the Old Madam said sharply. "Get on with it. Who is it. And what of Lord Genvere? What's his part in this?"

"Lord Genvere does not exist. I began to suspect it after Lord Crayle died. I began to believe there was no Genvere and that the killer was one of us. Then, I realized that if you take the letters of the name and rearrange them, they spell 'revenge.' That is what this is all about. These murders are about vengeance."

A few gasps of surprise came from the guests.

"I will not reveal the name of the killer now," Portia said. "I need one final piece of evidence. Once I have it, I will be able to prove a case against this person. I will be able to take it to a magistrate, and the killer will hang."

"But how will we get off this island?"

"There must be a boat on the island," Portia said lightly. "After all, once we were all disposed of, our killer needed a way to leave. The storm has passed and the weather is clearing, so we'll be able to leave the island. Alive and with evidence to convict the killer."

It was all a bluff. Even the bit about the boat.

What she hoped was this made her a target.

In her bedchamber, she had found Sinclair's box for his

dueling pistols. Within, he kept more of the small metal pistol balls and powder. She had loaded the pistol. She was carrying it now, tucked in her garter, under her skirt. So for the first time in her life, she was carrying a loaded pistol with her.

Horrifically, it was the very pistol that had killed Sinclair.

When would the blow strike? Her shoulders were knotted with tension. Her heart continued to thump so loud an attacker could probably stomp up behind her and she wouldn't hear.

She left the kitchen—left the other guests muttering to each other. The Duke of Saxonby accompanied her.

She stopped by the door that led to the gallery. No one would attack while the strong, silent Duke of Saxonby walked at her side.

She faced him with, she hoped, an expression of honesty on her face. "I . . . I must have some time alone. I need to think."

"My dear, you just put the cat among the pigeons," Saxonby pointed out.

"I just wish to walk in the gallery. It's deserted. The other guests are downstairs. I am sure I will be safe for a short while."

"Allow me to watch over you."

"No! No, I need some time alone. You must allow me this." Her voice rose in desperation.

The duke hesitated. Then nodded. "All right, Miss Love."

She left him in the corridor, went into the gallery, and began to walk its length. But first, she lifted her skirts and took out her weapon.

She moved slowly, hiding the pistol in the folds of her skirt. Her shoes tapped on the dark parquet floor. Weak sunlight was fighting to push between the clouds and filtered in through the tall windows.

She was sure the killer had followed her. She'd goaded enough.

Her footsteps echoed in the space, drowning out other sound. She stopped in the middle of the gallery and turned to the window. If Saxonby was the killer, if he came out and attacked her, she would shoot him. He didn't know she was armed. She had let him believe she would be bait without a weapon.

She moved closer to the window. One ray of sunlight sliced between clouds and streamed to the terrace.

Could she shoot a man in cold blood? Even to save herself and the others?

"So here you are." The voice shot into the quiet, making her jump. She turned toward the far end of the gallery. A figure stood there. Black mask. Swirling black cloak. A figure holding a gleaming, vicious, medieval ax.

Was it a woman confronting her? She couldn't tell. The person looked tall. Well-built and not fat or thin. That ax made her freeze.

Remember you have a pistol.

"You're a daft thing. A stupid fool." The killer's voice . . . rough, raspy, slightly high-pitched, but falsely so. She couldn't tell if it was a man's voice or a woman's.

The person stepped forward, holding the ax. "These other deaths had been too clean. I intend to make your blood run." Glee danced through those words.

Portia lifted her pistol, aiming at the cloaked figure. "Halt right there!" she commanded.

"You'll never hit me from there. I can see you shake."

The person began to run toward her, ax held high.

An explosion roared in her ears. She had pulled the trigger. And in her shock, she'd missed.

Mocking laughter rang through the gallery.

A second shot exploded. The killer screamed. The ax dropped with a clang and the killer clutched his—or her—right arm. Spinning, the figure ran away from her. Saxonby charged into the gallery from the door at the other end. He sprinted, holding a pistol, and she reclaimed her shocked wits and ran after him. The killer had vanished when they both reached the doorway at the end of the gallery.

She turned to Saxonby. "You saved my life. I . . . thank you.

I would be dead now if not for you. My foolish shot missed. Your shot actually hurt the fiend."

She was relieved. And in agony. Saxonby wasn't the murderer, obviously. Which meant Sinclair had thrown his life away for *nothing*.

"I am no hero, Miss Love," Saxonby muttered. "I ignored your request and instead took steps to protect you. But I was not the one—I mean, my shot unfortunately did not kill him. Why did you do this foolish thing? Make yourself a target. *Do you know who the killer is?*"

She shook her head. Sagged against the wall. "No, I thought I would make the killer come after me, and if I was armed, I would put an end to this. If you had not been there, I would have been dead. I feel Sinclair is dead because of me. He was so determined to protect me that he acted on impulse, in desperation. It was my fault and I wanted to stop this madness."

"I won't tolerate you taking more foolish risks, Miss Love," Saxonby said. "If Sin knew, he'd kill me. Damn it." With a sweep of his hand, he pushed back his longish silver-blond hair. "I don't know what in Hades I should do. I want you to go to your bedchamber. We'll search it to ensure it's safe. Then you are to lock yourself in there. I'll come for you soon. There is something I have to do."

Sin paced his room, the room in which he was supposed to be lying dead. Using his key, Sax had slipped in to confront him about firing that shot—the one that had saved Portia—and poured two glasses of brandy. Sin tossed back both of them, leaving Sax to pour himself another.

The brandy seared as it went down, but it didn't warm his heart.

Sax eyed him with disapproval. "You took a hell of a risk making that shot, Sin," he growled. "You could have been caught."

He stalked to the brandy decanter. Picked it up, then set it down. To try to warm his frozen heart and soul, he would end up pickling his brain. He needed his wits. But he was so cold with fear. And with something else—something that felt damn close to despair.

He turned on his friend. "What in hell was I going to do, Sax, stand by when she was in danger?"

"Obviously not, but—"

"So I have to tell her the truth. I have to let her know I'm not dead. Portia could have gotten herself killed. This is something I never expected. I've never had anyone care about me before."

"She cared, when she first agreed to marry you. Why shouldn't she care now?—you've devoted yourself to her safety here."

"I didn't think that was enough to make up for how badly I hurt her."

"We also care," Sax said gruffly. "The Wicked Dukes. We are your friends. That means we watch your back. And we give a goddamn if you get yourself killed. I don't know if you've noticed, but Grey and Cary are now concerned about whether we're happy—and believe we should find love, get married, and be happy. And you know I'd watch your back anytime."

Sax's words touched his heart, he had to admit.

"I know the three of you are my friends," he said, "but I don't have any damn clue how you treat someone you care about. I've never had the love of parents. I would have appreciated cold-hearted parents, as opposed to ones who sought to use and abuse me. The fact that they had to feed me made them believe I could be used as a whipping boy, an amusement, a—"

He broke off. Hell, what was he doing? He'd never revealed much about his past. The brandy was affecting him. Making him feel damned empty and lost.

"You don't have to talk about it, Sin," Sax said, running his finger around his cravat, looking awkward.

As boys they'd all known they were haunted by their pasts, but no one ever talked about it. And once they'd grown up, become men, they definitely had not talked about it.

Then, in his mind, he heard Portia's sobs again. Wrenching. Filled with pain. God, he couldn't stand it. He stalked around the room. Ended up at the fireplace, gripped the mantel with his hands and hung his head.

Behind him, Sax started to say, "I need to remind you, Sin, why we faked your death—"

"You don't," he cut in. "I did it so I could investigate while the killer believes me already dead. It meant I was no longer a target. It was also my intention to watch over Portia, protecting her without her knowing I'm alive. I just never thought my death would hurt her so much."

"Sin, the best way to protect her is to continue with the plan. Think logically."

His eyes stung. Guilt whipped him. The time he'd broken off their engagement, she had been so strong. So stoic. Just like she was when dealing with the children she rescued. He used to help her gather the children, and he'd been astounded at her courage. He'd never dreamed Portia was capable of crying like that.

Had she cried so hard over their broken engagement in private? God, had he made her feel like that? He would feel a hell of a lot better if he talked himself out of believing that. But he couldn't. He realized she must have cried like that, hurt that much.

"I can't let her suffer."

Sax's face twisted as if he was the one in pain. "At least she's alive and can feel something."

Sin turned slowly away from the mantel and clapped his friend on the shoulder. "I'm so damn sorry, Sax. I feel like I'm letting you down after you lost Georgiana. But I can't watch Portia grieve."

Did he stay with the plan to protect Portia? Reveal the truth? Reveal he wasn't dead and she'd know he'd lied to her. Betrayed her trust—again.

Would she forgive him?

"What are you going to do?" Sax asked, his voice hoarse.

"I have to confide in Portia. You're my friend, but I have to do right by her." He straightened. "Feel free to punch me in the nose if you want. Pound the tar out of me in anger."

Sax was staring at him like he was insane, Sin realized. "Why in hell would I want to do that?"

19

"There is something Sin wants you to know," the Duke of Saxonby said quietly. "Will you come with me? And promise you won't say a word?"

Portia stared at the duke, utterly lost. "What are you talking about? What could he want me to know . . . *now?*"

"Please trust me. It's important to Sin."

"Important? But . . . but he's gone."

"Trust me and come with me. No harm will come to you. And you will learn something that will make you . . . happier, I hope."

"You are speaking in riddles. Please be blunt."

"Even though we're alone, Miss Love, I can't."

Portia hesitated. They stood in the foyer. The other guests had gone into the drawing room, leaving her alone with Saxonby. The others were opening a new, sealed bottle of sherry. Would she be a fool to be lured away from the others, even by the man who had stepped forward to save her life?

She whispered, through a tight, aching throat, "I'll be quiet. What is it?"

But he just held his finger to his lips and clasped her hand. Gambling, she went with him. The Duke of Saxonby led her upstairs. They reached the door of the bedroom where they had laid Sinclair's body on the large bed. If Saxonby was going to try to kill her, she had to be ready. Maybe she could find a weapon in the room. Or maybe her last thought on this earth would be: *You are a blooming idiot.*

Very, very lightly, the Duke of Saxonby made three low coughing noises outside the closed, locked door.

"What are you—?" Portia began softly, but he held his finger to his lips. After waiting for several seconds, he coughed a fourth time.

She heard the soft click of the lock opening. The doorknob began to turn. Slowly, so it didn't make a sound.

Portia stared at it, stunned. Some of the children in the foundling home believed in ghosts. She'd always explained them away firmly, using logic. An old house, fluttering curtains, imagination . . .

But how was Sinclair's door opening?

Saxonby put his hand over the knob and turned it the rest of the way. In a low voice, but loud enough that someone might hear it if that person was trying to listen, he said, "I know you need to see him again, Miss Love. It's hard to accept that he's gone." He put his arm around her waist and propelled her into the room, using his broad shoulders to block the door from view.

The door closed behind her and the lock clicked as he turned the key. He stayed by the door, gazing at it, which was strange.

The bed curtains were drawn, plunging the room into gloomy dark.

Then something moved in her peripheral vision. A man's shape and she would have screamed but a large, masculine hand covered her mouth, and a soft voice said, "It's me, Portia. I'm not dead. Don't scream. You'll bring the rest of them running."

Sinclair's voice—husky, deep, and sincere. Just as he used to sound when he had made her melt and fall in love with him when she was nineteen. No trace of jaded wickedness.

For a moment, she thought it was all a dream—but that

hand on her mouth was real. The warm whisper of his breath on her ear was real. He was alive.

She grasped his wrist, pulled his hand from her mouth and whirled around. She was so close to his tall, strong body that her nose almost bumped his chest. He was there—soft chocolate brown hair, worried dark brown eyes, lashes that went on forever.

It really was him.

She surged forward and wrapped her arms around his neck, throwing her body hard against him. Her mouth bumped the warm skin. Stubble slightly scratched her lips, making them tingle. She laughed and sobbed, snuggled against him. She didn't care that Saxonby was a witness, and she realized that was why he was not looking in their direction.

Sinclair drew her back, lowered his mouth, and kissed her. His mouth caressed hers, teased hers. Then he tipped her back just a little, holding her, and his mouth commanded hers.

When he set her on her feet, she wobbled.

She was just a little afraid she was dreaming. "I don't understand. Saxonby felt for your pulse—he said you were dead. I felt for your pulse and found *nothing*."

He cupped her face tenderly. "I am so sorry, angel. I used some light card I found, colored it with pink-tinted face cream that belonged to Harriet, then shaped it into a curve. I slipped it under my cravat, keeping that tight so anyone who checked my pulse wouldn't be able to fit their fingers in far and wouldn't be able to see they were actually touching card. Also, Sax ensured he dragged you away before you'd touched me for long."

The matter-of-fact way he explained it suddenly made her feel cold. "That was tremendously clever. You certainly fooled me. I thought you were dead."

Sinclair winced, gazing into her eyes.

"We concocted the plan together," Saxonby added quickly. "Once Sin was 'dead,' he could investigate with impunity. We figured the murderer would be surprised, thrown off guard. Or get cocky. We hoped the fiend would give himself—or herself—away. That was the reason we couldn't let you in on the plan, Portia. We had to ensure the murderer was convinced of Sin's death."

She realized Saxonby was trying to take half the blame.

"Portia, I didn't mean to hurt you," Sinclair said hoarsely.

"But you did anyway." She pulled away from him, stepped back, and wrapped her arms around herself. What a fool she'd been. "You let me think you were dead without even a thought of what I would feel. You hurt me again, and you didn't care."

"God, Portia, I did care. It ripped my heart out to hurt you. I was afraid if you knew the truth, the murderer might see it in your eyes. And Sax promised to protect you with his life. He also promised not to tell you. I almost gave in and revealed myself to you. He talked me out of it once. Then Sax told me what you said in the kitchen. I guessed you were acting as bait to lure out the killer. I only wish my damn shot had gotten him—or her."

"*You* fired the shot that saved my life."

"I'm normally a damn better shot. But I was afraid to hit you. Portia, love, I'm sorry if I made you suffer. But I never thought you would hurt so much."

She gaped at him. "But why would you think that? Why would you think I wouldn't care?"

"I thought you still hated me, over what I did."

"I don't, Sinclair. I—" She couldn't say it, but she knew she loved him. But she was afraid to say it. He was wild and attended orgies. She was domestic and boring.

And apparently he didn't trust her enough to confide in her.

Saxonby softly cleared his throat. "I'll leave you alone to discuss things. Sin, you can tell her what we've discovered. Which isn't much. Lock the door behind me." Sax went to the door. He opened it and said, loud enough for any eavesdroppers to hear. "I'll leave you alone with him, Miss Love. To say those last things you wish to say. I'm sorry he's gone."

Then he closed the door. Sinclair took quick strides to the door and turned the key.

She watched his body move with lithe grace. She wanted to be angry he'd tricked her. She wanted to be hurt that he hadn't trusted her.

But she couldn't be.

All she could think was that he wasn't dead. Thank *heaven* he wasn't dead.

Something snapped in her. For days, she'd been surrounded by sex and by death and all she wanted was . . . was love. She wrapped her arms around his waist and pressed to his chest.

"Portia." With his words, his chest rumbled beneath her. His hands gently caressed.

No—she was tired of chaste embraces. She had thought he was gone. For twenty-four hours she'd been filled with pain. And . . . regret.

She arched up on her toes, grabbed the fabric of his shirt for balance, and kissed him. Wild and openmouthed and wanton.

Her lips caressed his, hot and demanding. She wanted to kiss him hard. She almost wanted to hurt him with her mouth. She wanted to make him be the one who was melting and begging and in pain.

Her hands ran over his chest, stroking his hard pectoral muscles through his shirt. He was so warm—warm and alive. She was heady with relief, panting with anger—how couldn't he have trusted her? But the anger made her want to touch him more.

Through his shirt, she found his nipples and she strummed them, tweaked them, played with them the way he had played with hers. She broke away from his kiss to put her mouth to his linen shirt and try to suck his nipple through the cloth. When he sucked her, it made her suffer agonies of desire and she wanted to do that to him.

Sinclair caught her shoulders and drew her back. "Portia, what are you doing?"

"What do you think I've thought about since I lost you? I kept thinking I could never hold you again. Never kiss you. I've thought of you in a grave—it's been agony."

"I'm sorry—"

"I've dreamed of what it would be like to make love with you for ten years." There. "I can't believe I admitted that. You'll laugh at me. You've done the wildest, most erotic things, and all the while you were doing that, I've foolishly dreamed about you. And now, I have you here. And I can do everything to you I've dreamed of."

"Portia—"

"I don't care about respectability. I thought I'd lost you forever. I thought I would never, ever make all those dreams come true. Then I knew I never would unless I made them happen."

Breathing hard, she put her mouth over his again. Her hands explored him, tugging his shirt, struggling to get it out of his waistband. She knew he'd never do this to her—undress her without her agreement—but she seemed to have gone mad. She wanted him desperately.

He pulled back, just enough to growl, "I used drink and orgies to try to blank out the pain of losing you. It didn't work. And when we figured I should pretend to be dead to flush out the murderer, I never thought you really cared, Portia. I'm not worth your love—"

"You're very worthy of this," she declared.

Her fingers touched the waistband of his trousers.

For ten years, she'd known she could never really have him, but she could fantasize.

Taking a deep breath, she slid her hands right down across the placket of his trousers, right to the bulge she felt there. Pressing her hand firmly, she ran her palm along it. Curled her fingers around it through the fabric. It felt alive—it swelled and moved.

She pressed tight against him before he could say no, trapping her hand against his growing erection. She felt it get longer. It was becoming quite enormous.

She dropped to her knees in front of him and pulled his trousers down with her. His cock, as he called it, sprang up. She inhaled the rich, intimate scent.

Then she opened her mouth wide—she'd never opened her mouth so big—and she bent forward and took his cock inside, marveling at the heat. Tasting his earthiness. Feeling him pulse and swell and grow so thick, she suddenly wondered if she really could do this.

"Portia, what are you doing?"

She sucked and he let out a long groan and she saw his legs shake.

She was going to do this until he collapsed in pleasure.

Sin almost fell over in shock as Portia opened her sweet, innocent mouth and his rigid cock disappeared between her soft lips.

Her silken lips slid over his sensitive flesh, rubbing and stroking and caressing the head. Then she took him deeper, her lips and tongue stroking his shaft.

He almost fell to his knees.

He cupped her face, knowing he should stop her. She was an innocent. Gently bred. Sweet and good.

"Portia," he muttered, "you shouldn't be sucking my cock."

She let it slide out and he cursed himself. Blasted honor. He wanted this—but he couldn't ask Portia to do something that only a courtesan should do. At the same time, he couldn't imagine being so intimate with anyone but Portia. Not anymore.

Her little tongue flicked across the head.

A gentleman should step away, but her hands clamped on his buttocks, holding him there. Bastard that he was, he didn't want to move.

Her tongue laved all over the head of his cock. Strummed the sensitive, tight piece of flesh at the notch in the crown.

"Portia, no. You're a gently bred girl."

She stopped. Eyed him with a raised brow as she slid his

prick out of her beautiful mouth. The loss of heat almost crippled him. But it was better that way.

"Why shouldn't I do that? You did it to me."

"That's different."

"Why?"

"Because you're—dash it, you're a respectable girl and you shouldn't know about things like that."

"Sin, I've seen far more than that in the last few days. Now, I don't see anything wrong with what we're doing. I don't see anything wrong with wanting to pleasure you. All I wish to do is make you feel good. And it gives me pleasure to do this to you. I rather like holding you in my mouth. It makes me feel strong, for you are rather vulnerable to me right now. But more than that—I find it very erotic."

How could he argue with that? He couldn't make any sound out of his tight throat louder and more coherent than a growl.

But she was an unmarried gently bred girl. And he should stop her before—

God. His hips bucked forward.

She had moved her head, opened her mouth, and was taking him inside as deep as she could. Sin watched his cock vanish, his fingers caressing her hair. Silk-soft hair as brilliant as flame. He'd always known that hair meant she was fiery. As much as she denied it.

She sucked him deep and hard. Pure erotic pleasure streaked through him. She bobbed on him and he moaned. Moaned the way a young man did the first time he felt sexual pleasure and didn't have any sense of control.

He'd had this done to him a few thousand times. Ten years of orgies meant a lot of cock-suckings. But never one like this. Never once had he felt his heart getting tugged with each pull on his prick.

Her hands found his balls and she cupped them. His most vulnerable place. He'd known what it was like to feel pain there, to experience sexual torture. He'd experienced that with Estella. He refused to let any woman touch him there. But he knew Portia was exploring. Her touch was so delicate, he could barely feel it. And that made it all the more intense.

He let her caress his balls.

Like a cushion, her lips pressed to the head of his cock as her fingers toyed with his balls, lightly squeezing them. The hairs tugged and that was damned erotic too. Her fingers traced the seam of them, then went lower, stroking the bridge between balls and anus.

Sin was holding his breath. He felt his muscles tighten, ready to shoot his come. Deep breaths. He needed them or he would lose it and come in her mouth. He'd never been so close to shooting his seed during oral sex in a long, long time.

Watching her was the most erotic thing. His chest rose with ragged breaths. She took him deep—deeper than any courtesan had ever done. Did that because she was genuinely exploring, genuinely trying to delight him. Then she sputtered and jerked back hurriedly.

He stopped her by gently holding her head. The poor sweet needed to breathe.

He drew back, pulling his cock right out of her mouth. "That was remarkable."

"I didn't mean to choke—I won't do that again."

"You took me so deep, love, I'm not surprised. But if you keep doing that, you're going to make me come. That would end our fun for a while—because it would take me awhile to recover from an orgasm that intense. I want to make love to you. Do you want that?"

Portia didn't try to take his cock back into her mouth. Her jaws ached a little from stretching around him. She could taste his earthiness on her lips and tongue.

He tasted . . .

A little sweet, a bit salty, a lot warm, and just a touch sour. He tasted . . . naughty.

She sat back on her haunches and looked at him. Sinclair's breath came fast and his chest rose and fell under his white shirt. Sweat gleamed on his brow. His eyes were bright, a deep glowing brown, and hazy with desire. His cock had bucked up when it left her lips and it stuck up and out from his body, rigid as a staff. The veins were prominent. It looked aggressive and thick and hard and beautiful, and she'd never seen it quite so huge.

Heat seemed to be washing over her too. When he'd said "an orgasm that intense" she had both blazed and ached inside. Had she made him feel so good?

She'd found it rather thrilling to do it. She never dreamed he'd want to go even further. And she knew exactly what she wanted.

"I want you inside me," she said bluntly. "I actually hurt inside, from wanting you."

Suddenly, he lifted her. Up in his arms and he carried her to the bed—one white sheet on a huge mattress.

Kisses pinned her there—his body over hers, his mouth kissing her lips, her throat, a spot behind her ear that made her squeal.

Then he moved, lifting up and off her. She wriggled in frustration and pain until—

In one fast motion, he pulled off his shirt, yanking it over his head. His body made her want to weep. Such a pronounced vee shape to his torso. Such muscles that bulged as he pulled his shirt free of his arms.

Portia gulped.

She loved watching his muscles move. She marvelled at the curve of his pectorals—so firm. His biceps bulged, too big for her two hands to grasp. His nipples were so tight and hard, like hers, but smaller. His cock bobbed as he moved, and it moved like it was heavy, made of wood, and she was sure it must hurt to have that huge thing swinging in front of him.

His trousers were already dropped down, caught at the swell at his thigh muscles. His shape was so different than hers—narrow hips with defined hip bones, and a flat expanse of abdomen, shaped by the rock-hard muscles underneath.

He pushed off his boots and slid his trousers down, baring his legs. Even seeing his naked feet was incredibly erotic. And so intimate. Maybe because this was the first time she'd seen his feet. Long and well-shaped, and thoroughly male, with elegant toes.

Every inch of him was delicious.

Then he turned to toss aside his trousers and she thought she might faint from the sudden stoppage of her heartbeat. His buttocks were naked. His cheeks looked so tight and firm she doubted her fingers would dent them.

She licked her lips, realizing she had actually drooled a little.

Then she thought of gripping Sinclair's hard bottom as he drove into her and she let out a little whimper.

He turned. "What's wrong, love?"

"Oh God, I can't wait any longer. Come here. Now."

His grin widened and she struggled with the fastenings of her dress. "Do you want to just pull up my skirt?"

He took over, leaning over her to undo her dress. "I want you naked. I want to taste you everywhere. Especially your sweet, juicy pussy."

She knew what he meant. Like before. When he'd licked her—her pussy and made her come.

"I . . . I don't want to wait that long." She wanted to be filled. She watched the sway of his cock and wanted to feel it filling her. Thrusting. Going deep.

Portia went weak with need.

She fell back on the bed, holding her arms out to him. She didn't know how to invite him erotically. How to look enticing for him. She had her legs spread, her knees up, ready for him.

But he lifted her, taking the time to undress her.

His hands brushed her skin as she did. She was almost ready to cry. She tried to help, pushing her dress up before he had all the fastenings done. She almost tore it getting it off her head, but she didn't care. So many clothes! It was driving her mad— stays, a petticoat, and a silly shift.

But then she realized she was completely naked in front of

him. Bare breasts and tummy and her private place. All exposed to him.

"God, you're beautiful."

The awed look in his eyes startled her. He looked as if he really thought she was beautiful.

She was slim. Rather too slim, but then she was always busy with work and her brothers were frugal with the allotment for buying food for the home.

She didn't know why she felt so shy. He'd seen her naked bosom before and he knew exactly what he was getting. Small handfuls with pink nipples. He'd lifted her skirts. But he'd never seen her completely naked.

His cock was leaking. She realized a thin stream of liquid fell from the tip.

He moved over her. As he did, he eased her back so her head landed on the soft pillow and she sank back into the mattress. His strong thigh slid between her legs. Then he was over her, all broad chest and rock-hard stomach and lean hips. His cock jutted out and bumped her tummy, leaving a sticky trail.

Lowering his mouth to hers, he kissed her. Long. Slow. His biceps bulged as his arms supported his weight. She felt small beneath him, small and delicate.

His lips caressed her neck. Ooh. She arched her back, lifting as pleasure struck. He suckled her neck and she writhed beneath him on the bed.

Cupping her right breast with his hand, he lowered his mouth to her nipple. She watched his tongue come out and tease it, drawing it until it grew long and flushed and hard. He did the same to her other nipple.

"Julian," she whispered. She was lost. It was as if she'd tumbled back ten years. She was desperately in love all over again.

He started to kiss lower.

"No." She moaned. "I want you inside me. I can't wait any longer. I feel all wet for you."

His smile was tender as he looked down on her. She watched his long fingers trail down her abdomen. Touch her nether curls, then caress and part her lips. She felt her moisture. She was slick with it, and his fingers grew slick and slid over her little sensitive bump.

She looked up at him, begging with her eyes.

"Patience. It's more fun if I build your anticipation. Let me play with your clit until you're ready to beg—"

"I *am* begging. Already. Please." She tweaked his nipples. Lifted underneath him. Reached down and wrapped two hands around his long staff and massaged his fluid into the soft but full and taut head.

"When you do that, I'm ready to come," he growled. He grasped his shaft too and pushed it downward.

"Doesn't that hurt?"

"It's worth it."

The full head pressed to her pubis; then he slid it lower, drawing it over her clit—as he'd called that place. Now she finally knew its name. She almost cried out, before she bit her lip, remembering she had to be quiet.

Her fingers curled into his biceps, gripping tight as he drew his cock lower, parting her lips again. Then he was wedged against her, feeling impossibly thick and full. His hands came back, bracing the bed on either side of her head. His hips moved, slow and coaxing, pressing his cock against her. She was so wet he slid in a little.

Oh! All that yearning need and now it hurt. It wasn't fair.

Gently, he kissed her. "There might be some pain. It won't last long. Then I'll make it good for you. That I can do."

She knew he could. She was certain of it.

The blunt pressure of his penis trying to go in was rather arousing. She moved her hips, somehow realizing she should. With her rocking and Julian slowly moving his groin, gently pressing into her, his cock slid in farther.

There was pain—a sharp, irritating shock of it. Why should she feel pain? Why should women?

Her fingernails gouged in. She couldn't help it. "Julian." It came out like a squeak.

"Sin. Call me Sin. I hate that name—Julian. It belonged to a young man I hate."

She wanted to know why, but his hips moved forward.

His thick cock slid in. Her toes curled. Her eyes almost rolled back in her head. So intense! He was in her. They were joined in the most intimate way. If she'd had a barrier, it was gone now.

Portia needed to be close to him. She wrapped her arms around his neck. "I want your body against mine. Everywhere."

He did as she wanted, lying on top of her. But still he held his weight. His chest squished her breasts lightly, his hard belly pressed to her softer one. His body had settled between her legs, stretching her thighs. And his cock was buried deep.

Then he started to thrust.

Oh, she'd had no idea. She'd seen people making love, she'd heard their cries. Now she knew why they screamed.

This was—

Delightful. Heavenly. Perfect. Sweetness and sin together.

She hooked her leg over his, pinning him to her. She moved her hips as much as she could, lifting to meet his thrusts. Slow and gentle thrusts. But getting stronger, harder, more demanding. Each smack of his hips teased her clit, sending shudders of exquisite sensation through her. So strong, she moaned and had to bury her face in his chest to muffle the desperate sounds.

As if he was losing control too, he nuzzled her neck hungrily. Kissed her lips in hot, fast, passionate kisses. His tongue teased hers, mimicking the magic thrusts inside her.

His hands slid down and he cupped her bottom and lifted her tight. His groin rubbed her clit. He was thrusting so hard into her.

"Yes," she cried. She reached down and gripped his arse. Felt the flex of the rock-solid muscles with the rocking of his hips. Sweat trickled off him, hit her lips, and she swept it off with her tongue. Salty. His.

"Bang me senseless," she gasped. "Bang into me so hard you shake the bed."

She was totally out of control. A wanton creature, moving with him. Wet with perspiration and slick with their juices. Hot and flushed.

He moved his hands again to brace himself. And he pounded so hard the bed did shake. He moved her whole body on the bed. It was too much—

No, it was perfect. Perfect—

The orgasm swept over her like a storm wave striking the island. She was awash in it. Her arms flailed. She slapped his buttocks. Buried her mouth into his shoulder. Oh God, she bit him.

She held him tight.

Then he groaned. His mouth tightened and his eyes shut. Pure agony sketched across his face. "Portia."

His hips bumped hers; then he shoved them forward, burying himself as deep as possible. She felt hot inside. A sudden flood of heat as he shuddered above her. He stopped moving and stayed on top of her. He pressed his face into the crook of her neck, gasping for breath.

A jerk of his hips withdrew his cock. A flow of hot fluid came out too.

And she knew at once what it was. His seed.

Huskily, he said, his mouth almost touching her lips, "You're mine, Portia. This marks you as mine. No other man is going to touch you. My come makes you mine now. Forever."

20

_____

Portia was *dying* with curiosity, but she couldn't make herself say the words. She was simply too shy to say: *What do you mean your come makes me yours?*

She made two attempts to speak the words. Each time, she looked into his eyes and all that came out of her mouth was a sound like, "Gah-ha."

She was no longer an utter innocent, but she was still too shy.

Sin rolled on his back. Portia hadn't liked that nickname for him, because she didn't like thinking of him as sinful. But sinful had proven to be a lot of fun. And it was the name he preferred. She'd never known that "Julian" made him think of bad memories. She wished he'd told her back then.

Grasping her around the waist, he lifted her easily and planted her naked body right on top of his. Her tummy pressed against his cock—which was wet, sticky, and growing hard again. "Goodness, you're aroused again."

"Having you naked on top of me does that to me, Portia, even though I just had the most intense climax of my life."

"I don't believe that. Clarissa hinted at the kind of things you do at orgies. You told me you like dark pleasures." She flushed. "How could just being with me be more arousing than that?"

His finger traced her lip. How she loved that. It tingled in her cunny even more than her lip. Then he arched his neck to lift up and kiss her mouth.

He lay back, grinning. "It's true, angel. You are special. Unique. Watching you come makes me come with the force of an explosion."

Knowing that gave her a glow of confidence she'd never had. So she ventured, "What did you mean that you hate the name Julian?"

His expression clouded. "It reminded me of things I'd rather forget. Losing you, for one."

"But why should you reject your name over that?"

"Ah, it doesn't matter, Portia." He nuzzled her neck. Nibbled her earlobe. Made her giggle. And gasp.

"Make love to me on top, Miss Love."

"On top of you!"

Sin settled his hands on her hips.

How she loved his grin—it spoke of wickedness, of wonderfully naughty fun, but of a special delight they'd shared. His eyes twinkled at her. "Sit up on me, love."

Sit up on him? He helped her up and she scrambled up, so her bottom rested on his groin. Thick and rigid, his erect cock wedged against her cheeks.

"What do I do?"

"You take my cock inside your hot, sweet pussy, love. Then you ride me. You could also take me into your ass on top of me, but we'll save that for next time."

"Next time," she echoed. The thought, the words, speared her.

Portia rose up, knees sinking in the bed. She had to press her hand on his chest to support herself. Wrapped her fingers around his hot, sticky cock, she made it stand upright. Slowly, she lowered on him—

"Oh, it rather hurts!"

His hands still rested on her hips, and he stopped her from moving down farther, from taking any more inside. Her fingers were curled around him, feeling how thick and hard he was.

"You'll be sensitive from making love, Portia. Sore. We don't have to do this. We can wait."

"But I want to do this. Now I want it so much, I don't want to stop. It's just that you are so huge."

"I love hearing that. You can tell me that anytime."

Suddenly he arched up and kissed her right nipple, leaving it erect and shiny with his warm saliva. His motion pushed his erection a little farther inside her. The pain had eased, that made it twinge a little again. But despite the ache, she wanted to feel full. Desire was more intense than nerves about a little pain.

Smiling into her eyes, he stroked her clit with his thumb.

Oooh! She had to clutch his shoulders. She loved his hand there. She tensed, because sometimes it was too much, but mostly it felt so good. But it turned her to liquid inside. Made juices flow. She was so wet she could take him in deep.

Somehow she knew to go up and down on him. With a moan, she lifted her hips, then lowered on him. Until he went deep inside and her bottom smacked his bollocks.

He'd thrust in her, she was bouncing on him. Up and down, hands braced against his chest.

Sin guided her. Coaxed her to lean back, which intensified the push of his cock head against a tremendously sensitive place inside her pussy. He brought her forward until her breasts dangled over his mouth. He caught her nipples in his mouth, sucked them.

She loved looking down, seeing her breasts, full and plump, hanging over him.

"Ride me, Portia. Touch yourself. Play with your clit."

She could, couldn't she? Moving up and down, she shifted her hips until she found the way that teased her the most. And she got to watch Sin while she moaned with each shock of pleasure.

"Fuck me, Portia."

Scandalous words, but exciting.

His fingers teased her, he licked her nipples, and his cock head rubbed her inner walls, rubbed a stunning place. There . . . oh! She tipped her head back.

It was so good. So good.

She rode him faster. Rising and falling, teasing herself. Her hair, tumbling free of her pins, danced wildly around them both. She was hot, sweaty. Panting.

His fingers caressed her. Then—oh!—he teased her bottom with a finger.

All the spiralling tension burst. Her hands fisted and pressed to his shoulders. She came.

She jerked on him. Writhed on him. Bit back a scream as pleasure claimed her. Then, the urge to go there again came over her. Greedily, she wanted another climax.

Lying over his body, she tried to work and wriggle herself to pleasure again. But she couldn't quite reach it—

Until he played with her with his fingers again. Sin slid his index finger in her bottom—like a second man's cock.

She came again, crying out beside his ear.

He roared her name. "Portia." He bucked underneath her, his hips going wild. Coming into her, he lifted her right off the bed.

Sin's brains had turned into mush. Intelligent thought left the instant he came. Portia was the only woman who'd ever made him feel like this. Even when he'd been nineteen, when he indulged in bondage, brothels, and orgies, his orgasms had never left him feeling like this. He'd used to be left exhausted. He'd never been left exhausted with a smile on his lips and a glow in his heart.

The look on her face had undone him. Her absolute shock when she came, then the utter delight. She wasn't faking it, as so many courtesans did, because they were too busy calculating to enjoy sex.

The way she'd sucked his cock, exploring pleasure with him—it had made him finally see real intimacy in sex.

He also felt a certain selfish pride. No other man had ever made Portia come. It gave him the desire to crow from the rooftops. But he would never do that to Portia, never boast about her.

She was special. Unique.

He'd never known such joy.

In the middle of murders, being hunted by a madman, he'd found joy for the first time in his life.

No—the second time.

The only other time he'd been happy in his life was when she'd said yes. When she'd agreed to marry him.

He'd let her go then, because he thought she deserved to find happiness with someone else.

Now, he owed her respectability. He owed her rescue. Not just from the killer, but from the sharp-clawed matrons and hypocritical gentlemen of Society.

But first—

Sin rolled her onto her stomach on their damp, messy bed. Rounded and tempting, her two sweet ass cheeks wobbled. She was so slender but curvaceous in delightful places—like her tits and sweet ass. He planted a kiss on both cheeks. Parted them and kissed her small, puckered anus. Lifting her bottom, he licked the bridge between pussy and ass, slid his tongue into her pussy.

His cock, which should be exhausted, was rising again.

He had to admit he was proud of it.

"Do you want more, Portia?" he asked. "Another orgasm?"

"I don't know," she whispered.

He heard the shy note in her tone. Sliding his hand between her legs from behind, he opened her nether lips and teased her clit.

She moaned. Lifted her hips to him.

He wedged his cock, now almost rock-hard, against her pussy. So slick, like heated cream. Her pussy would grip him tight, surround him with so much tight heat, he knew he wouldn't last long. He just wanted to make her come first. He needed to hear her scream with ecstasy.

Her hair was half out of its pins and he took the time to free her tumble of red hair completely. It glimmered, gold strands shining amongst the rich, exotic red. Burying his face in the silky thickness, he licked her neck. His cock was pressing against her silky pussy lips, with just the head drenched in her juices and held tight.

He suckled her delicate neck, sucked and kissed until she squirmed underneath him. Moaning for him.

Yes, this was what he wanted.

This intimacy.

God, yes. Sin groaned out loud as he slid into her sweet cunt. Pleasing her was his only desire. With his finger, he toyed with her clit and he slid his other hand over the rounded curves of her ass. Then up along her smooth sensual back. She was supported on her arms, and he moved his hand beneath her to her delectable tits. He bridged her nipples with thumb and forefinger.

Portia moaned at the teasing pressure.

She was so wet, one long, slow thrust brought his cock inside her. To the hilt.

Yes. Lord, yes.

He withdrew, until only the tip was wet, then thrust in again. Filling her. Diving into pure, sweet heaven. Over and over.

He kissed her hungrily, cupping her left breast, playing with her clit. She rocked with him, moaning, "Yes. Yes." Her ass lifted to him, a soft pillow for his groin to impact.

He moved his hand from her breast, ran down her, fingered her anus.

"Oh, Sin!" she cried. Her head arched. Her body rocked madly.

He felt it. The rush of heat and wetness inside her. The pulse of her muscles. But her moans and cries and writhing body let him know she was coming hard.

She sobbed his name. And he lost control.

His climax seared him, heart and soul.

Braced on his arms, he shuddered as the pleasure ebbed

away, as his come shot out of him, drained him. He withdrew, collapsed beside her. The bed jiggled as his weight hit. He was too exhausted, sated, to do more than just fall beside her. Then, he managed to wrap his arm around her. On her side, her cheeks pressed to the bed, she faced him.

Her gray eyes sparkled, brilliant as the sun on dew drops.

Sin knew what he owed her now. But under what terms? How could he do what was honorable, what was expected, and still make her happy?

He knew the words he had to speak.

But he couldn't make them come out. With them had to come the truth. The whole truth.

Her eyes shone at him. She looked at him with love. But with more than that—

Admiration. She looked at him as if he were a man worthy of her love.

Within minutes, that glowing light would fade, and he would lose her—the only person whose love he'd ever had.

He had cast aside her love once, had pretended he could fill his life with athletic sex and not feel the loss.

He'd been wrong.

Gently, he stroked Portia's shoulder. Skin like silk, sweetly damp from sex. Their scents filled the room—sweat and come.

The sweetest smile curved her lips. Breaking his heart. Because he knew, once they were off this island, she might become his duchess, but he would never see her again.

"I wish we could stay in here, with the door locked, and pretend that everything is well," she whispered.

"We can't, Portia. But I promise I am going to get you off this island alive."

"Such a promise is impossible. But working together, trusting each other, we can end this."

He had to explain why he had to let her go—

"Sinclair! I know you are in there—and alive! Open this door! At once!"

He bolted upright at the woman's desperate tone, despite

the hazy feeling in his head from three—still astounding to think of it—three intense orgasms. He went for his robe, threw it on. Someone knew he was alive—a problem. This intense knocking had to portend another disaster.

But he knew he was racing to the door to avoid telling Portia the truth.

Portia sat up, holding the sheets to her. She felt guilty, being caught in bed with Sin. Though in her heart, she no longer knew why. Why feel guilty about this? When surrounded by murder, how could sharing pleasure be bad?

Sin, wrapped in his robe of heavy, luxurious blue silk, opened the door. Only inches, so she could not see on the other side. She could only see his back, as he spoke to the person who'd knocked.

It was the Incognita. She'd recognized the woman's voice.

"How did you know I was alive, Clarissa?" Sin asked.

Portia heard the woman's laugh—but it sounded more strained than silky. "I assumed you were responsible for all of Miss Love's moaning and screaming behind the door."

Heavens, she'd never dreamed she was so . . . loud.

The Incognita ducked under Sin's arm and peeked in the room. Portia was caught in the bed, and felt her cheeks heat.

Then Clarissa smiled. "So you played a trick on us, Sinclair." The woman tapped her lips. "Perhaps you are the murderer— which is why I came here, armed with a kitchen knife. Perhaps you and Miss Love are in league. But I believe you're not. I believe you faked your death as a way to investigate, not as a way to lure the rest of us to our doom. So I have come because more people have gone missing. The last three women, other than me and your Miss Love."

"Nellie, the cook, and the Old Madam," Portia cried.

Sin glanced at her, then turned his attention back to the Incognita. "They've left the house, I take it."

"Not a trace to be seen."

"What do you mean by that?"

"All of their belongings are gone. I looked in their rooms.

Emptied," Clarissa said, sounding like a duchess about to crack.

"Has anyone searched the grounds?"

"Rutledge claims that he has done and saw nothing. But then, he could be the murderer. So I would not trust a word he says. I let him go and stayed with Saxonby. I held my knife at all times. We sat in the drawing room, at opposite ends of the room. But now there is only Blute, Rutledge, Saxonby, and me, and you and Miss Love left."

"It could be one of those women. Just because they aren't in the house, doesn't mean they are dead," Sin said.

"Oh yes. I did not think of that. I wonder—" Clarissa's dark eyes searched his face. "After all, you weren't really dead. . . ."

"You mean, what if one of the other previous victims was not actually dead?"

The Incognita nodded. "Only Willoughby is beyond suspicion, for his head was smashed to a pulp. But I have no key to those bedrooms, and Saxonby told me you and he had already entertained the thought and checked the rooms."

"That's true," Sin answered. "We did. They are all dead."

"So what do we do now? Do we simply wait to see who shows up to attempt to kill us?" The Incognita narrowed her eyes, which were rimmed with kohl to look massive. "I should think the killer will want to eliminate Miss Love. Since she claims to know who the killer is."

They both turned to her. Sin wore a grumpy expression. "You should not have done that."

"Actually, in the shock of discovering you alive and . . . uh, everything else—" Portia's cheeks felt as if burning. "I actually forgot about that."

"So, who was it?" the Incognita asked. "Or am I only to know when I am the victim?"

"I don't know," Portia admitted. "I bluffed."

"A ruse. Just like the one you pulled, Sin. It does intrigue me—what on earth made you think of faking your own death, Sinclair? I should never have thought of such a thing." Stepping closer to him, the Incognita smiled saucily into his eyes. "I have been fascinated by you ever since you came to London when you were just nineteen. Everyone thought you must be a naïve young man, raised in the country. But it was obvious to me that you'd had a lot more experience than that. So I learned everything I could about you."

In front of Portia's eyes, Sin paled. "Did you, Clarissa? Why? For blackmail? That's a damn dangerous game."

"Do you really think I would threaten you here? Now? My darling duke, I am relying upon you to save my life."

Portia was startled as Clarissa turned to her. "Sin can be quite the hero when he wishes to be. And I believe both of us will be safe. Unless you are the murderer. Wouldn't that be delicious? The least likely person. The sweet, innocent girl who looks as if butter wouldn't melt in her mouth. This is the first time I've seen you without your mask, Miss Lamb."

Shocked, Portia put her hands to her face. But it was unnecessary. She touched bare skin. "You know who I am?"

"Oh yes. I know your family's foundling home."

"How?"

Clarissa shrugged. "That is not important. Finding our three missing women is."

"Yes," Portia echoed. "One of the women might be a killer, but that means the other could be a victim. We must try to find them before it is too late."

They all searched together—Rutledge, Saxonby, Blute, Clarissa, her, and Sin. They scoured through the house, then over the island. All of them slowly walked along the edge of the island, looking over the cliff edge.

She and Sin took the lead. Sin tucked her hand in the crook of his arm, but she was not afraid of falling. She could face anything, now that she had him back.

"That part about Genvere being an anagram for revenge was clever, Portia," he said. "I never saw that."

"You heard that?"

"I was hiding behind the draperies, trying to keep watch over you. I almost launched out of there when you announced you knew who the killer was. I guessed it was a bluff, that you were making yourself into bait. Portia, don't ever do anything that mad again."

The pain in his gaze gave her a spurt of guilt. "I don't believe I will. I came rather too close to being killed." She said it lightly, but it had been terrifying. Yet what could she do? She couldn't sit back and wait to be murdered. Wait for Sin to be murdered. . . .

"I wish there was really a boat," she cried. "I suppose there isn't—the killer must have arranged to have someone come from the mainland when all of this is over."

"We'll be the ones to meet the boat," Sin said, his voice cool and firm.

She wanted to believe him. She *would* believe—

Then she saw it. A body, huddled on the ground by the cliff edge. She raced toward it, but Sin reached it before her. He turned, then turned the face back toward the ground. Portia knew who it was. Nellie, the young courtesan.

She bit back a sob. "But she was so young!"

"I know. The poor kid."

"Look there!" About five feet farther along the edge, a bit of gray cloth fluttered. "That must be from the cook's dress," Portia said.

She ran toward it. Sin raced after her, catching up to her as she reached the bit of cloth. His arm went around her waist, holding her fast. "Careful. This could be another trap, set to catch someone who found Nellie."

"But I must—"

"No, you won't." He shook his head. "You haven't changed. None of this has changed you. You're the same Portia who went into danger to rescue children."

"I suppose, for better or worse, I am. But I think you can put me down. If something was going to strike us, pushing us off the cliff, I assume it would have happened by now."

She knew he released her with reluctance. She took the bit of fabric from the twig. He moved closer to the edge, muttered an expletive.

And she knew. "It's her body, isn't it? At the bottom of the cliff."

"It is. You don't need to look," he said. But she peeked around him, his broad body trying to block her view.

In a huddle at the bottom, trapped in a small circle of jagged rocks, a bundle of gray cloth moved, pushed up and down against the rocks by the waves. From the height, she couldn't really tell if it was a body. It looked like the cook's dress. The she saw it—one spot of lighter color. A hand. A pale hand. Now she could spot a shape that must be the cook's head. A foot.

"Do you think she was thrown over alive? Or dead?"

Sin's arm went around her. "She's gone now, either way."

"And so is Nellie. And the Old Madam is missing. But is she also dead? Or is she the killer? Is she the one who had a child, and who is driven to get revenge for that child? We've searched the island with no sign of her—"

"If she went over the cliff, her body could have been dragged out to sea," he muttered. "We'll take the steps down to the sea. Your idea of a boat in a cave may have been a bluff, but I'd like to make sure."

He was armed with a pistol, with knives. They went down together, but they found no boat. They couldn't reach the poor cook's body. As they went back up the steps to tell the others, Portia could only think: Was the Old Madam lying in wait? Were they walking back into danger?

Surely, if they were careful, if they stayed together, watched each other, and focused on survival, they would indeed all survive.

21

"You're so beautiful, Portia."

At the soft, awed sound of a masculine voice, Portia awoke and opened her eyes. Sin was leaning over her in the bed they'd shared last night, naked, smiling softly at her.

She swallowed guilt. So many people had lost their lives, she felt terrible to be happy in Sin's arms.

"What's wrong?" he asked gently.

She explained, and he bent and nuzzled her neck, kissed her earlobe. "This makes it all the more important for us to celebrate being alive."

"Yes," she whispered. "I supposed that's true." She felt safe here, in his bed, their door locked.

She and Sin had returned to the house yesterday to discover the house apparently empty with no sign of the Old Madam. Another storm blew in, lashing the house with fierce winds and cold rain, forcing them all to give up the search.

The six of them—her, Sin, Saxonby, Rutledge, Blute, the Incognita—had taken food from the locked butler pantry and eaten in front of each other. Then they'd gone to their bedrooms and locked the doors.

Sin had spent hours making love to her last night. Even from behind, as she leaned over the vanity table. She sensed he needed to do it to forget the horror of what they'd found. Portia would never forget the erotic scene of him driving into her—and her coming—in the mirror. Perhaps it wasn't right, but she too had wanted to push aside thoughts of death and fear. And if she had very little time left, if the murderer did get her, she wanted to enjoy every second before that.

Sin drew away from her neck. He levered up on his side on the bed. "I'm going to marry you."

Portia blinked. Was she still addled with sleep? "I beg your pardon?"

"We're to be married, love."

"Are you asking me to marry you? You did that before, with rather disastrous results, Sin."

"Last time, I broke the engagement because I was not good enough for you. I'd fallen into a dark world of sex and orgies, and I couldn't be the kind of husband you deserve. You loved me and I hadn't lived up to that love. This time, it's not about love. I've taken your innocence and it's my duty and obligation to marry you."

She couldn't believe her ears. "*Duty and obligation?* I see. And I'm just supposed to put up with your shocking parties?"

"There won't be any more of those. I'm going to behave myself as your husband. I'm a decade older, a hell of a lot smarter. I owe you marriage, and it will be my duty to make you happy."

She'd had enough. Portia sat up, the sheets tumbling down. "I'm not a duty. I don't want to be an obligation. I don't care that I've given up my virginity. I knew perfectly well what I was doing. I'd decided I wasn't going to marry. I am happy running the foundling home. If I'm not going to marry, it hardly matters that I'm 'ruined.' So I don't need a marriage and I certainly don't want one where you've been forced to marry me."

The words squeezed her heart. Duty. Obligation. This wasn't about love. He didn't love her.

She pushed out of the bed. Forgetting, until she felt suddenly cold, that she was naked, standing in the middle of the bedroom.

Sin jumped out of bed too. "Portia, I hurt you ten years ago by not marrying you when I should have done. I won't do that to you again."

She crossed her arms over her breasts and stood behind the bed column, peeking around it. "I don't want to marry you, Sin. I just wanted to learn about pleasure." That wasn't true. He'd captured her heart again, but she was not going to tell him that. "I would never marry you."

His jaw dropped. "Portia, you deserve marriage. You deserve security, money, a position—I won't abandon you. It's the price—"

"Stop! I'm not a price. I don't want to be your lifelong punishment." This was the problem with being naked. She wanted to run out the door. Run away before she heard any more words that hurt her. But she couldn't run. And she shouldn't.

He was striding across the bedroom toward her. Naked. All lean, hard planes, except for his cock, which was soft and swayed as he walked. Shivers rushed down her spine as she watched him move. Sinuous. Graceful. So, so, so erotic. She wanted to touch him. Everywhere.

Marry him and you can do that.

But she would love him, while he saw marriage to her as a duty.

"There will be no marriage, Sin," she said firmly.

He came close and she trembled. He took another step and he was so close her nipples brushed his skin. The top of her head reached his chin. He bent to her, and his lips touched her cheek.

Sparks showered right to her toes.

But she fought for control. "You aren't going to seduce me into saying yes," she warned. "And we might not even escape this wretched island."

"We will. You will—I'm not going to let anything happen to you."

"I don't know if you are really in control of that."

He cupped her cheek. "Portia, there is going to be a wedding. I'm going to convince you to say yes."

There was a sort of desperation in his eyes. He really was determined to marry her. Maybe he felt he was making amends for hurting her in the past. This was his retribution.

"You do not owe me marriage. I can't marry you, Sin. We would both be miserable. If we survive this island, let me go back to my world, where I belong and I am happy."

Dejection showed in his long-lashed brown eyes. "You don't think you would ever be happy with me? You couldn't ever love me?"

She owed him the truth—she could not reject him without giving him the truth. He deserved better. "I love you now, Sin. That's why I can't marry you."

His brows drew together. He looked so vulnerable. "I don't understand."

"You don't love me. I won't marry you for duty. We'll both be terribly unhappy."

A muffled scream cut him off. It had come from outside. In the hallway, near their room.

"Hell, no," Sin muttered.

For one moment, they both just stood there. Then Portia pulled back from him. "Oh heavens, it's happened again. That was a woman's scream." She felt sick. Sick with horror.

Sin's strong hands gripped her upper arms. "You will stay here. It's not safe. I'll investigate."

She shook her head. "Haven't you learned by now that is not going to work? I am going with you."

Under his breath he muttered a curse. "You know, since you're so determined to be at my side," he muttered, "you *should* marry me."

He threw on his robe and left her to put on her gown, so he

could run out into the corridor before she was ready. She tried in vain to move faster.

Then she heard it.

As soon as he disappeared into the hallway, an explosion roared outside the door.

She knew what it was—a pistol shot.

Oh dear God. Sin had been shot! An image flashed instantly through her head: Sin lying on the ground, his shirt and waistcoat soaking through red. That time it had been red ink. But this time it could be real. Shock did something to her—it made her act. It filled her with rage.

She clamped the gown to her chest and ran for the door. She threw it open. "Damn you, I am going to end this now," she barked.

"Hello, Portia. What in the blazes are you doing?"

It was Sin. Dear heaven, alive. He'd launched back against the wall of the corridor. There was a charred hole in the wall two feet from his head.

"Get back in the room, Portia. Don't be mad. Your dress is falling down."

"I don't care. Someone shot at you."

"With a pistol. One shot. I would have gone in pursuit, except you began to open our door, and I wasn't going to move in case I had to shield you. Now, go back inside."

With that, he ran down the corridor, then charged down the stairs.

After him, she shouted, "Who shot at you?" He must have seen, mustn't he? But of course, he didn't answer.

Along the hall, doors opened. The Incognita rushed out, a wrap of silk thrown around her. Saxonby also came out. Rutledge and Blute stayed behind their doors and peeked out. Apparently they had no desire to step out boldly and risk being shot.

"Was Sinclair shot again? He's making a habit of this," Rutledge muttered.

"You could go to help him," she shouted, and she took off in pursuit before she'd finished the statement. She didn't care if the next shot was aimed at her. Sin couldn't face the killer alone!

Her legs shook, but she made them work. She was breathing in the smoke of the shot, the acrid smell of it. A male figure was rushing away from the darkened stairs. Why hadn't she thought of a weapon—?

Footsteps pounded behind her. "Miss Love, stop," shouted Saxonby. She ignored him.

She reached the bottom of the stairs, hesitated, trying to figure out where to go.

A figure emerged from the shadows. She didn't scream because she sensed, almost instantly, who it was.

Sin. He grabbed her, planting his hands on her upper arms. "You should not have come after me. I lost the fiend. Heard the front door slam shut. Then I feared it was a ruse to get me away from you, so I ran back. Cursing myself with every step in case you were in danger. I didn't see who it was. All I could see was the cloak the blackguard wore."

Then Portia realized what she had seen, what it meant. "I saw them all. Saxonby and Clarissa came out of their bedrooms. Rutledge and Blute peeked out. It must have been Harriet Barker. It must have been. What are we going to do?"

"Nothing tonight. With our doors locked, she can't get to us. She must have been the one to scream, hoping to lure me out. Or at least lure someone out."

"Couldn't we chase her? If you know she went outside—"

"Into the dark and a storm. We would be in too much danger."

"Then what are we going to do?"

"Go back to bed."

"What?"

"You said I couldn't seduce you into marriage. I plan to try. And I want to make love to you while I'm still alive to do it."

"But you could have been killed! Shouldn't we try to stop the Old Madam before she shoots at someone else?" Portia couldn't believe Sin had really returned to their bedroom, locked the door, and carried her to bed.

"We're safe until morning," he murmured.

"You can't know that."

"We are behind a locked door. The window sashes are locked. I was at risk because I fell for a ruse and went outside. In here, in bed together, we're safe."

"But Saxonby wanted to speak with you. He wanted to make a plan—"

"I need to be here with you, Portia."

Heavens, he licked her neck and it made her tingle everywhere.

Still, wasn't now a time to be serious? To plan for their survival? To plan to catch a vicious murderer? "How can you think of sex *now?*"

But he rolled her over and kissed the cheeks of her bottom. She had to admit—she really didn't want to chase a killer.

Not when his fingers caressed her rump and then slid into the valley between her cheeks. He'd stroked her there—in that forbidden place—when he'd made love to her from behind. Her whole body was poised in anticipation. . . .

Would he touch her there again?

He licked his finger—she saw him over her shoulder. Then caressed the entrance to her anus with his dampened finger.

"Oh, perhaps I shouldn't. Perhaps this is too wicked," she whispered.

"With you, I feel that nothing is wicked, Portia. Everything feels special. You deserve to experience and enjoy anything you desire. But I won't do anything you don't want."

Doubt hit her. He was tremendously experienced. Would he be disappointed if she proved boring—too afraid to do sexual things?

"Portia, there's nothing wrong with setting limits to what you enjoy."

"But you tried wild things."

"I needed to keep going for wilder, stranger sexual acts as I grew jaded. I don't want that with you."

Because he knew this was only for duty. That was what her heart told her.

"Touch me," she whispered. "Put your finger inside my . . . my bum."

There. She was going to be daring.

She held her breath as the tip of his finger stroked her in gentle spirals. She panted, her heart pounded, and her fingers curled up, mimicking the sweet tension inside her.

His finger had gone in just a little the first time he'd made love to her from behind.

This time—

Ooooh. He teased with just his fingertip. Then he thrust a little deeper. She felt her muscles resist, but it was the most erotic feeling. The tension built and she rocked her hips. Needing more. Fear and desire were an explosive mix.

Yes, more.

Oh, was she sure?

Yes, she was.

"Please," she whispered.

Deeper went his finger. Past tense muscle, to give her a jolt of pleasure that made her squeal.

He teased her, building pleasure with just the long, slow thrust of his finger. Her hands strayed down for the pressure in her derriere made her clit grow hard and ache. She stroked herself and he thrust with his finger. She felt rather like a virtuoso, playing with erotic skill on her body as he did the same.

"Two fingers," he growled.

She felt suddenly more full. And loved it. How could her ass take such thickness? But it did and it was so—!

Oh!

His cock slid into her while she climaxed, while her pussy pulsed and pleasure washed through her. Having him fill her then . . .

Her muscles clutched at him, trying to pull him deep. Braced on his arms, he thrust into her, and she rubbed her clit lightly, and came again. Came all over him.

"I'm going to lose control—"

He shouted it. Thrust hard and fast and she was so wet that she cried, "Harder. Oh, please."

Another climax burst, washing her with such intense pleasure she sobbed.

Then he roared. He roared loud enough to be heard on the mainland. And he came too.

He laughed roughly as she whispered, "That was so erotic. And I know we can't have any more—"

"You want more, love? I'm happy to try."

And he did.

22

She sucked him vigorously, holding his thick, hot cock in her mouth, savoring the taste of him. Portia was straddling his legs and her delicious Sin lay on the bed, and they'd made love for hours. For the whole day, except when the six of them had gathered for food. Sax and Rutledge had searched the island and the house for the Old Madam, but they'd found no one.

"What in hell do we do?" Sax had asked.

"A boat has to come," Sin had growled. "What we have to do is stay alive."

Then he'd hustled her back up to their bedchamber. Portia had wanted to know if they should do something, and Sin had said, "I will. But I want this day with you. One whole day with you."

The way he'd said it made her nervous. She acquiesced—for now—but she intended to stop him from doing anything foolish.

After so much lovemaking, she was sucking him because she was too spent for any more.

Suddenly Sin let out of deep, painted groan. His face contorted in the agony of orgasm. His thick cock pulsed in her mouth, growing impossibly hard and huge. But nothing came out.

Did she ask anything about it? She had heard men were terribly sensitive about lovemaking. She didn't want to hurt his feelings.

Lying on his back, he wrapped his arms around her and drew her to him so she was lying over his chest. Her hair was a wild tumble of curls, covering both of them like a shawl.

"I came dry," he said huskily. "I've run out of seed. Climaxed too many times. God, when I do that—it's almost agony, but its exquisite agony because it only happens when I've had too many orgasms and too much pleasure."

"You should have told me. I didn't know. Did I hurt you?"

He chuckled but winced. "You are adorable. I'm not hurt, but tired."

"You should sleep. So your body can recover."

He smiled at her, and it was such a tender smile, her heart lurched. She could agree to marry him and wake up like this every morning—

But without love, she knew they would not wake up like this together for long.

She heard a soft snore. Sin was already fast asleep. Eyes closed, his long, dark lashes curling against his cheeks, his lips soft and slightly parted. He looked so content and so beautiful, her heart gave a tug.

He was so exhausted he'd fallen asleep on his back, his legs slightly splayed, cock soft now and flopped along his left thigh. His right hand was outstretched toward her.

Portia knew she should snuggle against him and sleep.

But she couldn't. She'd had many, many wonderful orgasms, but her wits were whirling. They might be safe temporarily tonight, but what would tomorrow bring?

She lay on her back, trying to will her body into sleep.

But something nagged at her. From what Sin had told her the Old Madam had been afraid, but it must have been an act. She remembered seeing the woman wringing her hands. The woman had elegant hands with many jeweled rings.

Portia looked at her hands, curled over the top of the bedspread. She did much work at the foundling home, and her hands weren't soft and pampered.

If it was the Old Madam, why was she doing this? Had she had a child who had been hurt by all these people—?

Her hands. That was what was wrong! When she had talked to the cook in the kitchen, she hadn't really thought about the woman's hands. But now she remembered Mrs. Kent's hands were elegant. They weren't tough, reddened. She remembered how long-fingered and graceful they were when the cook touched her locket. And when the cook's hand had brushed hers in the kitchen, the skin had been smooth. She hadn't felt any roughness of calluses.

Those had been a lady's hands. Not a servant's hands.

But the cook was dead—

Or at least a woman's body, clad in a gray dress, lay at the bottom of the cliff, where they couldn't get to it.

Thinking back, Portia tried to compare the cook and the Old Madam. Both had large bosoms and were of similar height. The cook was dowdy and rather plump. The madam had a voluptuous figure and wore rouge, lip rouge, kohl around her eyes. But it was easy to look dowdy in a gray dress. The body at the bottom of the cliff could be the cook . . . or could be the Old Madam.

The cook was obviously not a cook. Certainly the food had tasted quite delicious, but no actual cook would possess such dainty hands.

She sat up.

"Portia, what are you doing awake?"

She almost leapt out of the bed. Sin sat up, the covers falling away from his beautiful, naked chest. The glow of coals in the fire gilded the lines and planes of his hard torso.

Stop thinking of his nakedness and think sense, Portia. "I thought you were asleep," she said.

"I was, briefly. I have to keep my wits about me and keep you safe, love."

"Sin, there's something I must tell you. Something I believe I've figured out about these crimes."

"What is it, my bride-to-be?"

"I'm not your bride-to-be—oh, let us stop arguing about that. Let me tell you about this."

He held out his hand and as she clasped it, he drew her closer to him. "Tell me, love."

"I think the cook is the killer. She's not really dead. She faked her death, just as you did." All her ideas spilled out madly as she outlined why she thought the cook was an imposter—and a murderess. "There was once she even lost her accent. She stopped saying 'yer' and said 'your,' but I didn't notice until now."

Sin listened. He never interrupted while she explained. Then softly, he said, "I think you're right."

"Then what are we going to—"

He put his hand over her mouth, cutting her off. She squawked behind his palm in protest. A muffled sound. He put his finger to his lips. And she heard a sound. Footsteps. Light and furtive outside the door.

She stopped sputtering—heavens, she even tried to stop breathing so they could hear. The steps continued past their door. Then came a soft creak.

"The stairs," Sin whispered against her ear.

He was getting out of bed. Portia put her hand on his solid, strong forearm. "You can't. Last time you were shot at. What if it's a trap? The cook luring you out. What if she shoots again and does not miss?"

"I'll be careful. This time I know what to expect." Naked, he walked across the room. Utterly unconcerned that he wasn't wearing a stitch, he opened the door slightly, glanced around. Then opened enough to slip out and closed the door.

She rushed to the door to follow, just as it opened. Her knees wobbled with relief as he came back in. "You went out naked."

He glanced down. "I'd forgotten." Frowning, he said, "It was Sax."

"Saxonby? Do you think I'm wrong—that Saxonby is the murderer? As you accused him earlier?"

"That accusation was false—to set up the false duel and my fake death. I've known Sax since we were boys. I can't believe he's guilty. He must be planning to hunt the killer alone."

"But that's utterly foolish. He must be stopped—"

"I'll do it."

Of course he would offer to do that. And she knew she must let him go. He went for his clothes and impulsively she rushed after him. Threw herself against him, pressing to his firm, hard, naked back. "Do be careful."

He turned, looking a little affronted. "I will be, Portia. I promise you."

She hugged him. She liked being pressed tight against him, her breasts against the hard muscle of his back, her cunny against his groin. She was afraid to let him go.

Even though she'd refused to marry him.

He actually had to pry her arms off him. "I'll lose him unless I go now, love."

With lithe movements he pulled on his trousers, then stuffed his feet into his boots, which were battered and muddy. He wore nothing under his trousers. There was nothing but bare skin. She held out his shirt, but he shook his head. "The white is too visible."

Instead he put on his dark coat over his naked chest. Picked up his pistol.

"You'll get soaked in the rain."

"A small price to pay to find out what's going on." He kissed her quickly. "I'll look out for myself. You keep the door locked."

He was grinning. He was enjoying himself. How could he be so thrilled when he was facing danger? He was like a boy, eager for adventure.

As he was closing the door noiselessly, he stopped. Whispered, "Lock the door behind me."

She hesitated.

"Do it. Don't follow me."

She knew she had no choice. She went to the door as he asked and just as he slipped out, he stopped her from closing the door. "When I come back, you're going to agree to marry me."

Then he was gone. She closed the door quietly and carefully turned the key.

He wasn't going to give up on marriage.

She paced in the room, arms folded over her chest.

She prayed he'd come back safely so they could argue about marriage. She went to the vanity mirror. There was still a faint glow of light from the coals in the fireplace—they had all been in charge of their own fires. It barely illuminated her face, but she could tell she was pale and haggard—

Oh!

Something moved in the vanity mirror. She looked up, heart pounding, at the mirror, but saw nothing. No, wait, there was something. Something draped in black.

She spun around just as a dark cloth slapped against her nose and mouth and strong hands held it there. She couldn't scream. She wildly grasped at the vanity table. There was a silver tray there. She tried to hit her attacker.

But the figure in black knocked the tray from her hand. It clattered on the floor, which was what she'd truly wanted. She was getting dizzy, losing consciousness, and she desperately swept everything off the vanity surface with her hand, making it all crash to the floor.

Then she remembered—her door was locked. Even if anyone heard all the crashing, a rescuer couldn't get in. Desperately she shoved against the arm and managed to push it back enough so she could breathe. She used all the strength she had.

Cold metal pressed to her temple.

"That's right," said a hoarse voice. A woman's voice. "This is a pistol. Now keep your mouth shut or I'll kill you now."

"Who are you?"

"You'll know soon."

"But where did you hide in here? We searched this room. Checked it . . . checked it before bed . . ."

Her voice was slurring. It was hard to form words. Hard to think . . .

The killer took advantage of her dizzied lack of strength. The rag slapped back on her face. She didn't have the strength to fight this time.

"Stupid git," the voice snapped. "You only glanced under the bed. The beds were all made specially, to allow a person to hide within the frame. How do you think we could hide and evade your search?

"We? There's more than one . . . ?"

She was fighting to stay conscious. She gripped the vanity, but her hand slid on the cool marble. The room was spinning—

Portia slumped then, falling to the ground. How could she be taken this way again?

23

Fighting across the muddy lawn, blasted by wind and rain, Sin could barely see through the downpour in the dark. At least Sax couldn't see either, so he had a fighting chance of catching up with his friend.

Ten years ago, Sin had come to London filled with guilt, trying to embark on a new life. Now he was scrambling through a rainstorm, fighting for his life. For Portia's life. Was her theory right?

"Stop there or I shoot," shouted a rage-filled voice. "Who's there? Tell me or I will blow your head off."

"Sax, it's me. What in hell are you doing out here?"

Saxonby stepped out of the darkness, into the faint pool of light given off by the lights in the house. Already, his unusual silver and black hair was plastered to his head, his clothes soaked. He lowered his pistol. "Sin? I got a note telling me to come out here if I wanted to find the solution."

Sin lowered his pistol also. "So you walked out, alone, likely into a trap?"

"I'm here alone, but armed as you see. This fiend killed Georgiana and I want justice. I figured it was time for a confrontation."

Sin grabbed his friend's shoulder. "This was a ruse to get you outside alone."

"I don't damn well care, Sin. I want vengeance. You're going to have to go back. The note requested I come alone."

"I'll come and stay hidden."

Sax hesitated. Then growled, "What have I got to lose? I don't give a damn if I live or die anymore."

"Don't talk like that. I'm fighting to survive, and I've got many more sins on my conscience than you. If there is anyone who has reason to sacrifice himself, who shouldn't care if he lives or dies, it's me."

"You have Portia to protect. It makes a difference. I've got no one now. And I have more sins in my past than you think." Sax turned abruptly. "The note said to go down the steps to the boat launch. To be there at two a.m. My plan is to be early, hide and wait."

Sin flicked his wet hair out of his eyes. "What if the killer is already there, waiting for you?"

"In a raging storm? My wager is that the killer is overconfident by now. Gloating with success."

"Portia thinks the cook is the killer."

"How could she be? She was at the bottom of the cliff."

"Portia believes the cook killed Barker, put her body in the cook's drab gray dress, and pushed her off the cliff, so we would assume the cook was dead. Mrs. Kent used the same ruse I did."

"Your Portia is a smart woman. Sin, you were a bleeding idiot to let her get away ten years ago."

"I know. This is my chance to make amends. For ten wasted years."

"Make amends?" Sax asked.

But Sin didn't answer. He looked back toward the house. Cold rain pelted his face. He could make out a few lights in the windows through the gray wall of rain. Did he keep going and follow Sax to protect him? Or return to Portia?

If he didn't this might be the last time he was going to see a friend he'd had since boyhood.

And Portia would be safe with the door locked.

Blast, Sax had vanished into the dark again.

Running in pursuit, Sin made his way to the steps that led to the boat dock. Rain made them slick and deadly. Below, waves smashed into the rocks, as if trying to devour human flesh.

He slowed his pace, moving with stealth. The moonless, rain-soaked night made him almost invisible. If he left space behind Sax, maybe he wouldn't be spotted by the killer. He couldn't hear his friend's steps on the stone ahead of him, but in the pounding rain, he likely wouldn't even hear Sax even if his friend was playing bagpipes.

There was something ahead . . . something white, that was visible even in the pitch-dark.

Sin reached it just as Sax picked it up. Sin pulled out matches and lit one, shielding it from the rain with his hand. The flame flickered, the feeble light revealed flat, rain-slicked stone. They had reached the flat landing at the water's edge.

"A lace-trimmed handkerchief," Sax shouted over the rain, unfolding it.

Words were written inside it. *Fooled you,* it said.

"What the hell—?" Sax growled.

The flame burnt Sin's fingers and he threw the match away.

Sax was walking around the flat area cut into the rock. "There's no one here."

Sin tensed, expecting a shot through his heart. A knife in his back. They were targets now, even in the dark.

But seconds went by—punctuated by his breathing and the thoughts whipping through his brain. Nothing happened.

"If Kent is trying to kill us," he muttered, "couldn't she damn well get on with it?"

He heard Sax let out a soft sigh. It had been long enough that his friend was starting to relax. High-strung tension couldn't last forever.

"Do you think she's going to show?" Sax said.

"I don't know." Was she lulling them into a sense of ease? Or was she just not damn well here?

What had been the point of the note to Sax? To get Sax out here—but why? By sneaking out, Sax had passed his room. He hadn't been sleeping most nights, too keyed up, too on edge. He'd heard Sax leave the house and followed.

The result was that he and Sax were out of the house. Two strong men were away from the house and Portia was alone in their bedroom—

"Damn it," he shouted. "Portia!"

Blind panic hit him. Sent him running up the stone steps. The intended victim could be anyone—or maybe the plan had been to get Sax out alone and his presence had foiled that plan. Anyway, Portia would not unlock her door. She would be safe—

But he felt dread like he'd never felt before. Not even on the most hellish moments of his life. When his parents were dead . . . when he faced his brother over pistols . . .

He tore into the house and raced up the stairs. He banged on his bedroom door. "Portia, open up."

No sound of footsteps. Not the call of her voice. Nothing.

He pounded harder. Tried to turn the knob again, even though he knew it was locked. He rattled the door. Slammed his shoulder against it. "Portia! Portia!"

If she was in there, she was unable to answer. The crystal-clear thought sent a bolt of crippling fear through his body.

Sax was on his heels, reaching him as Sin ran hard at the door, driving his shoulder into it. The door arched, pulling against both hinges and lock. He heard cracking, but it didn't give.

He went back and just as Sax said, "You'll break your blasted shoulder," he charged at the door again. The door resisted for a moment, then yielded with a bang. It flew open and Sin's momentum carried him wildly into the room.

No one was in the bedroom. A cold wind hit him at the exact

instant he saw the window was open. Everything had been swept off the vanity table. Broken glass, brushes, bottles littered the floor around it.

"No! No. Fuck, no," he roared, his language rough and blunt. He ran for the window. When he looked out, all he could see was rain and blackness. No sign of Portia. There was no smell of blood, thank God.

Sin ripped the room apart in seconds, searching everywhere. He stood, breathing hard, his heart beating so fast he thought it would explode.

Sax rested a hand on his shoulder. "She's not here," Sax said, stating the damned obvious.

Then the others were there. Rutledge. The Incognita. Blute, the blustering Corinthian.

"What's happened?"

"Why in hell did you smash the door down?"

"Where's Saxonby? He wasn't in his room."

They were all here. All the remaining guests. Could one of them have raced back and let himself into the room, making it look like he or she just came out? Or was it Kent all along?

Clarissa stepped forward. "Portia was taken?"

God, his throat was tight. Sin felt like he was trying to breathe through water. "It's the damn cook. It has to be."

"The window could be a ruse," Sax stated. "She could be in the house."

"Damn it." Sin whirled and drove his fist into the wall. Plaster and lathe exploded. Pain stabbed at his hand. He pulled out his fist. Blood oozed from his abraded knuckles.

Sax grabbed him. "That helps no one."

No, damn. He was going to find her. He couldn't be too late.

Portia stopped walking a few feet from the edge of the cliff. She stood on grass slick with rain. "I'm not going further. I won't go willingly to my death."

She faced the woman who had forced her to walk out here, far from the house. The woman who trained two pistols on her.

Portia thought of all the times she'd carried an unloaded pistol as a bluff. From the triumph blazing in Mrs. Kent's eyes, Portia knew these weapons were not a bluff.

The woman had killed ten other people and intended to kill her.

When she had come to, she'd discovered she had been brought out of the house. A woman was leaning over her, and had been slapping her face to wake her up. Slapping her so hard that her cheeks stung and her teeth hurt.

For moments, Portia hadn't even recognized Mrs. Kent. The cook looked completely different. Her face had been transformed from plump and ruddy to smooth and beautiful, with her eyes artfully made up. Her hair was elegantly styled, piled on her head, the coiffure protected from the rain by the hood of a thick cloak. An elegant jade-green silk dress could be glimpsed through the parting in her cloak.

Mrs. Kent had forced her to walk out to the edge of the cliff at this point far, far away from the house. Progress had been slow in the dark and pouring rain. Portia had been stumbling from the effect of the wretched drug that had knocked her out.

Now, she was desperately trying to shake away the woolly-headed feeling. She needed time to regain her wits. "How did you change your appearance?" she asked. "You were so clever. I can't understand how you did this." Her brain was beginning to work more swiftly, trying to piece it together.

"What fools you all were," Mrs. Kent crowed. "I kept all my lovely clothes hidden in the secret compartments I'd built in the thin mattresses of the cots in my servant bedchamber. I had secret compartments put in the furniture—that was where I hid my poisons, my pistols, the balls and powder, and the stage makeup I used for my disguise."

Behind Portia, the sea roared like a greedy dragon that yearned to feed. "But who are you really?" she asked, fighting to keep her voice calm. "I'm sure Kent is not your real name."

"No, this was a disguise, of course. Those wretched *gentle-*

men knew me, but they looked at me and did not recognize me. They saw a frumpy, dumpy servant. Once, I was London's most desired courtesan. I had dukes begging for my favors. My name is Charlotte Lyon. My mother was the most beautiful dancer in Paris, and she captured a duke's heart. With her encouragement, I became a powerful woman, using my voluptuous figure and beauty to entrance rich men."

"And you had a child. That is what this is about. A child—"

"My daughter!" Charlotte Lyon cried, impassioned anguish flooding her voice. Her right hand jerked on one of the pistols.

Portia froze with the expectation of being shot. Nothing happened, and relief flooded, making her feel both weightless and too weak to stand. But stand she did. She had to keep her wits.

"What happened to her?" she asked. Her voice was full of concern—because deep inside, she did understand why a woman would be in pain over losing someone. "Did you have to give her up?"

"She was taken from me! I was sixteen. My mother was furious when I became pregnant. I wanted my baby and she took the child away as soon as the babe was born. There was ample wealth to care for her. I could have visited her. I could have seen her grow up. But no, my mother made the infant disappear. For years, I searched for her. I learned what horrible things she suffered."

"What happened to her?" Keep the woman talking, Portia thought. Then what? She didn't know. She dealt with managing children, not murderers.

What did she do when one child lashed out at another? She found the reason. She talked to the child. She would be firm. She would be in charge. She would be compassionate.

"She *died*. My beautiful girl was only nineteen and she took too much laudanum. My wretched mother told me my child was to be condemned forever for taking her own life. There was no place in heaven for my poor little one, who had no one to protect her. My old witch of a mother was smug. But she wasn't so smug when I drove a knife into her chest. After, I felt I had done something to avenge my poor little girl. As I had searched for her, I had learned about her life. She had been hurt by so many people. I knew I must make it right. I would make them all pay. They were all selfish, arrogant, disgusting. I knew how to lure them to this island. It was so easy. I promised the gentlemen their perverse pleasures, or I pricked their pride. The women were easy—all I had to do was invite them to a party with titled men. For the servants, I bribed them."

The woman paused.

Portia stood close to the edge of the cliff. She feared she might shift her weight and slip off the edge. She managed to take a little step forward as the murderess brushed at tears.

"I am so sorry you lost your daughter."

"Are you? It was your fault! The fault of your awful, holier-than-thou family!"

Instinct told her to step back as the woman spat at her, but she couldn't of course. Instead she stepped forward, away from the edge. "What do you mean?"

"Don't come near me," Charlotte snapped. She leveled the pistols at Portia's heart again.

"What did my family do?" Was she goading the woman into doing something violent? But if she was going to die, she wanted to know why. "When we took in a child, it was with the best of intentions. We never hurt a child."

"You believed those children were less! You taught them to believe that!"

"I don't understand—"

"Then shut up and listen, Miss High-and-Mighty Lamb. Your mother took my baby into her precious foundling home. And took the money my mother gave for her care. Just agreed it was all for the best, then taught my daughter she should be respectable, she should be good. Taught her she would never be more than a wretched servant and she should be happy to accept that, for that was her place!"

"My mother meant the best for your daughter," Portia said.

"Mother would have ensured your daughter was educated, and she would have striven to give the girl a respectable future—"

"Your saintly mother turned my daughter into prey. And all the rest of them here—they were predators."

"What did they do to your daughter? She must have left the foundling home, then."

"Oh, she did. At sixteen, she went to what you would call a respectable house to work as a governess. The son of the house fell in love with her—you know him now as the Earl of Rutledge. The wicked little bitch of a maid, Ellie, worked to get my precious daughter fired, because she'd been bedding the little prick of a son. The butler found out who she was, so he blackmailed my poor daughter, taking every penny she earned. Then, when she was out on the street, that hag, Harriet Barker, dragged her into a brothel. As for Rutledge—did he do right by her? Oh no, once he got her into his bed, he decided she wasn't good enough for him! He stood by and let her fall into ruin."

Spittle flew from Charlotte Lyon's mouth. "The marquis, he visited her at that brothel and whipped her. She escaped that horrid place by becoming the mistress of the Earl of Blute. But he tossed her over. Then one night, she believed she'd finally found her rescuer. She still had some money and pretty gowns and jewels. But when she ventured out to a gaming hell in search of another protector, she was attacked. Viscount Sandhurst rescued her from a ruffian on the street. She fell in love with Viscount Sandhurst, but then he broke her heart. Not good enough for him." The woman gave an evil, reptilian smile. "But you know what that's like, don't you?"

Pain sliced through Portia. Yes, she supposed she was just like Charlotte Lyon's daughter in that way.

"Having her heart broken finished her. She fell into opium— she'd been introduced to it by old Barker. She tried to become a courtesan, but witches like Sadie and Clarissa kept her from finding a protector, out of jealousy and spite. Because she couldn't find anyone, she was forced to sell herself for pennies on the streets. That's when she met that young little tart, Nellie, who introduced her to her brother, Reggie. He was a footman in a grand house but got my daughter to steal for him. She was almost caught, and she felt like a sinner. A failure and a sinner. From your wicked family, she believed she had condemned her soul. That there was no hope for her."

"No! My family would never have taught her that."

"Oh no? All those places are alike! So noble, but inside, you're judgmental and cruel."

The woman was mad. They had never done such a thing. They tried to set children on a good path, but they would never condemn one for stumbling.

"If she'd come back, I would have helped her."

"How could she show her face when she felt as if she were worthless? I've proven she is not. She is worthy of justice." She leaned back and threw out a cackling laugh.

"How did you kill them?" Portia asked. Could she distract the woman and tackle her, taking the pistols? Would anyone find them out here? "Why didn't you just poison us all at dinner? Wouldn't that have been easier?"

The woman smiled, a smile bloated with evil. "I could have, but it wouldn't have been such fun. Poisoning the viscount was simple. I left a pill for him in his room, with a letter supposedly from Clarissa telling him it would ensure his sexual pleasure. That he must take it with his port after dinner. Of course, he fell for it. I destroyed the letter, of course. Crayle was easy. I'd put a sleeping draught in the brandy in his room. He had a drink, passed out, and I strung him up. Sadie ate the poisoned biscuits and the stupid widow drank poisoned sherry."

"What of the three servants?"

"None of them thought I was anything other than a silly old woman. It is so easy to attack when no one suspects you. Ellie took the tea I gave her. Then I hanged her. She woke up to the terror of a noose around her neck."

The delight in the woman's eyes was sickening. But Portia had managed to move a little closer to the cook while the woman spoke. "The butler—I took care of him by caving in his bald head. And you saw the footman. How terrified he was when I cut him up. I had to stab him to put him out of his agony eventually, but what fun it was to hear him beg that I not cut off his cock. He *deserved* it. He beat my girl, cut her and whipped her to make her do his bidding."

"Did Willoughby hurt her too? How did you kill him? He was a strong young man."

"It is all about the element of surprise, Miss Lamb. Look at that smug footman Reggie. He was young and strong, but not as strong as me!"

No, Charlotte Lyon had a madwoman's strength.

"I can see that you hated the others. But what did Sinclair do? And Saxonby?"

"My daughter went to Sinclair's orgies, trying to catch his eye. All she wanted was to be safe and dry and well fed. He rejected her, as did Saxonby."

"Surely they should not die because of a rejection—"

"You know nothing! If you knew what I know—" Charlotte broke off. She muttered under her breath. "Not to tell. Not to tell."

The woman was mad, driven by vengeance to do something unthinkable. But while Portia could understand the woman's grief and hatred, the sudden babbling scared her. "If your daughter was gone, how did you learn about all these sins?" she asked softly.

"Don't you understand your part in that? That's the blessing of what you did for her in that home. You taught her to read and write. Otherwise, I wouldn't have known who to make pay for her death. Now you are going to die. You are going to walk off the cliff."

"No!"

"Do it or I'll shoot you, then kick you over, Miss Lamb. Lamb to slaughter, that's what you are."

"You'll have to shoot me, then. I am not going to just walk off a cliff."

Charlotte Lyon leveled one pistol at Portia's heart. "Then I shall. This is for my daughter, my innocent—"

"What was her name?" Portia asked suddenly. She realized the woman had not used the girl's name once.

At the look of anguish on the woman's face, Portia swiftly understood. "You named her, but that was not the name she used. And no one told you her name. It must have been so hard to find her."

The pistol wobbled slightly, and Portia caught her breath. "I called her Madeline," Charlotte whispered, "but my mother insisted she was to be given away without a name, that the foundling home would give her a name."

"And no one told you what it was. For that, I cannot forgive my family," Portia whispered.

Charlotte let the pistol drop a bit. Then her face contorted with fury and she cried, "It's too late. You don't care. You are trying to fool me. Now you are going to die!"

A shot exploded in a roar. Portia expected terrible pain and a powerful blow that sent her over the cliff as the shot hit her. But nothing happened. Except Charlotte screeched and gripped her right arm as the pistol fell from her right hand. Her face went ashen. Then she took a deep breath and pointed her remaining pistol at Portia's chest. "Well, I still have this one—"

Another shot and Charlotte screamed and grabbed for her leg. She dropped her second pistol and crumpled to the ground.

Portia stood, frozen, then launched forward to the wounded woman who writhed in pain and wailed like a banshee. She knew someone had shot Charlotte, saving her life, but her thought was for the bleeding woman on the ground. "Stay still," she commanded. "I'll tend to those wounds." She got on her knees beside Charlotte and pulled up her skirts, searching for the hems of her petticoats—for clean fabric to use as bandages.

Suddenly, Portia found she was being lifted into the air, while behind her a masculine voice demanded, "What are you doing? The woman wanted to kill you."

That growling, deep voice. Sin! As he set her on her feet, she turned to him—saw his stark expression. "She's wounded, Sin. We must do something so she doesn't bleed to death."

He pulled her against him and his mouth, hot and commanding, seared hers in a kiss. He kissed her breathless. She wrapped her arms around his neck, holding him tightly.

When he broke the kiss, he took long, ragged breaths. "God, Portia. I was so afraid I'd lost you. How can your concern be for that witch of a woman? She's a murderess."

She pulled free of Sin's arms, knowing what she must do. "She deserves justice, not agony. I can't stand by and watch her suffer."

He shook his head, his hair spraying rain. "No, I guess you can't, Portia. You are just like the woman I loved ten years ago. Still every bit as noble and perfect. Let me help you."

She lifted her skirts a few inches to reveal her petticoats. "Tear off some of the fabric of the petticoat—it makes good bandaging. Try to find clean bits—the hems are very much splattered with mud."

Sin did so quickly, ripping off strips. Then he held the cook steady while Portia pulled fabric clear of the woman's wounds. "They are surface wounds." She looked up at Sin. "Was that deliberate? You were the one to shoot her."

"I was. At first I wanted to debilitate her, not kill her. But when she threatened you with the second pistol, I couldn't afford to be so careful. I would have killed her had it been necessary."

Portia saw the cool ruthlessness on his face. How much he'd changed from the young, sweet man of the country she'd fallen in love with.

Yet she loved this mature, wise, strong man even more.

Sin stabilized the woman as she wrapped her makeshift bandages around the wounds.

"I hate you both. Let me up. Let me kill you!" Charlotte Lyon screeched.

"Shut it," Sin growled. "You're lucky to be alive."

As Portia wound the bandage around the bleeding cut, she said, "I'll have to clean them properly at the house." Then she told Sin what the cook had said.

"I heard the end of it," he said hoarsely. "I reached you just as she was explaining all our sins toward her daughter."

"But how did you guess we were here?"

"I didn't. A note was left for me in the drawing room of the house. I was wild with terror, wanting to search for you; then Sax found the note. It was intended to lure me here, where she planned to kill me after—" He broke off. "Let me do that." He took over, wrapping a bandage around the woman's arm, tying it. "I learned this from when I was shot twice in duels." He met the cook's wild-eyed gaze. "You lured me here so I would watch you hurt Miss Lamb."

A mocking laugh, deep and thoroughly wicked, cut through the night. "No, she didn't, Sin. I did. The least likely suspect, that's who I am."

Sin slowly stood, turning to face the owner of the sneering laugh.

The barrel of a pistol was the first thing Sin saw. Then, beyond that, the face of a madman with golden hair.

"Willoughby. I knew you were involved in this," Sin said coolly. He had to play this game carefully—Will was pointing the damn barrel at Portia.

"You couldn't. My death fooled you completely."

"No, when Portia realized it was the madam who had been pushed off the cliff, not the cook, I began to realize the truth."

"You didn't." Will's eyes narrowed into dark slits. "You were fooled. You're bluffing."

"You've played enough cards with me to know when I'm bluffing. You know I'm telling you the truth now."

"You couldn't know. I was too clever."

Sin heard a soft squeak from beside him. Portia's eyes were huge with surprise and she'd made the little sound. She looked from Will to him. "You knew he was really alive?"

"You gave me the clues," Sin admitted. "When Harriet was murdered and dressed like the cook, we were fooled because we couldn't get close enough to identify her body. Then I realized there was one other victim who couldn't be readily identified. Will was the only victim to suffer so much violence he was disfigured beyond recognition." He turned back to Willoughby. "I went to your room, looked at the body that was supposed to be you. You used to joke about the heart-shaped scar on your back, put there by your father once when he hit you. That body had no scar. Who was he, Will? And why in God's name did you help this woman murder ten people?"

"He helped?" Portia repeated. "That was how she was able to perform such feats of physical strength. Willoughby did it. But why?"

Will took a few steps closer. He still had that damn pistol trained on Portia and Sin felt powerless. Will was watching him and he couldn't make any move yet.

"That body belongs to a young man I met on the mainland, a man was about my height with the same color hair. I brought him over here, drugged him, kept him hidden in the basement. You didn't search the house until after my 'death.' As for why I did it, pretty, noble Miss Lamb? Sin thought he loved you so damn much. He thought that your purity would save him. He didn't know a damn thing about real love."

"He does," Portia said, defiantly.

"Angel, don't let him goad you."

"Let her talk, Sin. Don't you think it's time she knew what you are?"

"She does know," Sin said angrily. "I lost her because of that."

"You told her you went to those brothels. You never really told her what you are." Will glared at Portia. "I knew everything about his past. You were no sweet, innocent, handsome young rube from the country. Why do you think I took you to the House of Discipline, Sin? I knew what you were."

Sin didn't say anything. Will wasn't paying attention to

him. His crazed gaze was fixed on Portia. If he jumped Will right now, they might both go over the cliff. But Portia would be safe—

"He slept with his brother's wife. Faced his brother in a duel over it. His own mother seduced him. He killed his own damn father. He grew up in a world of sex and perversion, and he lived in a private hell. I know what he suffered. I know," Willoughby shouted. "And I was trying to help him. Trying to lead him to see that he was not a sinner at heart. I was going to offer him love, damn it. Then he broke off his engagement and—"

"Love?" Portia whispered. "You loved him?"

"True love. With my heart and soul, I loved you, Sin. I'd waited a lifetime for someone who could return my love. I shared women with you to be close to you. I brought you to orgies because when we were making love in a crowd, it was like we were making love together. Then you rejected me—because you still loved her!"

"I didn't know how you felt, Will," Sin said quickly. He had to drag Will's attention and anger from Portia. "But I never would have loved you. Not because of Portia, but because . . . I just don't."

Just as he'd hoped, the pistol jerked around to point at him. Will's finger went toward the trigger.

A shot exploded—but it slammed into Will's back. Sin grabbed Portia and pulled her with him to the grass, to safety. In reflex, Will pulled the trigger, just as he stumbled forward, propelled by the force of the shot. His boots skidded on the wet grass; he howled in pain, then tumbled forward, off the edge of the cliff.

"No," cried the cook. She had managed to get to her knees. "Brother!"

"Your brother?" Portia gasped.

"My half brother. We shared the same father. I killed our father—he'd threatened to kill Will over his love of men. Called him a Molly boy, a sinner, a waste of flesh. I protected Will all those years ago, and in return, he came here to help me."

"You will swing for what you've done," Sin growled.

"I won't! I'll be with them now. I'll be with my little girl again. I've committed enough sins that I'll see her now!" The woman laughed manically and staggered to her feet.

Sin lunged forward to stop her, but he was too late. Lyon leapt off the cliff, her screams cutting through the night.

Damn, he was sliding toward the edge. The grass, slick with rain, sloped toward the cliff—

Hands grabbed him just as he managed to dig in his boot. He stopped his slide, wrapped his arms around Portia, who had stopped him from falling, and he got both of them several feet from the cliff.

He gazed into her huge gray eyes. The most beautiful eyes in the world, belonging to a woman who now knew the worst about him. Not everything Will had said was true, and he owed Portia the truth. Once she had it, he would lose her forever.

She cocked her head. She looked so startling beautiful with her huge pale gray eyes, her sweet freckles, her sensual mouth.

The most beautiful, sensual woman he'd ever known. Portia was precious.

"Portia—" That was all he got out because his throat was so dry and tight.

"Wait," she gasped suddenly. "The shot that stopped Willoughby—where did it come from?"

"That," he growled, "was Sax. Once I realized Will was still alive, I knew he would think I came alone. Sax armed himself, took cover, and waited. I was determined to save you, Portia, but I had hoped to be able to have Lyon and Will arrested. Of course, if I'd had to, I would have jumped him. Will and I would have gone off the cliff together, but I would've protected you."

"Thank heaven Sax made the choice to shoot, rather than you jumping off the cliff."

"In the end, Will left us with no other choice but to kill him. And he's gone."

"He was in love with you," she said softly.

He put his hands on her delicate shoulders and leaned close

to her. "I had no idea." That was the truth. In Sin's wild orgies, Will had been notorious for vanishing into bedrooms with groups of men and women. There was much speculation about what he did in there. Sin himself had played with other men, to delight women or when it had been part of the play at brothels. Will had obviously hoped for more.

Sin bent the last inch, kissed her.

Sax had not come out yet, obviously not wanting to interrupt this moment.

Sin drew away from the kiss, waiting for her to demand the truth. But she just reached up and stroked his cheek.

"You saved my life," she whispered. "Your planning, your cleverness saved me."

"Portia, about what Will said . . . aren't you wondering what he meant by those things?"

"I love you," she said firmly. "I don't care what a madman said about you."

Her faith in him stunned him. "I asked you to marry me because I owed you marriage, but I was certain that if you knew the truth about me, you'd never want to say yes."

She stared up at him, confused.

"Some of the things Will said were lies. But some were the truth. I don't know how he found out—he must have talked to everyone I grew up with. He must have figured it out somehow. I didn't kill my own father. My mother killed him—and she did it to protect me in her own warped way. And to save her own skin. When I was young . . . she did things to me that she had no right to. Things that were wrong."

His skin was hot, his heart pounding even harder than when he'd faced Will over a gun. "Sexual things. She touched me for years. Fondled me. Then she—hell, I can't even talk about it. My father found out, hated me, and she—I think she poisoned him because she feared he would punish me. That was how I knew the effects of poison when Sandhurst died."

Strange how he could talk about it dispassionately. As if it had happened to someone else.

"My brother was older than me. He was my half brother. I was twelve years younger than him. His mother died; then my father married my mother. My mother arranged the marriage between my brother and his wife, Estella. Estella was stunningly beautiful. She was also as warped as Mama, and soon after her marriage to my half-brother, Estella started coming to my bed."

"How old were you?" she whispered.

"Twelve, I guess. Old enough to know it wasn't right. My mother had been doing things to me for years before that—I don't really remember when she started. My father was still alive then. He was so busy with his own mistresses that he didn't care what was happening. My brother cared, though. He called me out. I was sixteen, facing my brother over pistols. The thing was—I wasn't sleeping with Estella by then. I'd refused to do it once I reached fifteen. I was away at school then, and she would try to seduce me on the holidays. But I said no. Out of spite, she told my brother. When we dueled, I missed my brother deliberately. But he didn't miss me."

"Oh my heavens," Portia gasped. "You were a child! None of this was your fault. How could he have shot at you?"

"I guess he hated me. He winged me. I wished he'd killed me. But afterward, he must have had a change of heart—he was so guilt-ridden over what he'd done that he took his own life. Estella died soon after when she fell and broke her neck while riding. My father found out the whole sordid truth; then he died of poisoning. And my mother . . . she paid soon after that. She died of a fever. I was the last one left. Then I learned I was the new duke. For me it was going to be a new start. I played a role when I came to London. I pretended to be innocent. I didn't want anyone to know about my past. What I wanted to do was forget it. But when Will took me back to the brothels, I found I craved wild sex. It flooded my mind so I couldn't think about the past. When I was having orgies, when I was drunk or in an opium haze, I was free of my past."

"Now I understand," she whispered.

"I proposed to you ten years ago because I loved you. You were like an angel to me, Portia. The most good and beautiful woman I'd ever known. I wanted to be worthy of you. But I'm dark and warped inside. That's why I can offer you marriage, but nothing more. Every time you look at me now, you'll see the warped man inside. I know I've lost your heart forever."

"Sin, I don't—"

She broke off and looked over his shoulder in surprise. Sin turned.

The other guests had come from the house—the Incognita and the two earls. Clarissa rushed forward with her arms open. "Saxonby told us everything. Dear Portia, thank heavens you are safe. You saved us all. Both of you. Oh, thank you."

She embraced Portia, then buried her face in Portia's shoulder and began to sob.

There was nothing more he could say to Portia now. He was going to insist on marrying her, then give her the freedom he knew she would want.

24

She was on the mainland again. On England's shores. Safe and alive, thanks to Sin. As soon as she stepped off the dory, Portia bent down and rested her hands on the solid surface of the quay. "I just have to make certain it's real."

Sin crouched beside her. "I'm tempted to give the thing a kiss, except there's likely been a pile of fish slopped there."

That made her withdraw her hands and he grinned. "It is real, though, Portia. It's all over. And I'm going to get you safely home."

He moved to his knees to cup her face tenderly. Then he kissed her—a hot, long, openmouthed, sensual kiss for the whole world to see.

Once she'd been a model of propriety. But that was before their scandalous night—nights—together. Before she'd thought him dead and discovered there were more important things than being proper.

So she wrapped her arms around his neck and kissed Sin passionately, in front of fishermen and sailors and fishwives.

When their kissed finally ended, she took fast breaths, and so did he. He stroked her cheeks so sweetly, she shivered. The wind off the sea tossed his hair about his handsome face, leaving the silky brown tresses as seductively mussed as after she and he made love.

"I know no harm can come to you now," he said softly. "And I know we survived because you are so good, because you deserved to survive."

He had been quiet on the boat ride back. He'd looked troubled. Now she knew it was because he'd been forced to tell her about his past.

Portia clasped his warm, strong hand. "You aren't bad. You were a boy, Sin, and others hurt you and took advantage of you."

"That does not excuse what I did. I knew right from wrong."

"Sometimes children are forced to do wrong by adults. It does excuse you."

He shook his head.

His heart was in anguish. He was tormented by his past. He'd offered marriage, but she couldn't bear to have a marriage in name only. She loved him and wanted him to accept her love. To believe in it.

Or did he simply not want a real marriage because he wanted to go back to his wicked orgies and brothels?

"It's time to take you home."

Sin lifted his hand, summoning a young lad to him. He gave the boy some coins to fetch his coachman, instructed other men to pile up his trunks.

Beyond the quay, the sea rippled. The waves sparkled in the sun that had broken through the clouds that dawn. Early this morning, discovering the sun glimmering and the sea calmer, she, Sin, and Sax had used a fire to signal the mainland and the dory had come out.

Now, safe on the quay, Portia turned away from the dark, foreboding shape of Serenity Island.

She would be going back to the foundling home. To the children she missed. She would see Mother and embrace her. It didn't matter that Mother wouldn't know who she was. She would be able to tell Mother she loved her, and that was what mattered most.

Surviving made everything seem so clear.

It made her know she wanted Sin.

How did she make him see they could have a real marriage?

The oarsmen were helping the other survivors off the dory. The Earl of Rutledge, whose expression had been filled with arrogance before, looked pale and fearful. The blustering, muscular Earl of Blute was shaking and trembling.

Saxonby got out of the boat and came over to Sin. His face was stoic. It had been a shock to him to lose Georgiana, but perhaps more of a shock to learn Georgiana's dark secret, written in a journal kept by Charlotte Lyon and hidden in the secret compartment of her cot. Georgiana had been the Old Madam's partner in brothels. She had obtained gently bred virgins for their houses of ill repute. That had stunned Saxonby and shaken his heart to the core.

Clutching a shawl around her, the Incognita alighted last. As Clarissa stepped onto the quay, her face went pale and she swayed. Portia understood—it was the delayed reaction of shock. She rushed to the woman's side, supported her, and Clarissa smiled gratefully.

"I should be jubilant now," Clarissa said. "But I feel so drained. Suddenly, I feel very scared. Isn't that mad?"

"Of course not," Portia answered firmly. "It just means that while you were surviving, your mind would not allow you to take in the horror. That protects us from great pain or fear. Now that you are safe, you are being hit by it all at once. You must take care of yourself."

"I thought I would want to go home at once. Instead, I want to go to the nearest inn. I want to drink far too much wine, collapse in a bed. I can't explain it, but I feel I need time before I return to . . . to real life."

"I understand that." For Portia didn't want to rush home either. Her actual life in the foundling home—teaching, carrying out the chores, managing the house—seemed almost unreal.

Clarissa clasped her hand, lowered her voice. "I overheard Sin and Sax speaking. Sin said he asked you to marry him and you turned him down. He is a duke, dear! Why ever did you do something so foolish?"

How did she explain it? Before she would never have revealed anything so personal, but what they'd been through had broken down barriers.

"I'm in love with him," she admitted. "Sin offered marriage because he ruined me, but not a marriage for love. He told me I could have my freedom. That he wouldn't bother me."

"So he can pursue his debauched life?"

"I don't know. I think it is because of his past—" She stopped. That was not her secret to reveal. "There is something that haunts him. He seems to think it will prevent me from loving him."

"He's annoyingly noble." Clarissa nodded. "So you have refused to marry him—"

"That was a mistake. I want to marry him. But I want love. I want to be with him. Sleep with him at night, wake in his arms in the morning. I have spent my life rescuing children, helping them to defeat their terrible memories and embrace their futures. That is what Sin needs. But if he does want to marry me, then leave me, I can't accept that. And what if . . . what if the reason really *is* that he wants wild parties and sexual games?"

"Then give him the wild sex life you think he desires," Clarissa said softly. "Just because you were raised to be proper doesn't mean you can't enjoy a little improper fun. I gather you have discovered that."

Portia admitted that was true.

"You should surprise him. Take him to an inn and spend a very wicked night with him. I suspect you can make him change his mind on marriage. If you follow my advice, and use some of the gifts I will give you."

"Gifts?" Portia asked.

Someone shouted, "Portia!"

She spun, surprised by the masculine cry. It was the Earl of Rutledge. He staggered toward her, but he was no longer pale. He wrapped his arms around her, startling her.

Around him, she saw Sin standing with Sax, and glaring in surprise at Rutledge's sudden, perplexing display of emotion.

The remaining guests, the survivors, all had learned her real name, but all had promised their discretion. Sin had insisted they vow not to reveal that she had been on the island, at an orgy.

"I owe my life to you, Portia." Rutledge released her and he kissed her hand gallantly, while gazing longingly into her eyes.

She was astounded. He was gazing at her as if—

No, that wasn't possible.

"Also to Sinclair and Saxonby," she said swiftly. "They stopped the killers."

"But you were the one who figured out it was the cook. Sinclair said I owe you my thanks."

"Thank you for them." She smiled.

"And now, to the nearest pub," he declared. "I intend to drink a toast to being alive. Do come with me, Portia."

"Oh, er, that is very kind of you, but I cannot, I'm afraid."

"Then marry me, Portia. You have captured my heart and my soul. You are lovely and clever. I feel you are exactly what my mother believes I need—a capable woman to make a worthy gentleman of me."

"Your mother?" She'd never dreamed Rutledge would... heavens... propose marriage. "I am very flattered, but I cannot marry you."

"You are going to marry Sinclair. A duke."

"No, you see, I already turned down Sinclair. And if I did that, I should not accept anyone else."

"I don't understand."

"I know. It is complicated. But I cannot marry you, Rutledge." She let him go.

He joined the others but gave her a longing look, and Sin came to her side.

"Why is he looking at you like that?" Sin asked darkly.

She gave an innocent smile. "Rutledge asked me to marry him."

"What did you say?"

"I said I would have to think about it."

He blinked. "You didn't say that to me. You refused me flatly." He stepped back. "Are you going to go with him?"

She knew she'd teased him long enough. After all they'd been through it wasn't fair. "I refused him, Sin, of course. I'm not in love with him."

"And you aren't in love with me either. Come, Portia, I'll take you home."

"No, there are two things you do not understand, Sin. The first is that I love you very much. The second is that I do not want to go home. I want to spend one more night with you, alone with you, at the nearest inn that will give us a bed."

Once she returned to the foundling home, she would return to her world where she had to be proper. They had to keep up the reputation of the home, for that ensured the children's futures. She could not have an affair with Sin. That would be impossible.

So this night was her last chance to convince Sin to have a real marriage. One filled with love. And passion.

They were in his carriage, heading toward an inn. Sin had turned his attention to the window. Now was the perfect time to surprise him.

Daringly, Portia reached over and stroked his cock through his trousers. Under her palm, it pulsed, twitched, straightened. All with astonishing speed.

And she absolutely had his attention.

She undid the falls of his trousers, bent down, and took him into her mouth.

This time, his cock was already hard and thick by the time it slid past her lips. Fluid bubbled from the full head, leaking over him to make him slick. She licked up those silvery, tart and sweet juices. Breathed in his scent.

"Portia, that's good," he growled. He fell back against the seat and gave a moan of pleasure that made her tingle to her toes. She ran her tongue all over the smooth, delectable head.

Now that she'd been so intimate with him, could she really go back to a life without any intimacy at all? That would be her future if she refused to marry him—or if they had an empty marriage. How could she wake up every morning, knowing she could never do this again to this wonderful, brave man?

Her heart gave a little hiccup. The hot sting of tears threatened.

At least, she had right now.

She opened her mouth wide and took as much of his magnificent cock inside as she could. And sucked him.

Lovingly at first. Then hard and wild and demanding, determined to pleasure him. Because making him moan and arch his hips and grip the seat cushions gave her pleasure too.

Then she reached down into his open trousers and cradled and caressed his ballocks with both hands.

To her shock, he pulled back, out of her mouth. He took her hands out of his trousers.

His brown eyes glowed like gold with desire. "Do that any more and I'll explode. I'd rather fuck you senseless first. Give you a half-dozen orgasms. Right now."

"That sounds rather good," she squeaked.

He was easing her back on the seat, drawing up her skirts when the carriage stopped.

"Damnation," she breathed, swearing aloud for the first time. "We've arrived at the inn."

The moment Sin left the room to fetch food for them, which he intended for them to eat in their rooms rather than in the dining room and tavern, there was a rap on the door.

It was safe to open doors now, Portia knew, but she still

opened it only a crack. When she saw it was Clarissa, she opened it fully.

Clarissa stepped into the room, clad in a thick robe of a sensible beige flannel.

At Portia's look of shock, she smiled. "I don't always wear scandalous gowns, you know. Even though the wealthy Earl of Rutledge is at the inn and ripe for seduction, tonight is just for me. A night with a book and a cup of cocoa. But first, I had to bring my gift to you."

Clarissa placed a velvet bag in Portia's hands. "This is everything you need to convince the Duke of Sinclair that you are not dull or sweet. This will completely entrance him and win his undying passion, I promise."

"Why are you doing this for me?"

"You saved my life. Anything you ask of me, it will be my pleasure to give."

"What am I exactly to do with these things?"

"There is something for you to wear that will surprise him. And something for him to wear that shall give you the chance to make him open his heart. Once he is vulnerable, he is yours to command."

"Sin? Mine to command?"

"When you've pleasured him, have you ever had moments where you have felt great power?" Clarissa asked.

"Well, yes. I suppose I have."

"Then take him to that moment. And use it wisely. Now, for your instructions." Clarissa drew the most astonishing thing from the pouch. Her explanation of what should be done with it was blunt. And thoroughly shocking.

In the mirror over the vanity table, Portia saw her face was brilliant red. Her hair faded into blandness compared to her scarlet cheeks.

To her surprise, when she finished her vivid explanation, Clarissa embraced her. A warm, impulsive hug. Clarissa stepped back and wiped her eyes. "Good luck, my dear."

With that, Clarissa left. Portia knew Sin would be coming

upstairs with wine and food. It had been a whirlwind since they'd returned to the mainland.

They had gone from the quay to meet the local magistrate, who interviewed them all about the events on Serenity Island. The tale had sounded fantastic, and Portia had seen doubt on the magistrate's face. Of course, he couldn't accuse two dukes and an earl of lying. But he had wanted to ask more questions in the morning and requested that they stay at the local inn. Willoughby was dead, but he was a viscount, and his crimes would have to be made public. The murders had to be explained. Families of the victims must be told.

She knew Sin had paid a small fortune to acquire the best room and hot baths—hers had been heavenly. He had ordered the best wine and brandy and food to be prepared and brought to their room.

Now, she had just a few moments to prepare before Sin came back.

Portia took the items in the bag and laid them on the vanity. Could she do this?

What she held in her hands was a harness made of supple leather straps and shining metal rings and buckles. It looked like a horse's bridle, but it most certainly was not a piece of tack. Secured to the leather, protruding out, was an ivory phallus. A fake cock that was long and huge and rather like—

Well, like Sin's.

Could she put it on and wait for him wearing it?

For a start, she could not even figure out how to put it on. She couldn't figure out which straps fastened through which buckles. She did it wrong twice—had the phallus sticking out behind her once.

Then she had it all fastened and she stood in front of the mirror.

Her courage failed. "No, I can't do this—"

The door latch clicked and she spun around in shock. She was standing nude, a fake ivory phallus sticking out from in front of her privates, as Sin walked in.

* * *

He was looking at Portia's lovely naked breasts, her rounded hips, her flame-colored pubic hair . . . with an erect cock sticking out.

His brows had shot up and Sin knew his eyes were as big as a young boy's as he stared at her.

She blushed. She looked down at her feet. Then she took a step toward him and the cock wobbled and she suddenly laughed, then sobbed. "What must you think of me?"

"Portia, where did you get that?"

That was not the best thing to say. Certainly not in a shocked, stunned tone of voice. He should have been hustling her to the bed for inventive carnal fun.

But he was so damn astounded.

"Clarissa suggested I try it. I was afraid . . . I was afraid you don't want a real marriage because you want to go back to wild sex and orgies. I wanted to explore wild sex with you. I want to share that with you, if we were to marry."

"You do?" He couldn't believe his ears.

He wasn't going to question anymore. He set down the tray of food on the dresser—the nearest surface. Staring at Portia, he tore off his clothes. She reached down and touched the fake cock, making it bounce, and his knees almost buckled.

Swiftly he got naked. His prick was almost as rigid as the ivory one.

He approached her, almost light-headed with lust. That had to be all his blood draining down to make his prick as thick and hard as a cricket bat.

He wrapped his hand around the shaft of her phallus. With wide gray eyes, she stared down.

"Now that is rather shocking," she whispered. "Seeing your hand wrapped around what looks like a cock. My cock. Which, of course, it's not really."

He slid his hand along to the hilt of the ivory prick, then realized it was a cunning device. The other end extended into her sweet pussy and it was also shaped like a prick.

"I thought you would find this fun. I . . . I wanted to be adventurous."

"And you got this contraption from Clarissa?"

"I wanted to show you that I can be exciting. I was shocked when she described it. Then intrigued. She said I could . . . oh, I can't say it." She put her hand to her mouth. Then she lifted her chin. "I *will* say it. In here, in this bedroom, I want to be improper with you." Her cheeks went bright pink, and she said, "Clarissa told me I should thrust it in your bottom. That it would give you pleasure like you've never had before. That men are tremendously sensitive there. She said that if I . . . uh . . . fucked your . . . your ass, you would be entranced with me. Bewitched by me."

"You were going to do that to me?" It was like being hit by lightning. He was shocked to the spot. But burning hot inside.

"I've shocked you, haven't I? I was afraid of doing that. I'm no good at this—"

"You are the most enticing woman I've ever known."

Curling his hand around her neck, he drew her lips to his. He'd been surprised, and his surprise had hurt her feelings. He was behaving like a damn prig. Like a prude, shocked that Portia had done this to please him.

"What do I do?" she whispered.

With his fingers, he stroked her clit. "Did she tell about lubricant?"

"She gave me a little vial of oil."

He gave the fake cock a jiggle and she gasped as the dildo in her pussy teased her. "Why don't you get that oil?" he asked. "I want to watch you walk with a cock sticking out from your lovely feminine figure."

And he did, his heart hammering with arousal. She returned in moments with a little glass container. Sin opened it and drizzled oil on his fingers, then hers. He showed her how to lubricate the head and shaft of the dildo. His heart pounded faster and faster as their hands worked together, sliding along the shaft.

"Now you have to do this to my ass, love." To show her, he caressed her rosebud anus with his oiled finger. Making her slick. His finger went inside an inch, pushing past her snug muscles.

He wondered if she would be too shocked. He was about to say he would lubricate himself, when she whispered, "I so want to do that to you."

He moved to the bed, got on his hands and knees. He hadn't been in a submissive position like that for a long time. And never with Portia. But this wasn't about some game.

This was about pure intimacy.

Soft, gentle strokes down his back made him want to purr. Her fingers slid down, then caressed his ass. She groped him. "My heavens, your muscles are rock hard. So different from my rounded rump."

"I love your ass, Portia."

Her finger pressed between his cheeks. He tensed in anticipation. Relaxing was the key to enjoying anal pleasures, but he couldn't help the instinctive tension. He'd been a party to too many perverse games when he'd been young. He'd learned the difference between being used for sex and savoring sex as he grew older.

He took deep breaths.

Her finger pushed slightly inside his ass. Pushing against his tight muscles.

"Oh, you're so hot and tight!"

He groaned. Now he realized why he was tense. Not because he didn't trust Portia, but because he was fighting for control. Playing erotic games with her had him on the brink of coming.

"You can try fucking me now. Take it slow, though, angel. My muscles are going to resist." His voice was a hoarse rasp.

"All right. What do I do? Get on my knees behind you? The bed is soft and it makes it hard to take aim."

He had to grin. As intense as his need for sex with Portia was, she made him smile. "Brace your hand on my back and take the cock in your hand, love," he said. Giving her instructions had him ready to explode.

The hard tip of the fake cock pressed against his anus. His muscles were so tight she couldn't push in. He told her to thrust—to push forward with her hand and her hips, then back off and try again. Finally, he held his cheeks apart and that opened him enough. In went her cock with a little pop.

Oh Lord.

"Thrust in me, Portia. Fuck me."

She braced her hands on his ass cheeks—a sensation that felt good. And her hips propelled the cock deeper in him. She fucked him slowly, until he begged her to go harder and deeper. Then he caught a glimpse of them in the vanity mirror—him on hands and knees, her on her knees behind him. Her breasts bobbed with each thrust. The shaft of the cock kept disappearing inside his ass.

God, he was going to come.

"Like having a prick of your own?" he said, lightly, though it came out sounding as if his throat was parched.

"This is much harder work than I thought. You are so tight."

He laughed gruffly.

Then she gave a sudden squeak. "Oh—when I do that, it teases me. Right inside."

"Then keep doing that." He grabbed his cock as he said that. The combination of jerking his rigid prick while his ass was being reamed . . .

His cock swelled in his hand. His every muscle went rock-hard. Pleasure exploded in his brain and he saw a heavenly light.

His come shot out all over his hand.

Portia cried out. In the mirror, he saw her writhe as she came over the fake cock inside her, with the other end of it impaled in his ass.

* * *

She watched Sin flop down on the bed, gasping for breath. His eyes were half-shut, sleepy from sex. He had helped her withdraw the fake cock and take the harness off. Now he flashed a grin at her, but Portia knew he was so exhausted, so drained by his orgasm that he could barely move.

She'd done that to him. She'd made him come so hard that he'd collapsed, smiling lazily at her. He reached out his hand and she knew he wanted her to lie down with him. But she shook her head. Portia knew what she was going to do—she was going to ask him to marry her. He might refuse. She might have wounded his pride too much—she now knew he was a vulnerable man who had been hurt when young and perhaps her rejection had hurt him also, and too badly. But she was going to try.

"I'm exhausted, my love," he said huskily, "but not too exhausted to do something very important."

He rolled out of bed and got to his feet. "Let me get down on one knee in front of you."

Her heart stuttered. He was going to ask her again.

He had to rest his hand on the bed to balance himself, which was utterly endearing.

Sin dropped to one knee. Portia held her breath, the word *yes* almost falling off her lips before he got the question out. Yes. Yes. Yes.

He leaned forward, parting her legs. The feel of his strong hands on her inner thighs got her aroused again, but she was too shocked to move. She'd thought he was going to propose. But he pressed his mouth to her cunny and licked and sucked and nuzzled her. She was squirming—his stubble teased her and she was soooo sensitive.

She was melting. Exquisite erotic tension was building and she clutched the sheets. But the saddest thought gripped her and wouldn't let go. Of course Sin wouldn't ask her again. She'd told him she would never marry him. Why would he even want to ask now? Why would he even want to marry her? He was celebrating life and that was all.

She would have this—one wicked night with her wicked duke—then it would all be over.

His tongue slid into her. How she loved that sensation, like being filled with silk. It was so intimate, to have him tasting her like that, more intimate than anything.

His lips closed on her clit. He sucked hard.

She closed her eyes. Stars exploded.

Oh! Oh!

Logically, she should be content. She belonged in her foundling home. The children brought joy to each day; they made her happy. She was doing good in the world. His family and friends had all thought she didn't belong in his world—and they'd worked so hard to end the engagement. Were they right?

His tongue slicked over her clit. Portia gripped his hair, moaning and writhing beneath him.

But she loved him so. Loved him so much.

She didn't want to lose him again.

She stroked his head, his lush, silky brown hair. His hands lifted her, cupping and squeezing her bottom. His tongue flicked over her, back and forth, exquisitely.

Then his finger dipped in the hot valley of her bottom. Teased the opening. Made slow, easy spirals. Until he finally dipped it in her anus. While he sucked her clit hard.

Oh! Inside, she wound up tight. Impossibly so and she knew the explosion of pleasure was going to happen—

He worked another finger gently beside the first in her ass and she exploded. Bouncing on the bed. "Sin! Oh, Sin!"

Her hands twined in his hair as she rode the waves of pleasure. She feared she'd pulled on his hair, but he continued to lick and suck her as she rocked underneath him, crying his name.

Then he lifted his mouth from her and arched up to kiss her. She loved tasting herself on him. So earthy. So scandalous.

"There's something else I want to do, now that I'm down on one knee," he said when he stopped kissing her. He held her hand delicately. "When I feared I'd lost you, I felt like my life was over. I want to be with you. For the rest of my life. You refused to marry me for duty. But the truth is, Portia, I love you. I loved you ten years ago and I've never stopped loving you. My life has been empty without you."

"Hardly empty. You've had all those shocking parties."

"I was trying to blank out the pain of losing you."

"And you're going to give them up for me?"

His brown eyes, dark and intense, gleamed at her. "Yes, I love you. Of course I will change for you."

She had always feared that men did not change. But she knew that Sin had changed very much. He had been an abused boy—he had grown into a noble, wonderful man. "Actually, I like you just as you are," she whispered. "And if you want wild orgies, I could . . . I could go to them with you."

"What?" He was looking at her as if he didn't understand a word she'd said.

"I shouldn't expect you to change so much. You like wild sexual orgies. And I—I felt aroused by the idea of them too. If I don't change, I will lose you. I'm sure of it."

"You won't—"

"I would like to embrace your life, Sin. I will go to your orgies too. If you wish me to." He looked shocked. "Oh dear, I'm too ordinary and plain, aren't I—"

"You are beautiful. You are my fantasy come true, Portia." He lifted her hand and kissed her ring finger. "That's in place of an engagement ring for now. In your honor, I will throw the largest, grandest party I've ever held. It will be . . . like nothing I've ever hosted before."

"You mean very wild?"

"Indeed." His eyes twinkled. "Extremely wild."

She swallowed hard. But she couldn't deny. She felt a tug of curiosity. And a sudden heart-thumping, burning arousal. "Oh goodness," she said suddenly. "We're engaged. We're going to be married."

"Regretting it?"

He actually looked uncertain and vulnerable.

"No," she said firmly. "Awed by it. I've loved you for ten years as well. If you hadn't asked me to marry you again, I was going to ask you."

His smile dazzled. "I'm honored. And we should be making up for lost time."

She looked down. "Goodness, you're hard again!"

25

Sin gently woke her when they arrived at her foundling home. Portia felt rather groggy and Sin had to help her sit up, for she'd fallen asleep curled up against his long, lean body.

"Let me straighten your dress," he said.

She looked down at it and sighed. "I think that is hopeless. It's dirty and crumpled. After all, I was kidnapped in this dress. I couldn't bring myself to wear the one left for me on the island. I left it behind and I hope it is burnt. Anyway, my family would have been scandalized to see me wearing it. As it is, I have no idea how I will explain what did happen."

"I will explain everything to your family," he said gravely.

"No, we'll try to explain everything together. I do not know if my brothers will believe this."

She tried to speak with calm, but she fluttered with nerves inside.

Sin jumped out of the carriage, then handed her down and Portia gazed up at the brick foundling home. Inside, all the children must be sleeping. That thought warmed her heart.

"You look delighted to be home," Sin said softly.

"I can't wait to see all the children. They'll be in bed now, of course. But I can look in on them." She met his gaze. "Thank you. Thank you for rescuing me."

"It was my pleasure. And privilege." And the honest, husky tone of his voice touched her heart.

Then Portia rapped on the door of her home, the home she had grown to love with all her heart because of the children within. She didn't care about the chores she did, if it meant that all these children were safe from the harshness of the slums.

It took several minutes, but the door was opened and Merry stood there. Merry's jaw dropped. "Miss! Where have you been? We were all terrified. We thought you'd been taken across the sea and sold into one of those harems!"

"I've had adventures, Merry, but they were on an island off the coast of England. And, Merry, I would like to introduce you to the Duke of Sinclair."

"Cor blimey," Merry gasped. "Miss Lamb, are you going to be a duchess?"

Sin watched Portia tell her maid what had happened on Serenity Island, her story careful to remove scandalous elements and to downplay the danger. Portia was warm and sweet with the maid, and efficient and brisk when necessary to keep the girl from getting upset. He'd always admired that about Portia—her strength and ability to take command. Even when his friends had insisted he should want to marry a rich, simpering girl, he'd known none could compare to Portia.

He should have been a stronger, better man back then. Told his friends to go to hell. Told Will to go to hell. Which sadly was where Will probably was now.

It had been ten years since he'd been inside the Lamb's foundling home. It had changed little. That revealed that the financial situation was not good.

"Portia! You've come back to us! Thank heavens!" A woman in a fashionable silk gown rushed forward and hugged Portia. This was her sister, he realized. Ten years ago, she had been a pretty blond girl. Now she was a lovely woman. And married.

"I am safe and sound, Rosamund," Portia whispered.

Two tall men, one dark and one fair, stepped into the corridor. They wore grim expressions. The blond man stepped forward, folding his arm over his chest. "Merry told us you had returned. And we recognized the Duke of Sinclair." The man glowered at Sin. "Will you explain to us what you have been doing with our sister for the last few days? Why was she abducted, and what do you intend to do to repair her sullied reputation?"

Portia blinked. "None of this was the duke's fault, Geoffrey. How can you greet me with a scowl? I was abducted, taken away to an island off the coast of England by a madman and a madwoman, where people were murdered. Sin—the duke and I were almost killed!"

"Is this true?"

"Of course it is," Portia cried. With concise efficiency, she told her brothers and sister what happened. "For days, I've gone through hell. Sin—and yes, that is what I call him and I don't care what you think of that—protected me. He came to my rescue. And we are now engaged. He offered me marriage to protect my reputation and I refused him. But then he told me that he loved me. I love him and I accepted."

Sin cleared his throat. "I asked clumsily the first time. I've loved Portia for ten years. I've always loved her. Now, I wish to ask for her hand in marriage."

"Portia, you will be a duchess," breathed her sister.

"Of a tainted, scandalous duke," muttered the dark-haired brother. He wore spectacles, which he removed and rubbed with a handkerchief. "Portia, we cannot allow you to marry this *gentleman*." He sneered over the word.

"Why not? I love him, Gregory."

"Your duty is here," Gregory said impatiently.

"There's no reason Portia cannot continue to come to the foundling home after her marriage, if she wishes," Sin said.

"And our mother? Your duty is also to her."

"What do you mean?" Sin asked.

"Our mother is ill," Geoffrey said. "She is becoming senile as she ages. Portia looks after her here."

"You're saying you expect Portia to remain unmarried, to work free of charge in the foundling home, living in it so you can carry on with your lives, and also nursemaid your aging mother?"

"She will be happier remaining with us than she will be in your world," the brother argued. "Is she really to stand by while you throw shocking debauches?"

"I love Portia," he said. "I won't hurt her."

"She belongs here."

"As a drudge," Portia whispered. "That is how you see me. You don't admire the work I've done here. You just want a servant. And you don't want to be troubled with mother's illness or pay for a nurse. I thought I was doing something worthwhile—"

Sin stepped in front of her. All she could see was his concerned face. "Portia, do not belittle what you've done. But also, believe in yourself. You are not a drudge. I won't allow you to be treated as one."

"We know what is best for Portia. She is respectable, dutiful, moral. Your world will destroy her," Gregory said.

"You're the one who would destroy her," Sin growled.

"You cannot marry him," chimed in the other brother.

"I will," she said fiercely.

"Then you cannot come back to the foundling home, Portia. You cannot work here or visit here. We can't allow it. For our reputation."

"That's damn ridiculous," Sin exploded. "She loves this home. She adores the children."

"She's chosen to marry you. We all equally have control of the home, but my brother and I have the deciding votes. To provide a proper home, we have to behave in an exemplary way."

"You can't force her to choose between the home and marriage," Sin roared.

"Please don't shout," Portia said. "You'll wake the children."

"It's hard not to shout," he said, but lowered his voice. "It's hard not to punch both of you idiots in the nose."

Geoffrey backed up behind his brother, but leaned out to snap, "It would hurt the children's futures if there is any question as to the moral training they've received at the home."

Sin realized Portia was too stunned, too hurt to defend herself. Rage boiled. "You damn bastard. She's been through hell and this is what you do? She's done nothing but serve this foundling home and be a good daughter and sister."

"Your language—"

Gregory shut up as Sin loomed over him. Behind him, Geoffrey squeaked, "We don't have a choice."

He couldn't take the home from her—she loved the children.

But Portia folded her arms over her chest and faced her brothers. "I am going to marry Sin. If it means these doors are closed to me forever, then that is the choice I have to make. I will leave now, after seeing my mother."

Sin watched her go upstairs, letting her go alone. He knew her heart was broken. She came down a quarter hour later, a look of sadness in her eyes. "She recognized me at least. She was happy to see me. But I don't know what will happen to her when I am no longer here." Portia took a shaky breath. "Let us go, then."

And she was walking out the door without a last look at the children she adored, which broke his heart.

She was going to be his. He knew then that was his deepest desire. To have Portia as his wife, to love, to honor. But she was paying a hell of price for it.

Could he ask that of her?

Portia could not quite believe she was homeless.

"I don't know where I will go or what I will do. I can't live with you before we are married, Sin. I can't."

"Don't worry, love. I have a solution. You will be the guest of my friends Grey and Helena."

It never occurred to her to ask more. She was too exhausted. Surviving that hellish island and finding love with Sin should have brought happiness, but now she felt sorrow over her family's choice.

The carriage pulled into a curved drive and stopped in front of a magnificent house. She goggled. Sin said carelessly, "Grey's house."

"And Grey is—?"

"The Duke of Greybrooke. Helena is his wife."

"I never thought—I'm not certain I'm ready to be a duke's guest. They don't even know me! What if they don't approve of me?"

"They will adore you, I promise. They may wonder what a remarkable woman like you sees in me."

She lifted her brow, not quite believing that, and let him lead her to the magnificent front door. A liveried footman opened it, bowing courteously. She looked like a bedraggled mess after the ordeal, and she wore Sin's greatcoat, which was warm and smelled deliciously of him, but was obviously too large. Her appearance must be raising questions in the servant's mind, but he looked impassive as he led them to a drawing room and sent a lesser footman to summon the duke and duchess.

Portia feared she would meet a couple who would be appalled at Sin's request.

But she soon discovered she couldn't have been more wrong.

She was astounded by how welcoming Helena, the beautiful duchess, was. Portia was thoroughly fussed over. She and Sin had partaken of food at inns on the way home, but Helena (she said Portia must call her that) insisted on having tea and cakes brought out. Portia was warmed her to her soul was how kind and friendly Helena was. Appalled to learn of the ultimatum given by Portia's brothers, Helena took Portia upstairs to see her slumbering child, a sweet young boy who was just over a year old.

Gazing upon the little boy beneath his lacy blankets, Portia felt her heart wobble. She'd seen many children, held many babies, cuddled toddlers, but for some reason this made her heart ache so much. Then she knew why—it was the happy glow on Helena's face. It made Portia dream of having her own child, but it made her remember that she would never be allowed at the foundling home again.

But she refused to appear maudlin in front of the wonderful, generous duchess.

The duke, who insisted she call him Grey, was just as kind. Impetuously, in their drawing room, she'd remarked, "You all have nicknames?"

"They all do." Helena smiled. "Grey, Cary, Sin, and Sax. Now, I think it is time for bed. You must be exhausted, Portia."

"I think I am," she admitted.

Sin bowed courteously over her hand, then muttered, "I need more than this. I need to kiss you." He gave her a toe-curling kiss, whispered "good night," and Portia followed Helena up to the lovely bedroom that was to be hers.

The next morning, a rap came on her bedroom door and then a maid breezed in, carrying a tray with a plate covered in a silver cover and a coffeepot and dainty cup. "Her Grace thought you might like your breakfast up here, miss."

Portia sat up. She felt tiny in the huge, canopied, beautiful bed. It was heavenly and comfortable. "The duchess is very kind."

"That, she is, miss," the maid responded cheerfully.

The maid set down the tray over Portia's legs. "Her Grace asked if you would be ready to receive her after your breakfast."

"Of course."

The duchess had loaned her clothing including a lovely shift of the softest fabric, a corset of luxurious, lace-trimmed satin, and a lovely pale day dress.

Now, being helped into her dress by the maid, Portia thought of the first time Sin had helped her dress. The mirror reflected her flaming blush.

To quell the flush in her cheeks, she put those thoughts out of her mind. Instead, she speculated on reasons the Duchess of Greybrooke wished to see her.

The real reason, she was not at all prepared for.

"Sin has told us he is a holding an enormous ball," Helena said, as she poured tea in the drawing room. "Something rather shocking, even for him."

Something shocking? Oh! Was he going to hold an orgy and want her to attend? She'd told him she was willing to go to orgies with him. Now that she was faced with the reality, she . . . wasn't sure.

"I don't know if I am ready—"

"Oh, you will do fine. Sin wishes me to take you out and ensure you find a proper gown for the event."

"They wear gowns?"

Helena laughed and looked at her strangely. "Oh yes. Gowns will be worn."

Portia spent the morning with two duchesses—Helena, the Duchess of Greybrooke, and Sophie, the Duchess of Caradon. Sophie's husband, known by the nickname Cary, was also one of the Wicked Dukes.

Both women were not at all what Portia imagined. Not stuck up or snobby. Helena, who had been a governess, admired her work at the foundling home. Sophie had one child by her first husband, who had been killed in battle, and was expecting her first child with the Duke of Caradon, known as Cary. Helena had lovely blond hair, beautifully styled, and wore a gown of rich blue. Sophie had silky dark hair, with twinkling eyes and a ready smile. She exuded optimism.

"We'll take you to Madame Latour," Sophie said. "She is the most sought-after modiste in London at the moment."

"I really am surprised clothes are so important," Portia said. "Don't they simply come off?"

"For this event, clothes are very important—or so Sin said," Helena told her. "It is to be a masquerade."

"Have either of you been to one of his parties?"

"After Grey married me, he never went again. And he wouldn't allow me to go. Grey became a reformed Wicked Duke when he married me." Helena had explained to her about the "Wicked Dukes," but of course Portia knew about them already. She had devoured every item about Sin that she could in the gossip sheets.

"I saw one," Sophie admitted. "It is rather a long story. But I went and I saw Cary there. It was before we married."

"What . . . what was it like?" Portia asked.

"Oh. Rather what you would expect. Of an orgy." Sophie blushed. Then she tapped her chin. "Do you think Sin needs you to be part of that world?"

She felt so comfortable with Helena and Sophie, Portia found it easy to be honest as the carriage rumbled onward.

"I knew I couldn't bear to be married to him if he wasn't faithful. I couldn't accept knowing some other woman was having fun with him. But I thought if I went to the orgies too, perhaps I could accept them that way. I want to be with him. I don't want to ask him to change. I like how sensual he is. And I don't want him to lie to me."

Helena nodded. "I see. That is very open-minded of you." She looked out the carriage window. "We've arrived. It is time to acquire a gown for you."

The other women looked so delighted. Portia was swept up in the fun. Exploring the fabrics—light-as-air silks, sensual velvets, shimmering satins—proved thrilling. The modiste described the design she had in mind as an assistant took careful measurements. Madame Latour was being paid a small fortune by Sin to finish the dress quickly.

Portia thought of some of the beautiful, tempting costumes she'd seen. "What of a peacock-inspired costume?" she began to suggest. "With a corset decorated in turquoise, blue, green, and gold thread and for the tail feathers—"

"No!" cried Madame Latour. "Monsieur le Duc has told me exactly what is desired. To match his costume, he said. He wished something beautiful for you. Worthy of his duchess."

"To match his?" She hadn't expected that and she consented, allowing Madame Latour to design what she wished. But Portia still couldn't understand why so much attention would be paid to clothes at an orgy. From the modiste's description, the design of the dress sounded as if it would be elegant and demure. Not at all what she expected.

"Is Sin up to something?" she asked them in the carriage, as they returned from the fitting. "I'm beginning to suspect there isn't going to be an orgy." She eyed Helena, who looked lovely and demure. Helena had been a governess and could put on the calm, inscrutable expression one often used with children.

Sophie was the impetuous one, who showed her feelings easily. So Portia turned to Sophie. "Is he up to something?"

"I'm sure he is not," Sophie said, but she blushed.

"You know something! I can tell."

Both women shook their heads. As one they said, "He may be up to something. But we have no idea what it is."

Was it far too impolite to accuse two duchesses of lying to her? Especially when they had been so kind? For the first time, Portia didn't believe she could be impetuous. She was bursting to say: *I think you do know and you must tell me.* But she restrained herself. As she did, she looked out the window of the carriage. What she saw made her heart lurch.

"Could we stop the carriage," she cried.

"Of course," Helena said at once, and she gave some kind of signal that brought the carriage to a swift halt.

They all had to grasp the seats not to be thrown, but utterly calmly, Helena asked, "What is it?"

"A child, obviously lost, wandering on the edge of the street," Portia said. She wanted to help but had no money with her. She saw the outrider coming around the carriage to open the door. "I could take the girl to the foundling home . . . but that door is barred to me now, because I am marrying Sin."

"What?" Sophie cried. "That is terrible!"

"Surely that is not true," Helena said.

"It is." Quickly she spilled out the story of what had happened, finishing just as the door was opened.

"Would you go and speak to the child? See if you can coax her to come into the carriage," Helena said. "We shall find out where she lives. If she has no home, I shall bring her back to the house, see she is fed. Then we shall take her to a home."

Portia's heart felt as if it had taken flight. She hastened down the steps to carry out the plan, knowing that both duchesses were wonderful women.

But there was pain deep in her heart. Could she give up the foundling home forever? She loved the children. Seeing this bedraggled little girl on the street made her determined to help. So did remembering what had happened to the cook's daughter.

As she coaxed the girl into the carriage, she felt a sharp jolt of fear. Could she marry Sin and give up the foundling home forever? Never see any of those children or her mother again?

Helena broke in on her thoughts. "We are also telling you the truth, Portia. We do not know what Sin has planned. He simply told us to acquire for you the most beautiful gown possible."

Elegant carriages lined the street, sleek, polished, and gleaming. Portia peered out the window. She sat beside Helena, and Grey sat opposite them. Since she was their guest, she'd traveled in their ducal carriage.

Could this really be an orgy? The other Wicked Dukes no longer attended such events, she'd learned. But Helena and Grey insisted that they did not know what Sin's party was supposed to be.

The carriage turned up the wide, curved gravel drive of Sin's Mayfair mansion. Footmen lined the stretch, torches in hand. They halted and the door opened. A young liveried footman held out his gloved hand. Portia accepted his help, stepping down onto the gravel drive.

Lights blazed in the dozens of windows of his enormous pale stone mansion. With Helena and Grey, Portia made her way up the wide stone steps. She lifted the hem of her dress, the silk exquisite beneath her touch and shimmering in the light. It was the most decorative gown, done in a style of several decades before, at the end of the last century, with a square bodice and a tiny waist. Lace roses decorated the bodice, framing her décolleté, looking sweet but also rather enticing. The sleeves were her favorite, elbow length and trimmed with ruffles that skimmed her skin.

If her costume was so delicious, what did Sin's look like?

Following Helena and Grey, she hastened up the stairs and stepped through the doors, held open by two footmen. Portia stopped in shock.

Hundreds of people filled the entry foyer and the stairs. They were packed on the curved staircase like cattle crowding Whitechapel High Street. They came dressed as kings, emperors, fairy queens, dairy maids. Several devils in black and red populated the crowd. One woman was a butterfly with enormous gauzy wings. Then Portia saw children as well as adults.

"I don't think this is an orgy." She leveled a look at raven-haired Grey, who bore an expression that was supposed to display innocence but didn't. Suspicion flooded her. "You knew!"

A servant approached her. "Miss Lamb? I am to bring you this way."

She followed the servant, and Grey called out, "This is Sin's idea of an engagement ball."

A what?

She had arrived here with her heart in a whirl and questions roaring in her head. Did she marry Sin and lose the home forever? Or stay at the home, which meant she couldn't marry Sin?

Portia followed the footman down twining corridors, along huge hallways. Past coats of armor, massive oil paintings, enormous vases spilling with bouquets of exotic hothouse orchids and roses. It was just as she remembered it from ten years before.

She was used to the foundling home and to struggling to make ends meet each month. How could she fit into this world?

"This way, miss." The servant opened a door and stood in front of it. "Your Grace, Miss Lamb. And the Duke and Duchess of Greybrooke."

As the servant announced Helena and Grey, Portia realized they had followed her. In the drawing room, she spotted glossy dark hair decorated with strands of glittering diamonds. Sophie, seated on a settee. Sophie's simple Egyptian-style gown flowed over her rounded belly. Beside her was a handsome man with golden hair, dressed as a pharaoh. He must be the Duke of Caradon.

Standing by the fireplace was Sin. Portia almost melted just looking at him. He looked more gorgeous than ever in late-eighteenth-century dress. He wore a pure white shirt with lace at his throat and wrists. How erotic it was to see the lace against the lightly stubble-covered, masculine skin of his throat and dripping over his long fingers. A frock coat and waistcoat of pale embroidered gold fit him as if painted on and set off his dark brown hair.

Across from him, seated in large, leather club chairs were—shock of all shocks—her brothers, Geoffrey and Gregory.

Sin came to her, kissed her softly on her cheek.

She met his gaze. "What is going on? All of the *ton* appears to have come for a ball, and I thought—well, the Duke of Greybrooke told me this is to be an engagement ball."

"You weren't supposed to tell her," Sin growled at Grey.

"Marriage should not begin with secrets," Grey responded.

"I didn't want her to know because I feared I would disappoint her. However, with the help of Caradon, I believe I am beginning to make these fine gentlemen"—he nodded to her brothers—"see sense. Care to add your position, Greybrooke?"

She noted he was being formal.

"Of course." Greybrooke stepped forward. "My wife, the duchess, has a special place in her heart for all children, especially those who are unfortunate. I believe Caradon has named a figure that he will donate to the home. A staggering amount, I believe it was?" He paused.

Gregory cleared his throat. "It was generous. However, such a gift means we have to take great care as to the reputation of the house. There have been rumors about Portia's behavior—"

"I am prepared to stop those rumors immediately," Sin said.

"There are rumors about me?" She goggled.

"Sadly, yes," Sophie said. "Simply because you were on the island with Sinclair, and it became known that you shared a bedchamber."

"I was kidnapped and taken to the island against my will. I hardly set up a clandestine affair while being knocked out by a drug and taken unconscious in a boat. Oh, I really do think Society is idiotic."

"I know you do," Sin said. "But you want to be part of the foundling home, which means these rumors have to end. I intend to end them this evening."

"Sin, I can't—"

"I will match the Duke of Caradon's donation," Greybrooke said. "That means thirty thousand pounds, including ten from Sinclair, will be put in trust for the management of the foundling home. That will only occur if three things happen."

Portia was too stunned by the amount to speak.

"Portia will manage the funds and the house as she wishes. You will accept this without complaint," Sin said.

"You will also accept any decision she makes in regard to her relationship with the Duke of Sinclair. And finally"—Greybrooke looked to her—"I am sorry to make this a condition, but Sinclair is my friend. I want to see him leg shackled. The money will be given to the home if you marry Sinclair, Miss Lamb."

Sin straightened. "Grey, I can't blackmail Portia into marrying me. The money is hers to use for the home, whether she becomes my wife or not. However, I will clear any smear on her reputation. And Portia will have access to thirty thousand pounds to run and expand the home, or purchase more buildings."

She couldn't believe what was happening. "I could have homes all over England with such an astonishing amount of money." She met Sin's eyes, with her heart heavy. "But I think I am better suited to that than to being a duchess."

"That is what would make you a perfect duchess," Helena said firmly.

"I agree," said Sophie. "Compassion and intelligence are far more important for the position than anything else."

Sin looked to her brothers. "Would you accept our marriage? I would authorize a stipend be paid to you for your work in managing the homes. Not as much as Portia would receive, but it would keep your families well, provide for daughters, allow sons to be educated at fine schools. If you perform your duties to satisfaction."

"To your satisfaction?" queried Geoffrey.

"Not to mine. To Portia's."

She saw the shock on her brothers' faces.

"But what about these rumors?" Gregory asked.

"I am going to tell the truth. Once Portia is a duchess and it is obvious that she's tamed me, there will be no scandal. This event alone will be proof that I've changed—that I've turned into a respectable duke for love. Because I have."

"Sin, I don't want to force you to change," Portia said. "I . . . I am willing to be disreputable with you."

For the first time that evening, Sin smiled. "In private, angel, we will be thoroughly disreputable. But like the other two Wicked Dukes, I realize I'm ready to be tamed. I don't want to share. And you are more alluring, more desirable than anyone else or any wicked party. I've realized that you are my ultimate fantasy, my deepest desire, Portia. I love you."

"I can marry you and have love, and still be a part of my family, still be a part of the foundling homes?"

Sin looked to her brothers. They both stood. Gregory spoke. "Of course, Portia. You must forgive us for our hasty words."

She was certain it was Sin's promise of incomes that had changed their minds. But she was happy regardless.

"Then yes, Sin. I want to marry you. But for one reason: because I am, and have always been, deeply in love with you. You are my deepest desire, my fondest wish, my greatest love. All in one."

He covered the distance between them in two strides. He lifted her and swung her off her feet.

And his kiss . . . it was what their love was about. Tender, poignant, happy, sensual, passionate.

At that moment a female voice cried, "Sinclair, what are you doing?"

Sin set her down as a woman in a high-necked dress of bronze-colored silk swept in. Jeweled necklaces roped around her neck and she held a lorgnette in front of her eyes. Portia bit her lip. Sin's older cousin, the current duchess.

"You are not—"

"Quiet," Sin growled. "You interfered once in my engagement. I know you spoke to Willoughby and agreed with his plan to introduce me to London vices. You did it in the hopes I would break off my engagement to Portia because I'd be so enthralled by that world. I was young and stupid then, but not anymore. I love Portia. If you don't accept her, you'll never be allowed in this house again."

Portia put her hand on his arm. "Sin, no—"

"I mean it. You deserve her respect. I won't tolerate anything less."

Portia remembered how he had once felt belittled by the resentful duchess. She saw how strong he was now. Willing to fight for what he believed in.

Her heart almost burst. He hadn't changed—he had gained the strength to be the good, noble man he was meant to be.

Impetuously, Portia stepped in front of Sin's cousin. She dropped into as elegant a curtsy as she could muster. Rising, she touched the woman's arm gently. The duchess, looking imperious, stared in surprise.

"I know I am not what you expected," Portia said. "I am not

from a grand family. There is nothing I can do about that, but I wish you to know you are most welcome in our house and our family. I wish to have you as a guest often."

Portia expected to get her ears blistered. To her surprise, the duchess curtsied.

"I have no choice but to accept. The boy has dragged the family name through scandal with his shocking parties. If you are asking me to be a guest, I presume you intend to change him."

"She already has," Sin said.

"Let us put the past behind us." Portia knew it must be hopeless, for why would the duchess accept a nobody?

"I made a mistake," the duchess said. "I should have not agreed with the plan of Lord Willoughby, who is now found to be a scandalous murderer. There are those who knew that I concocted that plan with him—the plan to take Sinclair to the more sordid places in London. Now I look like a fool. I wish to eliminate scandal. If you can make this boy stop his shocking parties, I will accept the marriage."

"Then be prepared to be invited for dinner, cousin," Sin said.

Portia had to giggle at the duchess's look of surprise.

Sin grinned. "Now we have to announce our engagement."

In front of hundreds of members of England's high society, all dressed in beautiful costumes, Sin interrupted the orchestra, halting couples in mid-waltz. The guests quieted, though whispers still buzzed in the crowd.

"I wish to make an announcement." Sin's voice sliced through the soft noise of gossip and speculation. "I would like you all to meet Miss Portia Lamb. Her family has run a foundling home in Whitechapel. Her father was a scholar. I fell in love with Miss Lamb ten years ago, but it has taken me a decade to get it right. Miss Lamb has agreed to my proposal. We are soon to be married and I am bursting with happiness. Another Wicked Duke has fallen to matrimony."

The buzzing increased.

"It has come to my attention there have been rumors that

something untoward happened between Miss Lamb and me. This is not true. We foiled a madman and madwoman who murdered several people. They had also kidnapped Miss Lamb. I was acting to protect her from harm. As we were engaged at the time, there was nothing untoward in my desire to protect her."

Portia had never dreamed he would be so blunt with Society. That Sin would make such an announcement.

"Miss Lamb saved lives without care to her own safety. And she is soon to be my duchess." He turned to the orchestra. "A waltz," he commanded.

Elegant music rose, soaring to the high ceiling and dazzling chandeliers.

"I've never waltzed before," she admitted.

"I have. But never with a partner I love. Just follow me, Portia."

Sin's hand settled on her low back and he drew her close. Her hand felt small in his—but warm and safe. He took the first step and she tentatively followed. His smile gave her confidence. Following him, flowing with the music, she began to understand the dance. Soon they whirled around the floor. Her heart filled with joy.

This was love.

This was her place. In his arms. At his side.

Then he leaned close. "I have some other wicked desires, you know. Let's slip away and I'll show you."

"That will start gossip."

"Damn, so it will. We'll have to wait."

It was almost dawn when they managed to meet unseen in the drawing room where she'd shared her first climax with him ten years before.

"Now." Portia laughed. "Show me all your wicked desires."

"My deepest desire is to make you happy. And to watch you come," he murmured. "I'm going to be your husband, but right now, I'm your willing slave. I'll do whatever you want."

She shook her head. "We're partners. What do you want?"

"I could ask you to put on that fake cock. Or I could have you tie me up. Or I could tie you up. But right now, I'm thinking I want to lie down on the Aubusson rug and have you ride me to pleasurable oblivion."

She giggled. "I was thinking we could go out on the terrace, and you could flip up my skirts and take me from behind."

"You don't want to ride me? Be in charge?"

"Standing up is rather exciting. But let's do it your way."

"I can't believe I'm arguing about how we're going to have sex." He grinned. Down went his trousers, so quickly she gasped. In minutes he was naked. Naked and beautiful and hers.

"I love you, Portia." They sank down to the thick rug together. "Another Wicked Duke surrenders to love. Very, very happily."

Portia kissed him, and Sin found he couldn't say another word. Though he did yell damn loud when he came. After his beautiful, perfect Portia had come twice, of course.

Enjoyed the naughty adventures of the Wicked Dukes?
Don't miss the other books in the series . . .

DEEPLY IN YOU

and

DEEPER IN SIN

Available now from Kensington Books

WITHDRAWN
BY
WILLIAMSBURG REGIONAL LIBRARY